Badder

Out of the Box, Book 16

Robert J. Crane

1

Before

"In my day, we ruled the world as gods, and all who beheld us quaked in righteous fear at the sound of our approach." Her granddad's voice always filled Rose with a sense of reassurance, that quiet desire to just put her chin in her hands and listen as he spun his tales. She looked up at him now with a smile of wonderment, eyes starry and glazed, as he talked of his own life and the days before. "We battled and fought amongst ourselves, and humans ran, fearful, from the clash of men and women so strong as to defy their ability to understand it in terms that didn't blast their heads off as surely as if a Brigid had done it for them." His thick Scottish brogue was the stuff of the Highlands, and it was deep, and rich, and Rose couldn't get enough of hearing it.

"Rose." The stern sound of her mam's voice made Rose jerk her head around. She found the lady herself standing there, disapproving, hands on hips. Her fiery red hair caught the midday light reflected through the window to the living room. Rose looked back at her granddad to see his eye twinkle, and he winked at her.

"We'll finish this later," he said, unfurling himself from the footstool where he'd sat and held court, telling her his tales. He stood, strong and tall, hair still dark and full. She knew he was already some two thousand years old. He didn't look it.

He didn't even really look a granddad, at least not compared to some of the other granddads around.

"No, you won't," Rose's mam said darkly, green eyes flashing, hands still firmly planted upon her hips.

"Ye're a wee scunner," her granddad said. "Ye're my daughter, I'm not your son." He didn't sound very serious, more mocking of the idea that she could command him than angry. The twinkle in his eye showed he had a good humor about it all.

"Aye, and she's mine," Rose's mam said, "and she doesn't need you filling her head with nonsense tales of the past." Her voice went a note higher. "Those days are long gone, Father. We don't live like that anymore. We have to exist with the humans now, and not try and rule them. You know that."

"I know that," he said, and waited for her to turn. "But it was better before," he whispered to Rose once she'd turned away. Judging by the slump of her shoulders, Rose's mam heard that, though. He clapped Rose on the shoulder lightly. "All right, enough o' that for now. Go on, then. Go outside for a bit, have some fun. Maybe go find Graham. No need to be hanging about inside on a beautiful day like today."

"Granddad, it's raining," Rose said, looking at the open shade over his shoulder. Grey skies were visible, and hints of moisture were coming out of the sky.

"But lightly!" he said. "That's what we call Scottish sunshine, and you better drink it up while you can." He favored her with a grin, then placed his hand on her back and gently pushed her toward the door. "Go on, then. Come back before tea. And don't go doing anything daft, you hear?"

Rose lingered, drifting toward the door. "I hear you, Granddad," she said, sighing as she left.

Outside, she discovered he'd been right about the sunshine. It broke its way through the clouds, revealing the sparse nature of the rainfall, only a few drops coming every square foot. It was a light drizzle at best, and the village was still awake, and still functioning in spite of the minor precipitation. Rose took in this overly familiar scene with a practiced eye; she'd lived here all her life, had yet to leave, and—well, really, why would she?

Over to the east stood one of the rounded hills that rose like a mountain over the village. It was tall and looked smooth, but it was easily climbable if you knew what you were doing. Hills dotted the ground to the west, too, and the sea was just a bit to the north. Somewhere south—far south—was Edinburgh and Glasgow, and beyond that England and Europe and—

"G'morning, Rose," Hamilton said, greeting her with that same twinkle she saw in her granddad's eye. "How are ye doing this fine day?"

"Aren't you a cheery bastard?" his counterpart said, Tamhas. He wore a grumpy look, eyes narrowed. He was always good for a grouse. Granddad had told her that this old silver-haired bastard had been the finest warrior he'd ever seen. Tamhas had a keen eye, like a hawk, always looking around; she knew he'd traveled all the way to Asia at one point and come back knowing every martial art known to man—or so Granddad claimed.

"How can you be unhappy on a day like today?" Hamilton asked. He was always bright of eye; an actor by trade, classically trained. He'd done quite a bit of work in Edinburgh, Glasgow and even as far away as London before giving it up and coming back home. That had been long before Rose's time.

"Because it's raining. Again." Tamhas seemed to sound like a hawk.

"Did somebody take a wee piss in your tea?" Hamilton winked at her.

"Good morning, Hamilton, Tamhas," Rose said softly, almost afraid to interrupt their banter. They were like this all the time. She tried to appear nonchalant, and asked, "Have either of you seen Graham this morning?"

Hamilton and Tamhas exchanged a look that made Rose's cheeks burn. They'd sussed out her intent, that much was plain. "Aye," Tamhas said, his cranky disposition suddenly lightened in ways that made Rose feel very sorry she'd asked. "I saw him go out that way, toward Miriam Shell's house." He put a hand up, pointing the way.

Miriam Shell was a widower. She'd married a human, so that was hardly a surprise. Rose's granddad had said she'd been born almost two hundred years ago now. He also said she was a randy old creature, and at that thought Rose felt herself pale.

Hamilton slapped Tamhas across the chest, drawing a sharp look in reply. Hamilton gave her a kindly look, his hints of grey hair matching the sky. "He was just helping her with some of her chores, lass. Nothing untoward."

"Mmm?" Tamhas seemed to get it now. "What? Oh. No, yes—didn't mean to imply anything." He lowered his voice, as though he could speak to Hamilton without her hearing it, his lips moving subtly. Rose caught it, though. "You know she'd have him splayed across the bed in two seconds if she thought she could get away with it."

"Aye, but you dinnae need to say it where the lass could hear you," Hamilton said under his breath—deep under his breath. "You know she and the lad have a thing going on."

"We do not 'have a thing going on'," Rose said, blushing heartily. Hamilton and Tamhas both looked up, quite startled.

"You…heard that, then?" Tamhas said. He looked ashen.

"Aye," Rose said, still blushing furiously. "There is nothing between Graham and me, I'll have you know."

"Sorry to suggest otherwise," Tamhas said with a little harrumphing. "You'll find him at Miriam Shell's. Perhaps you should run along now, just…check up on the lad." He seemed a bit…strained now, and Rose didn't know quite what to make of it. He nudged her, and pointed in the direction of Miriam's house. "Go on, then. Don't let us keep you."

Rose started that way, unsure if she should say something else, or just go. Hamilton and Tamhas were both watching her carefully, scrutinizing her as though she were something strange, a bizarre creature that defied explanation. Hamilton

4

nodded at her, encouragingly, but he couldn't hide the fact that he was watching her carefully as she started toward Miriam Shell's house.

She tried to put it out of her mind, but it was difficult. The village felt strange this morning, however, and Rose didn't know quite how it was so. An owl was hooting in the distance, birds were chirping, seemingly louder than they'd been before. She rubbed at her eyes; did the day seem especially bright?

Rose walked the short main street toward the outskirts of the village, only a few houses from her own, until she reached Miriam Shell's dwelling. It was an old house, but well kept, the shingles taking the drizzle well, little streams of water trickling down off the gutters.

"Good morning, Rose," Miriam said, stepping out of the house, her dark hair tousled. She watched Rose's approach with careful consideration. "You look a bit wet."

"It's Scottish sunshine," Rose said, feeling a little drop here and there between the rays shining down between the clouds. "Have ye seen Graham this morning? I heard he was helping you."

"Aye, he gave me a hand," she said, not sounding particularly pleased about it. "And little else, the thick lad." She shook her head. "You have a real prize there, Rose. A real prize."

Rose just stared at her. "I'm...nae sure what you mean..."

Miriam gave her a knowing look, full of mirth. "I'm sure you do." She shuffled on her feet, then announced, "Graham! Rose is here asking after you! What should I tell her?"

The front door opened seconds later, snapping hard back and rattling, then shutting of its own momentum. Miriam looked vaguely scandalized, and said, "Now then! Take it easy or you'll be back to fix my door soon enough."

"Sorry," Graham said, coming out of the house and almost tearing the door off the hinges as he did so. His hair hung to his shoulders, chestnut brown, and he was freckled in just the right ways, Rose thought. There was a single one that sat in the middle of his nose, and when she spoke to him, she'd look right at it. "So sorry, Ms. Shell—"

"It's Miriam," she said, with the air of a woman who had corrected him many times, and halfway through seemed to give up on correcting him any more. "I think we're done for today, though if you'd like to stop back after—"

Graham straightened. "After what?"

"Oh, I assumed you two were going to go for a walk or some such thing," Miriam said dryly. "Unless ye'd rather keep working."

"I'd love to go for a walk," Graham said, looking right at Rose, his hair catching a ray of sunshine stretching down from the clouds and giving a luster.

"Errr," Rose said, quite caught in between what Miriam had suggested for an activity and Graham's sudden leaping at an invitation she hadn't even proffered. But...would it really be so bad to go on a walk with him?

No. No, it would not.

"Let's go then, shall we?" Rose said, almost gulping as she said so, and Graham nodded, hurrying to reach her, as though Miriam might drag him back inside if he weren't quick enough.

"Do be careful," Miriam called after them. "You're of an age that two of you could quickly become three of you."

"What does she mean by that?" Graham asked as Rose felt the heat burn in her cheeks, and she quickened her pace to get away so she wouldn't have to respond.

"She was right about you," Rose said, cuffing him on the arm as she headed toward the road out of town. "You really are thick, aren't ye?"

Graham followed her as she led the way, down the village road and toward the winding path that forked from it, descending down a hill toward the springs where the village drew much of its water. It was a rocky creek, winding its way from the Highlands toward the sea in the distance. Rose walked a pace or two ahead of Graham, and he seemed to have to hurry to keep up, but she didn't mind that. The wind was brisk against her face, and she liked that, too, brisker than she recalled it being for how it had felt when she'd been standing still. Now it practically howled at her, coming at her with strength that it hadn't possessed when she—

"What in the hell are you doing?" Graham asked, and Rose tossed a look over her shoulder. He was fifty meters back, and struggling to catch up without breaking into a run. "I thought we were going on a walk together, but…" He stopped, drew up short, and stared at her across the distance. His mouth hung slightly open. "Rose…I think you manifested."

"What?" Rose stood up a little straighter. It seemed the grass on either side of the road was alive with bugs a-buzzing, things she'd never noted before. Her skin crawled with the chill of the sparse, sprinkling rain, the sensations filling her in a way she couldn't recall feeling before.

Graham strode up to her, eyes bright and wide. "Did it happen? Can you feel it?"

Rose swallowed, and even that mere act felt more…more rich, somehow. Everything felt brighter, louder, and more…more so. It was as though someone had turned the volume knob for her senses up to their maximum level, and she'd not really noticed it except as a distraction. "I…I feel a bit strange…"

"That's what it feels like!" Graham sounded as though he might wet his pants. He'd manifested his powers a few months ago, but then, he was also almost a year older than Rose. They were two of the only kids in the village. And at sixteen and seventeen, they were still kids to all around them, what with some of the adults, like her granddad, having lived thousands of years.

He studied her as though she were some novel new specimen. "Do you feel anything else?" He lowered his voice as he got closer. "Can you feel your power?"

"I don't know," Rose said, wondering what a power actually felt like. Her granddad and mam were both Thors, but her grandma had been a Poseidon. The line was hereditary, wasn't it? That's what her granddad always said in his stories.

She tried to imagine how it would feel to conjure lightning, and concentrated—

"Do you feel anything?" Graham eased closer and took hold of her by the forearm. It was such a little thing, but his eyes were aglow with excitement.

Rose felt flush with an excitement of her own. He'd touched her before, of course, but for some reason it had been awhile since, as though their budding self-consciousness were holding them back. They'd touched all the time when they were children. The only two in the village of similar age, it was as inevitable as them butting heads. And oh, how they'd butted heads, though mostly that seemed behind them now. "I don't…I don't know if I feel…anything…"

She closed her eyes and concentrated, but it was hard. Graham's palm felt delicate against her forearm. She was suddenly self-conscious about the little hairs that ran along her flesh. They were tiny, sure, and faint, but they were there, and she suddenly hated them furiously and wished she'd done away with them with her granddad's straight razor the way she did to the hair on her legs during summer, and under her arms. She flushed, feeling the dark heat roll over her skin—

Rose jerked her eyes open in time to see Graham's roll back in his head, his hand locked on her arm and his body shaking. Her skin was alive, was afire, and she felt hard breaths rolling into her lungs. Graham sagged to his knees and she followed him down, didn't want to let go, fear and fright mingling to work on her. There was a cold clutch of terror conjoined with this strange pleasure. It was almost akin to that she felt sometimes when she was alone, by herself, at night, and she reached down—

"Graham!" she cried, catching him as he started to slump. She lowered him to the ground, bearing his weight easily. She'd manifested, all right. Yesterday she couldn't have lifted him, couldn't have held him up like that.

But today…today she felt like she could have carried him for miles if she needed to.

And, she realized as he shook in her arms, she might just need to.

She touched his cheeks, placing both palms on them, and that feeling of tingling pleasure, that slow burn of fire across her skin in a way that she—well, she actually rather enjoyed it—had never quite felt before, ran through her like someone was ringing a pleasant bell that resonated through every fiber of her body. Rose shuddered too, her hands locked on Graham's cheeks, holding him against the storm that was surging through him—

"ROSE!" Her granddad's voice crackled like thunder out of the clouded sky, and she looked back to see him hurrying toward her, her mam in tow, and Tamhas and Hamilton following behind, along with Miriam Shell and a few others.

"Get your hands off him!" her mam screamed, and the command jolted through Rose so hard that she complied immediately, taking her hands off Graham's cheeks and skittering away from him, leaving him to stop shuddering all by his lonesome, as the others came thundering up.

"Oh, my," Miriam Shell said from a few feet away. She'd drawn up short, and observed the scene from a little distance like a detached spectator. She looked at Rose and seemed to gulp. "Oh, my."

"You've no need to gawp like an idiot, Miriam," Rose's mam said, staring at the widow with undisguised fury. "Save for the fact you are an idiot, in which case you still have no need to gawp."

"She nearly killed the boy," Miriam said in reply, though a bit hollowly.

Rose's granddad was on his knees next to Graham, as were Tamhas and Martial. "He's not dead," Granddad said. He looked up at Rose, and there was a spark of reassurance there, almost buried beneath something else—worry, she thought.

But worry of a kind she didn't remember seeing from him before.

"Miriam," Hamilton said softly, hovering over Graham

and looking down at him, "be a dear and go roust Caitir, will you? I think we're going to need her Persephone abilities for this. Ease the boy's spirit a bit." He turned to favor Rose with a weather eye, and she could see discomfort there, as well.

"What…what happened to him?" Rose asked, still sitting in the dirt where she'd moved away from Graham.

No one spoke for a long moment, and the only sound—other than Graham's ragged breathing—was Miriam's hard footfalls as she ran back to the village. They lessened in time, receding into the distance.

"You happened to him," Rose's mam finally said, and there was so much quiet judgment in her words. Even more in her eyes when she turned to look at Rose, hints of betrayal speckled in with the worry.

"Now, now," her granddad started, "you dinnae—"

"I do," her mam said, a whisper filled with fury. "I was afraid of this. That you'd take after…*him*." She said the last word replete with such disgust that Rose wanted to scamper back farther to escape any possible venom that might have spewed from her mam's mouth.

"You always knew that was a possibility," her granddad said with his usual air of quiet patience.

"I never thought she would, though," her mam said, and there was that streak of betrayal crawling through her words like snakes writhing in hay.

"No harm was done," her granddad said. "Nothing done here that can't be undone."

"Your granddaughter is a succubus," Tamhas said in a whisper so low that Rose barely heard it. Had the adults around her been talking like this all along? She knew in her heart they had, she'd seen it happen for years, heard the bare hiss, but never realized that they were having full conversations so low that she and Graham had never heard them. "I don't think that can be undone."

"Tamhas," Hamilton said warningly, and he was looking straight at her. They all were.

Rose felt like she'd been cracked hard over the head with a thick bough.

A succubus?

A damned soul eater?

Her?

Her skin tingled with cold, crawling over the warm feeling that had favored her moments earlier, when she'd been touching Graham. The world had seemed so pleasant then, so pleasurable—

Now it seemed like winter was going to set in any second, and a blizzard would bury her right here.

Her mam was staring at her with fury, and Rose stared right back. When she found her words, Rose said, "Why didn't you tell me?"

Her mam said nothing. Just looked away.

She looked at her granddad. "Why didn't ye tell me?"

He seemed to take a breath in, though just barely, movement so subtle he was almost a statue. "Your mam asked me not to."

"And when you have ye ever listened to her before when she's asked that?" Rose was on her feet now, steadier than she thought she could have been. Her skin was hot again, and she wanted to touch someone else.

They all seemed to recoil from her, and that made Rose hold back. She looked at Tamhas. "You didn't say anything. Just now." She stared at him, and he looked away. "You knew? You must have; you ran and got me mam and granddad right off when you realized I could hear you talking low, so…you must have known." She looked from Tamhas to Hamilton. "Didn't you?" The quiet accusation felt harsher to her than if she'd yelled.

Hamilton nodded, his face contorted with a strange regret. "Of course we knew. But…we all hoped you wouldn't end up as…well…you know…"

"As a bloody soul eater," her mam said, harsh anger bleeding out into the quiet air.

A thick drop peppered Rose's cheek, followed by another that landed on her shoulder.

The quickening pace of the rain seemed to reawaken the others. "We should get him inside," Tamhas said. "There's nothing to be done just waiting here. Moving him won't hurt him."

"Aye," her granddad said, and positioned himself at Graham's legs. "Let's be about it."

The clouds had given way now, crashed on each other, no Scottish sunshine left to see. It was all grey gloom above as her granddad lifted Graham by the legs, Hamilton got him under the arms, and they started back toward the village, Tamhas supporting him with an arm under the lower back. They didn't struggle at all under his weight.

They hurried, picking up the pace as the shower increased, fat drops raining down around them. They were out of sight in thirty seconds, disappearing up over the rise back to the village and leaving Rose alone with her mam.

That didn't last long, though. Her mam wouldn't look at her, and soon enough, she turned to leave as well, giving Rose the sight of her back.

Rose's eyes burned, but she stayed where she stood. "Mam!" she called out, when she could bear the quiet of her mam under the fury of the coming storm no longer.

Her mam stopped, but only for a second. "You're such a disappointment," she said, and that was it.

And soon enough, she, too, disappeared over the hill.

Quietly, six strangers watched it all happen. Among them stood a man with sandy blond hair, and the stir of familiar feeling came through him at the sight of the exchange, a peculiar similarity that verged on deja vu.

*

"This all seems…familiar," Zack David said, running a hand through his hair, ruffling it. His hair wasn't actually here, but then, neither was he; the events they'd just watched play out must have happened years ago. They were most certainly not of the now, though he couldn't put his finger on an exact year, at least. The village looked almost timeless in its way, and by that token seemed frozen in time. He stared at the red-haired succubus in the storm, rain pouring down around her. She stood there alone, the girl who'd just lost everything she'd ever had, and…

He almost felt sorry for her.

Almost.

"I imagine you've seen this story play out somewhere before," Aleksandr Gavrikov said stiffly. He wasn't wearing his habitual skin of fire, but he hadn't worn it habitually for quite a while. When Zack had made his acquaintance— briefly—in life, he had scarcely gone without it. Now, as he stared at the Russian, whose eyes betrayed nothing but sadness most of the time, he felt a hint of pity for him, too. Gavrikov's gaze met his own, and the Russian smiled, faintly, as if to acknowledge their shared plight.

Trapped in the head of an unfamiliar succubus. Prisoners.

"It does have some incredible parallels," Zack said. The red-haired girl was just standing in the rain now, soaked to the bone as they all watched her. "There was more snow in Sienna's tale. And the first time she touched my hand, I didn't pass out, just felt lightheaded." He spoke somberly, because damn if he didn't feel somber. Dead for seven years, and now he'd been passed off from his familiar respite of Sienna's mind into someone else's.

And she…this Rose…did not seem friendly.

"So far I'm not enjoying the dime tour," Gerry Harmon said with his usual sarcasm. He was unflappable, a bit of a cipher when he didn't want his emotions to show. Zack imagined that would have been incredibly useful during his last job—President of the United States—but now it was distinctly annoying, because it always felt like Harmon was cut off and above it all.

Well. It *had* felt like that. The occasional note of fear was creeping in here and there, and that was hardly unexpected. Harmon had seemed to just get used to being one of Sienna's souls, and now...

Now they weren't anymore.

"I don't like this bitch," Bjorn said, almost snorting his anger. Rose had greeted him with a distinct lack of kindness, ripping into him with a kind of agonizing touch that Sienna could have imparted at any time, but never did—or at least hadn't for a long, long time.

"Join the club," Eve Kappler tossed in. Her arms were folded, her eyes set and hard. "She called us 'boring.'"

"At least she did not hit you with torturous pain," Bjorn said, sounding a little resentful. The grey Scottish sky hung over them, and below, the redhead shuddered under the chill of the blowing winds and now downpour. She was so thin, so sad...she looked a bit like a wet cat left out in the rain.

"We are not on sound footing, that's for sure," Roberto Bastian said. The former squad leader carried a sort of military precision and a reserve of his own that seldom cracked. It was showing some signs of strain now though, with their familiar ground ripped away from them—quite literally torn out of what had been their home for, in most cases, years—and now landed here, in an unfamiliar mind, witnessing unfamiliar spectacles.

"What did she do with Wolfe?" Zack asked, chewing a lip that no longer actually existed. "That's what I want to know."

"He's her new fair-haired boy-toy," Harmon said with dry amusement—or perhaps a sarcastic lack thereof. "I don't think we'll be seeing him again."

"He's living life on the Lido deck," Eve said, "and we're down in the bilge pumps."

"This is bilge all right," Bjorn said, seething. He locked eyes on the redhead in the rain. "If I could, I would go down there and pound her until she was nothing but blood and bone strewn over these rocky Scottish grounds."

Harmon stared out at the thin figure in the rain. "You should go try that."

Bjorn seemed to take it as a dare. "Perhaps I will." And he turned, thundering off toward the memory of Rose.

"Now that we've eliminated most of the idiocy," Harmon said, glancing at Bjorn running toward Rose in the distance, "can we have a discussion about what's next that doesn't involve vague and stupid threats? I'd like to talk about this clear-eyed."

"His eyes certainly aren't clear," Zack said as Bjorn passed through the past Rose, still standing there alone. Bjorn sailed through her in a tackle that didn't land, as though she were mist, or he were. "All he sees is red."

"What do you think is going to happen here, Harmon?" Gavrikov asked stiffly.

"I think it's obvious," Harmon said, and Zack detected a measure of reluctance. "Rose is going to go after Sienna. She's going to try and kill her. And with Wolfe on her side...she might well succeed."

Zack's face burned like Gavrikov had lit off a fire within it. "Lots of people have tried to kill Sienna. No one has succeeded yet."

"No one else has been this well matched," Harmon said. "Think about what Rose has been doing. She's created metas specifically for the purpose of draining them and stockpiling their powers. She is the meta equivalent of a nuclear bomb." He looked apologetically at Gavrikov. "No offense intended, what with you previously occupying that role."

"I saw it as more the meta equivalent of a Swiss army knife," Eve said, pensive. "Because of the versatility."

"No offense taken," Gavrikov said. "But I agree with Zack. Many have tried to kill Sienna. All have failed. This Rose? I do not think this time will be any different."

"It will be different," Harmon said, "because *she* is different. Think about it. Whoever she is, whatever her axe to grind, she has planned this for years. She set a trap for Sienna, drew her in, got close to her, and managed to cloud her suspicions long enough to pull off the greatest sucker punch since 1941. Now Sienna's back to being a vanilla succubus, none of us to aid her."

"That's happened before," Zack said. "And she wiped out the people that came after her then, too."

"I'm starting to agree with the President," Bastian said, snugging his arms tighter around him. "Think about it, Zack. In any engagement, there are factors for and against you. Maybe you've got favorable weather and your opponent doesn't. Or you've got a strategy and you ambush them on ground that works to your advantage. Sienna had powers that others couldn't or didn't have. The ability to heal from almost any wound. The power to throw fire or blow up like a bomb. To net up her enemies in twine of light. Or even," and here he seemed to turn away slightly, "go dragon if all else failed. She's got none of that now, so on Sienna's side—she's lost her advantages. At the same time, on the other side of the equation, Rose has stacked them up. And when it comes to locale, we're on unfamiliar ground to Sienna, so…" He shrugged.

"You think she's unbeatable," Eve said, "because you want to believe she's unbeatable."

"Because no one has beaten her yet," Zack said.

"Yet," Harmon said, "being the operative word. But no one has ever stacked the deck this hard against her. She has little left to rely on."

"We're not going to settle this right now, today," Eve said as they all watched Bjorn pick himself up and promptly attack the image of Rose again, to no effect. He turned on it once more, and this time seemed to content himself with punching at it, hands slicing through the face, the body, without any contact. He did not stop though, continuing to attack with merciless wrath the girl standing there in the increasingly pouring rain.

"I don't think we can settle this at all," Gavrikov said,

looking around at each of them in turn. "What were we ever able to do from within Sienna, after all?" He stared into the distance, the mountain rising above the village looming.

"You used to set her hand on fire all the time," Zack said, trying to breathe a little hope into them. "And Harmon—you can use your telepathy, can't you?"

"I can't," Harmon said. "She has an empath, and they seem to be blocking me, either intentionally or by proximity." He looked around. "That said…Zack has a point. We're inside the enemy fortress right now."

"I think we've all noticed that," Bastian said. "Can any of the rest of you…just feel the seething rage around us?" He looked around. "The hills are alive with a whole lot of pissed-off people."

"I feel it, yes," Harmon said. "I think it's the other souls she's taken and pressed into service. There must be… thousands."

"And we thought Sienna was a killer," Eve said darkly. "Figures Wolfe would switch his allegiance to this Rose."

"I wouldn't have called that, myself," Zack said, truly feeling the disappointment and surprise combo, rolling through his—well, he didn't have a body, as such, so it must have rolled through his soul. "He always seemed so loyal, right up until—"

"Until we came to Scotland," Harmon said. "Then he got sullen. Withdrawn. Stuck in his own head—"

"Or lack thereof," Zack muttered.

"We can't worry about him right now," Harmon said. "We have problems of our own."

Zack could agree with that. The cold rain was coming down around them, and he looked up at the grey sky. It was complete and total, from one side of the horizon to the other—Scottish sunshine indeed. "What the hell are we supposed to do now?"

"We wait," Harmon said, though he did not sound sure. The others, still gathered in their little circle, shifted uneasily.

Gavrikov evinced a hint of worry, one of the few times Zack had ever seen that from him that did not involve his sister. "Because really…there's nothing else we can do right now…"

2.

Sienna

My mother had a favorite quote when she used to train me: "There's always someone bigger and badder than you." In the way of all teenagers, I just thought she was stupid. Drunk on my own teenage invincibility, I didn't think I'd ever meet that bigger and badder person.

There was a pain in my shoulder. It radiated out along my arm, the product of getting dragged beneath a truck for hours. It wasn't the sort of thing that you could call deleterious, but it still ached. It had been worse a few hours ago, before I'd caught some sleep under some bushes on the side of the road, but it was still present, like a reminder that I'd not only gotten my ass kicked last night, but kicked well and truly.

The sound of car engines was a low buzz in the distance, and I raised my head. I'd slept in the dirt, the remainder of my tattered clothes now covered with grains of sandy soil. I brushed the bottom branches of the tree above me, rattling the boughs such that I bristled, stiffening like I'd heard something. I had, and it was myself, and even that was enough to send a thrill of fear all the way through me.

I didn't know it at the time, but my mother had a "bigger and badder" person in mind when she said that little ditty. His name was Sovereign. I eventually ended up fighting him and beating him, and since that day, six years ago, I had gotten in a lot of fights.

Actually, saying "a lot" might be understating it.

I had gotten in a heaped shit ton of fights, and I'd won every single one of them in the end. There wasn't a person who'd stood against me that I hadn't bested or let walk away. I kicked more ass than the proverbial Chuck Norris, whom the internets had suggested, lightly, was perhaps my father. There were a whole slew of jokes about it.

And then I'd come to Scotland…and man, had I gotten my ass whooped.

I finally found that badder person Mom had promised, and she turned out to be a real—

"Son of a bitch," I said under my breath, the sound of my voice piercing the early morning calm. There was little noise of nature in this thicket of trees, overcome as it was by the nearby road. The sun was either up and covered by clouds, or still working on rising. I was in Scotland, which meant it could go either way, really. I sat up, dragging the ragged ruin of my shirt along with me, a tragic tangle of cloth that hadn't just seen better days, it had pretty much reached the end of its effective life as any kind of cover for my body. It lacked an entire sleeve, just as my pants were missing a whole leg.

The wilds of Scotland did not answer my comment. I was in a seemingly endless forest that stretched off to hillocks on either side of me, trees giving me cover in this little valley that was pierced only by a road some hundred or so feet to my right. I was probably less than an hour outside Edinburgh, though it was hard to tell. I'd been in a rough state last night, shock and trauma having done their part. I'd been hanging on the bottom of a truck, lucky I didn't get wrapped around the transaxle, holding tight to the chassis like Indiana Jones, for however long it had taken me to get to this point. I'd dropped to the ground when the thin sliver of the world I could see from the undercarriage had been green for a long time, and then rolled off the road to come to rest in the underbrush, where I'd remained until now.

And if I could have…I probably would have stayed there a lot longer.

The pangs of hunger were doing their work, though. My stomach felt like it was filled with a thousand living bugs that were crawling within, scratching and biting and trying to get the hell out. It was a beyond-uncomfortable sensation, and I wanted it to end in the worst way. I almost considered grabbing a handful of sand and trying to swallow it, just to shut my belly up—it had been a long time since I'd had a meal—but that was stupid. Trying to gut down a handful of sand wasn't going to solve the problem. Nor was chewing on tree bark or leaves or any of the other nasty options available to me close at hand.

Normally, I would have been up and moving by now, in this situation. My brain was screaming at me to put some distance between myself and the road, to get going and haul ass away from here. I'd left tracks by the road side when I'd rolled down the embankment, and some sharp-eyed soul could maybe have picked them out. Movement was a compelling idea—

But it wasn't compelling me. Not enough to move me.

Not right now.

I listened to the silence in my head. It was impressive, and total, and…

Lonely.

I'd had souls in my head for as long as I could remember. As a succubus, I could drain the life out of my enemies. I'd used the power sparingly, adding only four of the seven I ended up with willingly. The other three were forced upon me in some way, but they were still…mine.

And now for the first time since I was seventeen years old, my head was filled with a breathtaking silence. Left alone with my own thoughts, I had never quite realized exactly how much background noise that those souls had added to my life.

Car engines hummed occasionally in the distance. A bird tweeted somewhere to my left. A wind rolling through stirred all the tree branches before departing and leaving them shaking, a few overlapping ones clacking together.

Silence.

And not a silence I was used to.

"I have to move," I said, saying what I thought one of them might say in this circumstance. I focused, the cool morning air prickling at my skin. It was midsummer, but it was Scotland, which meant that it was still chilly.

Silence. No reply in the depths of my mind.

"I have to go," I said, trying to muster up the will to get to my feet, to get moving. My own voice seemed inadequate to the task of motivating me to action.

A car in the distance applied its brakes, and I could hear it squeaking to a stop. I listened, my ears perked up, as it slowed and finally came to a rest, engine idling. It wasn't far away, maybe a hundred feet, close to where I'd gotten off the truck last night.

Doors opened, then slammed shut.

A voice cracked in the morning. "You check over there, I'll look over here."

"Aye," another answered, "I think I see what the helicopter spotted. The ground's all turned up over here, like someone crawled."

Helicopter? Had I missed a helicopter in my sleep?

"Could have been an animal," the first voice said.

"Could have. I'm calling it in anyway."

"Aye, best be safe than sorry."

I was on my feet now. A helicopter had spied where I'd crawled off the road, barely able to move because of injuries from my last fight, and the dragging wounds I'd suffered while riding the bottom of the truck. For all I knew, there was a trail of blood leading right to me. A bloodhound could probably follow me easily.

"I thought you said you were going to call it in?"

"I am, I am; just a wee second."

I clenched my fist. I couldn't let them call it in, whoever

they were. They'd bring all manner of hell down on me, and now that I'd lost my voices—my souls—I'd lost the power to fly the hell out of here in a hot second, to heal myself nearly instantly after a grievous wounding—hence my spending the night under the bushes—and nearly all my power to fight back.

Nearly all.

Choosing my path carefully, I set around the edges of the bush, snaking my way hurriedly but carefully back up toward the road. I had to stop them before they called for help, or else they might summon more trouble to me than I could possibly handle.

3.

Reed
Eden Prairie, Minnesota

It was just before midnight, and all of us had been glued to the TV in the bullpen for countless hours. I'd watched the footage coming out of Edinburgh with alternating fear and horror wrestling like twin snakes in my belly. Someone had turned loose metahuman powers in a major way, but naturally all the blame was going to Sienna, even though everyone on the planet knew she didn't have the ability to shoot giant red exploding forcefield beams out of her hands (I don't know how else to describe them). It was a subtle narrative trick, but one that the news anchor providing breathless coverage of the chaos—which hadn't had an actual news update in about six hours—had well in hand by now.

"Again, we are coming to you live," the head anchor—head wanker, more like—said, "and this is a BREAKING NEWS ALERT." He got very self important as he said this, slight double chin wobbling, his bald head gleaming under the studio lights. "Sienna Nealon has been involved in rogue metahuman action this evening in Edinburgh, Scotland. Details are still scarce—"

"Hasn't stopped you from talking about it non-stop for the last six hours though, has it?" Augustus Coleman said, his patience with this twenty-four-hour news bullshit as thin as my

24

own. "I mean, really, people. Just shut up for a little while and let some facts roll in before you go running your mouths."

"Well, that's the hazard of humanity, isn't it?" Jamal Coleman asked, quietly pensive. He was standing back, had been on his feet the whole time, occasionally walking back to his computer and giving it a tweak with his electricity powers, probably downloading the whole internet into his brain and coming back to stand, nervously, around the TV with the rest of us. "We always operate from incomplete information, but it never seems to stop us from arriving at our judgments. About our actions, about others…we've got an opinion on everything, but when you stop and think about it? It's breathtaking how little we actually know."

"Speak for yourself," Guy Friday said. "I know lots. Lots and lots. I know so much you could fill books with it." He was still wearing that black mask that he always seemed to wear, everywhere he went—which begged the question to me of how he didn't get in trouble with stores when he did his shopping—but judging by the thin, pursed line that was his lips, showing through the gap for his mouth, he was as worried as the rest of us. You could kind of tell by the quiet. Under normal conditions, he wouldn't shut up.

These were the first words Friday had said in about three hours. He had a hand on his chin, and he'd chewed his fingernails down to almost nothing, a ragged edge left on the tips.

Someone eased up to me, his curly, dirty blond hair visible by dint of the way he'd lowered his head, like he was doing some serious pondering of his own. "What the hell do we do about this?" Scott Byerly asked, voice so low that it wouldn't be blazingly obvious to everyone else in the room that we were even talking.

"Yo, I can hear you," Augustus said, not turning around. "Scotty. Meta-low talking only works around people who ain't metas."

"We're not doing anything," I said, answering probably a

little too quickly. Every head in the bullpen turned to me.

"Yo, chief," J.J. said, "this is Sienna we're talking about."

"She's a big girl, though," Abby said, giving a flash of her pink hair as she turned to speak directly to J.J. himself. "She can deal."

"Hey, guys?" Chase Blanton asked, a little tentatively. She was the newest member of our team, and had only been with us for a couple months. She'd come recommended by Sienna. To me. In a dream. And as strange as that sounds, it was good enough for me. "I'm gonna head out, okay?"

"Sure," I said, trying to be as quietly magnanimous as possible. We were way after hours here, and I hadn't even considered how some of these people might have been hanging out because I was, following in the example of the boss. "Anyone who wants to go, seriously, guys, you can leave any time."

"Yeah, we know that," Jamal said, keeping his eyes fixed on the TV. "Angel and Miranda left hours ago."

I looked around. I didn't even know Miranda and Angel had gone. But then, I'd been a little distracted with what was going on with the TV and the complete lack of new news.

And here I was, left with a core group that had all—mostly—worked with and knew Sienna, and we were all standing around the bullpen with the hour hand creeping closer to midnight on the wall clock, watching a pointless news broadcast that would tell us no more than it had six hours ago, the last time they'd actually had something to report. The live broadcast from Scotland showed signs of the horizon lightening behind the reporter, grey skies showing themselves in full, UK glory.

I looked up; Chase had disappeared out of the exit to the lobby without another word, and that left those of us remaining all staring at the screen. No one was wavering, no one was looking around, trying to figure out when it was polite to make their exit. There was concern, there was worry—surprising, I know, coming from Friday, but it was there—and there was—I think—just a little fear.

Maybe that was just me.

"I'm heading out, guys," I said, trying to put a pin in this before everybody stayed up til unholier hours for news that wasn't forthcoming. Sienna had probably found a place to lay low, a nice hole she could crawl in and say, "To hell with the world," until it forgot about her for a bit. Maybe she'd even jetted off to another continent. She could be almost to Australia by now, for all we knew, after all.

My announcement seemed to break up the party a little. "Say hey to Isabella for us," Abigail called.

"You're such a sweet and considerate person," J.J. said. They leaned forward and kissed. Then again. Then—

"Yeah, I'm out, too," Augustus said, on his feet at meta speed double time.

J.J. and Abby broke for air, and he winked at me, like he thought he'd done me a favor by clearing out the bullpen. "Just as well," J.J. said. "You wouldn't have wanted to see where it goes next."

I cringed, not because of their inappropriate PDA, but because I saw one of our people had drifted over to them, leaning against over the top of the cubicle wall they were sitting in front of. "I'm interested," Friday said, leaning over casually. "Go on. I'll watch."

"Time for me to call it a night," Scott said, and bailed for the lobby.

"Yep, it's late," Jamal said, right after him.

"Too true, gents," Augustus said, looking right at me. "Shall we?"

I looked at J.J., who appeared completely stricken, looking with paralyzed horror up at Friday. Abby was slightly cooler, but there was a sense of panic hiding in her eyes, one which I couldn't find myself too sympathetic to, given how many times they'd pulled this geek love PDA trick to get us out of the office.

"We shall," I said. "Later, kids." And I walked out with Augustus, leaving them to their fates.

"Uh, Reed?" J.J. called after me.

"Just lock up when you guys leave, okay?" I called over my shoulder, and disappeared into the short hallway that led to the lobby. Augustus walked at my side, trying to keep a straight face.

"Okay," Friday said after we left, "let's get this party started. I'm thinking you can start by kissing her, like down the neck, and then you, girl whose name I can't remember—"

"It's Abigail," she said coldly.

"Whatever. You bite his earlobe. Like you mean it. Like a raccoon with rabies, you know? And then—"

"This isn't an adult movie, Friday," Abby said. "We don't need a director." There was a short pause. "Oh...oh, God. Why did I even have to explain that to you?"

"I'm thinking severe brain damage has something to do with it," J.J. said.

As soon as Augustus and I were out the front door, Augustus dissolved into a fit of snickering. Jamal and Scott were waiting just outside, watching the door like they knew we were coming. The sky was black like poured tar, a few streetlights scattered around the parking lot holding the night at bay around us. It was a warm summer night, one of the few in Minnesota where it felt like it wasn't going to get cool at all, maybe.

I came to a stop, feeling a little like I'd walked into an ambush. "Why do I feel like you guys are about to draw guns and shoot me down right here?"

Augustus shifted nervously next to me. "Dude...you were dead silent in there, for like...hours."

"We were just wondering if you were okay," Scott said, and his lips creased with a supportive smile.

"I'm fine," I said, folding my arms in front of me. "I'm not the one being chased by John Law on another continent."

"It's okay to worry about her," Augustus said.

"Didn't know I needed permission for that," I said as lightly as I could given the subject matter, "but thanks."

"He just means that what you're feeling, what you're thinking—it's all normal," Scott said.

I tried not to be a dick, but I probably missed the mark. "It's normal to have your sister be the subject of an international manhunt? Interesting. I should look into support groups for that, then. Find some people who understand."

"Reed…" Augustus started.

"Guys," I said, pre-empting what I was sure was going to be a very kind set of thoughts that I'd end up somehow throwing back in their faces, "it's okay. *I'm* okay. And I'll see you all tomorrow." And with that I turned to walk away, a gnawing pit of worry still writhing in my stomach.

4.

Sienna

I didn't have much time, so I tried to focus. Worry was the enemy of intelligent action, because it used brain cells that you needed in order to be on the top of your game. I slipped through the Scottish underbrush, bushes barely touching me as I went past, heading for the voices ahead and the road I'd left behind when I'd crawled this way the night before.

Moving like a metahuman meant running at speeds most people couldn't really conceive of. It was like being an Olympic sprinter times two, my legs pumping so quickly and crazily that when I'd seen myself filmed running, it looked absurd, like someone had kicked the video into high speed. I was doing that now, leaping over a sapling here, dodging under a low branch there, assessing the threats to me and avoiding them quicker than the human eye could normally even process them.

The smell of rich, green forests was thick in the cool, morning air. The fresh air would normally have been an incentive to—I dunno, go for a run or something if you were into that. And I was certainly running this morning, but the incentive in this case was to bust the living crap out of an officer of Police Scotland before he got a chance to broadcast my location to anybody and everybody this side of—oh, I dunno, Scotland, pick a frigging city. Inverness. That one was big back in the day, wasn't it? Macbeth took place there, didn't it?

Up ahead I could see the vegetation clear; green branches and light brown boughs gave way to grey skies beyond. I was sprinting up the embankment below the road, and I heard a male voice start to speak, following a hiss of static as he thumbed a microphone. He must have heard me coming, though, because he hesitated before saying anything.

I burst out of the trees and hit him like a freight train. I wasn't aiming to kill him, but I assaulted that police officer hard, keeping on after I kicked his legs out from beneath him. They flew up, leaving him as my violent sweeping kick landed, and I was moving on to the next target, figuring hesitation was my deadliest enemy in this fight. I grimaced and said, "Sorry," as I rammed into the second officer. He'd been grabbing for a baton the moment he'd seen me, but he didn't have a prayer. I'd only had to cover about ten feet once I left the cover of trees, and that was simply too much for human reflexes to deal with. He'd needed to draw his baton, deploy it, and then raise it and bring it down on me. He'd gotten to about halfway through deploying it when I jacked him in the jaw. The light went out of his eyes and the strength went out of his legs, and he sagged. I caught him and let him down slowly, then turned my attention back to the guy I'd cut the legs from beneath.

He was moaning, but coming back to himself, so I took a couple quick steps over to him and punched him right in the forehead. It hurt me, it hurt him, but it put his lights out and I didn't break his skull, so I considered it a win overall. He was probably going to wake up concussed, but he'd wake up, and that was important for reasons of his health and my conscience.

I looked around. We were down in a ditch just off the roadway, probably about ten feet down the slope. I could hear a car or two coming by, but I couldn't see them from where I was standing, and that was damned good luck, the first piece I felt like I'd had in a while. I stood there for only a second catching my breath after the run and the—uhm, assaulting a police officer—and reflected that it was already time to go back to work.

It only took me about ten seconds to load a cop over each shoulder and then carry them back into the woods. I didn't want to go too far, so I stopped about ten feet in, where there was enough cover that they wouldn't be immediately visible from the road, but they weren't totally out of sight, either. I figured a helicopter with thermal gear would be coming this way once their higher ups figured out they were missing, probably go along their patrol path. Here they'd find them, if a passing motorist didn't hear the screams first.

These were the judgments I made in seconds, and I defy you to figure out how to make better ones.

I took the clothes off the shortest one, including his boots and that stupid reflective vest. I rolled up the cuffs of his pants and put them on, then did the same to his shirt. I laced his boots up tight, and sucked it up as I pulled his belt as tight as it could go. Fortunately (or maybe unfortunately, given that my waistline allowed me to wear a man's belt), that fit fine.

"Guess I need cardio after all," I muttered under my breath. Usually that was the sort of line that would provoke a good gout of laughter and commentary from the voices in my head, but...

I didn't have any more voices in my head.

Shit.

I put the stupid cop hat on after cramming all my hair up underneath it in an unrestrained bun. The hat did a fine job of holding it back, fortunately, and I only hoped that it'd changed the look of me enough that people wouldn't be shouting, "That's Sienna Nealon!" as I passed. It was the most I could hope for at this point.

I had several problems to solve, but the most pressing was that without Aleksandr Gavrikov rustling around in my brain, I'd lost my ability to retreat effectively. Time was, I could turn on the supersonic flight powers and be in Zimbabwe by now, all worries about Scottish police in my rearview.

Without Gavrikov, though…I was a sitting duck for patrols like this. Well, maybe not exactly like this, but certainly any patrols that came armed would have a better chance of bringing me low now that I was as close to powerless as I'd been since that time I'd been gassed with a drug that suppressed metahuman abilities.

Taking short breaths to calm myself, I started back up the hillside toward the road. I'd taken the other cop's gear and tossed it aside after cuffing them both around the tree in their undershirts and boxers. "I miss undressing a man for the fun of it," I said aloud, again forgetting that I had no audience for my brilliant wisecracks now. Which was a shame, because the edification of a laugh track in your life almost made me understand why stupid sitcoms put them in.

Honestly, though, there were a lot of things in my life that I missed at this stage of the game, having been an international fugitive for however many months (like seven or eight, but who was counting other than the news channels?). Being able to have breakfast with friends. Sitting in my living room, watching TV without worrying someone was going to come bursting in to arrest me. Sleeping at night without having paranoid dreams about waking up in a jail cell—or not at all.

My feet crunched the dewy grass as I came up on the road next to the police car. It was another shoe-sized car, like all of them over here seemed to be. I missed pickup trucks, and SUVs, and the glorious American cars that stated plainly that if you didn't get the hell out of the road, we would run you over and you would die, instead of suffering a tragic injury to your big toe where it scraped the bumper.

I missed home, I realized for the zillionth time as I opened the wrong door to the police car, and had to circle around to the driver's side. Someone came by at about twenty miles an hour, and I waved to them as I turned my head away, trying to make sure they couldn't see my face. They kept going, which I hoped meant that I'd succeeded as I slid into the driver's side, which was, because it was the bass-ackward UK, on the wrong damned side of the car.

It started up with a choking sputter, sounding a little like I'd turned on an RC car, and I sighed again, deciding it would be best to avoid getting in any high-speed chases. I scoured the car quickly, and found no joy in the form of hidden handguns or the like. I hadn't expected to, but I still found it unfortunate, because I'd had one last night, but it had gotten lost somewhere in my fight with Rose.

Rose.

Here was a name that stirred questions and provided no damned answers. I was so tangled that even thinking about that red-headed bitch made me want to throw every thought of feminist cooperation and empowerment back in someone's face along with a hard damned slap, the sort that wouldn't just rattle their head but bust it clean off.

Rose had played my friend and fan better than anyone I'd ever seen do it before. There was something about people that shone through, that hint of malice you could see when you looked in their eyes.

There had been none of that for my pale, red-headed "friend." I'd taken her power at face value, ignored the fact that I couldn't read her mind because the story she presented seemed oh-so-logical, and because she'd taken a bullet for me. That was a commitment to the art of deception I'd never been prepared for. People who wanted to trick me usually kept their plans simpler.

Rose, though—she'd gone for the gold. She'd stayed by my side long past a time when she had ample opportunity to kill me without resistance. She could have snuffed me in my sleep, multiple times. She had enough power she could have turned me into free-floating atoms any one of a hundred times I turned my back on her.

But she didn't. She didn't even give me a sour look, nor a kick in the duff, not even a cross word…until she was ready to end the charade.

Shit, that was some deep planning. It bespoke of a hostility that was almost otherworldly in origin, the kind of white-hot hate and scary levels of self-discipline that I hadn't seen outside of…well, Mom, I guess.

And Rose was a succubus.

"Shit," I said under my breath, lowering my head. She was Scottish-born—if her story to me could be trusted, which…I guess it couldn't. So maybe she wasn't Scottish at all. She'd said that her meta powers came from her drifter father, but now I had to doubt that, too. I'd thought she was young, younger than me, but now every single thing she told me about herself was thrown into doubt. Her name might not even have been Rose, for all I knew. It could have been Frito Bandito.

But probably not that. I'd given this Rose problem some thought while contemplating the underaxle of a truck last night, and the number of conclusions I'd come to was roughly zero. All I had was that she hated me enough to run the longest con of all the long cons I could remember, short of maybe Sovereign or Old Man Winter, and all in order—in her words (if they could be trusted)—to "know me."

Why the hell would she want to know me?

Who the hell was this girl?

And, I wondered, not nearly the last of the questions I had, but the one bubbling most fiercely in my upset, rumbling, hungry stomach…What was she doing right now?

5.

I drove along a scenic Scottish road, and by scenic I meant mostly covered in trees with the occasional overlook of a lake, or loch, I suppose they called it, because when you're at the northern rump end of a country, why not just call things whatever the hell you want?

The sun was barely visible through a thin string of clouds, shining down on the loch like it was going to be a quasi-beautiful day for everyone but those of us being actively pursued by law enforcement. I stole glances at the sparkling loch while driving and trying to orient myself, because I had no idea where the hell I was and even less idea of where I was going, save for, "the hell outta here," and as quickly as it could be arranged.

Fortunately, I had an idea about that, and was debating how best to execute said idea. I had stolen a cell phone from one of the cops I'd mugged (yeah, I mugged them, let's be honest about what happened), several, actually, both personal and work ones, and luckily a couple of them were smartphones. I was under no illusions about how long I could actually hold onto them; I planned to get the info I needed and ditch them into the nearest loch as soon as I could find a scenic overlook that would allow me to pull off and do some web browsing.

I found it about a half mile ahead, a little paved area that was fenced to keep anyone from tumbling their ass down the hill and into the water, and nosed the car into a parking space and shifted the little go kart into park, phone already in hand. I dialed a number from memory, one that was international, to a burner phone that would have to be, well, burned, after this call.

"This is Fritz," a male voice answered on the other end of the line. He spoke in a thick accent, Germanic in style, though I'd never heard him speak German.

"You're not keeping banker's hours today, Mr. Fritz," I said. Truth was, he never kept bankers' hours, even though he was, in fact, a banker. My banker, in fact, in cozy Liechtenstein.

"Ms—" he started.

"No need for names," I said coolly. I wasn't sure how sophisticated the Brit version of the NSA was, but they were probably monitoring cell phone calls for my voice, and I didn't need a name tagged to go along with it. That would just speed up the ID process.

Fortunately, being a banker to the wealthy and somewhat criminal, Fritz caught on quickly. "I understand you've had a spot of trouble."

"You could say that," I said, tensely, looking at the lake—loch, whatever—and trying to use its placid surface to give myself a peaceful feeling that was not so strangely lacking in my life today. "I need cash and transport the hell out of this country."

If he thought my request strange, he didn't deign to mention it to me. "Anything can be arranged for the proper…incentive. What sort of transport were you thinking?"

"Private plane," I said, thumbing on the other officer's smartphone so I could browse while I chatted. Luckily, neither one of them had bothered to set a passcode. Silly of them, really. "I'm about an hour outside Edinburgh, apparently. How long will it take you to get a private plane—a trusted one—to, say, the airfield at…" I started to scroll my Google results for "airfield."

"I have an airfield near Lochty, assuming you want to stay

out of Edinburgh, given the circumstances," he said casually, like he arranged illegal transport for fleeing felons all the time. For all I knew, he did. He didn't technically work for the bank itself, after all. I'd have to call my actual banker, Nils, and arrange payment after he quoted me a fee. "It is just a field, though, a grass strip in the middle of nowhere. Does that work?"

"That works," I said. "Also, for planning purposes, I might need some, uh…toys." I really didn't want to be specific here, because if I said, "I need grenade launchers, rocket launchers, machine guns, a nuclear bomb, etc." I was pretty Brit NSA would be all over that shit, no matter how lousy they were at their job. A fricking third world knockoff NSA consisting of two guys and one of those old long-range microphones would pick up on that kind of conversation.

"I see," he said, still cool about the whole thing. "Have you run into a difficulty that is beyond your usual abilities?"

"Yeah," I said. "You could say that. I need some special shopping done. From the kind of markets that, uh…well, would be easier in the US, but most difficult in Europe." I hoped that was subtle enough for the Brits, but clear enough for him.

"I believe we can accommodate such a request," he said. "For a modest fee."

"Tell me how much you need, and I'll call Mr. Nils and have him wire the money." I braced myself, because I knew this was going to hurt.

"I think five million should cover it," came the answer a moment later. "Top to bottom."

I wanted to say it was highway robbery, but I was sitting on the shoulder of a highway and I had zero ability to throw flame, light nets, fly, heal my wounds rapidly, or turn into a dragon if need be. If someone came along to highway rob me right now, my recourse was to beat their skull in. I didn't like that, because I'd come to enjoy having other abilities at my fingertips for when trouble (inevitably) came a-callin'.

"Done and done," I said. It wasn't like I'd earned that money, and I could smell the danger I was in right now. A private plane out of the country and some serious hardware for five mil? I'd pay that price, get the hell out of here, and regroup, make my plans for revenge, and come back to bushwhack Rose when she least expected it. Or else find a way to lure her to me and into a trap, throw her off her game and finish this fight that way.

No matter how I played it, though, getting hounded by Police Scotland until they ran me to ground? Not an effective way of dealing with my Rose problem. Thorny little bitch.

"A pleasure as always," Fritz said, and then he hung up, presumably to deal with the problems of arranging a private plane for an international fugitive and lots of guns to be smuggled into a country that didn't really truck with that sort of thing.

My next call was also from memory, and was answered on the third ring by a curious voice. "Hello?"

"This is, uh," I started, hoping he'd recognize my voice. "Well, I hope you know who."

"I think I recognize your voice," Nils said. "And I somehow thought I might hear from you today."

"You're a smart guy when it comes to knowing your customers and their needs, Mr. Nils," I said. "I need a payment to Fritz. Five mil."

If he was surprised at the sum—larger than I typically moved, but I had somewhere near half a billion still sitting in his bank—he evinced no surprise. "I see. I will arrange it immediately."

"Thanks," I said. I might have chitchatted more, but neither he nor I were chitchatty people, and I suspected he was as busy as I was. "By the way, this number—"

"I assume it won't be in service much longer?" he asked, but he did so in the manner of a man who already knew the answer.

"Safe bet," I said. "As always."

"Til next time, then," he said.

"Thanks," I said, and as soon as the call was disconnected I broke the phone in half, looking around to make sure no one was watching, and rolled down the window and tossed it into the loch. I finished my browse, finding out that there was a nearby town just up the road, and then broke that phone in half too. I'd been careful not to plot any trips, instead figuring out where that Lochty airfield was by visual inspection only, then after busting that phone followed it with the two police cell phones, which were just plain flip ones. I thought about tossing the radios too, but those couldn't be tracked (that I knew of) and I'd been listening to the low-level chatter of their manhunt, hoping not to hear anything like, "She's stolen a police car and is on Route Blankety-Blank, on the shore of Loch Rainyland." Because that would be bad.

The last of the things I needed disposed of now gone, I popped the car into gear. Still getting used to driving on the other side of the road, I eased back out into the light flow of traffic along the scenic lane and took a left. Hopefully the village ahead would continue to provide me a respite for trouble, and I'd be able to grab what I needed, swap cars, and get the hell out of Scotland before anything else bad happened.

But somehow...I had a feeling it wasn't going to be nearly that easy, because with me? It never was.

6.

The Scottish village wasn't really much of a village. It was more like a collection of houses that were grouped casually together with a church, a petrol station, as they called them, and little else.

Luckily for me, there were woods nearby, and I took full advantage, ditching the cop car after I wedged it between two trees in a parallel parking situation right out of Austin Powers. I didn't do the parallel park myself, of course; I actually picked up the car and moved it there, partially to take this particular instrument out of Police Scotland's arsenal, and mostly to test my own succubus-level strength, because it had been a while since I'd done anything without Wolfe power.

I was still strong enough to lift a car, so that was good. And it wasn't even the full height of my powers, luckily, because I had a feeling that if the dread that was building in my belly gave way to an actual reason for being rather than just a nervous residue of the ass-kicking I'd received last night, I'd be needing that strength.

Hiking back to the village only took a short while, a quick run over uneven ground. I surveyed it while remaining hidden in the trees, trying to figure out where I'd do my respective misdeeds.

I needed, in this order: another car, preferably one that wouldn't be missed for a while; clothes to disguise me; and possibly some petty cash and/or a meal. Because I hadn't eaten since either yesterday or the day before (sad that I couldn't recall), and my stomach was whining in hunger as well as fear, though it was getting hard to tell the difference.

Making my way out of the trees, I tried to walk as casually as possible. I was up on a high approach to the village, and it seemed likely someone was going to see me at some point. There I'd be, a police officer strolling down out of the heights. I wanted to try and make it look casual, no big deal, just out on patrol without a police car anywhere in sight. To that end, I didn't run, I just walked like I had all the time in the world, because furtive movements would do a lot more to give me away than casual action. The entirety of Scotland was now in a manhunt for Sienna Nealon. Watching a lady cop walk out of the hills was weird, but it would be a lot less weird than seeing one come darting out of the hills like she was trying to play spy. That kind of thing got the cops called on you, even if you were a cop.

I strolled down into the backyard of the nearest house and vaulted the fence lightly like I owned the place. I'd read that in Scotland there was something called the "right to wander," which meant you could basically cross private property without consequence so long as you didn't mess with someone's cattle or do something similarly dickish, and so I just kept my hands at my sides and walked like I had nothing going on this morning as I strolled toward the small blue house ahead.

Other houses were a ways off, probably fifty yards to my left and right. There were only about ten homes in the entirety of the village, so if someone saw me, I was under no illusions about how fast word of my appearance would travel. Hell, it was probably already fully spread through this place.

Coming up to the somewhat ragged back door of the house, I gave a polite little knock, then tilted my head to look at the picture window to the right of the door. A dog barked inside, and I could hear its claws drag the carpet as it scampered toward the back door to…I dunno, lick me to death or something.

Once again, I looked to my left, to my right, and then behind me. I couldn't see the houses on either side, and behind me there was only a slow hill climb up to the woods, so…this was about the best I was going to get, especially since there was no sound of a human from within the dwelling.

I reached down and broke the door, cracking the mechanism right out of the frame and pushing it in slowly. I didn't want to turn Fido into a skidmark on the entry carpet, so I took my time and the dog yelped, skittering around and barking furiously. I debated letting the pup out, but instead I slipped inside and then closed the door behind me.

Greeting me was a pug that was probably no bigger than a double burrito from Chipotle. His barks were low, and a little wheezy. "Hey, big guy," I said, and he sniffed my pant leg, putting aside the barking. Dogs liked me, and I had little idea why, because I was pretty neutral on them. Maybe it was all the meat I ate, oozing through my pores. *This is a kindred spirit and meat sister!* they'd be thinking, and then try to lick me until they got all the good stuff. That was the only explanation I had.

This pup was no exception, and he dutifully followed me around after I stooped down and offered him my hand, fist closed, extending it for him to give a lick or two. He backed off first, then trudged forward experimentally and gave me a couple of sloppy, cool slurps with the old tongue. After that, the barking was done and we were fast friends.

I was pretty sure no one was home, judging by the fact that no one answered the door. That was hardly conclusive evidence, but I'd also not heard anyone, and given my super hearing, that was a little closer to proving my thesis correct. I made my way through the house quietly just in case, sweeping from the hallway next to the rear door and into the main living area. I listened carefully, trying to hear over the pup scampering along the wood paneled floor behind me.

The whole house was dark, but, judging by the outside, not terribly big. I'd assembled a mental sketch of it from the exterior, and it looked long and linear, all the rooms built sideways with the front facing the street, and the back, obviously, facing the wilderness I'd trekked through to get here. I'd entered on the left side, and there didn't seem to be much room for anything other than a bathroom and a coat closet on this side of the house, which I quickly confirmed as being the case before turning right and entering a small kitchen and living room combo.

There wasn't a light on, and the place smelled of stale cigarettes, which made me cringe. I hated the smell of smoke, and it doubly bothered me because of my meta sense of smell, which enhanced almost everything, allowing me to partake in secondhand smoke (fortunately not a health risk to me, just stinky) from what felt like miles away. I'd caught a whiff of this from outside, but what else was I going to do? It was the house best angled to prevent people from seeing my B & E, and it didn't seem like anyone was home…

That changed quickly. I heard something stir in the bedroom, and for a brief second I hoped it was another dog; just another pup, happy and friendly as this one, but more lethargic. Getting some zzzs, maybe. I froze halfway across the living room, my tiptoeing act coming to an abrupt stop so quickly that the pug following behind me collided with the back of my ankle. It would have been comical if the little shit hadn't surprised me in doing so.

I squelched the desire to let out a yelp of surprise, but the dog did not. He caught my calf and Achilles tendon right in the face, and although it couldn't have hurt much, he seemed offended by it, and let me and whoever else was in the house know it with a series of barks.

If there was someone stirring in the bedroom, they were either hiding—possibly having called the actual police before doing so—or else they were the heaviest sleeper in the history of man. "Archie! Shut the hell up!" someone bellowed in a heavy Scottish accent. It took my brain a second or two to translate that.

Archie took off, apparently so offended by my sudden stop and his own clumsiness that he was going to run to his master. He shot around the corner, yelping all the way, like a kid going to tattle to mommy. "Traitor," I muttered low enough that only the dog and I could hear it. I was probably the only one who could understand it.

The dog jumped on the bed with a squeak, agitating his master further. Heavy Scottish brogue that I couldn't make head nor tails of came from behind the bedroom door across the way, and I tiptoed across the living room in the interim, wondering how best to solve for this problem. I could have left, I supposed, but this problem of mine related to clothing wasn't going to go away anytime soon, and—as the Brits might say—in for a penny, in for a pound. Hell, Americans said that, too.

"Police Scotland!" I announced, trying to throw on as general of an Edinburgh accent to my words as I could. "Come out with your hands up!" I said it bullhorn loud and forceful, and it produced an immediate reaction from inside the bedroom.

Archie let out a fury of barks as he hit the floor, preceded by a yelp that suggested he'd gotten bounced from the bed in his master's haste to exodus the tangled sheets. The smoke smell was even heavier over here, and my already uneasy stomach was moving toward queasy. A burst of furious Scottish came out the open door to the bedroom, and I took a second to loosely translate it as, "What the hell?" It didn't really sound like that, though.

"We know you've got methamphetamines in there," I shouted. "Come out with your hands up and make this easy!" I knew no such thing, but I knew it'd get one of two responses, and I hoped for it to be the one that most harmonized with my needs.

"I don't have *meth* in here," the outraged Scotsman said, coming around the corner with his hands up, and speaking a little more clearly, but not much. I'd crept up to just next to the door while he'd made his way over to it, and as soon as he emerged, ready to protest his innocence at what was clearly a huge mistake, I jumped him.

There was a difference in how I approached this guy versus how I would have approached a bad guy, and it was night and day. I caught his arm and dragged it down, clamping my left around his wrist as he walked out the door beside me and wheeling him around to put my right forearm squarely against his left elbow. If he didn't move where I wanted him to move now, I could really do some damage to his joint, and like most people do when you put them into a painful situation where their arm could break in about two seconds, his gut got the point before his brain caught up.

I whirled him around and put his face in the wall—but gently. Mostly. "Hi," I said, once he was good and planted there, not moving. "Know who I am?" I dropped the Edinburgh accent.

He nodded sharply. "Uh huh." That I understood instantly.

"I'm going to take some of your things," I said. "Some clothes. Some food. And I'm gonna hang out here for a while. I might borrow money when it's all said and done. You're okay with all this, right?" I asked extremely sweetly, though I did still obviously have him in a position where I could shatter his arm like a candy cane against concrete.

"Uh huh," he said, nodding as best he could with the wall in his face. He really rubbed against it, like he wanted to shave the first layer of skin off. "Take whatever ye want." Man, his accent was thick.

"I'm going to tie you up now," I said. "Don't scream, and you won't get hurt. Fair enough?" He nodded. "Do you live with anyone?" I doubted he had a girlfriend by the state of this place—clothes were strewn across the floor, dog toys everywhere—but he surprised me with another nod. "Who, and when will they be here?"

"Kytt," he said, smacking his lips together. "She gets home from work around six."

"Okay. That's fine. I'll be out of here well before Kytt gets home," I said, nodding along with him. "So she'll find you here tied up, and you'll have a fun story to tell all the reporters. You'll be famous." For about five seconds, I didn't bother to add, *Until I assault some other poor schmoe, or wreck a town while passing through, and the media forgets about my last grievous offense in favor of the next one.* "What's your name?"

"John," he said, blinking. "John Clifford."

"All right, John," I said. "You have any rope I can tie you up with?" He shook his head and I sighed. "Clothes it is, then."

I trussed him up with a bunch of old flannel shirts, tying them tight enough that he wasn't going to easily get out, but not so tight it'd cut off circulation. The truth was, clothing was a terrible choice for binding people, because ideally whatever you used would produce chafing and resistance so they didn't try and worm their way out. Clothing was too smooth for that, the fibers easier to rub up against repeatedly in the course of wriggling your way out, but I did the best I could with what I had and knotted it meta-tight, to the point where the sleeves sounded like they were going to rip off.

Once I was done getting John all bound up, which was mostly for psychological effect since he could most likely have escaped them with concerted effort, I led him like a submissive puppy into the next room. "Do you have any duct tape?" I asked, something I should have asked earlier. Duct tape wasn't much better for binding than clothes, honestly—you could escape duct tape with a reasonable amount of torsion against it—but there was a profound consequence to mentally surrendering, and I wanted John to experience it fully, so that he wouldn't do something dumbass like try to escape. Because that would really put a kink in my plans for how today was going to go.

John nodded toward the kitchen, and I dutifully led him back there and found the duct tape. I wrapped him up tight around the wrists, then checked the knot on the clothing. It wasn't coming off easily, and he seemed fearfully impressed, so I just left it along with the double precaution of the tape. I led him back toward the bedroom, not willing to let him out of my sight for long. Once there, I started to raid his closet.

Well, Kytt's closet, anyway. John was too tall for me.

Kytt looked to be a few sizes too tall for me, but unlike Goldilocks, I didn't have a "just right" third option to choose from, so I made do by rolling up Kytt's pant legs. Archie wandered around the entire time, not looking particularly upset by the fact that I'd bound up his master and was now raiding his mistress's wardrobe. He came up and gave me a sniff, like he was trying to decide if whatever scent Kytt offered—it smelled a little lilac-y to me—was better than the sweat of meat that was my signature. He didn't seem impressed either way, and licked my ankle until I put my shoes back on.

I'd kept John's face in the wall while I changed; no threat or anything, just a subtle physical reminder as I turned his head for him that I could break him into tiny, tiny pieces if he pissed me off. I wasn't going to threaten him at all verbally, though he would probably not realize that until later, if ever. Words were slower than pressure applied to a sensitive joint in getting a point across, after all.

"Mind if I hit up your fridge?" I asked once I was done, pulling John off the wall and pushing him toward the living room/kitchen again.

The sound he made was awfully discomfited, but it squeaked out politely enough, and clear, thankfully. "Help yourself."

"Thanks," I said, and pulled him along, Archie trailing in my wake, to finally, *finally*, get something to eat, and settle in for a few hours until I needed to make my way to the airfield so I could get the hell out of this country before anything worse could happen.

7.

Reed

To her credit, Isabella didn't ask me if I'd seen the news when I came walking in. She probably didn't need to, because we'd been together long enough at this point that I was sure she could see the gears turning just by looking at my face. The smell of her perfume wafted lightly through the air of our small apartment in Eden Prairie, just a few short minutes from my work.

And the gears were turning. They'd been turning the whole drive home.

"How was your day?" she asked instead, her Italian accent ever present. I didn't notice it most of the time, unless she was yelling. Then it tended to get really pronounced. She asked neutrally, without a hint of irony, or leading, like she really just wanted to know.

I pondered my answer as I plopped down on the couch next to her. My white collar was already unbuttoned, my tie loosened appropriately, as though I'd been swilling liquor behind the cafeteria at a school dance with the other guys, instead of crammed in a hot bullpen watching cable news report over and over that my sister was the subject of a manhunt in another country for more crimes that I was pretty sure she didn't commit.

"Like someone wiped their ass on my toast," I said, picking

a random metaphor out of the air. It made her frown in contemplation, which I took as a failure, because I'd been hoping to lighten the moment. "Like crap," I said, and the frown lessened a degree.

She nodded. She didn't have to ask if I'd seen. "What are you going to do?" she asked instead.

"Nothing," I said, parroting back what I'd told the boys outside the office. "Sienna's a big girl. She can take care of herself better than any of the rest of us can, our new boosted powers notwithstanding. She did kick all of our asses, minus Jamal, last time we fought, remember."

"It would be hard to forget," she said dryly, probably thinking of how I had disappeared after that for a while. "But…just because she can handle the problem doesn't mean you're not going to agonize worrying over it. How do you feel?"

I put my head back against the soft, white leather couch. It sank back slightly, but I was still able to meet her gaze, even with my head tilted just so, my neck angled uncomfortably. "Powerless," I said. "You and I know this thing, this hunt for her, it's all a farce—"

"She does a fair amount of damage wherever she goes," Isabella said, playing devil's advocate once more. Though, honestly, if she were advocating for the devil, you'd think she'd be on Sienna's side, at least based on the way our world's theology was tilting. Sienna was rapidly achieving boogeyman—or boogeywoman—status. But not woman-who-boogies status, which was a shame, because seeing her dance? Hilarious.

"But that's not why they're after her," I said, shoving up off the couch and taking care not to overturn it, and my paramour, with excess zeal as I did so. "They know she didn't mini-nuke Los Angeles. The government knows she didn't blast the crap out of Eden Prairie for the heck of it. Those criminals were after her, were going to kill her, and President Harmon—"

Isabella held up a hand to her lips, a single finger stretching across their rich, lustrous red. I'd almost let it fly with everything there, and admitting that Sienna had confronted Harmon, resulting in his death, was probably not the sort of thing it'd be wise to say here and now. We were pretty sure the FBI had us under surveillance as part of their general Sienna Nealon investigation. At first it had been really awkward, but after a while we'd simply adapted to the fact that we were probably being constantly listened in on.

On the plus side, I suspected now that Isabella had a bit of a voyeurism fetish, based on her rise in—

Never mind.

Gross.

Anyway. I changed course mid-speech. "It's not fair that she gets blamed for what happened when those crooks came after her. Or what happened to Harmon, because—I mean, let's face it—no one knows what happened to him." I knew what happened to him, at least in general terms, actually, but it wouldn't do to say aloud on an FBI recording, "Yeah, Sienna inadvertently killed his ass, and boy, did he deserve it," however true all that might have been.

"Yes, but people have reason for their suspicions," Isabella said, patiently. Which was funny, because, of the two of us, I was generally the patient one. "Everyone knows she's killed people before. And not just killed them, but cold-bloodedly murdered them. Clyde Clary. Glen Parks, Eve Kappler—"

"I know their names," I said, looking away at the TV, which was dark, thankfully. The last thing I needed at this time of night was to get sucked back into the news cycle.

"She's done so much damage," Isabella said. "The YouTube video of her assaulting a prisoner—"

"I know. I was there, and Eric Simmons could have used a good punching after that—"

"That reporter she slugged—"

"Geez, they blindsided her—"

"I could go on," Isabella said quietly, but seemed to resign herself to not pressing it. I knew she was right anyway. "Everything she's done, right or wrong…it's all bricks in the wall they've used to block her in. Box her in, I guess you could say, if you were feeling…what's the word…ironic?" She made a face that expressed her distaste. "Your sister is a scary person to those looking from the outside. However much good she's done—and I'll admit it's a lot—it doesn't erase the bad, you know."

"I'm not so blinkered I don't see that." I pushed my fingers against my forehead and cheekbones and gave a solid press, battling against sinus pressure that wasn't actually there and a headache that was. "I don't view her as some flawless goddess, all right? But she's saved the world a few times, and she's put a lot of criminals away." I pulled my fingers back from my eyes. "She's fought against people who have no ethical line, who have—in some cases—practically no limits on their power. I mean, look at this Edinburgh thing." I gestured to the black TV screen. "Whoever she fought there, they've got a power tailor-made for massive amounts of destruction." I thought about that red beam ripping through the city on the shaky, camera-phone footage. "How are you supposed to bring someone like that down calmly, without it getting wild?"

Isabella shrugged. "How do you do it?"

I sighed. "Wildly. And sometimes it gets out of control. Recall that I ripped apart a commune outside Orlando earlier this year with a custom-made hurricane. People like us…" I bowed my head, taking a long breath. "We're not human, but we're subject to human laws, and sometimes it stinks, especially when you meet a person who's hell-bent on destruction. I don't think I have to explain to you that there are just certain people out there whose only allegiance is to wrecking everything they possibly can, to hell with who gets hurt in the process." I tried to let out another cleansing breath, but it didn't really cleanse me. I felt as tired, and knotted as ever. "Sienna puts herself up against those people all the time, and she doesn't really get much credit for when things go right, only for when they go madly wrong. Sometimes I wish…" I put my head back again. "Sometimes I wish that she hadn't been found out, that metas had never gone public. Or that she hadn't been around when they did, that we just had a few years of this rising chaos without a Sienna Nealon around to ride herd on it. Let people see what the world would be like without her for a while, let people know what they're missing."

Somehow, speaking this simple truth let some of the sting of all these months of injury, something I'd not ever been able to put my fingers on exactly before, let loose a tide of feeling I could finally put a name to.

Stinging anger at the world's ingratitude toward the person who'd saved them more times than they'd ever know.

"You should be careful what you wish for," Isabella said, taking my hand gently, our living room quiet now, our eyes meeting over the distance between us. "You might just get what you want…and then you might find…it was not what you wanted at all."

8.

Sienna

John's fridge had been inadequately stocked, at best, and between the t-shirt I was now wearing that proclaimed Kytt's allegiance to some (presumably) UK band named (I am not, as Dave Barry would say, making this up) "The Stranglers," and the near-lack of anything life-giving available to eat in this house, I started to suspect this chick's judgment was off.

John himself didn't help that suspicion. He was, as one might expect from a hostage, by turns sullen, and scared, and then verbose in that I'm-a-nervous-Scot-and-you-can't-understand-a-thing-I'm-saying sort of way. For the last half hour, as I'd alternated watching Sky News and the BBC, John had favored me with a hash of his opinions of various topics, including how America was getting it wrong in so many ways. Even though I couldn't disagree with him in many regards, it was still a perpetual irritation to hear your country run down in front of you, and I wondered if he thought he was ingratiating himself to me or was just too nervously stupid to know he was pissing me off by the second.

I was chewing the last meat off a chicken bone, and my patience was wearing thinner than my Stranglers t-shirt, which I suspected had been made by infants in a sweat shop somewhere, such was the quality. Still, of all Kytt's clothing, it fit me the best, probably because it fit her the worst, if I had to guess. All her jeans had holes in the knees for some reason, and, thinking back, I recalled seeing twenty-something girls with exactly that look in Edinburgh. Apparently the American eighties had come late to Scotland.

"I just don't know why you Americans don't—" John started to say.

"Shut up, John," I said, not as lightly as I might have on a truly full stomach. The one leg of chicken and a few slices of stale bread hadn't done much to alleviate my stomach's pissiness. I was about two steps away from opening a can from the pantry described as "Spotted Dick," because there wasn't much in there other than that, and the fridge was now bare save for a bottle of HP sauce, which I had honestly contemplated drinking just for the calories. I gave it a sniff and decided it wasn't worth it. "If you don't stop shit-talking my country," I said, giving John my full attention again, "you're going to see what Merle Haggard called, aptly, 'The Fightin' Side of Me.'" His eyes swelled, and he swallowed visibly at that threat, then nodded. "I need a map," I said, staring him down.

"In the car," he said.

"Great," I said. "Cash?"

"Wallet in the bedroom."

I was ticking through my mental list. "How much?"

"Fifty pounds, maybe?"

That'd do. It would have been better if it had been thousands, but I was beggaring, not choosering. "How full is your gas tank?"

He stared at me curiously for a second, then got it. "It's about half full of petrol. I should warn you—it's not a new car."

"I don't care," I said, because I didn't, insofar as if it moved, I'd work with it. The UK had some sort of rigorous emissions testing standard anyway, so if the car was a giant piece of crap, it probably wouldn't have passed that, leaving me feeling confident it wasn't a total garbage bucket. "I'll try and keep it intact so that the police are able to return it to you whole after I'm done with it." If he took solace in that, he didn't give any sign, still looking like a frog I'd squeezed too tight in the holding.

"Are…are you leaving soon, then?" he asked, doing a little fishing when he found his voice.

"Soon enough," I said, and flipped on the TV in the corner of the living room. It came on to the news, and I was treated to a man staring right into the camera, dressed up in a suit and looking quite coiffed.

"—again, announcing that Police Scotland—" his accent wasn't too bad "—are seeking assistance with their manhunt for Sienna Nealon." He paused, looked at the camera and said, "Err…I mean…womanhunt? Personhunt?" He tried 'em all out, apparently worried about offending someone, presumably not criminal me. He blushed, and went right back to reading.

"Hmph," I said, paying little attention to what was going on now that he was just blathering. "Let's hope they don't find her." I flipped the TV off and looked at John. Archie came up to my ankle again, breathing heavily. "Does he need food before I go?" I dropped down and gave Archie a good petting on the back of the neck. "Who's a good boy? You are. Yes, you are."

"Uh, no, he's fine," John said. "You can go anytime, no worries about us." He smiled, the most forced, plasticine thing I'd ever seen.

"All right," I said. "You're sure about that map in the car?"

"It's in the glove compartment," John said with a swift nod. I meandered over to him as he talked, and he watched me with a wary eye like I was going to strike him dead or something.

I checked the knots and bindings. "You sit your ass in this chair until Kytt gets home tonight," I said, yanking a little harder than was strictly necessary on one of the flannel shirts I'd bound his feet to the chair legs with. It was snug; he might have to cut through it, which he'd have a hell of a time doing given his hands were now bound behind him and anchored to the chair independently. I'd used the clothes, and duct tape, trying to achieve some measure of binding that wouldn't cause him to lose a limb to lack of blood but still keep him tied up for a while as I made my escape from Scotland. "In that time, if I were you, I'd think about how great she is, and how lucky you are to have her, and how many other women in this world are ever so much worse and more fearsome." I threw that last part in because what the hell, he needed to occupy his mind on gratitude, and drawing a contrast between hellish me and his lovely significant other seemed like a safe way to do so.

"Oh, yes, I'm a lucky man indeed," he said, nodding his head fiercely.

"Damned right," I said, and gave Archie another pet as he wobbled up to me. "All right, boy. Stay. Both of you." And Archie dutifully plopped down next to John as I headed for the exit, grabbing the car keys off the ring by the door as I plunged out into the daylight. "Making friends everywhere I go," I muttered, mostly to myself, as I swept out into the weak summer sunshine.

9.

John's car was functional, and that was about it. Another of Europe's ubiquitous shoe cars, it had the virtue of at least being not too old, I guess, though I suspected from the smell it had been used to haul livestock, however one would manage that with only enough passenger space to carry a lamb if it had been butchered first.

I took the winding roads east, following the map, having found the destination immediately upon getting my hands on it. I'd quickly sketched out the route, which was pretty much back roads the whole way. I had it spread out on the seat next to me, giving myself plenty of time to get where I was going. And it was good thing I did, too, because the airfield was not on this map, so I was basically going by my recollection of what I'd seen on the phone screen before I'd broken it.

That was fine, though; I had time to drive in circles around the area I knew it was in, tracking it down. It was out on a kind of half-ass peninsula north of the Firth of Forth. Bordered to the east by the North Sea, and with St. Andrews up north of it, I had a solid idea of where I was going—roughly. I'd caught the name of the town of Lochty, and the road the airfield was on, and from there I just drove until I got to that locale.

The cloud cover was heavy overhead for most of the trip. I tried to stick to back roads, which slowed my progress but helped me avoid any police entanglements. In fact, I didn't see a single cop anywhere along my route. Looking at the nature of the car, I didn't have to worry about GPS tracking or LoJack in the thing, for which I was also grateful. I turned on news radio and tuned it out for the most part, listening to the continuing excitement over the fact that Sienna Nealon was in Scotland, which was apparently the most thrilling thing that had happened since the Haggis disaster of '07 or whatever passed for major news around here.

The hilly countryside was pretty, and I was lucky in that although there were a lot of blind corners coming around hillocks, I didn't run into any police roadblocks along the way. I was slightly tense as I drove, the maddening silence inside my head chipping away at my resolve. Until today, it had been a while since I'd actually driven a car, and I'd never done it on the wrong side of the road.

My mind settled into a steady rhythm as I got on a long straightaway, and finally my thoughts veered into a territory I hadn't wanted to contemplate: my missing souls.

"Dammit," I muttered under my breath. This silence was killing me.

I hadn't even known another succubus could steal my souls, but in fairness, I hadn't exactly dealt with many of them. My aunt Charlie, my mom, and myself—those were the three succubi I'd known before Rose came into my life. I cursed myself again for not having listened to my suspicions about her, the same suspicions I get for everyone, but damn! I mean, she was a good actress. I'd been around a lot of criminals, and I'd yet to meet one that could perform like her. That was some classically trained stuff right there, and I didn't wonder that hard why actors from the UK ended up so famous lately. Maybe she'd been in theater when she was young.

My thoughts wandered back to my souls. I knew what a succubus could do to a soul if they wanted to apply pressure. Agonizing pain was a tool at your disposal, if you wanted to break one of your captives. You could basically turn your brain into a 24/7 torture dungeon for them, if you had a little help.

And based on the number of powers Rose had, and the

number of corpses she'd left behind...I guessed she had a lot of help at her disposal.

Every single soul she took was another centurion in her personal, mental army. I'd seen it happen on a very small scale with my own souls when they'd taken a run at Harmon one night when he'd first arrived in my mind. There was a horrific, howling noise as they jumped him, one that had woken me out of a sound sleep with the horror of the screaming. I'd put a stop to it, of course—Bjorn claimed it was just hazing, but I'd heard what I'd heard, and Harmon, though quiet about it, had been less insufferable for a few days afterward. That told me that no matter how fine he said he was, whatever they'd hit him with—their combined wills, near as I could suppose—it must have hurt quite a lot.

That was six against one. Rose could have thousands of souls ready to pour the fire on my few.

Wolfe could take care of himself, I knew. He'd probably been through worse.

Then again, when I'd killed him...he'd screamed and begged just like anyone else would. He probably wasn't used to taking pain anymore, having become the guy who more often dealt it out.

Bjorn, Eve, Bastian, Gavrikov...they all were pros who knew the score, like Wolfe, a little, in that regard. Harmon, too, to a lesser extent. Pretty much every one of them had been in meta battles at some point, and they'd be familiar with the way things went, with the way of the world, really. Might makes right, and Rose had a lot of might on her side.

I wasn't under any illusions about this turning out "right," though.

My arm was rested against the window, the warmth of the sun feeling pretty good against the skin, a far cry from the fiery feeling I'd experienced when Rose had put her hands on me and ripped the souls out of my body. I shivered a little at the thought, hands shaking on the steering wheel until I got myself back under control. No one had dominated me like that in a long time, and it felt...

I nudged the car to the side of the road for a moment and took long, steadying breaths. I was fine. Physically, I was fine. A hundred percent, even, for my own powers.

But if that were true…why did it feel like a huge chunk had been carved out of my flesh?

I was keenly aware of that missing space inside, a hollow center that made me feel like Rose had cut me open and ripped out a few internal organs. Sure, maybe I could survive for a little while without them, but sooner or later I'd keel over dead without what was missing. It was a gaping, empty hole within, a painful cavern inside me that echoed every time I spoke, resonating with a kind of agony that I hadn't fully experienced, even when all my friends had betrayed me and the US government had turned on me.

It was the feeling of being…alone. Actually, truly, completely alone.

"You bitch," I said in a voice that sounded very, very small.

I imagined her face in front of me, and right there with a desire to punch it, squarely, in its freckled paleness, was another desire—to not hit her. To quail away, to turn and run.

I hated that feeling, and the shot of worry that it sent rushing through my veins. It was a physical reaction to the thought of Rose, a sense of fear that was like a hobble fastened to me, cramping my desire for action.

She'd made me fear her. That made me hate her even more.

I spent some time composing myself. Not a single car passed me during that interval, which made me feel like I'd picked the right roads to traverse. I wiped my eyes, cursing the fact that I was actually despairing, alone, in a damned European shoe car, on the side of the road in Scotland. I felt so wretched I could barely put words to it, and I was on my way to a rendezvous that would see me fleeing this country for safer ground.

I think I hated that worst of all.

It took a while to get myself back together, but I finally did it. At least I hadn't full-on ugly-cried, I thought to myself, reveling in this one small victory as I nudged the vehicle back on the road, my destination bleary but visible in the map next to me. I'd held it in, for now, keeping all this fury and sadness and loneliness and isolation buried inside.

I resolved I'd keep it buried until the next time Rose and I crossed paths, when I was ready for her.

And then…I'd find some way to make her give me back what she'd taken from me.

10.

I found the airfield about an hour and a half before my plane was supposed to land. It wasn't much of an airfield, more like a grass strip in the middle of miles of farmland, but it was nestled in a little valley, and there wasn't a ton of cover nearby save for a grove of trees to the west.

Parking the car miles away seemed like the wise, cautious approach, and now that I was missing most of my godlike powers, I needed to be more careful. So I hiked across the farmland, exercising my right to wander across endless fields, and snaking my way carefully through the woods once I reached the western approach to the airfield.

I crept through the woods slowly, taking care not to crunch a single leaf. Fortunately it was summer, not autumn, so there weren't too many leaves on the ground, though there were enough that it required some caution. I listened with every step, avoiding rustling the underbrush. The trees were tall, reaching high into the sky, and I contemplated climbing one, maybe jumping from bough to bough and observing the field from a distance at that height.

But that was more of a thing for the old Sienna, the one who could cancel out gravity. Not this one, who would probably break a tree branch loudly and send herself plummeting helplessly to the ground to break a leg, thus ensuring that I'd be waiting nicely for Rose and her police helicopters to eventually find me if they passed this way. I wasn't sure they were going to, but I was paranoid enough to not want to chance it.

I spared a thought for Alistair Wexford, my contact in the UK government. I felt bad that I hadn't touched base with him in a few days to explain what was happening up here, but he hadn't exactly given me his phone number, so it was at least partly his fault. I wondered if he had any idea what was actually going on. Probably not, given that he'd sent me into the thick of it, but then I'd been betrayed already in the last couple days, so I wasn't prepared to fully write off the idea that he was involved in Rose's scheme somehow, though I was still extremely muddled on what Rose's scheme was, other than beating the hell out of me.

Once she'd let the mask of her acting drop, I'd seen a real hatred in her eyes, the kind that was breathtaking to behold. Whatever I'd done to her, it had put a bee in her vagina, and she seemed pretty raw about it. Whatever she had in mind for me, I had other plans. In fact, I wanted to be as far from her when she executed her plans as possible. If I could have caught a rocket to the moon on that day, I would have taken it.

Nah. Nah, I wouldn't. I didn't even want to run now, not really. But I needed something to beat her—some help. Wexford's name floated to my mind again. Another idea came up, too:

Suppressant.

Suppressant was a drug the US government had developed in order to deal with metahumans. It suppressed the powers of any metahuman for a period of hours once they'd been injected. Regular use would render a meta like me pretty thoroughly human. Which was a scary thought for a meta. I'd been under its influence once, a few years ago, when a group of Russian mercenaries hired to break someone out of the prison I guarded for the US government had stumbled on the wise idea of disempowering Sienna Nealon before they tried to rip something away from me.

It contained echoes of what was happening now. Those

Russian mercs hadn't known what hit them when I'd proceeded to kill every single one of their asses without any powers at hand. I'd gone full *Die Hard*, and shown the world that the powers didn't make the woman.

This, though, was a little different situation. When that had happened, I'd had guns, explosives…what the military called "force equalizers." Here, Rose had superpowers and I had my own two hands and feet. She had super strength, speed, dexterity…I had those, heightened, but no match for hers, I suspected. I'd been working out, sure, but she could probably draw on strength enough to lift mountains while I topped out at—well, I actually didn't know where I topped out with just my own succubus powers. I wasn't going to be Crossfitting with mountains, though.

But if I could hit her with a dose of Suppressant…she'd be human, and I'd be superhuman. My meta power would probably override hers, then, which meant I could maybe drain my souls back without having to worry about her ripping the life out of me. I could give her a taste of her own bitter, shit-tasting medicine.

I took a steadying breath. I was kneeling about a hundred yards inside the treeline that overlooked the airfield. It was quiet. The grass strip looked like it had been freshly mowed, and I wondered if they'd done it in order to accommodate my plane, which would hopefully be arriving soonish.

Getting my hands on some Suppressant wouldn't be overly hard. Every police force in the US was ordering it nowadays, now that metahumans had gone epidemic in America. Finding someone selling a dart gun and doses of Suppressant was probably going to be worlds easier than actually delivering it to Rose, which would involve sneaking up on her like she was a wascawy wabbit and tranqing her when she wasn't looking.

Now I had a plan, at least. Get Suppressant, dose the bitch, take back what was mine. Easy peasy. Sort of. I wished I had had this brainstorm earlier; I could have had Fritz send some along to this meet. It probably wasn't quite as prevalent in the

EU territories, given that they weren't yet having the meta problems the US was, but there had to be some on hand in order to make sure their ban on our kind was enforceable. Because as far as I knew, they didn't have a meta team of their own to deal with flare-ups.

I stared out at the green airstrip, long grass waving between the edge of the woods and where it waited. I doubted my ride was going to be a Gulfstream or something similar, not at this tiny airstrip. Not if they knew what they were doing. They'd need to bring in a prop plane, something that wouldn't have a jet engine to suck up foreign object debris. Something like...

A Cessna buzzed in the distance, making its approach. I had a feeling they didn't get a ton of traffic here, but it was hardly a guarantee that this was my plane. If it was, though, I was looking forward to getting my hands on a gun, if only for the reassuring sense that if Rose showed her face, I'd be able to pop a dozen rounds in it from long range. Seeing her grimace in pain would be so joyful right now.

The plane swayed in the cross-breeze, the winds rustling the trees around me as I crept closer and closer to the edge of the woods. I didn't know who exactly I was looking for, but I knew that they'd find a way to make it known that they were here to meet me. I suspected I'd need to approach them, play it cool, start a conversation. If they didn't evince surprise at the sight of me, they were probably my crew.

The Cessna bumped as it landed, but hugged the ground, the nose tip prop spinning so quickly I couldn't see terribly well through it. I could tell it was a guy at the controls, though, and the way the plane bounced made me think it was carrying some decent weight on those axles considering he was the only one in there. That could have meant he had my hardware, or it could have meant he had a crate of heroin in the back. Either or.

It taxied to a stop and rolled toward the tower and administration building—the only building on site, really—and when it finished, he waved over a guy who was standing there, waiting. They spoke, briefly, and the pilot wandered off toward the admin building while the airfield employee went and got a hose and started to fill up the plane. I watched as the guy spent some time fueling it up, then put away the hose securely. The bunkers for the fuel must have been under the ground, because there were only a couple hangars and they were both open, and definitely not meant for big planes.

I had a plan. (Actually, I had a few plans, including an escape one, but hopefully that wouldn't become necessary.) When the pilot came back out, I was going to watch his actions for a few minutes before I approached. The fact that he'd disappeared right into the admin building—a squat, one-story building no bigger than a small house that was connected to their stubby tower—didn't necessarily mean anything. He could have really needed to pee after a long flight. He probably had to pay for the fuel and landing fees and whatever other ancillary charges there might be to land at a field like this.

If he left the admin building and immediately started to take off in his plane, he probably wasn't my ride. If, on the other hand, he lingered around…

Well, then I'd make my approach.

The sound of the trees rustling above and behind me in the wind was a nice symphony. I looked for signs of trouble, but I wasn't seeing any. Other than the guy who fueled up the Cessna, there didn't seem to be anyone here. Someone was up in the tower, maybe—it was hard to tell because there was a fierce glare on the windows—but it was pretty close to the ground, maybe a story or two up at most. The admin building could have hidden some people in it, but not that many. It was safe to say there wasn't a regiment of troops secretly hiding in its confines, but it would have been able to house a SWAT team or the like fairly easily.

Doubly good reason to watch the pilot carefully when he came back out. If he was being pressed by Scottish cops right now, he'd probably show some sign of it if he emerged. Of course, I didn't think they were here, but I hadn't thought Rose was conning me, either. Now that I'd found my judgment suspect once, I'd be second- and third-guessing myself every time, at least for a while, because that girl had rendered a harsh lesson unto me.

Just when I was starting to wonder if maybe the pilot had died in there and nobody had bothered to call an ambulance, he came bopping back out, just like normal. Or what I thought was probably normal for him. There was no hitch in his giddyap, no sign that he was more nervous or worried than when he'd come in. I finally got a decent look at him. He had olive skin, wore dark sunglasses (probably unnecessary given the weather), had black hair that was well styled, and was dressed in a polo shirt and jeans, with the tail untucked—very casual, his loafers black and shining against the green grass as he made his way back to the plane.

The fueling attendant had made himself scarce, and that was good for me. I caught a glimpse of him tinkering around with a plane, no sign that he was paying attention to anything other than his work on a small two-prop job. That was a good sign for me that this place wasn't under serious scrutiny, or at least that it hadn't been infiltrated by hordes of Police Scotland agents under Rose's control. The mechanic started working on one of the plane's engines and didn't even spare a glance out the open doors of the hangar, which convinced me he was who he appeared to be.

The pilot stopped a few feet from his plane and surveyed the ground around him. He cast a gaze over the flat, open space that surrounded the airfield, like he was just taking in the weather. He shuffled around the plane for a few minutes, stretching his legs, then opened the door and pulled out an apple. He started to eat really slowly, which made me think this was either my guy or he wanted an extended break before starting on the next leg of his trip, wherever that may have led him.

It was time to chance it. I broke cover, wandering out of the woods completely casually. It was about a hundred yards to the edge of the airfield, and there was no perimeter fence save for a low one about four feet high that I vaulted when I got close. I didn't even have to go meta on it, I just climbed over it like a normal person, in case anyone was watching from a distance. No point in drawing unnecessary attention to myself by sprinting or leaping like a gazelle over the thing. Motion draws the hunter's attention to the prey, after all, and I knew to keep my actions measured and normal. I was just a girl out for a walk, so far as anybody knew.

The pilot caught sight of me when I was only about fifty yards away from him. He cocked his head, looked at me over his sunglasses, and after an interminable pause in surveying me, lifted his hand in a very small wave, once he had checked in either direction to be sure no one was watching us.

We were clear, and I was pretty sure this was my guy.

I drew closer, picking up the pace a little. "Hey," I called out to him when I was only about twenty yards away.

He nodded at me. "How's it going?" European accent, somewhere in the Mediterranean area. Spanish, maybe, or Greek. Tough to tell by his English.

"It's been a day," I said, now only about ten yards away. I slowed my pace further. "You waiting for someone?"

He smiled thinly. "Not anymore. Get in and let's get out of here."

"How was the view from inside?" I asked as I passed him, never once taking my eyes off him. I climbed up into the plane through the pilot's door and crawled over into the passenger seat, not wanting to board the aircraft in clear view of the admin building or the hangars.

"Sleepy," he said, getting in and fastening his seatbelt. I didn't really want to fasten mine, because it restricted my motion, but I also didn't want to get thrown from the aircraft now that I couldn't fly or heal myself either, so I did the ostensibly smart thing and buckled up. "Only a clerk to process paperwork," he said. "Maybe another in the tower for ATC. Why?"

"Just paranoid," I said, and he smiled again, thinly. He was a pro, probably a smuggler, but I didn't care what he did right now. I just wanted to get the hell out of Scotland intact. "You got my gear?"

"Big bag in the back," he said, nodding over his shoulder, before positioning a boom mic in front of his face from a headset. "I'm told it contains everything you asked for. I was also told to ditch it if I was in any danger of getting caught."

"Yeah, this isn't the sort of stuff you want sitting on the passenger seat when the cops roll up," I said, turning back to see a big military duffel and a smaller one next to it. "What's in the other bag?"

He didn't look back. "That's for me." I caught the hint of a smile. "In case of trouble."

"Oookay," I said, "well let's hope for none of that." I suspected it was a handgun or something of the sort. Maybe a knife if he was the overly cautious sort. My instincts of him being a smuggler seemed more and more likely by the minute, which meant if he was carrying a rocket launcher for me and machine gun, an assault rifle…carrying a pistol of his own, even in the UK, wouldn't exactly have been a tremendous addition of trouble with the law.

He brought the plane around in a bumping taxi, and I looked out the window at the air traffic control tower as I passed. He was talking to them in his headset, requesting permission to take off. There was a little bumping as he guided the plane, the ground uneven on this landing patch. Not terrible, but it was no airport runway, that much was plain.

"Where are we headed?" I asked. And when he cocked his head at me for asking, I said, "You know, in case we get separated in flight." Which was a joke.

He let out a grim smile. "A field south of London to refuel, and then past the Channel into mainland Europe."

"Where's my final destination?" I asked him over the sound of the prop spinning, chopping through the air like the world's most hellacious fan. It was loud, even through the headset I was wearing.

"We're heading to—" He stopped, and I caught the flicker of motion ahead a second after he did. It must have originated behind the tower, because there'd be no sign of anything the moment before, but now—

There were choppers.

Two of them.

They looked like old Hueys, the military helo that America had made famous in Vietnam. They were still painted in the olive green of a military helicopter, but their age was showing, and they could have belonged to anyone. There were men with guns inside, hanging out of the big open bay doors, and a voice crackled through the air, aided by a loudspeaker on the side.

"Sienna Nealon! Surrender now, or you will be killed!" Judging by the hardware the black-tac-geared guys within were carrying…they could do it, too. Several times over. I saw Stinger missiles, a couple of M249 Squad Automatic Weapons, a machine gun that could fill the air with 100 rounds per minute without breaking a sweat, and a dude with a big fifty-caliber sniper rifle that could put holes in a human body the size of a Gatorade bottle. And not one of the small bottles, either.

Something about this setup trickled through me with the dim creeping of fear that made its way from my brain into my stomach, churning the acid in mere seconds. It wasn't the weapons, though I had plenty of reason to be fearful of those. They could kill me easily now, after all. And it wasn't the second helicopter, which came sweeping in behind us, similarly laden with men with guns.

It was, I realized, the fact that when they'd shouted their message of surrender, these heavily armed men…it hadn't been with a Scottish accent.

It had been an American one.

The US government had found me.

11.

Reed

I was awoken in the middle of the night by the call, jarring me out of a fitful sleep. Isabella was breathing softly by my side, but even she was wakened by the buzz of my phone. I rolled over in the peaceful darkness of our apartment and fumbled past my hand lotion (they get dry in winter in Minnesota, come on), the pad of paper and pens, and finally to my cell phone charger next to the bed. I damned near fumbled it in my sleepy clumsiness, but managed to hit the unlock button and push it to my ear. "Hello?" I asked blearily.

"It's Miranda," came the calm voice at the other end of the line, and for a second my stomach dropped, remembering that when last I'd left consciousness, my sister had been on the run in Scotland. My brain decided to jump to conclusions, and as my breath stuck in my throat I wondered if her next words were going to be, "I'm sorry—she's dead."

But they weren't. Instead: "We've received an emergency request for assistance from a little town outside Odessa, Texas. They've got a hostage situation involving a metahuman."

My heart, a second earlier feeling like it was thudding toward two hundred beats per minute and an explosion, suddenly stilled. "Okay. When do they want us there?"

"Yesterday, if you could travel through time," she said. "They've got the place surrounded, but this person—the hostage-taker—they've got a family barricaded in a house. Mother and small children."

I rubbed my eyes. "Okay. I can catch a plane when the airport starts up—"

"No." Her voice was solid, iron in the middle of the night, like a wall I was running up against. "I've already booked a private jet. It'll leave as soon as you get to Eden Prairie airport. Pack lightly."

"Who's riding shotgun with me?" I asked. Technically, I could pick anyone I wanted, but I guessed that she'd have already called or texted someone else to get them moving, and I had a suspicion who it'd be.

"Angel," she said flatly, and I rolled my eyes a little, but shrugged. Angel was all right, I guess, but I preferred Jamal, Scott or Augustus to watch my back, mostly because I'd been working with them for years and Angel for about six months. She was a fireball, but I could see the advantage in sending her. She spoke Spanish fluently, which had been useful on more than one occasion in Texas, and she was Miranda's cousin.

Downside: she liked to drive. Always. And she was dangerously good at it, but it felt like she was always about half a heartbeat from putting whatever rental car we were in through the highway dividers and off the road into the ditch. She was that kind of maniac, the kind that liked to play with the manual gear-switching feature on high-end cars. Personally, I let my car make those sorts of decisions for me, but not Angel.

"Okay," I said. "You know, I could just fly myself. Grab one of the guys on the way—"

"This will be faster, and, as a side benefit, legal," she said, and I didn't feel like arguing. I didn't really love gliding through the clouds at high altitude without a plane to protect me anyway, not over long distances like Minnesota to Texas. I could do it, but I didn't love it.

"I'll be there in fifteen minutes," I said, and hung up, clicking the lamp next to the bed as I rolled over the side. I rubbed my eyes, the bedroom shown in dim light.

"Where are you going this time?" Isabella asked, turning over in bed to look at me. She was still beautiful in the middle of the night, her makeup all rubbed off before bed and a pair of woolen pajamas with a sky-blue-with-white-polka-dots pattern not at all like the old Victoria's Secret Collection she'd worn to bed every night when we first started sleeping together.

"Somewhere in Texas," I said, rubbing at my eyes. I kept a ready bag packed, so that was going to be easy. All I had to do was throw on some clothes and get the hell out of here. Maybe I'd fly myself to the airport—no. No, it'd probably be better if I didn't, since Governor Shipley had technically cancelled my flight privileges over the state at the same time she'd yanked Sienna's. She was up for re-election this year, and I was voting for the other guy.

"When will you be back?" That Isabella asked this at all was a measure of how much this Sienna situation had knotted her up without my realizing it. I looked back at her, and for once I could see the concern playing through the coolness she wore like a second skin. I couldn't tell whether it was because she was worried that I'd worry while on assignment and end up getting myself hurt, or because just the general pervading sense of concern that Sienna had gotten in trouble overseas reminded her of my own mortality. Either way, there was something here that I hadn't necessarily seen in other departures I'd made.

"As soon as I can," I said gently, and leaned over to kiss her. "Ever since we took out the supply operations for that cartel that was bringing the meta serums from Revelen, business has been slacking off. We could use this payday."

"It's not worth your life," she said.

"It's not just my life on the line," I said. "This crook, whoever it is—they've taken hostages."

She seemed to take this information in, and then she nodded, inscrutable. "Hurry back," was all she said.

"You know I won't linger," I said with a sly smile, and

leaned down to kiss her again before I got up, heading for the closet to get dressed. I didn't have long, after all, and I couldn't afford to spend my time distracted about Isabella's worry, or Sienna—whatever was going on with her.

It was time for me to get back to work. And Sienna, wherever she was…she'd be just fine.

12.

Sienna

Things were not just fine.

Having a Bell UH-1 Huey drop down in front of your plane while you're taxiing for takeoff to reveal lots of men with guns and rocket launchers and the like has a way of causing a great deal of clarity in the mind, very rapidly. Vague concerns get amplified, and they manifest verbally.

Like so: "Holy shit!"

That was the pilot, but I was thinking along similar lines. He'd slammed the throttle to bring the Cessna back to idling, and we were just sitting there, me with my hands up, palms facing inward, toward my head so I couldn't be interpreted to be aiming a fireball at them or anything. In a situation like this, signaling surrender was the wisest course, and the only one that might save my life.

It was weird, because as far as I knew, the US government had given up on wanting me dead or alive and was now firmly in the camp of, "Dead is fine." They'd proven that during our last encounter in Montana.

Yet here we were, with a bunch of Spec-Ops-looking dudes, armed for bear—no, scratch that, they were armed for a reprise of James Cameron's *Aliens*, but in it to win it, this time—and all my weapons were well out of reach, in the back, zipped up in duffel bags. Not that it would have mattered if

I'd had my SCAR H on my lap. There was no way, even with meta reflexes, I was raising that thing up and drilling every single one of these guys before they punched my ticket with a Stinger missile or one of the underslung grenade launchers I saw sticking out of the chopper behind me.

"Come out with your hands up!" the loudspeaker boomed. "Do not make any threatening moves!"

"I am all over that," I muttered, bumping the door handle with my elbow. It sprang open, and I slid out, feet hitting the ground a heartbeat later. I kept my hands up and bobbed out under the wing, keeping them pointed skyward, and well away from the helos directly in front of and behind the plane.

I tossed a glance at the guys in front of me hanging out the side of the chopper. They had the look of soldiers long in service. I realized, though, that whoever was doing the talking was probably in the cockpit, and I hadn't heard any of these guys speak. For all I knew, this was a merc team. Hell, it probably was, because the US government likely wouldn't have wanted to deploy their own forces over a friendly country. Likely. Hardly definite. We'd done worse.

Standing under the plane's wing, I got my instructions. "Walk out in front of the plane. Slowly."

I complied, taking my sweet time in order to make sure they didn't think I was going to do something untoward. Before I'd gotten even with the spinning prop, the loudspeaker boomed again. "Pilot, shut off the engine and get out of the plane."

My breath stuck in my throat. I hadn't really consulted with the guy before I'd gotten out, but I threw him a glance now. He was wearing those aviator glasses, and I couldn't see his eyes, but his mouth was a thin line, and there was sweat beaded on his forehead like he'd been sitting outside in Mexico City in the middle of summer, chowing down on a burrito filled with ghost peppers or worse. I got another little tingle in my belly just looking at him, and I took a long and not subtle sidestep away from the prop, and then another one, keeping my hands up as I edged away from the plane without trying to defy the orders I'd been giving by the men with guns.

"Pilot!" the helo loudspeaker boomed again. "You have three seconds to comply or—"

I heard the engine throttle up before the speaker had even finished delivering the ultimatum. Whoever that pilot was, he was clearly a desperate man, and he did not mean to be captured here. I didn't know whether he thought he was going to be arrested, or bagged and dragged with me out of the UK, but he definitely panicked.

There was no further warning from the helicopters before they opened fire. It was like thunderous Ragnarok descended on that Scottish airfield, grenades and Stinger missiles and machine guns all belching in the afternoon sun. I threw myself to the ground and tried to roll away, my hands still over my head, maintaining my surrender even as I attempted to clear the ground zero of the damned plane that was supposed to be my ride out of this sun-forsaken country.

It was hard to separate out the cataclysmic, cacophonous noises that followed a second later. One that I heard for sure was the WHUMP! of a Stinger missile hitting the plane's engine. A shard of propeller landed about a foot from my face, sticking out of the ground like a mile marker on the side of a highway.

At least two grenades found their way into the Cessna's cabin and exploded with a dull WHUMP! of their own, and then an overpressure wave jarred me from the boom as I was sprayed with glass from the windows and fragments from the body of the aircraft. One of the doors flew past my nose as I was rolling, missing me by less than a foot.

The sound of the guns firing was like every trip I'd ever taken to the gun range, all wrapped into one. Hell, it was like every gun on the planet was firing at once, and all in close proximity to me. The two helos hosed the Cessna with fire, walking their bursts across the cockpit, the remains of the engine, shredding it as effectively as if a giant had reached down and ripped the plane apart.

I covered my ears and came to a rest, putting my head down. I was about a hundred feet from the plane, and trying to make it very clear that I was not with stupid, that I was not making a run for anything, that I was really just trying to preserve my life and my hearing so that I could comply with whatever instructions were next going to come my way. I only hoped that whoever they had tasked with keeping a bead on me wasn't the sort with an extremely itchy trigger finger. I had a feeling they weren't, because I wasn't dead yet, and by all rights, given my reputation, I should have been perforated with a thousand bullets the second after the pilot gunned the engine. Yet here I lay, palms squeezed against my ears to try and ward off what was left of the apocalypse as my ride out of here and the guns that I been counting on crackled and burned in the wreckage of the plane.

Well, that was five million bucks I wasn't going to get a refund on.

Also, my situation was looking pretty dismal, unless these guys were secretly my guardian angels. I didn't hold out a lot of hope for that though, because I could count on one hand the number of times people had blown up my escape plane with a million guns while trying to befriend me. Maybe even no hands. (My life was funny; it could have happened and I may have forgotten it. So many explosions.)

"Put your hands up!" the loudspeaker blasted out again, and you better believe I had those hands up lickety split. My ears were ringing, but I heard the command even still, and suspected it was a kind of test to make sure I wasn't getting buyer's remorse and thinking of throwing my lot in with the pilot. Not a hard sell considering his lot was now in flames and probably shredded to pieces back in the cockpit. I couldn't see his remains through the flames, but I was fairly convinced that there was no way in hell he'd gotten out of there alive.

I raised my head slightly, enough to see that the Huey in front of me had changed position. It was backing up, slowly, the pilot a real pro at handling the thing. That screamed Spec Ops to me, and the outdated Huey gave the US government plausible deniability. It damned sure wasn't the Brits or Scots, because here on their own soil they'd fly a different bird and have an accent. I bet there wasn't a single scrap of identification on the soldiers or the weapons that could tie them back to America, which was smart. And the trigger discipline of whoever had been assigned to shoot me in case of emergency—probably someone in the chopper behind me—bespoke of serious training and badass gravitas. A commitment to the mission and the rules of engagement that you didn't find in a guy that was just looking to collect a paycheck and get his ass home safely. That guy and his five comrades would have doused me in bullets and called it a day. Maybe even nuked me from orbit because it was the only way to be sure.

My curiosity was up about the guys in the chopper behind me, but I didn't let it get the better of me, keeping my eyes squarely ahead. "Get on your knees," the next command came, and I followed it less than a second later, without removing my hands from the air. Better safe than sorry, and I had enough ab strength to pick my ass up out of the dirt without my hands. It probably looked weird, though, like I was a snake rising up to bite.

"Looks like you're going home," the voice over the loudspeaker said, and I could hear the chopper behind me throttling down, ever so subtly. They would probably put guys on the ground, then dose me with Suppressant, bag me, drag me, and off we'd go for a chopper ride to—hell, I dunno. One of the RAF stations the US Air Force staged out of over here if they were feeling cheeky. Maybe an American base in Germany, Spain or Greenland if they were playing it safe.

They encircled me quickly, but only partially, from behind, in order to keep from making a circular firing squad. I kept on my knees, hands straight up in the air. If they were expecting me to go dragon, or launch flames, or shoot light nets out of my ass at them, they showed no sign of it. Which suggested to me...

Somehow…they knew I couldn't do any of those things anymore.

It was the only explanation that made sense for this sudden change of tactics. Somehow the US government already knew I'd been disempowered, and they'd seen a chance to sweep in and take me off the board without nearly the worry I'd caused before.

Assuming these guys were US government. Assuming they didn't work for—

One of the guys to my right burst into flames, his M249 SAW ripping off a blast skyward as he staggered back, burning. A guy just to my left carrying what looked like an injection gun that had a chemical vial sticking out of its handle staggered and jerked, a red laser perforating his face and replacing it with nothingness. His neck just ended above the collar, and he slumped back, body not realizing what had happened to its driver. His injection gun vaped up a second later, the plastic and metal turning to slag under the onslaught of that same meta laser beam.

Suppressant. Right there, just a few feet away. It lit off and burned to nothingness like my hope of easy escape.

Screams rang out behind me, and I didn't dare look. I threw myself to the ground as bullets spanged and shot in long strings, the men who had been about to capture me all dying in seconds, bloody seconds.

When everything paused for just a beat, I pushed my chin up out of the dirt, and rolled over halfway, just to confirm what I already suspected.

Rose was hovering over me like an avenging angel, about ten feet off the ground, favoring me with a smile that bordered on a sneer, hands aglow with her meta powers. Instead of a benevolent goddess here to save me, though, I saw an angry one, a furious one, lording it over me that she'd swept in at the last second to keep some other bastard from getting me before she could.

"Hi," she said.

13.

Rose

Rose awoke with the morning light peeking in between her curtains, and there was a sick feeling lingering in her belly, like she'd gotten nauseous overnight.

Of course, she was awakening with that feeling every day lately.

Rose lifted her head off the pillow. It had a smell about it now, the smell of hair unwashed for days, of the pillowcase unlaundered. The bed had the same scent, because her laundry had stopped being done for her and she had no desire to do it for herself.

She sat up in bed, looking at the ceiling. Smooth, white, it had once been reassuring, a familiar thing to awake to every morning. She used to keep lying there, staring up at it, thinking about her day. Thinking about her lessons, thinking about Graham, about the village...

Now she still thought about all those things, but...differently.

Rose listened. Dim whispers reached her ears from outside her room. Quiet talk in the kitchen between Granddad and Mam, she decided at last. That was all they did nowadays. Quiet talk when she wasn't around. Quiet talk when she was.

It was all anybody did around her these days.

She arose, putting her feet over the side of her bed. She felt sticky all over, hair still limp and tangled where it hadn't been fiddled with for days. Weeks, maybe. She only made a cursory effort anymore to address her looks, her hygiene, because…what was the point, really?

Rose dragged herself out of bed, still wearing the jeans and shirt from the night before. She opened the door to the hall and heard the voices in the kitchen quell. Stepping across the hall, soft as a mouse, she closed the bathroom door and relieved herself, making this one solitary concession to hygiene.

When she was done, she left the bathroom, flushing, again, a small concession. She opened the door to silence, and worked her way slowly down the hall, shuffling, almost like a zombie, toward the quiet living room and kitchen.

She found them standing awkwardly in the kitchen. Granddad was next to the fridge, arms folded, grey bushy eyebrows furrowed heavily, and eyes pointed at the floor. Her mam had her back turned.

Mam always had her back turned these days.

Rose thought about conditioned response, the theory that you became accustomed to, acclimated, trained to respond in certain ways by certain stimuli. In her case, it'd be days and weeks of silence, strained words to convey small points, and overwhelming quiet the rest of the time.

Today looked to be no different, with the two of them silent and immobile as statues, not even looking up or turning around to acknowledge her.

A sudden urge of wild abandon tweaked at her, like a raw nerve tinging at her spine. "Good morning," she said, softly. In the quiet it was like a bomb going off.

Her mam did not react, did not move. Why would she? She had a good streak going, having not spoken to Rose since…then. The day of.

"Morning, Rose," her granddad said, also softly. He did not look at her.

"I think I'll go out for a while," Rose said. No reply.

After waiting a good half minute, Rose went for the door.

She opened it slowly, hoping someone would say something—anything, really.

Silence was all that lingered within the house.

The sky was sunny, for once, a peculiar turn of events if ever there was one. It had been sunny the last few days, even more peculiar still.

Rose didn't care for that. She wanted grey skies to reflect her dark mood. The more opaque the clouds, the better, in her view. Twenty-four hours of night per day wouldn't have been out of line.

Hamilton went past, on the crossroad up ahead next to the Macdonald house, and Rose raised a hand to wave, reflexively. Apparently her response hadn't been completely conditioned out of her, but Hamilton caught sight of the motion and hurried on, not daring to stop or even look back once he realized who was waving at him.

Rose turned to walk toward the path out of the village that she'd followed on that day—that awful day, the one that changed everything.

The one that ruined her life forever.

She trudged, feet against the road, the worn soles of her shoes protesting that they were thin and in need of replacement. Her feet protested, too, catching a rock that popped up through the sole. Rose grimaced, but didn't complain aloud.

It was the least of her problems lately.

She was walking past Miriam Shell's house when the door opened. Rose slowed, figuring she might try saying something. Reaching out, trying to make some human contact, at least—

Graham stepped out through the door, pulling his shirt on. His trousers were undone, and a voice carried behind him on the wind.

"And you can come back tonight, if you'd like." Miriam emerged behind Graham, broad smile beamed at him. She wore a thin, silken sort of gown. "I wouldn't mind at all." She stepped out onto the porch and ran a hand over his bare, smooth shoulder, then, catching sight of Rose before he did, turned him around. Graham went along with it, and she drew his lips to hers for a long, full kiss.

Rose just stood there, watching it, dumbstruck and horrified.

A part of her, distant and in the back of her mind, wanted to scream, to cry, to do anything but stand there silently as her mind assembled the pieces that had been thrown out on the table before her like a puzzle box overturned.

Instead, she watched in silence as Miriam parted Graham's lips and put her tongue in his mouth, obvious as the sun in the bloody sky, and then broke from him with a wide, satisfied smile and a sidelong look at Rose to make sure she'd caught it all.

She had. It would have been impossible to miss.

"I'll see you later, luv," Miriam said, stroking Graham's chest and letting a gentle sigh as she admired his physique. She turned and headed back inside, casting one last look of smug satisfaction at Rose.

Graham, for his part, was smiling. That faded the moment he turned and saw Rose standing there. His shirt fluttered in his hand. His trousers, though fastened, were still unzipped.

He hadn't spoken to her since the day it happened. She hadn't dared say anything to him, either. Now they just looked at one another, Graham's cheeks blossoming red.

"Hi," Rose said stupidly, and hated herself for it. Her own cheeks flushed hot, like a lit fireplace, and she turned her gaze away from him, standing shirtless and shamed on Miriam Shell's front porch, the truth of what had passed between him and Miriam written obvious across his face for her to read, obvious to someone who'd known Graham from the time they were both toddling infants.

Rose broke into a run, down the road to the village. Behind her…Graham said nothing.

He did not come after her, no quiet footsteps or running feet reaching her ears over the sound of the wind, which was picking up.

And the wind did howl the closer she got to the cutoff that led down the hill to the spring. She hurried down it, wanting to get away, away from anyone, away from Graham, away from her mam, away from Granddad, away from Hamilton, and that damned Miriam Shell, the whore.

Graham had been hers, dammit. Hadn't he known? Hadn't the whole village known? Of course they had. There were jokes about it. They'd circled each other for years. At night, when she'd...touched herself...it was Graham she was thinking of. When she imagined her future, it was him that was in those thoughts.

And when she pictured kids...he was always there in those dreams, too. He'd make such a good da, she'd always known it...

It felt as though someone had punched through her ribcage, giving the ol' heart a solid tug. It would come free easily enough these days, withered and dead as it seemed like it must be after all these weeks and months of silence, of quiet hate, of fear and disgust. Someone had spat on her the other day, caught her flush in the eye. It was little Ronnie Gordon, not even ten, and he ran off before she could scarcely reconcile herself to believing it. She'd babysat that little shite, had known him since he was knee high to a cricket.

Rose almost stumbled, her head down, not paying a whit of attention to the path. Something stopped her, though, a solid bump against a solid object. She raised her head as she stumbled back, and almost fell over.

It was Tamhas, looking at her with one eyebrow cocked. "You all right there, Rose?" He even asked it in a normal tone of voice.

"I—" She hesitated. It had been so long since anyone had spoken to her like she wasn't some broken thing that would break further if they raised their voice to a normal volume. Her usual inclination, had someone asked her this, before things had gone so badly skewiff, would have been, "I'm fine, thank you."

But things were not fine, they were not fine at all. She'd been shot in the bloody heart by Graham this very morning, Graham and that harlot Miriam Shell, and it, when coupled with everything that had happened these last years, was more than she could contain. "No," she said, it all coming out in a hot rush, "no, I'm not all right at all."

Tamhas just stared at her, eyebrow fixed, thinly streaked with a few stray greys mixed with the black hairs. "No," he said at last, as if pronouncing a judgment, "I reckon you're not."

"They all hate me," she said, letting it gush out. "Every last one of them." She didn't even care that he had been so noncommittal in his response. He'd bloody well talked to her, asked her if she was all right, and that was a sight better than what anyone else had done of late. "Everybody. And Miriam Shell and Graham are together now, and—"

"Haud yer weesht, lass," Tamhas said, holding up a hand to stay her babble. "What's that about Miriam and Graham?"

"They're shagging," Rose said, and it came out boiling with hatred and self-pity and every other sort of bubbling emotion she could produce. Hot tears of rage were already soaking her cheeks, and as hard as she'd tried to hold back from weeping in sight of others, the steady stream of insults, of hatred, and finally this—this damned abomination—this last insult to cap all insults, Miriam Shell shagging her man—this was it—

Tamhas reached up and scratched his thinning hair, skin tingeing slightly red from the neck up. "Aye, I suppose that was inevitable now that…things have happened the way they have." He drew a long breath, not meeting her eyes, and said, speaking to the damned ground, "You have to understand, Rose…people are scared. And when people get scared…they catch a case of the stupids."

"They're scared of me," she said, feeling like it was all judgment, pronounced from high above and raining down on her, handcuffed, in a dock.

"Not just you," Tamhas said, keeping his distance. "You

and other things. It's a tense time, you know. A bad time to be one of our people in Europe."

Rose blinked tears out of her eyes. "What's that?"

Tamhas stirred, having settled in thought after his last pronouncement. "Hm? Oh. Our cloisters, our communities… they're going quiet all over Europe. Most of us who've been around awhile, we have family, friends, all that…all over the place, really. When you're keeping a secret as big as the fact that we have superhero powers…it helps to have an interconnected support web, you know? But those other cloisters, in other countries…" He reached up and scratched his eyebrow. "Well, we're getting no answer when we call. No return letters when we send—or emails, or whatever it is you kids nowadays are using." Tamhas sunk into a momentary silence. "So I wouldn't go taking all the blame if I were you. People are scared of you, surely. Always have been, of your type, since the…olden days." Tamhas's eyes glimmered a little here, not with warmth, but with some knowledge he seemed to be holding back. "They'll get over it, though. They know you, Rose." Now he favored her with a hint of a smile. "And you haven't changed, really. You are who you always have been. They'll come around to that, in time."

She sniffled, feeling the sobs die a strange death inside. It still stung, no doubt, that deep-drilled pain that rolled all the way to the core of her. But something in Tamhas's words rang true, and she managed to get out, "Thank you."

He nodded, and started back up the slope, hands cupped behind him. He was a man at peace, though clearly things were on his mind, and he walked back up the hill toward the village while Rose just watched him go, not feeling good, by any means…but feeling more reassured, and perhaps even slightly at peace…in a way she hadn't felt in months.

And there, high above her, watched the six strangers.

*

Zack could almost taste Rose's isolation from back here, and it was a bitter flavor. The sheer hope that had swelled in her when Tamhas had spoken to her had been like a drink of water on a hot day, and he'd felt it almost as acutely as she probably had in the moment.

"I always wanted to see Scotland," Bastian said, blowing air out between his lips, amusement almost glinting in one eye, "but I gotta say…this isn't the tour I was hoping to take. One little town, one little tweener girl's feelings, and not a drop of Scotch to soften the bludgeoning."

"I think she's technically a teenager," Eve said, her own arms folded, and no sign of amusement. "And a dramatic one at that."

"All teenagers are dramatic," Zack said, feeling like he was forced into the position of defending her. He stood there, in the waist-high grasses, feeling the chill of the air prickling at him, annoyed that he was feeling anything at all.

He was dead, for crying out loud. Why did this illusion or memory or whatever feel so damned real?

"This one is experiencing events of a slightly more dramatic nature than most," Harmon said, hands in his pockets, examining the ground, maybe because he was sick of the same scenery and the same faces around him by now. Zack understood that. Harmon looked up. "She's been shunned by everyone she knows and has ever cared about. This town is like a prison for her, and the only things keeping her here are the fear and uncertainty of how things could be any better out in the cold world beyond its borders."

"What is the point of this?" Gavrikov asked, still as pale as ever. He wasn't shaking, though, which was a good sign. Occasionally he did, but his lack of flame to cover himself seemed to bother the Russian more than witnessing these events unfold. "She has a sad story, yes? Why are we seeing it?"

"Yes, I don't recall having to experience the last girl's sad-sack backstory when I was murdered into her head," Bjorn said. His eyes were dark, a pained malignance lurking behind them. "This is some form of payback. Torture because she doesn't need us."

"You know a succubus could torture us way worse than anything we've seen so far here," Zack said. Bjorn inclined his head slightly, as if conceding the point. "Something's going on here. Maybe she's showing it to us to keep us distracted."

Eve laughed, a loud bark. "We are prisoners in her head. Why would she need to distract us?"

"Prisoners can cause problems from within prison," Harmon said carefully, giving them a sly look. "We certainly did within Sienna."

"You said your telepathic powers weren't working in here," Eve said.

"They aren't," Harmon said. "But I'm hardly the only one of us here."

"Are you suggesting we try and use our powers?" Gavrikov asked. "Trigger them from within? Because we're blind right now. She is keeping us out of her current thoughts, which is maybe why we're here." He extended his arms to indicate the idyllic village around them. "When in Sienna's mind, she let us see what was going on at all times—"

"Almost," Eve said, a little pouty. "She tended to put us away when she was entertaining male company." She snorted.

"With that exception," Gavrikov said, "and I didn't mind that—she let us have the run of her mind the rest of the time. We could access her memories, see what she saw, offer counsel." He looked around the broad, grey Scottish skies. "Here…we are truly prisoners, but in a prison of different construction—a prison of her past."

"If I have to keep living this," Bjorn said, "I'm going to go insane. Or start a prison riot."

"Good luck with that," Harmon said.

"To hell with your luck," Bjorn said, and spat on the ground.

"If we're prisoners," Zack said, trying to get them back on

some kind of track, "then our first obligation is to escape." No one argued against that, which was surprising, because all these assholes seemed to do was argue. "To get back to Sienna."

"While I heartily agree that conditions were better in our last host mind," Harmon said, "let me play devil's advocate for a moment. Why would we go back to Sienna?"

"You answered your own question already," Bastian said, frowning. "The conditions were better."

"I think you're missing my point—we're prisoners either way," Harmon said. "Why lock ourselves into a course of action like, say, trying to get back to Sienna?"

"Are there other options available?" Zack asked.

"Almost certainly," Harmon said with a glint in his eye.

There was a moment of silence. "Care to share with the rest of us?" Bjorn asked.

"After Sienna got shot in the head," Harmon said, coolly, almost conspiratorially, "I used my telepathic powers to transfer memories she'd stolen from Byerly back into his own mind."

"I remember," Zack said cautiously. "What does that have to do with—"

"What if I could transfer all of us?" Harmon asked, with a mischievous element of drama. "If we're going to escape, why go back to the same old, same old? Why not pick a new host body? Metahumans have notororiously strong wills, and Sienna probably takes first prize in that competition, perhaps topped only by this girl." He indicated their surroundings again, and Zack took his meaning. "Why fight that? Let's find a nice human body, one we can dominate together."

"Can you even do that?" Bastian asked. "Transfer all six of us—"

"Seven," Bjorn said, and when everyone looked at him, he said, "Wolfe will be back."

"I'm not so sure about that," Eve said. "He seems to have—how do you say? 'Drank the Kool-Aid'?"

"It was actually Flavor-aid," Bastian said. "At Jonestown, I mean."

"It will be difficult," Harmon said. "But…yes, I think I can. Transfer us into another body. But not until I get my powers back."

"Why haven't you mentioned this before now?" Eve asked, getting a little heated. "We have been prisoners in Nealon's head for years. And you had an escape route?"

"She was a good warden," Harmon said, shaking his head. "It never would have worked with her watching over us. But here…" He looked around again. "We're alone. Unsupervised." He smiled thinly. "I say we get into some real trouble."

The world felt like it was shuddering and shaking around Zack. His head spiked with a sudden ache contemplating this new possibility. "You cannot be serious."

Harmon cocked his head. "Why wouldn't I be serious?"

Zack held out a hand, trying to find a way to indicate the world beyond. "Those are people out there. Actual people. They're not rental cars just waiting for you to drop in and take them for a drive."

"What about coma patients?" Gavrikov asked. "We pop into a coma patient, take them over?"

"They have actual physiological damage to their brains that would essentially seal us in there as well," Harmon said. "It has to be a healthy person."

"What if it was a…bad one?" Eve asked, shrugging her shoulders lightly. "Say, like, this Rose? But, you know, without the superpowers? What would be wrong with taking her over and…making her a vessel for us?"

"You have got to be joking," Zack said, clenching his eyes tightly shut. It did no good; he had no eyelids, could not shut out the stimuli of the Scottish village and the grey skies, the cool air, none of it. "We're dead." His head sprang up. "Our time is over."

"We're going to have to agree to disagree on that one," Harmon said. "I don't think our time is necessarily over. We're not dead. We've just been in purgatory, earning some links off our chains so we could have a second chance." He held up a hand. "I think we're closer on this than you might believe. I have no desire to take over an innocent person. But Eve brings up a good point. There are plenty of very bad people out there who have, frankly, done things that should have made them lose their freedom and their shot at life—"

"I thought you campaigned against capital punishment," Zack said.

"—and that's where we could come in," Harmon said, easing back a step. "A second chance for us."

"I don't see how this even matters," Bastian said.

"Because we could get our lives back." Bjorn leaned in. "Our bodies would be different, but…" He paused. "Could I be a beautiful woman? I mean, a bad one, obviously, but with enormous—"

"I'm still not going to like you, even as a woman," Eve said.

Bjorn smiled. "You never have liked me. That hasn't stopped you from—"

"The point," Harmon said, cutting that madness right off, "is that we need to be looking for an opportunity if this is something we want to do. We need to look for a way out of this…" He glanced around. "Well, 'hell' seems to be the right word for it—"

A subtle rush of wind around them seemed to come from all directions at once. Zack felt it bristle along his skin, causing it to tingle and making him shiver in a way he couldn't recall really doing since before he'd died. It raised gooseflesh on skin he no longer had, and almost made his non-existent legs wobble.

And then a voice spoke, quiet, and slow—and most definitely not Rose:

"There is…no…way out."

"The hell was that?" Bastian asked, looking around, already planning his defensive perimeter; Zack could tell because he knew the man.

Harmon was the only one who answered, face screwed up in intense thought. "I think it's one of the other inmates."

"The voice of experience, then," Zack said, relaxing just an inch. It hadn't come off as a threat. More like a warning, and it repeated once more, quiet and low, and with more fervor and feeling, as though whoever was speaking knew exactly what they were talking about.

"She will never…let any of us…go…"

14.

Sienna

Rose's greeting didn't last long; the other helo started firing, and she was immersed in bullets and grenade blasts and all else. Rose disappeared under a shroud of smoke and shrapnel, and I leapt to my feet in a dead sprint, not giving a damn if I got shot now, because if I stayed to wait this out, I was probably going to end up dead or as good as.

It was time for Plan B.

I'd studied the maps of this place on that phone before I'd chucked it in the loch, of course. On it, I'd noticed a certain element of the design that I'd explored a little further when I scouted the area before I'd pulled in behind the woods and ditched John Clifford's purloined car.

Now, sprinting for the cover of the air traffic control tower, explosions going off behind me as the US Spec Ops team tried to avenge their fallen brothers against the hellbeast that was Rose Steward (might have been a fake name, like everything else about her but her boobs—those weren't significant enough to be fake), I was going to find out if my scouting and suspicions were going to pay off.

Personally, I was kinda rooting for the Spec Ops guys to win.

I dodged between the admin building and the tower, bouncing off one of the walls and leaving a very slight smear of blood as I did so. Must have gotten hit by some shrapnel, I reflected, but there was no time to worry about it now.

Besides, the second part of Plan B would help take care of any wounds, if in a somewhat oblique and less than satisfactory way.

An explosion signaled that the first chopper had blown up, probably. I was on the other side of the buildings now, but it came through loud and clear. Nothing those military guys had been carrying could have made a boom like that, and I doubted it was the Cessna's aviation fuel going up, though I suspected that was coming soon, too.

"SIENNA!" Rose shouted, voice booming over the airfield. "Where did you go?"

I spotted a gully hidden just beyond the parking lot of the admin building, the midday sun sliding behind the clouds. I wasn't going to have long. Speeding for the gully at meta speed, I hoped—hoped—hoped that the logic I'd followed in drawing up my plan B, that straightforward thinking and scouting was about to pay off in the form of an ace I was going to pull out of my sleeve unexpected.

A drainage culvert, only a few feet wide, yawned open at the bottom of the gully, and I sprinted for it, launching myself inside as Rose shouted, still a ways off, "Where are yeeeee?" all singsongy and crazy.

I hit the ground inside the culvert and didn't wait. It was mostly dry, a hint of moisture touching my elbows and running up my body, down my chest, all the way up my thighs to my feet. I lay longways in the culvert, only an inch or two of clearance to my left, and maybe a little less on my right. If I raised my head up, I'd bump the corrugated metal above me, so I kept it down and started belly-crawling as though my life depended upon it.

Because it damned well did.

"SIENNA!" Rose cried. "Are ye in the woods?" The unmistakable sound of a blast of fire being unleashed, and another, and another, made their way, muffled, down the tunnel. I was in about a hundred yards already, speed-crawling, and judging by the tiny pinprick of light in the distance, I had about five hundred more to go. The culvert had a downward slope, being meant for drainage in this hilly country, after all.

Lucky for me, it didn't look like this part of Scotland had experienced torrential rains in the last couple days.

"Come out, come out!" Rose's voice was getting fainter. "You can't hide from me, luv. And if you don't come out, you're just going to burn to death, and that'd be a shame. I want to have words with you."

She wanted to have words with me, all right. Or at least one word:

Death.

I was wise to her game, though, and while fully aware that I couldn't outpower Rose—not now, anyway, with my order of weapons burning in the Cessna and my chance of grabbing Suppressant melted to slag—I picked up my pace and started to sink into my own head as my body got into the rhythm of crawling.

My stomach bumped against rough, jagged rocks, and so did my knees, my stolen pants not doing a lot to protect them. I could feel the bruises forming, the steady aches beginning in the bones where I was thumping down hard, over and over. My elbows were complaining too, and I was covered in grime from head to toe. The light in the distance was getting brighter, though it was doing so slowly enough that I wondered if I'd get out the other end before Rose got wise to the fact I wasn't hiding in the cluster of trees she thought I was.

I didn't dare breathe very loud for fear that she'd hear it, magnified, from some distance. Thinking, though, that was an even greater hazard. She had to have a telepath available to her, didn't she? She'd mentally jammed Harmon when he'd been in my head, and we hadn't been able to read the minds of any of her thugs, either. Harmon had been pretty firm that an empath couldn't do that the way she had.

So…if she could read my mind…why wasn't she on me right now like a tick on a hound?

I put that thought aside, because I couldn't suspend my escape on a premise that might have been false, the idea that she was some all-knowing force. Maybe she had a telepath, maybe she didn't. Maybe her telepath was weak and couldn't have read Guy Friday's meager thoughts.

But...wouldn't she have broken Harmon by now?

I couldn't look back, but I kinda wanted to, not that it would have done any good. What I really wanted to do was have looked back when I had been running away from the conflagration that was Rose's "rescue" attempt. Those Spec Ops guys had lit her up good, but she seemed to be flying around fine now. How'd she pull that off? Some kind of meta power that turned away bullets? Some ability to create a shield around herself with energy that dissolved them? I'd seen Gavrikov put up a wall of flame that melted bullets before they could harm him. Did she have something similar?

Or was she now in possession of Wolfe's healing powers?

The light was growing brighter ahead, and my knees and elbows and chest were damned sick of being rubbed roughly against uneven ground and rocks that had washed their way down this culvert only to get lodged in the dried silt at the bottom of the pipe. I was probably only a hundred yards from the end now, and though I could hear Rose shouting faintly in the distance, I could no longer tell what she was saying. My entire world was the pipe, and only a dull hum pervaded this place, that and my labored, steady breathing as I exerted myself to GTFO of here as quickly as I could.

The air was stale, and dry, and even though I'd probably only been crawling for five minutes, it felt like I'd been in this darkness forever. My head was still spinning, and another question presented itself. Rose had turned an entire Police Scotland station against me back in Edinburgh, and she'd done it without even having to expose herself as the villain pulling the strings. How had she done that, if not telepathy?

I had another theory, of course, but it now had a big hole in it. There was a type of meta called a Siren. I'd never met one myself, but an old friend of mine—Breandan, an Irishman I'd met the first time I'd come to the UK—had a girlfriend who he claimed had that power. I had no reason to doubt him, because she'd died in the war, taken by our enemies and killed, like so many metas had been. He'd said that she could control men with the sound of her voice alone—not women, only men—that she could wrap them around her finger surer than any seductress.

If there was a male counterpart to those powers, kind of in the same way that my powers had a male counterpart, an incubus, then Rose could have absorbed those, and that was how I explained the fracas in the station in Edinburgh.

Except...

If Rose had the power to compel obedience by speech, or by using her mind (telepathy)...

Why the hell hadn't she used it on those Spec Ops guys just now? Or me? Why bother wasting time fighting them or chasing me?

Unless she *didn't* have those powers.

I was getting closer to the light now, and it had morphed from a pinprick to the size of a bowling ball. The culvert was reaching its end, and the dust I was stirring up with each scrape of my elbow against the ground was puffing up in my face. I couldn't see any water at the end of the tunnel, just light, and I had to concentrate to keep my body in its rote habit of crawling.

Behind me, the faint sound of Rose's fury still echoed, as I pulled myself from the hole in the ground and got to all fours. I sucked in a greedy breath of fresh air, smelled the greenery all around, and looked up at the iron grey sky above. I'd come out in a copse of trees, a little mini-forest down the hill from the airfield. Ahead of me, the dried-out drainage path went on, down to a pond.

I stood there, trying to orient myself by the sun. I didn't dare say anything, afraid that she was listening somewhere in the distance, and that even the slightest sound would stir her to my presence.

Maybe she hadn't tumbled to the idea that Harmon was a powerful ally that could help her immensely yet. Maybe she didn't have any other telepaths. Maybe—

Maybe, maybe, maybe. If I was lucky, she was just being dumb, and was ignoring the mind reader in her midst.

But I couldn't count on luck.

I didn't bother to brush myself off, because I was just going to get dirtier in the next little while. I looked back at the culvert, the little metal tube sticking its way out of a concrete earthwork, and then set my course—due south.

Let's go, let's go, I said in my own head as I broke into a run. Not a hard sprint, but a metahuman jog, one that would cover some serious ground. I forgot for a moment that I would receive no answer, and I tried to bury my disappointment— my loneliness—at the lack of reply somewhere deep inside under the fatigue, under the weariness, and under most especially the gnawing, creeping sense of fear that seemed to get larger with every confrontation with Rose.

15.

My heart was pounding, a relentless, steady rhythm, the only companion I had within my own body anymore. Listening to it beat out its fury at this string of abuses—Rose's ambush of my plane, crawling through a culvert for five hundred yards, and now this—I'd probably run four or five miles, heading south—was strangely soothing now that my head was emptied of all voices but mine.

The Scotland countryside was picturesque, and might have been pretty if I hadn't been running for my freaking life. I'd heard the buzz of helicopters overhead, and I was seriously afraid for what would come if I got seen. Most of my run was over hilly farmland, and I worried I wouldn't see a helo coming until it was too late.

As a consequence, I was zigging and zagging between wooded areas. I'd stop for a second, take a breath, and get my ass through the woods until I could see another wood, preferably one that was mostly south. Then I'd haul said ass toward those woods, as fast as my meta self could run. If anyone saw me, they'd know instantly I wasn't human, because humans couldn't run that fast. But I hoped that I'd be to my destination before they realized what I was doing, being as I was giving all villages a wide berth and only popping into sight of farmhouses for a few minutes between forest sprints.

Why was it always the cardio I regretted not getting enough of? Not the strength training, because my strength was desperately down without Wolfe. No, it was the damned cardio I'd slacked off on during my stay in the UK, because training cardio as a meta in your hotel room is not the easiest of things to pull off. Sure, I wasn't in terrible shape, but I wasn't in peak condition either.

These were the struggles of the metahuman fugitive. Also, I effing hate cardio. Who wants to gasp like a fish?

I was between open stretches, on a high hill, when I saw it below: the Firth of Forth, that river estuary that emptied into the North Sea. I'd been running south to find it, and here it was, day's end not quite approaching, but not terribly far off. Looking out across the gleaming water, I could see a few ships, tankers and cargo vessels, probably from Edinburgh, or bound to Edinburgh, passing by at slow steam.

Standing there, catching my breath, I was reminded that the next phase of my getaway plan was perhaps the most dicey now that I'd evaded Rose. The Firth was less than a mile away, and I could cover that mile quickly if I didn't continue to zig and zag looking for tree cover. It had been a while since I'd heard a helicopter, after all, and it had been my good luck (there was that word again) that they apparently hadn't been using infrared or heat sensors during this manhunt.

There was tree cover to the west, and farther cover after that, but it looked like it was starting to get sparser the closer I got to the Firth. I swore under my breath, because that left me with a choice—break cover and run for it, chancing a helicopter or farmer seeing me as I did so, or take the safe route for a little longer.

It was probably a measure of how rattled I'd been by Rose these last two days that when I broke cover, I sprinted for the next copse of trees instead of going bold and making for the Firth. Finding myself under their shade a minute later, I took another breath, soothing myself for what was to come. Soon, I wouldn't be getting a break for a long time. I stood under the shade of the trees, not that I needed shade on a day like today. There wasn't exactly a lot of sun right now.

I took in the smell of the trees as I stood there, put my hand on one of them for support. I thought about lying down, but if I did, I might not get up again for a while and I needed to be well out of here before I collapsed. In fact, given that they were using search helicopters, next time I slept it needed to be either indoors or else under a car, somewhere that my IR signature would be masked in case they did start to employ sensors in their search.

Because that had to happen soon. They couldn't just keep sending helos overhead in hopes they might blindly stumble onto me.

I broke cover and ran for the next set of woods a minute later. I was timing myself, making sure I didn't spend too long in any one place. I hadn't heard the sound of a helicopter in a few minutes, but I could dimly hear one now, chopper blades churning through the air behind me. I poured on the speed, my legs throbbing, screaming, really, as I broke into a metahuman band of exertion that probably made me move in a blur.

I zoomed under the shade of the next woods, and came to a sliding stop before I burst out the other side. This was a small wood, maybe a hundred or two hundred trees, nestled in the middle of farmland. I went all the way to the southern edge of it and stared south, hoping to find my next checkpoint down the hill toward the Firth.

Instead…I found the end of my freaking cover.

There were no more woods between me and the Firth, just a bunch of fields and what looked like a park with a bunch of camping trailers in it. There was human activity within, and I didn't want any of that, so I chose my course accordingly. I'd break straight for the Firth once I was sure the chopper was clear.

If the chopper got clear.

I could hear it back there, doing a sweep. I didn't dare peek out at it from within the safety of my concealment. It seemed to be sweeping straight toward me, maybe a mile off to the east.

That was concerning.

The steady beat of the blades against the air was a cheery sound, like death approaching on wings of steel. I tried to control my breathing. It was loud, furious, agonizing in its way, trying to keep it under control. I wanted to suck in gasps of oxygen and expel fearful breaths, but I couldn't. I kept it quiet, as though somehow they could hear me from above.

I waited, the sound of the chopper first starting to fade, then receding. I didn't know how they'd chosen their course, but apparently they'd chosen poorly, as Reed was so fond of quoting. Once the blade noise had died down, I set my last checkpoint.

Right on the shore of the Firth.

Plunging ahead at a dead sprint, I ran for it. I headed for the water with breakneck speed and complete abandon. I cleared fences with a single leap, like a champion hurdler, and cut through farm fields hard enough to harvest a part of their crop. My feet hurt, my legs hurt, and my lungs were like a pair of balloons that someone had inflated inside my chest. Foreign, painful, they hung there in discomfort within me.

And the consolation was…there was no consolation, because what was coming next was going to be so. Much. Worse.

I reached the bank of the Firth and came surging down, carefully. I had nothing but some cash on me, and I'd stowed it in my pocket, deep, in preparation for this next thing. It didn't do any good to wait, so as soon as I reached the shore, without hesitating…

I plunged into the Firth of Forth.

The shock of the cold water was like death washing over me. Okay, maybe not that bad, but it was freaking colllllllllld. My teeth started to chatter, but I didn't let a little thing like death and impending hypothermia stop me.

No, I had an escape to make, and freezing waters were not going to deter me from my plan.

The frigid chill settling into my bones, I plunged deeper

into the Firth, and started my swim south. I'd estimated by the map it was something like ten or twelve miles.

If I hurried…I figured I could make that in about an hour.

My heart sinking—at the cold, at what I was having to do to survive, at the general unfairness of the world presently—I steadied myself and started my long swim south.

16.

Reed

Odessa, Texas was more or less what you'd expect when you think of Texas. I hated to say it, but most of the TV shows meant to depict Texas had been shot in California at one point in time, because saguaro sagebrush country looked more or less the same to the untrained eye. It was long stretches of what I'd call desert ground—kind of a sandy tan, with most of the greenery more of a deep brown, they were the main sign of life around here.

Other than, y'know, the town.

Odessa itself wasn't too big. Wikipedia had estimates of a population of 160,000 or so. If they had a sign declaring that number, I'd probably missed it while playing on my phone. The Odessa PD had sent a driver for us at Midland Airport, and Angel and I had made our way here in the back of one of their cars. Well, I'd been in the back. Angel had been up front, twitching like she'd wanted to be in the driver's seat until I had zoned out and started scrolling the internet.

Looking for news on my sister, of course.

There was no actual news, just a metric ton of analysis. It wasn't like they'd caught her between my flight and my arrival. Police Scotland weren't even saying anything, just keeping tight-lipped about whether they'd encountered her at all. Tips were pouring in, they said, and having been involved with the law enforcement side of those kinds of manhunts, I was reasonably sure they weren't lying.

The problem with that kind of tip was that you got a lot of static. It seemed like everyone who had encountered a short, dark-haired girl in Scotland this last week would probably be calling, and the investigators would have to sort through which of them were credible leads, and which were fanciful farces. Usually that was made somewhat easier by tagging your target's location at a given time and drawing concentric circles outward from that locale based on the time of travel it took to move from one place to another. That allowed you to eliminate a lot of the noise, because if they were in, say, Dallas at 10a.m. today on a Walmart security camera, and you got a tip saying they were in Honolulu at a pizza place with kids and a family at noon, you could pretty much write it off as bullshit if they were your average fugitive, because your average fugitive does not dare try and pass through TSA security checkpoints and the like while wanted. They're restricted to ground travel, and Honolulu ain't in the ground travel path from Dallas within two hours. Or ever, until they get around to building a bridge between LA and Hawaii.

What Police Scotland was bound to discover—if they hadn't already—was that such a weeding out was not really possible with Sienna. She could fly at supersonic speeds, which meant if they got a tip that she'd shown up in, say, Vienna, Austria an hour after they'd caught her on security camera footage in Harrods in London, that was totally possible. *Everything* was possible, which meant you couldn't toss away these probably useless tips out of hand.

I would have felt sorry for them, but I really, really wanted them to fail.

The cop car bumped to a stop, mid-morning sun blazing down above us. We should have been here hours earlier, but the flight from Eden Prairie had seemed to take forever, and the Midland airport seemed to be as far from the part of Odessa where this hostage drama was unfolding as possible. It might not have been, but with the Texas heat beating on us even inside the air-conditioned car, it sure felt like it.

"We're here," Angel announced, as though I were still in my electronically induced coma. She turned her head around, leaning an arm on the back of the seat to look back at me in my caged seating area.

I put my phone away slowly, calmly. No point in acting like I hadn't done this a hundred times before. "Okay," I said, and nodded toward the door. "Let me out."

She broke into a half smile. "Time to free the beast." And she got out of the passenger side to let me out.

The deputy who'd driven us looked at me with an air of uncertainty. I hadn't said much on the trip, and he looked like maybe that had worked his nerves over, riding with two quiet metas for an hour in his car. "Just a figure of speech," I said, trying to put him at ease. It did not seem to relax him.

Angel opened the door, and I said, "Thanks, Jeeves," as I got out. She favored me with a scowl—it didn't take much to get Angel to scowl; she was like the opposite end of her cousin, Miranda, being that Miranda—although not a smiler—didn't scowl. Both of them seemed to take a lot of effort to move from their natural emotional state. Miranda's was a kind of stoicism.

Angel's…was most definitely not. Her natural state was irritation, and she let it show often. She didn't shut the door for me, instead leaving it hanging wide, already walking away.

I got it for her, because I'm cool like that.

That done, I followed her toward the nearby officer in charge. Angel was wearing one of those modern all-business kind of lady suits, with the grey skirt, blouse beneath for a splash of color, and a jacket. I was clad similarly, but the male version of it—dress shirt and suit, but all black and white because the contrast looked good on me (Isabella said so). Angel was wearing heels, not flats, which would have been a mistake for most people and most metas in our line of work, but…

She could handle it. It's what she did.

The man in charge was evident by the fact that he was standing in the middle of the scene. He tipped his hat to Angel as she approached, then nodded at me, talking in a broad Texas accent as we came closer. "Ma'am," he said, taking a lot more deference to Angel. He just met my gaze with a fair amount of the reserve you tend to encounter in law enforcement when your superior has called in some outsider to come paw up your turf. "Reckon you heard we had a problem."

"Lay it out for us," I said, and he beckoned us over to where a bunch of house plans were sitting weighted on an old Crown Vic-style police cruiser hood. I made my way to the other side so I could take a gander without anyone else standing in my personal bubble.

"Got a 911 call in the late hours of last night," he said, putting his hands on the hood and then looking up at us, all seriousness. "Lady's voice. She was ordering a pizza."

"I remember seeing that on one of those domestic violence PSAs," I said. "Not a bad idea."

The sheriff seemed to think otherwise. "When my men showed up, we tried to take it easy, but this, uh…well, you know—"

"Metahuman," Angel said stiffly. Her arms were already folded in front of her.

"A-yep," the lawman drawled. "He opens the door and starts firing at my boys—well, and girls," he said in a seeming concession to Angel, who did not look amused. "Blows up a squaddy—" he nodded at the ruin of a new police Explorer on the curb, still smoking "—and my people go running for safer cover. This chickenshit hostage-taking son of a bitch, he ducks back inside, and stays in there with the curtains drawn. We hear some screaming, try and establish contact via the phone—" all this sounded like standard operating procedure "—and he informs us not to come in, not to make a move, but to charter him a private plane so he can get away clean. And that's it. No sound inside since, no demand for it on a timeframe, just…that." The lawman finished, and straightened up, crossing his arms in front of him. Now we had three people standing, one at each point of the hood, not one of us apparently wanting to be here, and all of us with our walls up.

"Okay," I said, since I was probably supposed to figure out what to say here. "There's been no threat of violence if his demands aren't carried out in a certain timetable?" I thought I'd heard the man right, but in a hostage situation this was pretty crucial stuff.

"No timetable," he said. It was probably a sign of how he felt about us that he hadn't offered his name.

I frowned. "That's a little odd. Did he specify what he'd do if you didn't comply?" The lawman shook his head again. "Have you called him back?"

Here, his expression darkened. "We were told by our higher-ups not to contact him again until you arrived."

"Well, we've arrived," I said, unfolding my arms. "When was your last contact?"

"Four, five hours ago," he said. "Haven't heard a peep from inside since then."

"All right then," I said. That wasn't great news, but it wasn't world-ending either. "Let's give 'em a call. Got the number?"

He handed me a cell phone after he'd already punched the number in. I pushed talk and held it up to my ear.

The sun beat down on me as I stood there, the black phone hot against my ear like it was about to explode. It was shaping up to be another Texas summer day, dry and fiery. My feet felt like they were going to melt their way onto the pavement, the soles of my shoes sticky against the rocky black aggregate.

"Hello?" someone answered, jarring me out of my heat-induced lapse into silence.

"Hi there," I said. "My name is Reed Treston, and I'm working with the local police. Who am I speaking with?" Using my Grade A phone manners, like grandma taught me to.

There was a nervous silence, and for a second I wondered

if the voice would answer. It was male, sounded young, cagey. "This is Peter."

And I had a first name. It was progress. "Peter, how are you doing in there?" I lowered my voice to a calm octave, trying to be all soothing and pleasant.

"Fine," he said, short, clipped, to the point. He didn't sound greatly agitated, but there were definitely a few things on his mind.

"That's good," I said, trying to be smooth. "We're all rooting for this to turn out well, you understand? We don't want anyone to get hurt—and that includes you. All right?"

He seemed to ponder that one for a second, then to take it onboard. "Okay."

"So…Peter," I said, repeating his name as often as I could to try and establish familiarity and rapport, "I talked with the Odessa PD officer on the scene, and I took over. I'm in charge now, okay? They're backing me up. And he kinda suggested what you want, but he was a little vague about it." I tried to adopt a conspiratorial, "he's over there, and it's you and me against him," kind of tone to put us on the same side. "I don't know what exactly he said to you, but I want to know exactly what you want, so I can get to work on that for you, because—again—we just want this all to work out and nobody to get hurt, okay?"

"Okay," he said again, and the wheels were turning really slow in this guy's mind. I tried to keep my voice even, but either he was on something, drug-wise, that was slowing his cognition, or he was flat-out dumb. It could have been either, and both were worrying.

"So…what do you want, Peter?"

Peter was quiet for a few seconds. "I want to get out of here. I want—I want a plane. To get me out of this country."

"Okay," I said, once I'd allowed a few seconds to be sure I wasn't going to end up talking over some request he made after a brief pause. The last thing I wanted to do was cut over this guy. I needed to listen, full, attentive, and long. It was amazing how many times you could actually talk someone out of doing something stupid just by listening to them. "We can do that," I said, giving him a little of the can-do attitude. "I will need something from you in return though, if that's all right." Gentle. Conciliatory. "And it's not tough; you don't have to really do much—I just need to talk to the people in there with you, and make sure they're all right." I hesitated, and went for the gusto. "Are they all right, Peter?" I asked as non-judgmentally as possible.

"Yeah, they're fine," he said, and a mild hint of agitation cut through in the strain of his voice. It wasn't a terrible amount, but enough that I found it…worrying…that it came out when I mentioned there might be harm to the hostages.

"Okay, good," I said, trying to sound relieved, which was not hard. "Can I talk to one of them, please, Peter?"

He chewed that one over. "Yeah, okay," he said, and then went silent.

There was a sniffling on the other end of the phone, and then a voice, female and cracking with fear, said, "Hello?"

"Hello," I said, trying to keep pouring on the soothing. "This is Reed Treston. I'm outside, with the police. Can I ask your name?"

"Elvira," she said.

That one took me aback. "Elvira?" I mostly repeated it so that I could confirm I got it right, and would have done so even if she'd said, "Jane."

"My mom was a fan of—never mind," she said, sniffling. "Elvira, yes."

"Okay, Elvira," I said, almost a whisper. "Is there anyone else in there with you besides Peter?"

"My kids," Elvira said, voice straining as she held back a tide of emotion.

My stomach plummeted like an elevator in the Empire State Building with the line and brakes cut. "What are their names and how old are they?" I asked, fighting off the emotion that threatened to creep into my voice. I needed to keep that at bay, because if I didn't, if I let feelings infect me, it had the potential to damage my discussions with Peter. Because it was really tough to talk to someone with decency and respect when they were a chickenshit who took kids as hostages.

"Elijah is six," she said, sniffling a little. "Barry is four. Annie is two."

"Elijah, six, Barry, four, Annie, two?" I repeated it and watched as Angel jotted it all down. She'd been listening in and taking notes all throughout my conversation. "Is there anyone else in there with you, Elvira?"

"No. Just us and Peter."

"Okay," I said. "I just need you to hang on, Elvira. We are working on this, okay? We are going to do everything we can to make Peter happy and settle this problem so everyone's okay. All right?" I wanted to end on a peppy note, give her some hope, because people without any hope tended to do desperate, terrible things. That went for Peter as much as it did for her. "You can hand the phone back now, okay?"

"Hello?" I heard Peter's rough voice again.

"Hey, Peter," I said, "thanks for making that happen." I complimented him on his can-do ability to be in charge, because that kind of thing worked wonders on a man's ego. "I'm gonna go talk with the sheriff and get things rolling for you on that plane, okay? It's probably going to take a while, though, because—I don't know if you've ever dealt with the airlines before—" I threw in a fake chuckle "—but they're pretty particular about people asking to borrow their planes." I hoped he wouldn't dive too deep on this lie, since the government owned plenty of planes we could probably easily commandeer, but he didn't seem the deep-thinking type. "But I'll get to work on that right away, see if we can cut through some of the red tape for you." Everything was for him, and I'd throw this in over and over again in our conversations, because I wanted him to see me as his advocate, on his side. I was working for him, fighting the man for his benefit!

Fearless, tireless, against all odds, I'd be working into the late, late hours trying to answer his needs. And it would go into the late hours too, because my job was to keep him from doing anything stupid while we waited for him to go to sleep so we could take him unawares. Or wear him out so he'd surrender without hurting anybody.

I glanced at the scorched squad car. Yeah, making sure he didn't hurt anybody was very important.

"Is there anything else I can do for you, Peter?" I asked. "Anything else you need? Food? Drink? Anything? Gatorade? Steak? It's Texas; we can get steak a lot easier than a plane."

"No," he said, and it was a pretty snap decision. "I'm good." He sounded...mild. Not like he was aiming to cause a shitstorm, but not embarrassed about it either.

Humility and the capacity to see that what he'd done here was breathtakingly wrong would have been preferable, but I'd take quiet acceptance and be happy with it now, because it beat the hell out of him getting belligerent and throwing around threats. Besides, the fact that he'd shown some grace meant that now I could get on to making my eminently reasonable request for a fair exchange considering all the wonderful things I was about to go and do for Peter.

"All right, just one thing then, Peter," I said, right before I sensed he was ready to hang up. "I'm going to go do this for you, but in return...I need something. And...really, it's no big deal. I just need to show the Odessa PD, and you know, the other people out here—" the cops, the governor, whatever authority Peter most identified as his antagonist—guys with man-buns, maybe "—what a good guy you are.

"Peter," I said, trying to build up to it, "can you let the kids go?"

The answer came back in a half second, flat and firm, devoid of emotion. "No."

I drew a deep breath. It was a big ask, and I decided to explain. "Look, Peter...I get that, I do. But these are kids, man. They need diaper changes." I heard no agreement, which I suspected was a tacit kind of agreement. "They need food, naps—you don't want that kind of trouble, do you? Crying, whining kids? Because they're gonna do that. We just want to make sure they're safe, and that everything goes as easy as possible. You keep Elvira in there, and you'll still be safe. We want this to end with everybody okay, right? But the kids…come on, Peter…you don't need the kids. They're going to be more trouble than good for you, don't you think?"

Presenting it as a question was part of trying to change his thinking. I'd listed out the bad points, obviously, and glossed over the good—that cops were terrified of shooting into a building where there were kids, because the potential for disaster was enormous. No one wanted to take the chance for a stray round offing a kid, not even the hardest hardass.

Peter seemed to think about it, like he was weighing my points. "No," he said again, still flat. "Get me that plane."

And he hung up.

"Shit," I said, taking a deep breath. I looked over at Angel, and her face was frozen. She'd heard. Maybe even suspected what I did. The Texas sun was still beating down on me, but it had nothing to do with the sudden sweat I found breaking out—on my lips, on my forehead, and everywhere from my scalp on down.

Peter was determined and not all that bright. He also had hostages, including three children, and a complete unwillingness to surrender even one of them.

This…was a formula set up for complete and total disaster.

17.

Sienna

Oh, man, did I have plans for my next nap. Big plans. Huge plans. Plans that defied the scope of the universe itself…

Okay, really, I just planned to make sure I dreamwalked to Reed or Zollers or Wexford or—hell, the list was starting to really mount up.

But also…I could have really used a nap.

Swimming across the Firth was not as easy an endeavor as it might have been had I attempted it at Edinburgh. There, the two banks were only a short distance apart, maybe a mile or two.

Here? Where I was now, the distance had to be ten, twelve miles. It wasn't exactly marathon distance, or Cuba to the Florida Keys, but it was a long swim for a girl who typically didn't get in the pool.

Also, cold. Still really, really cold. My nipples were practically cutting through the water for me on every stroke. Brrr.

I wished I'd removed my draggy, stolen clothes before I'd jumped in, but then I'd have been a shining beacon of white that could have been spotted from space, even as the day dragged to a close. I cursed the fact that Scotland was like Minnesota in its long days during summer. I bet the sunset wouldn't even happen until close to nine o'clock, and that was probably hours off (I didn't have a watch or phone—not that either would have survived the water). All I had before me was the swim.

The long, long swim.

Well, okay, not that long. I was probably halfway there, and I'd been going for a little over a half hour.

I'd lost sight of the bank behind me, but the bank ahead, I could see in the distance. My arms were weary and tired, and my legs were screaming and protesting my sorry efforts. They wanted to quit and let me sink, and I was tempted to let them. I was threading my way through the channel at an hour best suited to being anywhere else, where visibility was high and if a ship passed, I'd surely be seen.

On the other hand, if a ship passed and I could get aboard, I should probably do that, even if it went to Thailand or something, because frankly, my original strategy of retreat on a chartered plane and arm up, then come back at Rose with Suppressant and bullets had badly, badly failed.

And while I'd done a reasonable job of coming up with an alternate escape plan, I was kinda shit out of luck when it came to what to do next. This part of the plan that I was currently implementing was still all about the evasion, about getting the hell away. Unfortunately, once I had gotten the hell away—as far as I could, in this case—I was still going to be in Scotland.

Which was not nearly far enough from Rose for my taste. Not when my bag of goodies had gotten torched in the Cessna.

I put one arm in front of the other, churning my legs like a shark. I was cruising along at a good clip, probably looking a little like a jet ski as I buzzed through the water. I didn't make an actual buzzing noise; it was probably more like a gurgling, from my efforts and the sound of me throwing my head to the sides to breathe as I sucked in hungry, greedy breaths on each stroke. Paddling like a junior wheelboat wasn't exactly light on the oxygen consumption.

Plan. I needed one. Getting to the bank of the river was a start, but that didn't get me out of Scotland.

So, what could I do?

Well, in order:

a) Evade on land. If I made it to the south bank, I would have increased the search radius so broadly that Rose's helicopters would have a hard time tracking me. If I could avoid creating any other John Clifford-like entanglements—which was to say little bombs of info to shout out, "She was here!" in my wake once I landed—Rose would have no idea I'd reached the southern shore, or even that I'd gone for a swim at all. She'd just be sitting at a map table somewhere in her evil lair, wherever that was, and every hour that she didn't have a bead on me, the circle that indicated her search radius would get wider and wider.

She'd have to assume I got my hands on a car too, or hitched a ride on the back of an unknowing truck. Boom. That'd carry me farther away. Not as far as if I could still fly, but far enough that she and her minions—I assumed Police Scotland was co-opted based on the amount of overhead helicopters I'd seen after me post-airfield—would struggle to cover all the ground as the radius got wider and wider.

b) My second option, which I dismissed almost out of hand, was to evade by going out to sea. Assuming I could maintain a bearing of due east without any reference point but perhaps the sun and stars, and could survive the freezing cold of the North Sea, in about five hundred miles I'd make landfall in Denmark. Optimistically, I could maybe make that in two or three days. With no sleep. In the freezing water. (Not actually freezing, it just felt like it.) So I'd wash up on the shores of Denmark half dead and probably collapse right there, assuming I didn't drown on the way.

As a side plan, call it "b2," maybe I could latch onto a commercial ship of some sort like a barnacle and hitch a ride to elsewhere in the world, lying low in a lifeboat or something. This felt like more of a long-odds plan, and I dismissed it, too.

c) Land, lay low. That was less evasion, which I considered to include movement, and more sheltering in place. Break into a house like with John, take a hostage and keep them for a few days. Downside: taking hostages meant exposing yourself to the risk that the people you took would be missed. Over the course of several days, this became more and more likely, and produced the offshoot result that even if you imprisoned them as I had with John, unless I killed them and hid the body (which I was unwilling to do) they'd eventually rat me out.

The other alternative to this plan, let's call it "c2," was the idea that I should find a cave or other natural formation, a spider-hole kind of thing, and pull the earth in over me. No movement, no food, nothing, just stay there until some of the heat subsided. Major downside: a few days without food and water and I'd get weak. Especially water. If I could find a place that had water it was slightly more feasible, but when I did come out, I wouldn't be in peak fighting condition.

Not that fighting had been much of an option thus far, but…still. I wouldn't be in peak running condition either.

I turned my head and took another gasping breath. The shore was drawing nearer and nearer, sand and sea meeting in a glorious symphony of salvation. I couldn't quite hear the crashing of the waves yet, because my own splashing was heavy in my ears, but I dreamed of a moment when my feet would touch dry land again, and I could stop swinging my arms like I was a motorboat, maybe spit the saltwater out of my mouth and not have it seep back in again.

Modest goals.

I didn't like plan c at all, nor plan b. Staying still or evading by sea seemed like non-starters to me. Even the idea of trying to catch a commercial ship relied heavily on the idea that I wouldn't get caught, or that I could somehow bribe the crew. It seemed unlikely I could survive without water in a lifeboat, so I gave up on that idea.

It was going to be plan a all the way. Which begged the next question:

Where should I go once I made landfall?

I needed to get the hell out of Scotland, that much was sure. Here, Rose was on her home ground, and however she had done it—I was doubting the Siren explanation, but I had no reasonable alternative—she seemed to exercise a certain control over portions of the populace. Or at least the cops in Edinburgh.

Which meant if I could avoid it, I should stay the hell out of Edinburgh.

That left me with a few avenues. I could try for the Channel Tunnel. That was really the only convenient ground route out of the UK. I could potentially get on a ferry at Dover. Maybe there were others, I didn't know.

Or I could try and get a plane. Though we'd seen how that worked out the first time around.

Which brought me to another question: How had Rose found my rendezvous point at the airfield? Just simple luck seemed right out, especially since a US government team had shown up at the same place, same rough time.

That suggested my fears of some sort of NSA cell phone hacking might be well founded. Shit. When I called my banker again, I'd need to use a landline, for his safety and mine. Less chance of interception that way. I'd have him make arrangements this time, leaving it to him to make contact with and to get money to someone who could.

I didn't want to rely on Fritz again for transport, given what had happened last time I'd put my future location out there. Which meant exfiltrating the country was on me. A commercial flight was pretty much out, because even if I could procure fake ID—which seemed difficult, again, owing to the trouble that came from having to rendezvous with people and giving away my location in the bargain—I doubted if I'd be able to pass the scrutiny of a security checkpoint given that I was the most wanted fugitive in the UK right now. They'd be on high alert, and watching for me.

The tunnels and ferries? Maybe I could sneak through there, though that was kind of suspect too. I would have laughed in the face of the EU meta embargo now, at the thought of crossing into France only to be arrested there for being a powered person, but…it wasn't that funny.

Either way, if I wanted to get into position to do that, I needed to get the hell out from under Rose's nose.

I needed to get the hell out of Scotland.

Car, rail, or on foot. Those were my main options for getting back into the south of the country. Once there, maybe I could exfiltrate myself. Hell, I could swim the English Channel. Though, maybe I'd be better off making contact with Wexford—in person, or via landline somehow, or even better, dreamwalk—and letting him sort out my escape, given he probably didn't want me caught here.

Hopefully, anyway. If Wexford was off my side…

Well, then I was really alone.

The shore was in sight now, my excessive thinking roiling in my brain like my arms were doing to the water around me. Only a few hundred yards to go and I'd be out, out of this frigid wash, out of immediate danger, out of…

Well, not out of the soup, because I was still in deep shit, but…closer to a break, at least.

And I needed a break.

I couldn't see anyone on the beach, and suddenly I was thankful for the utter lack of sun overhead. Hell, if it wanted to break loose and start pouring, that would only aid me, really. So long as the choppers weren't flying with IR sensors, I was safe as houses in a downpour, though I'd look suspicious if anyone peeked out their window and saw me hotfooting it across the hills in a tempest at metaspeed.

Dragging myself through the rough surf near shore, I fought against the breakers that threatened to knock me over. Apparently the tide was high. Who would have guessed, given how late it was probably getting in the afternoon?

The exhaustion was sweeping; it had me from toe to head. My brain swirled in a slow eddy of worry, looking up and over my shoulder for helos. Still none in sight. There were ships out in the Firth, but none that had gotten terribly close to me. As long as none of their crew picked up their microphones and called in the sight of a crazy person swimming like mad through the water...

I couldn't rely on that. Up on shore now, I was dripping across the clumped, tan sands and occasional rock like I was the sky letting loose. My clothes were clinging to me like weighted chains, threatening to drag me down. They weren't actually that heavy, especially to a meta, but to a meta who was battling exhaustion?

Yeah. They felt heavy, soaked and cold and clutching at my skin like an industrial-strength full-body suction cup that had been licked by someone who'd just taken a drink of ice water.

I dragged myself up on the beach and forced myself to go on, kicking up the sand as I went, my feet barely lifting with each step. I needed to keep going, just a little farther inland, somewhere that I could find a safe spot to take a break...

And maybe pass out for a few hours, before I ran myself to death, maybe literally.

18.

I was pretty damned sick of running through the Scottish countryside by now, but at least it gave me the ability to dodge the hell out of the Scottish people, for the most part. Being this far out from most of the cities and towns meant fewer people, which was good.

Because right now, there was a deep uncertainty factor with people. They weren't all Rose's servants, but the fact that she seemed so annoyingly ever-present was…concerning, to say the least.

Out here in the middle of nowhere, I felt strangely safer. Avoid people, avoid Rose, because, obviously, she was a people. A person, I guess, if you want to get all grammatical about it.

I hooked the long way west, avoiding a pretty good-sized town that I spied from a hilltop. Skirting my way around the edges of fields, running low over fences and hedgerows, I knew my luck had to be running short. Sooner or later, someone was going to see me bolting through the fields, and that'd spell disaster.

Finding a place to lay low until nightfall? That was my new plan.

Farms were good in that regard. If I found a farm that had a few outbuildings, odds were I could slip into one and find a hiding place, maybe in a barn, buried under some hay, and spend a good portion of the afternoon and night all sacked out there, unconscious, and wake up around midnight. Under cover of darkness, I could start moving again, less worried about getting spotted out in the countryside because almost everybody would be asleep at that hour. I could cruise through the fields in the (hopefully lack of) moonlight, and get my ass heading on toward the next destination.

Which I had yet to pick out. Because I needed to try and make plans again.

Cresting the next hill, I found another of the seemingly endless farms out here in the countryside. This one didn't seem to be in production, the fields filled with hay—which, I suppose, was a kind of production, but not the kind you had to assiduously watch and care for, necessarily—and otherwise a little overgrown.

The barn was old and rickety, and next to it was another squarish building, what we in the midwest would have called a pole shed. This one had a wide bay door that was open, and inside I could see it was set up like an auto shop, with a car inside. There was a mechanic standing outside, smoking a cigarette and facing the other way. He was just standing there, minding his own business, about a hundred and fifty yards away. And playing on his phone.

I came creeping down out of the hills, taking a dogleg path around so I could approach from behind the building. It was getting late in the day, my run and swim having burned most of it. I estimated the sun wouldn't set for hours yet, but here I'd found a nice little set of buildings, and an automotive shop would be an ideal place to hide for the night, especially if this guy were to knock off soon and call it a day.

As though someone was sensing my thoughts, I heard someone call, "Angus!" from the farmhouse, and I reached the cover of the back of the automotive shop just as he started to head in. I couldn't see him, hunkering down in the shadow of the building, long grass tickling at me where I crouched, but I could hear his footsteps as he headed toward the house.

"What is it?" he asked as he opened the door and let it slam behind him.

"Did ye hear from Mactaggart?" a female voice asked him, muffled by the fact that there were now house walls and an automotive shop between us.

"Nae," he said. "Did he call?"

"Aye. Said he'd been trying to reach ye for hours."

"Did he call the shop?"

"I don't know. Just he's been trying to reach you."

"I bet he called my mobile, the daft prick. He should know I can't hear it when I'm working."

"Aye, he's a bit thick. But you should call him back."

A bit more disgruntled: "Aye. Tomorrow, though."

She seemed to perk up, this unseen woman. "Oh? Are you done for the night, then?"

A pause, then he answered. "Aye. I want to see what happens next on *Stranger Things*."

"If we hurry—" she sounded hopeful "—we could squeeze in an episode before *Great British Bakeoff*."

"That's what I was thinking, too." He seemed enthusiastic. "Let me lock up the shop." I heard something else, and it took me a second to realize it was kissing. "I love you."

"I love you, too."

More kissing. Yeesh. Get a farm, you two.

This seemed like my chance. I darted around the building and into the automotive shop. There was a big under bay beneath the car that was parked within. The car wasn't lifted up at all, no jack or hydraulic lift, so it seemed like maybe Angus just did all his work underneath. I spied stairs going down in the corner, and I headed for them, darting down quickly, pausing a couple steps beneath the start and just sitting there, waiting.

It actually took a few minutes before the guy came in. He was humming, and I got a feeling he was a pretty happy fellow. I listened to his hum morph effortlessly into a whistle, and couldn't help breaking into a smile myself. He had a fun night ahead of him, watching a TV show he liked next to a woman he loved.

Must be nice.

The door of the shop clanged shut a second after the lights went out, throwing me into darkness. A few high windows cast a little grey light over me. The smell of oil was thick in the air, stronger beneath the car where I suspect an oil change had actually been in progress before he'd decided to call it a day for some Netflix and chill time. I waited a few seconds before moving, until I could no longer hear him whistling, and until I heard the door to the farmhouse slam.

Finally, I was alone in the dark.

I scouted the pit beneath the car first. It was dark, but I could see well enough to notice the vat of oil. I'd need to avoid that, but otherwise the pit seemed like the place to settle down for a nap when the time came. It was nice and dark, even compared to the rest of the shadowy shop, and it was under enough cover that an IR scope would have a hell of a time picking up one human body heat signature under all that concrete and the chassis of the fairly large farm truck that was on the rack above.

I crept up the stairs, figuring there was no point in being loud. There was a fridge in the corner, and I immediately headed toward it as though it contained the secret of life. Which it sorta did, because I found a few beers, something called Irn Bru, which came in a can and looked like a beer also, or maybe an energy drink.

No food, though.

I checked a cabinet just to the side of the fridge, and jackpot. Terrible-for-you snacks were stockpiled here like some brilliant ant had seriously readied himself for winter, a wise precaution in Scotland given the length of those suckers. I busted into them like they were food and I was a starving person—both true things, because I hadn't really eaten since John's house earlier today, and not very well.

Cracking open an Irn Bru, I took a sniff and decided, yeah, this was probably an energy drink of some sort. I mentally flipped a coin and decided to pass on it for now, figuring the potential caffeine wasn't worth the risk. I was going to have enough trouble sleeping as it was; no need to compound the problem.

Instead I chugged a different soda to rehydrate, then found a sink and drank straight from the tap. I didn't want to make enough of a mess to get the mechanic thinking someone had been in here, so I carefully cleaned up after myself, leaving the Irn Bru out, fizzling quietly on the bench; I'd chug it before I headed out later tonight. Everything else I put in the trash can, taking care to try and bury the food wrappers under other stuff so it wouldn't be blatantly obvious someone had pigged out in this guy's stash.

Cleanup done, I started looking around the quiet, hazy shop for the phone the mechanic had mentioned earlier. I found it on the wall, and dialed that number I'd memorized for Mr. Nils. I waited a few seconds, hoping that I hadn't messed up the dial as I always seemed to here in the UK, but within a few seconds, it started to ring.

"Hello?" a voice answered on the other side. No familiarity now, which would have been irksome under normal conditions.

"It's me," I said, still avoiding saying my name, just in case the wired UK telecom system was set up for easy listening. Hopefully the NSA or whoever had tipped off the military types that showed up at the airfield weren't tapped into it. That left open the possibility that Rose was, but I had no time to worry about that right now.

"Ah, yes," Mr. Nils said coolly. "I was wondering when I would hear from you."

"The answer is now," I said. "Listen—I need you to place an order for me with a different supplier. Whoever you want to use, whatever it takes, within reason. I mean, I don't want you to give away the whole—"

"I'm afraid I can't do that," Mr. Nils said quietly. "Your account has been locked."

I froze, the quiet of the shop seeming to develop into a blaring silence, one that echoed in my ears. "I'm sorry, what? Locked how?"

"If you'll wait just a second, I can transfer you to the party responsible."

"No, I don't want a transfer, just tell me what—"

Bzzz. Bzzz. The bastard had already put me on hold.

I almost considered hanging up on him, but I didn't, my curiosity sparked by the feeling that I'd been gut-punched. I'd had my money with this bank for years, and they'd always been on call for me, the way you would expect when someone puts almost a half billion dollars with your bank. This "Account Locked" thing was bullshit, pure and simple, because they'd put me in touch with so many shady people over the years when I needed something illegal or damned near done that the idea that they were suddenly becoming moral crusaders against the evil of Sienna Nealon was laughable, frankly.

"Hello?" a bright female voice answered on the other end of the line, a faint, lilting accent.

"Yes, I'm sorry—" I started to say, and then froze, my blood turning cold.

I knew that voice.

"Hello, Sienna," Rose said on the other end of the line. I could almost see her smile, even in the dark of the auto shop, miles between us counting for nil, as I heard the joy in her voice at having cut off another of my avenues of retreat. "I hear you're having some problems with your account...the biggest of them being...it's not yours anymore." She cackled lightly. "Because, like those souls you had, and everything else that's yours...it's just become mine."

19.

I slammed the phone down almost hard enough to break it. I didn't need to hear any more.

No taunts.

No laughter.

No further conversation.

I drew a ragged breath in the darkness of the automotive shop, and rested a hand on the farm truck sitting at its center as I wobbled away from the phone. That money was mine, my ace card, the thing I kept in reserve as a surprise and a hedge against all the troubles I'd faced the last few years.

It felt like someone had yanked the rug from beneath my feet, and without Gavrikov's power of flight to save me, I had come crashing down to the hard concrete floor of life.

"Oh no," I gasped, feeling like maybe I was having a heart attack. Or a panic attack. Or just death coming straight for me like a Hades reaching out with his powers and ripping at my soul.

Sure, I was technically immune to that power, but still...it felt like someone was tearing at me.

My brain was wheeling, whirring, again speeding at a thousand miles per second. I grabbed the Irn Bru I'd left open and chugged it, taking it down swiftly, then tossing the can in the garbage. I looked at the window high above the workbench at the back of the shop. It faced away from the farmhouse, which was good, because I'd heard the mechanic lock the door, and I didn't need to deal with him looking out later and seeing it open.

I jumped up, grabbed the window ledge with my fingers and hoisted myself up, tugging with my baseline succubus meta strength. It was easy enough, and once there, I unlatched the window and popped it open, sliding out and landing in the tall grass behind the building.

Rose had been on the other end of the phone from me, and could easily have gotten caller ID on the landline I'd just used. It would have been simple, presuming somehow she'd co-opted Nils. And I had to assume that, because how else would she have locked my account?

This was her manifestation of control again, this power she had over others. I was thankful I'd hung up on her, thinking again of her possible Siren abilities. She could have talked me into surrendering myself, maybe, if I'd kept chatting.

And even if she couldn't do that, she could damned sure have dispatched most of Police Scotland to the origin of the phone number I'd called her from, which meant I needed to put some serious distance between myself and this auto shop, and quickly.

The sky was still an unrelenting grey as I sprinted toward the nearest fence, on a hilltop about three hundred yards away. I kept the auto shop between me and the farmhouse, just in case the couple within had come up for air from *Stranger Things*, I'd best not accelerate the process of getting the cops on my ass.

Once I reached the fence I hopped it, trying to control my breathing, and scouted the land on the other side. No buildings in sight. I started forward again, heading west along the fence line. I'd just run using this cover until I found another obstacle.

I did that all the way to the intersection of the fence, some two miles down the way. There, I found myself steeped in a wood, weary and breathing heavily again. I crept through, crunching a few stray, fallen leaves, shivering, less from cold than from constant exertion and fear creeping in. My heart was hammering and I was exhausted. My eyelids were trying to creep down on me. I hadn't gotten a lot of restful sleep last night, I'd run and swam for miles and miles today, and had been kicked in the ass by adrenaline more times than I could count.

Mopping my sotted brow, I tried to figure out what to do next. There was another farm below, this one with just a barn, a farmhouse, and one outbuilding. The farmhouse looked abandoned, but that was hardly a guarantee. The grounds were overgrown, which was another mark in their favor, but again, no certainty that this was empty.

There was no sound of helicopters overhead or in the distance. I felt certain that Rose would have tracked back my call by now. I definitely hadn't known how to block the caller ID, not here in the UK. Hell, I could barely figure out how to dial their phones. It would have been a smart skill to learn before coming over here, or during the months I'd spent in London, but you couldn't anticipate every possibility. Brushing up on the telecom systems of the places you visited? Ranked somewhere below daily cardio and martial arts practice.

I couldn't stop at this farm, but I did decide to make a break right through the middle of it. It was a risk, but a calculated one. If I stuck to fence lines, I'd have to really take the long way around, and I needed to put a ton of distance between me and that automotive shop before I did hear the helos overhead.

That in mind, I sprinted out of the trees and bolted over the field, heading for the stone fence that waited on the other side of the farm.

I covered the ground in a matter of sixty seconds or less, which seemed considerably longer since I was in the middle of open fields, not an ounce of concealment anywhere nearby save for a couple of scraggly bushes not far from the farmhouse. I kept my distance from the buildings, a plan I was willing to change if I heard a helicopter's buzzing.

It didn't come though, and I made it to the other side of the property without incident.

The longer I stayed out in the open and the more time elapsed between when I'd hung up with Rose and now, the more likely it got to be caught out in the open. My breathing was coming furiously, my already exhausted body having reached the point of quitting. There was exertion—say, running a marathon, or a triathlon, both of which I'd kinda done already today—at a human pace, and then there was doing all the above at a metahuman pace.

I was an impressive athlete among humans. I could win just about any event at the Olympics without putting much effort into it, solely on my natural gifts. (Which had become a problem the IOC was dealing with.)

But today I'd done far more than just a normal human run, or even a superhuman run conducted at a human pace.

I'd run a marathon at a meta pace, sprints, stopping and starting constantly.

I had gone for a swim that lasted less than an hour but covered something like ten or fifteen miles.

And I'd experienced more stress and adrenaline and fright and hell and trauma in the last twenty-four hours than I could recall facing—with the possible exception of that time I caught a bullet in the brain, and even that was debatable—maybe ever.

It felt like I was dying, like my legs were going to give out on me at any second, like my lungs were taking their last breaths. I was well conditioned for a human, maybe even for a meta, but my body had reached the wall and I was now being thrown back, hard. If I'd gotten a decent night of sleep last night, maybe—

No.

This was it.

I was crashing.

I'd had nothing to eat but what I'd raided from John's fridge this morning and the sugary crap I'd taken out of the mechanic's junk food stash since...hell, I'd been starving myself in Edinburgh yesterday, too. I probably hadn't eaten a real meal since the day before, and exerting this many calories on a near-empty tank…

It was beyond unhealthy. It wouldn't be fatal, because I didn't think metas could die that way—I knew of high-level ones like me that had been asphyxiated and starved for years or even centuries that had somehow survived, albeit badly brain damaged—but it would mean the end of my run.

I had to rest. There was nothing else for it.

There was an agonizing stitch that had sprung to life in my side, screaming like someone had taken a knife and plunged it in. Rose sort of had, I guess, but that was more of a back wound, and not a literal one.

I scanned ahead, hoping for some sign of—

There.

In the distance was another farmhouse, this one well-kept and the fields growing sprouting, green crops that were about a foot out of the ground. I couldn't tell what they were, and I didn't care unless I could eat them as I went by. I might not even have had the energy to chew them at this point. There was a barn here, and it, too, was in good repair. And out from the barn a little bit…

Was a covered car port, with an old truck parked beneath it. There were no walls, and it was exposed to the elements, but the truck didn't look like it had been moved in a long time. In fact, compared to the rest of the farm, it was in dismal shape, the hood all rusted and at least two of the tires flat as Iowa.

I belly-crawled over the distance between us, probably close to a mile, trying not to disturb the hay that hid me at first, and then keeping myself between the rows of the budding crops on the final approach. No helicopter sound echoed on the horizon, but my breaths were still coming furiously.

My hands were numb as I scraped along on my elbows and knees, like some sort of wounded dog. My brain had slipped into a twilight state, the corners of my vision blackening, a tunnel forming in my sight between me and my objective. My legs seemed to be seizing up, painfully, aches screaming at me as the muscles gave up the ghost.

I fought them back into action, always one more pull forward, always just one more elbow ahead. I swayed from side to side with each motion, always in danger of tipping over.

Somehow I made it out of the row of crops and onto the manicured lawn. There were only ten or fifteen yards between me and the old truck now, and I felt every single one of them. I tried to stand and failed, crumbling back to my hands and knees. Running had been a thing I took for granted this morning. Moving normally had been possible only an hour—had it only been that long since the call? I thought so—before.

Now I strained to get the last few feet. When I reached the concrete floor of the car port, I dragged myself across it, not caring that I was leaving a dirt trail, a blood trail. The next good rain would wash it all away, I hoped. Maybe that would even come tonight, if I was lucky.

Ha.

Me.

Lucky.

That was a good one.

I dragged myself beneath the truck, and just in time. My whole body quit as I did so, my neck muscles giving way and my face crumpling gently to the concrete. There was an oily smell lingering here too, but not as strongly as the automotive shop. The lingering orange, metallic flavor of Irn Bru was stuck on my tongue, and the pavement grain felt like it was burning at my brow.

I didn't give a damn about any of that.

I was safe as I could be.

There were no choppers buzzing in the distance.

Every inch of me hurt, was sore, was tired, was shutting down from exhaustion.

I felt like I was forgetting something. To escape, maybe, but that was impossible now. I couldn't have run any farther if I had to. My heart could have been pumping wildly—hell, it still was; I could hear it—and I couldn't have traveled another inch right now.

I was in for the night. The grey horizon was barely visible beyond the shadow of the truck above me.

And as I lay there, mind almost blank from fatigue, from fear, from the complete and total mental exhaustion that went with the physical, a single thought came to me.

Reed.

And with that last, stray thought, I plunged into the darkness of sleep.

20.

Reed

The day was dragging, because there wasn't anything else to do except call Peter every once in a while and let him know all the things I was working on doing for him. So I was doing that every hour or two, after having received his permission to do so, and offering food, and gently requesting—oh so reasonably—that he give us the youngest kid. Just the smallest. Make your life easier. Give us a sign of good faith, I would say, as I baked in the hot Texas sun, sweat rolling down my face in great rivulets.

And the answer was always, "No."

Some thoughtful person who'd clearly been in Texas law enforcement for some time had set up a tent for us to hide under while we waited. It was just a simple canopy, but in the summer heat, the shade was appreciated by me and everyone else. Angel and I were sweating through our suits, and I had big ol' beads dripping out of my thick hair every few minutes.

I wiped my brow with my shirt sleeve, admiring the new, translucent shade the white broadcloth had turned from absorbing all that moisture. It was not a trivial amount of sweating I was doing, and suddenly I wished Miranda had called Scott instead of Angel. He could have set up his version of a misting device, drawing moisture out of the air and blowing it over us to defray some of the life-choking heat.

But as Teddy Roosevelt said, "Do what you can, with what you have, where you are."

I doubted he'd been standing in a suit in the sweltering summer sun in Texas when he'd said it, but anything was possible I guess. Those guys were crazy back then. They wore suits all the time, and everywhere.

"Getting close to the hour," Angel said, a quiet, tense reminder to me that the moment was coming up for me to place another call to Peter.

We'd managed to identify him, finally, after a little more coaxing allowed me to get his last name out of him. Peter Upton, age twenty-six, a troubled lad with a troubled life. He had a rap sheet for petty stuff, but I hadn't seen the kicker until Angel pointed it out to me.

Peter Upton was five foot six, and as near as I could tell he had all the brains to match his stature—which was to say, in both these ways, he was below average.

Every one of his prior convictions read like something out of *America's Dumbest Criminals*. Robbed a liquor store, no mask, using a squirt gun—that was yellow. When the clerk laughed at him, Upton proceeded to beat the clerk with the squirt gun, giving the man some serious contusions. But the clerk did fight back, and ultimately drove Upton out of his store and into the arms of a police patrolman who happened to be driving by just as Upton ran out with the offending squirt gun, wild-eyed and slightly bloody.

That wasn't even the best highlight in the reel, at least in my opinion, but it was pretty emblematic of Upton's history. Dumb, easily angered, cruel when he thought he had power over others. He felt like my worst analysis of humanity, all the regressive genes rolled into one person and illustrative of the least favorable part of our natures. He'd kept a somewhat even keel so far in his dealings with me, but he was not bright enough to realize how dumb he actually was.

Which made him extremely difficult to deal with.

And somewhat sensitive.

"Yeah," I said, stirring to wipe my forehead for the millionth time. I'd shed my suit jacket and so had Angel, who was sweating through her blouse. Honestly, Angel in a blouse and suit didn't seem quite right to me for some reason. She was a tense, terse woman who would—again, I suspected—rather be wearing a tank top and boots than heels and a suit. It wasn't that she didn't wear them well—she did, and Isabella hadn't taken my eyes away so I wouldn't notice—it was that she didn't look like she wanted to be wearing them, that she was generally stiff all the time she was in them.

Her bare, dark arms showed signs of sweat as well, little beads hiding on her biceps and forearm, companions to the ones that she, too, kept wiping off her forehead. "You don't sound excited about this," she said, not exactly bringing the thunder in the enthusiasm department herself.

"I'm not so sure stalling is going to work with this guy," I said, giving her my heartfelt assessment. "He's dumb, but I'm not sure he's dumb enough to realize he's being played. And he's stubborn enough that I think he's probably stuck in a mode where he just wants what he wants, no room for compromise in his head."

"Dangerous profile," Angel said. We'd worked together for a while, and I still had no real idea of her background. Her hiring had predated mine, brought to the team when Sienna had reorganized it after Harmon had torn us apart. Sienna had done so using Miranda as the guiding force through which she'd done everything, which made sense given that Sienna was on the run from the law at the time. I'd come in to a ready-made team, but it had included Angel as part of the bargain, hired by her cousin Miranda.

That choice by Miranda had made me curious. Angel's performance these last few months had given me no cause to think her hiring had been motivated by nepotism. She was steady and did her job, kept a cool head in crisis situations, and didn't gripe about stupid stuff like the heat in Texas on a summer day.

But I didn't really know her, and it bothered me in moments like this, when she offered a hint of experience with this type of person, and then just shut it down before saying anything else. She looked away, maybe catching sight of my deeper ponderings about what was going on in her head.

"I think this guy is a Revelen-made meta," I said, glancing at his file again.

"Oh yeah?" Angel was pretty non-committal about her reply, like she'd lost interest in anything going on here.

"Yeah. I was thinking specifically of that time he'd robbed the store with the squirt gun, since it happened last year." I brandished the file. "Why not use your cop-car frying laser power instead of a yellow squirt gun?"

"Why not paint the squirt gun first so it looks like a real gun?" Angel asked, seemingly unimpressed. "This guy's a moron."

"Yeah, but if he had laser powers, he's surely not dumb enough to forgo those in favor of a yellow squirt gun. And he assaulted the clerk with his fists. Damage wasn't anything meta-like, given that the guy was bruised up and fighting back, no hospital visit needed."

She nodded once, and it was clipped. "You're probably right."

I was used to a little more argument. "Hopefully this means he got his dose of the serum before we rolled up that meta-making operation." I put the file down in anticipation of picking up the phone. "Otherwise…"

Angel got it, credit to her. "Otherwise someone's setting up a new one."

Yeah. That was a scary thought. We'd just started to see our troubles start to disappear, too. Meta crime was going down month over month since we'd crashed that party back in May.

No time to dwell on that now. I picked up the phone and dialed the house number. Wiped my brow of another round of sweat as I waited for it to ring.

It was picked up a few seconds later, and this time, the agitation in Peter's voice was new—and obvious. "Hello?"

"Hey, Peter, it's Reed," I said breezily, trying to make it sound like all was right in the world. "I've got some great news—"

"Do you have my plane?" I could hear a baby crying in the background, loud, unmistakable. It was a terrible sound, and I wondered why I hadn't heard it through the house. It wasn't some small, sniffling cry like Elvira had been making, a little tension sprinkled with a lot of fear. It was top-of-the-lungs stuff, loud as you can get.

"Almost," I said, realizing very quickly I needed to give him something. "That's why I was calling you," I said, trying to put on a smile so he'd hear it in my voice. "We need to figure out how you want to get to the plane."

The baby wailed in the background, and Peter said, strained, "Just land it on the street."

My mouth fell open, but fortunately he couldn't see that. "Uh…Peter? We can't land a plane just anywhere." I looked up and down the street, which was a small and quiet residential one complete with light poles on either side every fifty feet or so. As far as emergency landing strips went, it was a poor one for many reasons, the poles being only one of them. The shortness of it—it was an angled cul-de-sac that was only a hundred yards long or so—being another crucial one.

"Yes you can," Peter said, the agitation straining through in his answer, baby still crying in the background. "Get me one of those ones that does the up and down landing and takeoff." He sounded like a caged beast, pissed off and wanting to get free.

I tried to translate. "You mean like a—like a VTOL—vertical takeoff and landing? Like a Harrier? A military plane?"

"Yeah, get me one of those," Peter said. I could almost see him nodding, blissfully dumb, inside the house.

"Peter," I said, trying to keep my voice in the reasonable range, "you have to understand—those are military planes. The one I was getting for you was a—well, a civilian one—"

"I know that," he snapped, telling me that he did not, in fact, know that.

"And I almost have it," I said. "But if you want me to get a military plane that can…take off and land here…" I was choosing my words carefully, because this conversation was heading in a bad, bad direction. "That's going to…well, I don't know if I can do it. The military doesn't turn over its planes like an airline would." That was a lie too, inasmuch as if I was going to cave and get him a plane (I wasn't) it'd have to be a government plane of some stripe. Delta or Southwest was unlikely to volunteer use of a jet in a case like this, after all, and you couldn't just seize their property without a court's permission. But getting a military jet for this guy?

It'd be a cold day in hell before they'd turn something like that over, especially to some cowardly hostage-taker who wasn't smart enough to drive a car, let alone fly himself anywhere.

"If you want that," I said, "we're going to have to start over again." I looked at the sky above, and the sun was heading toward the far side of the horizon, though not nearly quickly enough for my sweating ass. "It's going to be hours. Longer than it took this time." Forever, actually, because no one was going to give this dickhead a Harrier or whatever that new plane was that did VTOL. Sienna would know.

Peter's voice came back over the line now with a nasty tinge. "I don't think you're telling me the truth."

"Oh, believe me, I am," I said. "The military doesn't loan out their equipment, Peter. They tend to be pretty protective of that sort of thing, try and keep it from falling into enemy hands, you know—"

"*I want a plane*," he said, and the agitation in his voice was now laid bare, and it was terrifying. It didn't contain a whine, or a whimper, or an ounce of awareness that the thing he was asking for was impossible. It was wounded anger, patience run out, and I heard the real threat in it about a second too late.

"Okay, we'll get you a plane—I've almost got one, but it's—"

The front of the house exploded in a blast of red energy that surged toward the cop car parked about twenty feet in front of me.

"Reed!" Angel shouted, and she was already moving, faster than me, faster than anything I'd maybe ever seen other than Colin Fannon.

It wasn't faster than the speed of light, though, and that was the speed at which Peter's laser traveled from out of the front of the house and into the cop car nearest me, where it hit and blew up the engine, catapulting me backward into the pavement and knocking me into the hot black of unconsciousness.

21.

"Reed?"

I was in the darkness a second after I hit the pavement, my head aching in the black. There was a dim light around me, a faint feeling of familiarity like I'd been here before. My skull hurt like it had been used as a stand-in for one of those machines where you test your strength at the fair, and some big guy comes along and wins his girl a stuffed animal by bringing down a sledge to ring a bell. My head felt like the bell and the sledge target, both at the same time, and I tried to shake off that cloudy feeling that seemed to persist in the darkness.

I knew that voice though, as clear to me as my mother's own. "Sienna?" I asked, looking around. I didn't see her at first, but maybe that was because of my recent skull trauma. "Where are you?"

She stepped out of the darkness a moment later, lingering in the shadows, tentative. She was watching me like it was some kind of trick, a cloud of suspicion hiding under her eyes. It evaporated like an afternoon rain within a second, and she surged toward me, hitting me right in the center of my chest and sticking there like a suction-cup Garfield, arms around me and snugging me tight. "Reed," she whispered, face buried in my shoulder.

"Uh, hi," I said, a little—okay, completely—taken aback. "How's it going?"

She didn't let go, and didn't answer, at first. She just stayed there, cheek pressed tightly against my shirt. I let the uncomfortable silence linger for a few seconds more, then cleared my throat and said, "That well, eh?"

With some seeming effort, she pulled back from me, and when I saw her face...

I knew that things...were most definitely not all right.

"What happened?" I asked, staring at her. My brow furrowed so thickly it felt like a series of deep ridges were dug in on my forehead.

"I screwed up, Reed," she said, looking ashen in the shadowy dark of the dreamwalk. "Really bad."

"Worse than accidentally nuking Eden Prairie and making a crowd of reporters shit themselves from fear?" I tossed out a joke, figuring it might take some of the tension out of the situation.

It did not.

"What happened?" I asked, my hands clutching her sleeves, which were...damp? In a dream? Probably a reflection of her real-world state, but still...a little weird. Not that Sienna didn't go swimming from time to time, but...

"The UK government," she said, almost choking as she started. "There's a man named Wexford I met last time I came here—"

"Yeah, he's the Foreign Secretary," I said. "He offered you asylum over there. You told me about him."

"He sent me to investigate a series of murders in Edinburgh," she said, and now she seemed to be rushing to speak, hurrying to get it out. I let her talk, trying not to interrupt. "They said—they thought they were incubus- or succubus-related because of autopsy results from Wolfe—"

"Huh?" That was a tangled thread. My mission not to interrupt lasted all of three seconds, but I shut my mouth again. Clarity on this probably wasn't that important.

Sienna didn't seem to notice my interruption, so deep was she in spitting out her own thoughts, like a poison she was trying to excise from her system. "So I went to Edinburgh to see for myself, to try and track down the killer." Her eyes flared, seemed to get dazed. "There was a guy named Frankie, and he seemed like he was the one. I was getting help from a local named Rose—she took a bullet for me and saved my life a few times—"

I processed through that one. People didn't tend to take bullets for you all willy-nilly, but people also didn't generally go jumping out of their way to save the life of a woman who was an international fugitive, even a super famous one like Sienna. I kept these thoughts to myself.

"—and it turns out that this killer was producing metas using the Revelen serum, Reed," she said, her eyes ablaze now, fear and horror burning within her. "They'd been creating them—and then draining them for their powers."

"Holy shit," I said, because what else do you say to that? "How many?"

"Thousands," she said quietly. "Tens of thousands, maybe. She'd been killing them for years—"

"Wait," I said, feeling like I'd missed something. "I thought this Frankie was the killer—"

"No, it was Rose," Sienna said.

I hesitated, thinking for a second. "Was Rose the local helping you?" She nodded. "And she took a bullet for you? Watched your back?" More nodding. "And now—"

"She's trying to kill me," Sienna said. "But that's not the worst part."

Uh oh. If that wasn't the worst part, what could be so bad that it would render Sienna Nealon, the most fearsome warrior I know, into a pale, shaking, near-whispering wreck of a human being—

"She stole my souls," Sienna said, almost under her breath, but it was loud as a gunshot to me. "She's the stronger succubus, Reed, and she tried to drain me and…she stole my souls."

"Which ones?" I asked, feeling icy fingers of alarm creeping up my spine from the small of my back, chills snaking their way up the back of my neck and across my scalp. They tingled like the skin was rising into mighty—not even goosepimples, more goosetowers, gooseskyscrapers on my skin.

"All of them," she said. "Wolfe, Gavrikov, Bjorn, Zack, Eve, Bastian...and Harmon." She was quiet for a few seconds as this sunk in. "She took them all from me. She took...everything."

And now the bottom fell out of my stomach, like it had been held up by some decaying wooden slats and someone had just come along and kicked them right out from underneath, sending my stomach on a twenty-five-story plunge down the length of my body and then maybe down an old mine shaft afterward to boot, once it reached ground level. It felt like instant freefall followed by queasiness when it came to a plummeting stop. "Okay," I said, trying to process through this new info. "Okay, so you have to get out of Scotland—"

"I tried," she said, still near-whispering. "I called my banker and my fixer. I chartered a plane at an old airfield near where I was. The US government must have intercepted my call, because they were waiting for me with a Spec Ops team. Rose showed up a few minutes later, killed them all." She said this with quiet authority.

"All right, well, you can try again," I said, mind racing wildly. "Or I'll book something for you—"

"And when I called my banker back...she'd wrapped him under her control and locked off my accounts, Reed." Sienna's voice was quiet and hollow. "All the ones in Liechtenstein are gone now. She took all that money."

I smiled faintly. "But not the one you set up in the Caribbean to finance the new agency, right?" She shook her head. "I mean, even if so, that's not a deal breaker. The agency has its own accounts now, and up until this last month or so, we'd been showing a nice little profit. I can book a private plane, meet you in Edinburgh—"

"No," Sienna said, almost choking on it. She put a hand on my chest, brushed against the white broadcloth shirt, which was sweat-damp even in this dream. "She'll know, if it's in Scotland. You don't understand, Reed. She controlled the entire Edinburgh police force. Through a—a—like a third party person—it was through Frankie, and she was controlling him the entire time—gah, I don't know what you call it—"

"Like a sockpuppet account online," I said.

She just stared at me. "Yeah. Okay. Sure, that. She controls people like they're her own personal suckmuppets—"

"Sockpuppet," I said lamely, because suckmuppet was actually more fitting, but I didn't want to laugh.

"Whatever. She controlled them all, like a puppetmaster, and I didn't even see any strings." She was getting more animated as she spoke, and it was obvious this Rose, whoever she was, had hit Sienna in a way she hadn't been hit before. It was more than a little disquieting to see my sister knocked onto the back foot like this, because even when President Harmon had turned all of us against her and made her a fugitive, she'd at least still had her massive, invincible superpowers and endless bank account to draw on.

Now…she was just about down to her sparkling personality, which was…alarming, since her personality only sparkled like a particularly sharp knife, and for just about the same reason.

"You can't come to me in Scotland," Sienna went on, quiet, firm, filled with conviction. "She owns this place, lock, stock and five hundred smoking barrels, since she has the cops."

"Okay," I said, running through my mental map of the UK from my days operating all over Europe with Alpha. "Newcastle-Upon-Tyne is the first English town past Scotland—"

"Too close," Sienna said, shaking her head.

"York is halfway between London and Scotland," I quickly amended. "There's an airfield there. I'll charter a private plane and swoop in, pick you up. All you need to do is show up, and we'll GTFO, make for a non-extradition country, maybe in the Caribbean or something."

She was silent for a long moment, like her brain was

chugging along at half speed. "I don't want you to get hurt."

I smiled. "I'll be fine. This succubus—does she have a telepath or something? Like Harmon?"

Sienna shook her head, frowning. "I don't think so. She couldn't seem to detect me or my thoughts. But she was definitely pulling the strings on people somehow. I was thinking a Siren, but…I don't exactly know what using that power looks like."

It was my turn to frown. "Breandan told me about it one time, because his girlfriend was one. Said that it was like when they spoke, people oozed to try and answer their requests, polite or not. Said she could really pour on the honey, make it feel like you were the only man in the world." She stared at me with one eyebrow cocked, and I cleared my throat and looked down. "What? It was just a couple guys talking. I mean, I've never felt it myself, obviously."

"I don't know if that's what she has or not," Sienna said. "Maybe. It'd be tough for me to tell, not being a guy, but…there were women in Police Scotland that were coming after me too, and it was more…frenzied. Like when those reporters went feral on me in Eden Prairie." She seemed to be giving this some thought. "It wasn't cops on the job, it was wild dogs on the hunt, you know?"

"I think I get it," I said, at least understanding the broad strokes based on her explanation. "Look…whoever this Rose is, and whatever she wants—"

"She wants me. Dead." There was quiet certainty in Sienna's voice.

"Why?" I asked, and she looked at me funny. "What did you do to piss in this girl's cornflakes?"

She just shrugged. "I honestly don't know, Reed. I have no idea. I've never met this girl before. I didn't even know there was a succubus in Scotland. It seems like she's been planning this for years, if what she told me before she turned on me is true. I mean, this grudge—it's deep, like I killed her entire family or something."

Something about what she'd said tingled in the back of my head, but I didn't know why. "You've never even been to Scotland, have you?"

"No," she said, shaking her head, arms folded across her chest, frowning in thought. "The closest I ever even got was the first time I went to London, when we were thinking about coming up here to visit that meta cloister and protect it from—" She froze. I knew from looking at her that she had maybe discovered the source of my ill-found tingle. "Oh, God, Reed."

"You think she…?" I asked.

Sienna closed her eyes. "She's a succubus." She put her head in her hands. "How could I be so stupid? She's a Scottish succubus." If there had been a wall around, she might have punched it.

"It's okay," I said, trying to rally her back to the moment at hand. "We're going to work through this."

"Thousands," Sienna whispered. "Thousands dead. That she killed. Because of me. Because—"

"Not now," I said, seizing her by the shoulders, feeling the damp fabric of her shirt between my fingers. Whatever had happened to soak her to the bone, I bet it hadn't been fun. "There will be time for guilt later. We don't know for sure that…THAT…is why Rose is very, very angry with you—" She gave me a "you're-an-idiot" look, which I ignored, because she was my sister, sarcastic to the nines, and I was used to it on all occasions. "And we can't do anything about it either way. It happened years ago, Sienna, and there was nothing we could do about it at the time. We made the best choices we could, and now—now we have to…to keep doing that." I took a breath, trying to breathe some conviction into those words, because I wasn't necessarily feeling them right now. "Can you get to York?"

She looked rattled, answered quietly, "Yes. I think so. I've evaded Rose for a hundred miles or more so far. York can't be that much farther. I'll find a way."

"Get to York," I said, squeezing her shoulders tight. "Get

to the airport." My voice built in intensity, because something was happening around me, noise and fury, the quiet darkness fading as I returned to consciousness against my will. Sienna was right in front of me, scared, feeling like—like she was helpless, almost for the first time since I'd known her. My fearless sister, and here she was, filled with toxic fear. There was a roaring tempest around me, the sound of staccato shots being fired, the low whine of something sizzling its way, screamingly searing through metal like a laser— "I will be there, waiting. Come to me, and together we'll get you—"

The darkness broke, and I felt like I was seized from this unconscious vision and hurled back into the light. The last thing I saw before I woke up was Sienna's face, pale, ashen and afraid.

And seeing my sister...my fearless sister...afraid, really, truly afraid, for the first time in years...

It scared me more than I had ever been in my entire life.

22.

I awoke to the gunfire of a dozen Texas cops pouring it on, huddled behind cruisers and shooting at Peter. My head was against a curb, and the sound of the gunshots was like a heralding of the apocalypse. I blinked into the bright sunlight, shining down on me with the intensity of a heat beam, or maybe one of Peter's lasers, and something shook me, shoving my shoulder.

"Oh, good, you're awake," Angel said, smudged with sweat and some other black substance across her forehead. "You know what you were saying about a peaceful resolution…?" She looked significantly, almost theatrically at the chaos unfolding around us. "I don't think it's going to happen."

My head was hard against the curb, the endless blasts of gunshots painful to my meta ears. I blinked a few times into the sun, trying to recall what had just happened in the dream, way more vivid and real than this battle I found myself in. The police cruiser next to me, that I was hiding behind for cover, was scorched and blacked. A few more were on fire, flames crackling quietly, unheard under the gunfire.

Peter was out there somewhere, blasts of red giving away his position behind me. I sat up, the ruined cruiser acting as cover between me and him, and I rolled to my knees, my dream now coming back to me, afresh.

My sister was afraid. Scared. On the run. In a strange, foreign land.

I had to save her.

"What the hell are you doing?" Angel asked as she stared at me. "You must have taken a harder hit to the head than I thought. You should lie back down while I take care of this."

"Peacefully?" I asked, rolling to my knees and shaking my head. I couldn't get the image of Sienna out of my mind. She just looked so...

Afraid.

"Like I said, I don't think it's going that way." Angel was not trying hard to contain her distaste for this situation. "I'm going to try and flank him—"

"Stay right where you are," I said, reaching out with my powers. "I'll settle this."

"Peacefully?" Angel said with a fair amount of mocking.

I found what I was looking for on the side of the house: an air conditioner unit, intact, and several hundred pounds of steel and internal components.

"To hell with peace," I said, and concentrated.

Creating a vortex was a tricky thing. I did it all the time, of course, with varying levels of strength. Before I'd been super-empowered—boosted, I guess you could say—I could create a hell of a tempest when pressed: walls of wind that moved a hundred or two hundred miles an hour in a pinch, sustained over the course of a few minutes. Maybe even create the kind of tornado that could lift a car.

But since I'd gotten my power boost, that had become old news.

Now, the new hotness was creating massive tornadoes, F5, F6 and over, a thing that didn't exist in nature, and even—once—dispelling a hurricane before it landed on Haiti. The weathermen had looked stupid that day, at least as stupid as they did most other days, since they tended to be wrong almost as much as political prognosticators. Both still kept their jobs in spite of that appalling track record, which was one of the mysteries of the universe as far as I was concerned.

I didn't need a tornado, or a hurricane, to deal with Peter, though.

I just needed that air conditioning unit.

It wrenched free without me having to apply much power to it, a few hundred pounds of metal lifted into the air by a vortex under control of yours truly.

And then I reversed the current, redirected it a few feet, and lifted my head up to make sure I knew where it was going.

Peter was standing on the front lawn, aglow with laser light shooting out of his hands and chest. It was a stunning red beam, and he was howling, directing it any which way it pleased him. He locked his eyes on me, and I on him, and surveyed him with a cold fury worthy of…well…

Someone in my family. Not usually me.

"I gave you a chance to get out of this peacefully," I shouted across the lawn, which was an apocalyptic wasteland of devastation. The house, fortunately, looked to be mostly intact, and I hoped the hostages were, too. "I tried to work with you, Peter, tried to help you get out of this alive."

"Get down here!" Angel was seizing at my pants leg, tugging it, but gently, probably realizing that if she yanked it, I'd just let her rip it and keep doing what I was doing.

Peter cocked his head at me, like he was seeing me for the first time. He opened his mouth to speak, and a red glow started within it. Laser powers out of every hole in his body. Cute.

"But you didn't want peace," I said. "Or you were too stupid to take it." That got his eyes glowing, and I was speaking rapidly now, furiously. "I don't care either way, but you missed out, bub. You wanted war? Fine. This is war.

"Now reap the whirlwind, bitchnuts."

I brought that air conditioning unit down on him like the wrath of God itself descending from the heavens, a meteor out of the sky with no fire to streak behind it to herald its arrival. A few hundred pounds of air conditioner made its landing on Peter's head and he disappeared beneath its bulk as I slammed it into the earth and stopped it there, walls of wind arresting its forward momentum so it didn't go bouncing into the police barricade or the houses beyond.

The only thing left to mark Peter's passage was a splatter of blood and a couple of twitching feet.

"So long to the wicked Witch King of the South, no?" Angel was beside me, staring at the end of Peter. He did look a little like something out of *The Wizard of Oz*, now that she mentioned it, minus the cool footwear.

"I have to go home," I said, turning from her and looking for my ride.

"Wait, what?" Angel was after me in a hot second. "Reed, you can't just leave now that he's dead. There are hostages—" As if on cue, a woman I took to be Elvira came bursting out of the shattered front door, two kids beside her and one cradled in her arms, squealing to beat the band. "And we've got—paperwork, and reports and—"

"Screw it all," I said, still looking for my ride. "I have to get home. Right now." My jaw was set, and so was my determination, and Angel must have seen it, because she didn't argue. "All that other stuff can wait. I have to go. Now."

"Home?" Angel asked. "Why?"

I didn't answer her. All I could think of was that look on my sister's face. I needed to get home, right now.

And then I needed to go to York.

To save the only family I had left.

23.

Rose

The silence might have been the worst part.

It was in the still of the night that Rose seemed to feel it worst of all, the quiet stretching like a heavy, suffocating blanket over her. She lay in the darkness, looking up at the ceiling, and wondering if it would be like this forever. It had been months, and she'd wondered, based on Tamhas's comments, if maybe, just maybe, the village would start speaking to her again.

So far, though...it just hadn't happened.

Nighttimes were the toughest part. She would have figured it'd be walking down the street. But it wasn't. The hardest part was to lie awake in the wee small hours, thinking about the future she didn't have any longer, at least not here, where she'd expected to. Thinking about Graham, about her mam and granddad, and wondering what she could have done that was so wrong—

Rose tensed. There was a sound in the night, faint and distant, like a bird hooting, or perhaps squawking. It was a bit of an odd noise, not one she normally heard at night. Birds slept at night, didn't they? Unless they were owls?

Perhaps she just usually wasn't awake at these hours. That was the real challenge. She'd gotten into a pattern where, with nothing to do during the days, she'd sleep until whenever she felt like. And then take a nap in the afternoon. And why not? It wasn't as though she had anything else going on.

No friends.

No appointments.

No future.

She rustled against the sheet, chasing sleep again and failing. She put her face against the pillow, seeking a cool spot and failing to find one, as though every inch of the pillowcase had been heated in the oven. Rose let out a little sigh, adjusting her thin white t-shirt and shorts. They rode up uncomfortably, and she considered simply tossing them given that it felt stifling in here.

An idea occurred, and she got up on her knees, bouncing against the spring of the bed, feeling a little like she was on the moon from the bounce. She threw open the window a few inches, and the night air came in with real chill. Rose shivered, her skin instantly rising in gooseflesh, even from so small a gap as she'd made.

A small trill of delight ran through her, and she slipped back under the covers with the closest thing to a smile she'd worn in months. Winter was on its way, she could feel it in the air, though it hadn't come quite yet. There'd been a snowfall or two, sure, but they hadn't stuck, and had melted away shortly after arrival, which was strange. It wouldn't have been unusual for them to have a few inches by now, but all they had thus far was a nice, brisk chill to the air.

The wind picked up and rushed into the room like an uninvited guest—except she had opened the window, so she supposed it was invited after all. Either way, she pulled the blankets up to her chin and shivered in mildest pleasure, the room infused with the scent of the outdoors, of the coming cold, of—

Another high, trilling bird caw came, louder now, and Rose froze in her bed. It sounded closer, didn't it? Or had opening the window just made it seem so?

Rose took a deep breath and watched it appear in front of

her in a heavy mist as she exhaled. This had always been her favorite time of year, going toward the days of frozen chill, heading toward Christmas, toward that time when everyone on the village street seemed to greet each other with a little extra joy, as though it were a reminder of how fortunate they all were to have one another—

That didn't seem likely to happen this year though, did it?

This year she'd be walking the streets by herself, if this new tradition continued. No one would look her in the eye. They'd all rush away, grabbing their children—the few there were—and pretending she was a disease carrier in the street.

No, it was best—

The hawk trilled again, loud, almost earsplitting, and Rose stirred, craning her head back to try and look out the window. There was nothing but black and starry sky above, no sign of this bird that seemed to be continuously trying to—

There it went again. Loud, like it was trying to—

A door slammed. Then another.

There was movement in the streets; Rose could hear it through the open window. Someone was out there—now another someone—more doors were opening, and voices melded together in the night.

"What do we do?"

"Is this it?"

"—now come to us?"

"—thought we had more time—"

"—not ready."

It was a cacophony of action, like every house in the village was emptying its contents, its residents. Someone was ringing a bell, loud and clanging, and it hurt Rose's ears. She'd only heard them ring it very occasionally, when there was an emergency, perhaps.

What, then, was this?

She got up on her knees and stuck her head out in the window, grimacing against the cold chill that caught her as she did so. The night's darkness was nearly complete, a few exterior lights on houses casting shadows over the trees in her garden. The buzz of conversation was thick in the air, so thick it was like a stew of melted rubber, almost impossible to do anything with.

Graham's voice drifted to her through the din. "What do we do?"

Rose frowned, the heavy lines creasing her brow. What was this?

A door slammed closer to her, and she heard her granddad speak, audible by dint of his proximity to her. "All right, then, you lot—"

"It's happening." Hamilton's cool, calm voice split the night like an axe split cord wood.

Her granddad hesitated, probably contemplating his answer. "Right now?" he asked. The conversational buzz was fading to silence.

"Yes," Hamilton said. "Right now." A pause. "Where is she?"

"Inside," Rose's mam answered, strong, resolute. Had she gone out with Granddad?

Just what were they talking about? "She" was inside—?

Oh.

Rose.

"Come on then, lads," Hamilton said, grimly, and the quiet spurred to life once more. "And lasses," he added, as though in apology to someone who'd taken offense.

Rose could feel the change in the atmosphere of the house this time as the door opened, as though a groan ran through the entirety of her home from the change in pressure, the shift in the wood frame hidden inside those plaster walls. She was still half-out the window, listening, when she heard the footsteps coming toward her door.

She scrambled, like an animal panicking at a predator's approach. They were coming for her, many of them, strong, confident footsteps echoing down the hall like thunder on the approach of a storm. Rose's mouth went instantly dry, and her skin turned colder than any blustery winter wind could have managed in the space of a second.

Her feet rustled against the sheets as she started to propel herself out the window. Her only thought was of escape, and she knew not from what. There was only the threat of something, of the villagers coming after her, the target of their ire of late. Their scapegoat, they had alienated her so effectively that if she'd heard this entire conversation only a few months earlier, she'd have thought they were planning a party for her.

Now, her stomach roiled in blind panic as she lunged for the window. The only party she reckoned they were planning for her now was the kind where her neck would be at the end of a thickly knotted rope while her feet danced a good margin above the ground.

Rose hit the window sill on her way out, lower back thumping as she slid roughly against the window. She hadn't raised it high enough; it wasn't as though she'd planned to do anything other than get a little breeze. She certainly hadn't planned to use it as an escape exit—not when she was in her nightwear. Her chest scraped against the sill on the way out and her lower back ached from where it had made hard contact with the window at the squeeze point of her pelvis and her arse. She'd gotten just a little too deep at that part of her body, and she couldn't turn it sideways to get out like she had her head.

"What's that?" someone said, muffled, through the door.

Rose felt a note of panic. They were almost—

Someone threw open the door, a booming noise that was like the arrival of death itself, and she looked back to see shadowy figures through the dirty glass. They were in her room now, standing inside, and Rose was here, briefly trapped with her damned arse stuck...

"Get her!" someone shouted, and someone else shouted back inside, thunderously loud, "She's trying to escape out the window!" There was a frenzy of motion inside as Rose tried to wriggle her way through, out, away from this shite, blind panic settling over her now even as strong hands grabbed at her legs, clamping on and trying to yank her back. She kicked out madly, trying to free herself, but they had grips like iron, and they were on her calves, her thighs, and holding on tight enough to bruise the skin.

Someone yanked a hand away, and then another did, and a brief thrill of hope ran through her. Her powers! They couldn't hold on, not if they wanted to—

"She's burning me!" someone shouted. The voice was low and deep.

"Use the bloody sheets! Get a hand on her!"

Footsteps were coming around the house now. Rose's stomach seethed. She struggled against the window even harder, and it slid up a few inches, allowing a little margin for her to try and slip out, butt bumping it again as it hit the widest point of her arse cheeks, pelvis thumping against the sill on the down side. And then—

She was free, worked loose of it, and tipping toward the earth and a good drop a few feet below. She could see the dark ground start to rush up at her—

Someone grabbed her by the ankle, arresting her momentum as she started to tip forward. This grip was strong, but strange, a cloth texture wrapped over the fingers. Another came a moment later on her other thigh, fighting hard against her body's forward motion.

Rose hung there, almost out the window, and those grips dug in tighter to her skin. She cried out, unaware that she was even whimpering now, trying to escape this—this—whatever it was.

They seized her and dragged her back through the window, all pretense of being gentle dispensed with. She struggled as they reeled her back in, and someone punched her in the back after she'd rattled the window fearfully by bucking against it. The glass shattered and showered her with a few flecks that cut at her, but she ignored the pain. She was crying already.

Someone threw the window frame open full, and now there were enough cloth-clad hands on her that they dragged her back in easily.

"Get a sheet over her!" someone shouted, and the other shadowy figures worked to make it happen. A sheet was thrown over her immediately, and she saw her mam's face before it came over her, and had the dim realization that her mam was, in fact, the one who'd done it.

The hits that followed were breathtaking. "Don't kill her!" someone offered as guidance between the blows. She was screaming, crying, trying to fight back but not having an ounce of luck. She couldn't see except dimly, through the cotton, and the hits—they kept coming, hard and fast against her sides, her back. Something broke, and the fight went out of Rose, and she lay on her bed, covered in a sheet, crying and sobbing, face trying to suck breaths through a cloth wet with her own spittle.

"Drag her out," a voice commanded.

It was granddad's.

Rose's mouth was frozen open in a long, whimpering scream. It came in a low whine though, instead of a fearful, forceful cry. They carried her out, people on every side like it was a funeral procession, carrying her sheet as though it were to be her casket.

Dark thoughts swirled around her. Maybe this was the end. Maybe they'd had enough of her now, and they were going to just get over with the things they'd been thinking about behind her back for months.

It would almost…almost…be welcome.

They dragged her outside, the slight warmth of the house giving way to another round of cold chills that filtered through the sheet. She expected cheers of triumph and jeers of hatred from the assembled townsfolk when they brought her out. But it was silent instead, the quiet hum of any conversation simply dying when they brought her into the middle of the crowd and then pulled back the sheet.

Her mam was standing right there, one of her "pallbearers," stone-faced and uncaring.

Granddad was at the other side, and his lips were pursed, face knitted with worry. "I'm sorry," he said, and she couldn't tell if he meant it or not.

Rose was on her haunches in a sea of legs, a sea of people staring down at her. Her shoulders were heaving up and down involuntarily with her fear, her eyes darting to see implacable gazes shining down on her like beacons from above, watching, judging…

The hawk cawed once again, louder now that she was out in the open air, the frosty cold rolling across her skin, her shorts and thin tank top inadequate to protect her from the frigid late autumn weather.

"We've got her," Miriam Shell crowed from somewhere behind her, and laughed like a great crone, some mixture of relief sprinkled in with…fear? Rose wasn't sure she heard it right, her heart was pounding so hard.

Rose was crying, her nose running as the wetness froze on her cheeks and her lip. She tried not to show weakness but it wouldn't be held back. Not even here, among these people who hated her. The pain and terror was pressing in hard, like razors against her, and all she could do was look around at them as they stood like forbidding statues, all of them looking down at her.

"It's coming," her granddad said, looking around in the darkness.

"Can you feel it?" her mam asked, face frozen like the chill had dragged it into a death mask, white as pale snow.

"Nae, but it's about to happen," he said, rubbing his hand against his chest. He glanced down at Rose.

The hawk called again, and it echoed over the village. Rose looked up, peering at the bird of prey. It was circling, and she wondered if it was a bit out of place here, and at this time of night.

Graham edged into view, not looking at her but for a brief

second, and then he looked away. "I wish we could just get this over. If it's going to happen—" He didn't finish his thought, and no one else finished it for him.

Rose swallowed, feeling like a boulder was trapped in her throat. She wished it would get over with too. If they were going to kill her…

Her friends, her family, her neighbors—

…she wished they'd just be on about it. Hang her from a gibbet and be done. The chill was biting, and it wasn't just the weather. She'd lived here all her life, and now these people— she'd once have thought *her* people—had turned on her.

To the last.

Her granddad tensed at her shoulder, and she looked back to see him stricken, his face a pained shade. A grunt behind her jerked her attention away, and then someone cried out.

"It's coming!" Hamilton shrieked, and he lunged through the crowd at her, hand outstretched.

Rose let a little shriek of her own as he reached for her, hand open, palm extended. Someone else grabbed her from behind, landing a heavy, sweaty palm on the back of her neck. Someone seized her hard by the arm, someone else by the back, lifting her. Someone grabbed at her back, clawing at her. Their hand pressed against her and their nails dug in to rip her apart—

She was lifted high now, up in the air, and everyone wanted to clutch at her, to rip at her, fingers digging in like they meant to tear her apart. Her mam found purchase somewhere in there, she could tell by the cold fingers at the small of her back. Her shirt was ripped off without ceremony, there one moment and gone the next, and replacing the cloth were a dozen hands lifting her up, frigidly cold on the small of her back. They pulled at her legs, her arms, ready to tear her to pieces—

Rose screamed, and screamed, and—

She was held there, up in the air, above the heads of the crowd, the freezing night air biting at her belly and chest and throat and face and toes and fingers, and what felt like a thousand grabbing hands on her body as she was trapped there, lifted into the air with no power of her own. She kicked her legs and it did nothing; hands caught her again, anchoring to her as they came back down.

Rose let out another wild scream, and someone hit her in the back of the head. It was like the time she'd leaned over to see what was in the bottom of Granddad's cedar chest, and the lid had come crashing down on her. She saw stars then, a flash in the cold night, just as she did now.

The back of her head ached where she'd been struck, and thoughts were slower to come. Her mouth was cottony dry and the hands—they were everywhere—clutching at her, grabbing at her, holding to her, her skin burning where they touched...

Burning.

Where they.

Touched?

Now other screams were filling the night, and the crowd was wild and surging, Rose carried on them, her voice blistered and raw. Her skin itself felt like it was on fire, and she looked over to see Mam staring up at her, mouth open in a scream of her own. Rose could almost feel her there, her presence, and then suddenly Mam's eyes went dark and her body went limp. She reeled away, gone, somehow; Rose knew, could feel her— her entirely—inside the mind, now, and someone else stepped into the void and laid a cold, rough hand on Rose's skin by her ribs.

They were falling away like dead flies now. She watched Hamilton's eyes roll back in his head hard, death come for him, and he fell over. Graham's eyes were flittering up, only the whites visible save for the peak of his spasms, when a tiny edge of the pupils could be seen, a hint of the brown which she'd once thought she could stare into forever. Then he fainted away limply and crashed, and someone else surged in, trampling over his body to lay hands on her.

"Had to be this...way..." her granddad said over the

screams and cries, and she looked over at him just as he keeled over, and she knew he was dead too, his hand leaving her body as he fell. Her skin felt as if it were aflame, hard fire running over the flesh. She half-expected her skin to be glowing in the night like a midnight fire's last embers, but she was as pale as ever, and nearer to the ground now.

A pitched cry came from behind her, and somehow she knew Miriam Shell had fallen, her day now done, and the stray thought passed through her mind—was that what she had sounded like with Graham?

Rose's very head was splitting, her mind now lit afire, as though someone had gone and crammed too much in its bounds. There was a mad whirl to it all, a very mad whirl that made her wonder how she could possibly endure this feeling—this burning feeling—even one minute more—

And then it stopped, and she realized she was on the ground, or near to it. She rolled and found a body, another body, bodies piled on top of others. She rolled and saw her granddad's face, still in death, eyes open and staring back at her, and she wanted to scream, but something else shut that instinct down. Her mam was just there, buried under another body, face invisible, but there was a clear view of her sleeve that Rose could hardly forget. She knew her mam's wardrobe, every stitch.

The hawk sounded again, and the riot of noise in Rose's head stilled, listening for it. There was a raging energy in her mind, an indistinct mass of howling that Rose could scarcely make out between the screaming of her nerves, ever single inch of her flesh howling at the feeling it'd just been overwhelmed with. She'd never felt anything like it, that burning feeling. The closest thing she could think of was—

You dirty little harlot.

The voice burst out of the din in a distinct shock of outrage.

Rose stopped dead, her slow writhe stunned into quiet and stillness by that voice that sounded like a bullhorn out of the heavens.

It was her mam's voice.

We have to go now, her granddad said, and it was as though he were there, next to her, or louder, even. She rolled to look and—

There was no one there. Above, the hawk was the only thing that was moving, and it was circling lower, like a carrion bird over a corpse.

Rose tried to push herself up and failed.

Come on then, you.

Move it, girl.

Useless thing.

We have to go, now!

The cacophony was deafening, a chorus of voices with an utter lack of unity. They screamed and squalled in indistinct directions, and Rose clapped her hands over her ears, cold fingers against frigid lobes, trying to shut it out but only making it louder in the process.

Go, you stupid girl!

Get us out of here!

Her mam's voice cracked through it all, sullen and resentful and filled with icy hate. *Idiot child. I should have thrown you off a cliff the moment you were born.*

Rose got to her feet, wobbling on unsteady legs. Somehow that voice drove her, and she looked up at the hawk, which sounded once more and then—

Something long and sharp buried itself in the bird, appearing as though by magic, a skewer straight through the creature. It arced and fell, thudding to the ground just beyond her house.

Go, you idiot! someone shouted in her head, and Rose staggered forward, trying to find the fallen bird. She traced a path around the house, but when she came to where she thought it might have landed—

Tamhas lay there, a long spear sticking through his middle, and his breath coming in sharp gasps. Rose stood there, at the edge of the house, and then took a tentative step toward him.

He met her eyes, and gasped, and motioned her forward.

She came, strangely drawn to him as he lay there, dying. She knew just by looking at him that his time was short. The spear, whatever it was, had pierced him clean through when he'd been a bird. It hadn't stopped piercing him now that he was a man again. He raised a hand to her, and something urged her forward, a thousand voices in her head telling her to take his hand.

Rose took his hand, and knelt next to him. The smell of his blood as it pumped out onto the cold ground filled her nostrils, metallic.

His hand was cold against hers, another against her this night. "Needed your…help…" Tamhas whispered, and when he spoke blood oozed down his lips. She cradled his hand, thinking of the kindness he'd shown her so recently. Speaking to a body was a strange and small kindness, yet it was the only one she'd received of late. "You're the only one who can…" His eyes fixed, pain setting in from her touch, and she started to pull away, but he clutched her hand, like the others, shaking in the night against her skin.

He didn't last long, his shuddering done, his blood stilled. And Rose dropped his hand, feeling him this time, another voice in the chorus, but not loudly. Like a pebble in a pond, the ripples coming out from it, but the rock itself so small and indistinct as to be lost in the volume of water.

Now go, you idiot! someone shouted in her mind.

Go! Go!

Go!

Get, you fool!

Run!

Rose staggered to her feet and did run, making it to a thicket about fifty yards away before she collapsed into them, leafless branches stinging her, hiding herself from sight and feeling the jagged pains of the night like swallowed glass, writhing around inside her with all these new voices. She whispered, almost, to herself, sobbed quietly, even as the chorus of howls screamed in her head to—

Move!

Go, stupid!

Get out of here!

You're going to kill us all!

But they were already dead, weren't they? Rose wondered as she knelt there on the frozen ground. It seemed impossible that they weren't; she felt them in her mind, that frightful sick feeling that she'd—

Well, she'd—

She'd eaten the souls of every single person in her village.

And they'd bloody well lined up and forced her to do it.

The first voice in the night was like a stilling calm, icy and laden with contempt for everything. She couldn't see the speaker himself, but somehow she knew of him immediately, a vision thrust into her eyes about what he looked like—mop of wild, dark hair and shadowy eyes, his face filled with a barely veiled look of contempt. Tamhas's voice supplied the name, *Weissman*, and Rose listened to him speak in the quiet night.

"…turned out pretty well, Raymond," Weissman said with dripping contempt. "This is the last cloister. And look at 'em! Other than the shifter, they're all…" He strolled into the middle of the town, Rose watching him from behind the bushes. "…well, good and dead."

"People don't just keel over and die like this," the second man said, following slowly behind Weissman. Tamhas seemed to hand his name to her: *Raymond.* He must have overheard it while watching as a falcon.

"Au contraire, Raymondo," Weissman said, all full of vicious energy, like he was glorying in the pile of dead Rose had crawled out of. "And you should know, you lil' Hades scamp, you." Weissman spoke in an American accent, and the lack of formality between them told Rose everything she needed to know about who was boss here. "How many times have we walked into a scene such as this, dead everywhere—I mean, this is your *raison d'etre*, Ray. This is what you do, keel people over and die 'em."

"I didn't kill these people," Raymond said softly. She couldn't see him well, but he seemed like he was…struggling with the bodies, all piled together. Rose could see the corpse of Ronnie Gordon, his youthful face already adopting a grey pallor in death. Someone had lifted him up to touch her, too, and she could hear him seething inside her, slithering in the back of her mind like an angry little snake.

"Hm," Weissman said, not really seeming too interested. "Well, they're dead, and that's what counts. I'm thinking… mass suicide. Like Heaven's Gate."

"I was trying to pull them from their bodies, and then, suddenly, they were just…gone," Raymond said, with soft regret.

"Who cares?" Weissman called into the still night, like the cawing of a crow, black hair like a shining shadow, brighter than the dark around him. "They are dead. Mission accomplished. Let's move on with our lives like they have. No. Wait. Not exactly like they have, obviously…"

"You're going to care if a certain succubus who's been foiling your London operations got ahold of old souls like these, some of whom might know what her power can actually do if she were to…*unleash* it." Raymond's soft voice was like a grenade exploding in the night, and it shut Weissman up hard.

Rose's ears pricked up. What was this about a succubus?

"I honestly did think Sienna Nealon would be here for this," Weissman said, and now he was quieter. "That she'd try and stop us, at least." He laughed bitterly, but it sounded hollow. "My spies still put her in London, hunkering down and waiting for us to come back. I guess she doesn't give a damn about Scotland, but then…who in London does, really?" He cackled, but again it lacked any real feeling other than a malice that made Rose shiver in the night. "So…she ain't here. It was probably just poison."

"Do you see any cups?" Raymond's soft question was laced with accusation.

"Shut the hell up, Raymond. You're stepping all over my triumphal mood, you downer lowmarket jackass." Weissman seethed in the dark. "Can't you just let me have this moment? If I could stop time to savor this minute, this second, without pissing off Akiyama, I would do it just so I could breathe in this triumph. We have wiped out every cloister in Europe. Every one. They are all dead, all of them—with that, you know, glaring exception of the country of Revelen, but who cares about them? We'll get to them. Sovereign will get to them," Weissman amended. "But Europe—the old redoubt of metahumankind? It's ours, Ray." Weissman slapped him, genially, across the back of the neck. It didn't seem very friendly, even to Rose, who had just been handled much more roughly. "Now let's go deal with your not-so-great niece and put this whole continent away, okay?"

They started away, Weissman again in the lead, and Raymond giving one last subtle look around. He seemed to stare into the dark, and then, placidly, quietly, gave an indistinct wave at the darkness, but not at her. As though he could not see her, but somehow suspected—or knew—she was there. Then he, too, turned and started after Weissman.

"Something I've been meaning to ask you, Ray," Weissman said, their voices receding into the dark. "Why can't you use your souls like Sovereign does? Seems like a thing that you'd want to do. Power untold, right at your fingertips? Why not seize it, Ray ol' boy?" Weissman adopted a British accent—a terrible one—for the last bit.

"Because it's forbidden," Raymond said, raising his voice slightly, as if trying to project the message backward, to Rose. "After Hades died, his offspring were warned, in no uncertain terms—do not seek this power, or you will be annihilated, swift and sure. And they did some annihilating, too. My brothers and sisters—"

"Yeah, I got the story from Sovereign," Weissman said, already sounding like he was losing interest. "Still…haven't you ever at least been tempted? I know you've got to have some serious souls rattling around in there, Ray. Why not just…keep it in reserve, you know?"

The answer came back, muffled, not given for her benefit: "Because my father never taught me."

Weissman was quiet for a moment, then let out a peal of laughter. "Daddy issues? Join the club, Ray." And they vanished into the night.

Rose huddled behind the bushes, listening. They were talking still, in the distance, and she could hear them all the way up until they reached a vehicle and she heard the engine start. She sat there listening, until it faded from sound, from audible range, and was gone in the night.

When it was gone, she stood. The village was silent, dead. And her mind…

…her head…

…was not.

The question, unasked, on her lips, was asked instead, in a dozen voices, in her mind, all at once, a cacophony of confusion and fear and worry:

What now?

We have to get away, her granddad said. *Have to survive.*

What if they come back?

We need to be elsewhere, her mam said.

Where do we go? they all asked.

Edinburgh, Tamhas said. *We vanish. Blend in there. Wait. We'll be safe in numbers.*

Rose just stood, listening, buried in her own thoughts, the thoughts of the entire village.

You carry the fate of us all now, her mam said, seeping disgust. *Try not to cock it up, you little whore.*

You should get going, Tamhas said, a bit more kindly. *You can take Miriam's car.*

Aye, Miriam said with loathing that was apparent, even in Rose's head. *The keys are in the house on a hook. She's topped off.*

"I…don't know how to drive," Rose said, muttering into the dark, speaking to herself? It felt so strange.

Miriam knows, Tamhas said. *So now you know. You know everything we know, and can do everything we can do. Hamilton's acting…my martial arts…it's all at your disposal now. For the good of us all.*

Did you hear what those two were talking about? Granddad asked, sounding a bit shrewd. *About—*

Her using our powers, Tamhas said, with some calculation of his own. *Aye, I heard it. Sounds like something we should look into as well. I knew it was possible for Old Hades to do it, but…this is an added wrinkle, isn't it? Explains why her kind—* he didn't put any meanness into it, like others in the village might have when talking about Rose *—were so hated after he died. It became quite a stigma.*

Aye, it's a wrinkle, all right, mam said. *But what's my useless daughter going to do with our knowledge, our powers? Other than likely burn herself to death with Augie's?*

Tamhas was quiet, was calm, but when he spoke, a ripple of excitement ran through them all. *Why…she's going to get revenge, of course. For all of us. Because…* And she could almost see him smile in the dark of her mind. *…that's our way.*

*

Zack just stared, stared at the dead bodies, and a cold unrelated to the winter's chill ran through him, top to bottom. "Oh…my…my God…"

"This…changes things somewhat," Eve Kappler said in quiet voice, staring at the dead, and the girl who stood frozen in the middle of them, talking to voices in her head that they all could hear. "Weissman and Raymond killed her family."

"They tried," Gavrikov said, the Russian seeming to shiver in the chilly Scottish night. "But did you not see? The entire village sacrificed their own lives to Rose in order to save themselves from Raymond."

"It'd be hard to miss that mass suicide disguised as a midnight wilding," Harmon said, looking around a little cagily.

"This little scene bringing back memories?" Bjorn asked Harmon with a nasty sneer.

Harmon snapped around to look at him. "Why, yes, yes it is. When it comes to throwing yourself on a succubus to avoid death, I'm very familiar with the process. Though even I have to admit, watching an entire village mob make that choice at one time to avoid being drained by a Hades? Well…I thought I was jaded, that I'd seen it all." He looked over the dead. "This…this is new."

"It's not new," Zack said quietly. "This must have happened…seven years ago now. Look at Rose here. She's a teenager, probably about Sienna's age. She's got that thin, reedy look, malnourished. Reminds me of—well, Sienna, when we pulled her out of her house." He looked away. "It's starting to alarm me the similarities I'm seeing between them."

"Her people were wiped out by Century during the war," Eve said, nodding at the dead. "How many voices do you suppose this scared, angry girl has in her head right at this moment?"

"This moment we're viewing?" Harmon asked, looking away. "Or this moment right now, that we're not living because we're among the dead trapped in her head, reliving the tragic high points of her life?"

"Explains why is she crazy, no?" Gavrikov asked.

"The sooner we get out of here," Harmon said, "the better."

"Now all we need is a body to jump ship to," Eve said. "And a chance to do so."

"You assholes," Zack said under his breath. "Bastian…you cannot possibly think this is a good idea?"

Bastian's ghostly form was standing silent in the moonlight, arms folded across his massive chest. He stirred in the dark. "Leaving this place behind? Why wouldn't we want to? This girl's made a hell in her own mind and we're living it with her. You bet your sweet bippy I'm getting out of here if I get a chance."

"Sienna has been our—" Zack started.

"Horse?" Eve asked.

"Vessel?" Gavrikov threw in.

"Prison," Bjorn said.

"Our *home*," Zack said, "for lack of a better word. And you guys are talking about leaving her to die at the hands of this crazy—"

"She could already be dead," Gavrikov said, but there was a slight catch in the way he said it. He swallowed, visibly, uneasily, "for all we know. We can't see outside this place. She may well be a corpse, cold, and gone. Our loyalty should be to—"

"To her," Zack said, feeling the fire of the feeling.

"I don't think we're going to come to a consensus on this," Harmon said stiffly. "But if it makes you feel better, remember this moment. And when we jump ship, and I have access to my powers again, we can send this memory of Rose's to Sienna, if she's still alive." He spoke smoothly up until he said her name, and there...he seemed to catch a little as well. "Maybe the knowledge of what Rose is, how she came to be...maybe it'll help her. But beyond that..."

"This is not our fight anymore," Eve said, eyes cool. "We're not sharing a body with Sienna. We never really shared a mind with her. She has goals to save the world from all these dubious criminals, most of whom don't actually want to destroy it. They just want to cut their little slice out of it, and I'm content to let them have that piece—so that I can have peace." She shrugged. "Is that so bad?"

"It's depraved indifference to human life," Zack said. "Yes, that's generally considered bad."

"I'm not human," Eve said. "Hell, I'm not even alive anymore."

"I'm indifferent," Bjorn said with a split grin, crooked at the corner of his mouth. "And depraved."

Bastian broke his silence. "I'm not indifferent. But this mano a mano thing that Rose has got going with Sienna..." He looked right at Zack. "You think our place is in the middle of this fight? We're on the bench at best, out of the arena at worst. Rose doesn't want us, and Sienna…" He shrugged. "She's not in our Area of Operations, okay? Much as you might want to help her…what do you really think we can do from here?" He looked around, as if taking the emotional temperature of the others, who were nodding in quiet. "It's our obligation to bust out. After that, if you want to help Sienna…" He shrugged again. "Maybe we can get you your own body, and off you go." He looked to Harmon for approval. "Right? Let the man pursue his interests."

"We are going to need many fresh bodies," Gavrikov said.

"I'm certainly not opposed to trying," Harmon said smoothly. "I don't wish Sienna any ill will…at this point." He seemed to stiffen again. "If you want to go help her once we're out…I won't stop you. Just don't expect me to get involved. Rose is a small threat to everyone else—"

"She's killed five thousand people, man," Zack said, disgust welling within him. "That's not a small threat and that's not a small number—"

"It is in the long history of mankind," Harmon cut him off. "You want to get involved? You may. Leave me out, all right?" He looked around, caught a few nods. "Leave *us* out of it, I should say. Because it looks to me like a grudge match. Like Rose powered up to kill Sienna. What's she going to do once she's done? Hm?" He paused, waiting for an answer Zack didn't have to give. "Probably nothing."

She will not stop, a quiet voice seemed to whisper in the wind.

"Oh, good," Eve said dryly, "the disembodied voice again. Look me in the eye when you speak to me, voice." She looked around, as if expecting something to jump out of the shadowy bushes. "Hm? Or are you a coward?"

"Yes," came a voice as a silhouette slipped out of the dark, appearing before them as if shimmering like falling water. His face was clear, handsome even, and the earnestness that had been there before was replaced by eyes that were dark and shadowed.

Graham.

"So you are in here with us," Zack said, looking him right in the eye. There was a sadness there, one that hadn't been present when last he'd seen Graham, in this very memory, grabbing hold of Rose and letting her rip his soul out of his body to save himself.

Graham just looked at each of them in turn, and then stared at Rose, still huddled in the bushes. As they watched she stood, turning, and started down the lane toward Miriam Shell's house, as if spurred to life by their discussion of her. She wobbled, unsteady on her legs, but gained strength with each step. She avoided the bodies, picked her way around them, and disappeared into the night behind a house that was freshly painted and shone blue in the moonlight.

"This…" Graham"s voice was quiet, full of sadness, and some strange, foreboding menace. "This is not all." He looked at each of them in turn, and Zack could see in his eyes a pain, a callousing to his soul, a wounding that years in Rose's mind had left him with—something that Zack himself did not feel, could not feel, even after years of his own imprisonment in Sienna, a longer sentence than Graham's.

And it worried him.

"This…" Graham said, and it seeped into Zack like the rising chill of Scottish winter as the wind ran through, rustling the bushes around them, "was just the beginning…"

24.

Sienna

I woke up in the middle of the night, under the car, cold seeping in on either side. It was probably in the seventies or sixties, Fahrenheit, based on the chill that had sunk into my bones. I was shivering slightly, metal underbody of the old farm truck above me, the concrete parking pad beneath me, and the sides open so I could breathe in the cool night air.

Obviously I'd been at the point of deathly exhaustion when I'd crawled beneath the truck seeking shelter, but now that I'd awoken, other than the open sides and fresh air coming in, it kind of reminded me—what with the shallow confines above and below—of the time I'd spent in the steel box my mom used to imprison me in.

No wonder I'd fallen asleep so easily. It was like a little slice of home away from home.

My muscles ached, but not impossibly badly as they had when they'd seized up before I'd conked out. That oily smell beneath the vehicle was now oddly comforting, like something I'd gotten used to. I tested my arms, and they worked again, which was fortunate. My legs did the same, bending on command. My abs felt a little sore, and my inner ear seemed to be still experiencing the feeling of rapid swimming, even though I'd concluded my flight across the Firth many hours ago, a sense that I was bobbing in the waves still thrummed through me.

"Oh, gahhh…" I mumbled, my face pressed into the concrete parking pad. I hadn't felt it when I'd collapsed, probably a little too focused on being completely spent rather than worrying about the fact I was using concrete as a pillow. For my cheekbone.

I lifted my head, but carefully, very aware that there were tons of metal lingering just above me. I'd drooled in my sleep, one of those qualities that made me so super attractive, I supposed. No wonder I was beating the men away with the stick these days. A headache lingered, lightly, behind my eyes, and I figured it was my body's revenge, along with the other aches, for pushing myself so desperately hard with so desperately little over these last few days. I was living on nothing and adrenaline before Rose had stolen my powers, and since then it had basically been junk food, adrenaline, and Irn Bru, which was not much better.

Hardly conditioned to live the high life, I had nonetheless become accustomed to a certain lifestyle these last few years, and it mostly included decent food and a bed to sleep in. Waking up on concrete and marathoning and swimming for miles and miles? Not something my body was super jazzed about, I could tell from the pain.

Sorting through the aches, I came back to the memory of my dreamwalk during my sleep.

Reed.

I'd talked to Reed.

I rose so quickly I did clang my head against the undercarriage of the truck, and in the distance, what sounded like miles away, a dog started barking. "Oww," I muttered under my breath. I hadn't dinged myself hard enough to split the skin, fortunately, I could tell by running my fingers over the point of impact, but neither had I done my already aching head any favors.

I'd talked to my brother.

And he was coming to get me.

The weakness that filled my arms, the pain that had

replaced the agonized muscles and screaming tendons, gave way to a surge of strength. I belly-crawled out from beneath the truck like it was just another short length of the culvert I'd struggled through yesterday, filled with new purpose.

I had to get my ass to York.

I'd forgotten so much in my attempt to pass on information in a hurry to Reed. I'd forgotten to tell him, "Bring Suppressant." I hadn't mentioned my plan for getting my souls back. I hadn't begged him to bring a bevy of weapons with him.

But none of that mattered, really. I needed a ride first and foremost. I needed to escape, to regroup, to get clear of Rose and the police and all the other trouble that hounded my footsteps here in Scotland.

Once I was clear of all that, I could start my planning. I could come up with a real strategy, maybe even set a trap for Rose, since she seemed so keen to come after my ass.

All I had to do was get to York, and get the hell out of the UK.

And that started with getting the hell moving.

Once I was out from beneath the truck, I looked up. I'd used the sun all day as a reference point for directional heading. It was easy enough, so long as you knew about what time of day it was. But now it was night, and probably around midnight, my gut told me. There was no sun, and I was deep in the countryside, with no bank clocks to tell me what time it was, or a compass at hand to give me direction.

Surprisingly, in all the years my mother trained me and taught me, trying to impart survival advice to her wayward and listening-only-because-the-alternative-was-no-TV daughter, she went pretty light on anything related to surviving in nature. Orienteering was right out, except in theoretical terms, probably because I wasn't allowed outside. For a woman obsessed with trying to prepare me for every dangerous scenario, she left some huge gaps in my knowledge base, all related to what to do when you're alone with nature.

Fortunately, my mother hadn't been my only source of instruction. Glen Parks had come along after her, and he hadn't been lacking in knowledge about surviving and thriving in the wilds. It was hardly my favorite thing, preferring firearms training and martial arts and all that other hitting and hurting people stuff, but I had some knowledge of navigating now.

I looked up, lying on my back on the concrete pad, the metal roof of the truck obscuring my view of the stars. I let out a slow sigh; I didn't really want to move that much, but there was work to be done, and my new plan—to get to York to meet Reed so I could escape—was enervating me.

Creaking as I got to my feet, my joints popping as they resettled, I started to wonder if this was what normal people felt like after a particularly laborious workout. It certainly wasn't normal for a meta, and probably wouldn't have been happening right now if I'd managed a few more hours of sleep.

But it was good that I hadn't, because I'd need all the time I could get to travel under the cover of darkness.

I eased out from underneath the shed roof, carefully making sure I went in the opposite direction of the nearby farmhouse, just in case there was anybody home. Once clear, I looked up into the sky…

And beheld a wonder of stars, a plethora, like diamonds sparkling across the night sky.

Too used to the light-polluted cityscapes of the places where I hid, it had been a long time since I'd been out in the middle of the night in a place where I could really see the stars. This was most definitely such a place, and I made a mental note that once this whole Rose bullshit was over, I needed to make my next hideout in a place that was a little more rural so I could appreciate this kind of view for a while.

It took me a few minutes of staring, breath taken away by the sight of all that wonder, before I shook it off and got back to my search. I was looking for something specific. Something important.

And there it was.

The North Star twinkled down at me, a guiding light that shone brighter in the sky than any other in Ursa Minor. It had acted as a navigational beacon to generations of human beings, and now it was going to guide me.

Because now I knew which way north was, and it was just as easy this time as it had been when Glen Parks had first taught me.

I drew a breath, and took one last look up at the stars. There was work to be done, miles to cover before I collapsed again, and places to be before the sun rose. Trying to keep my eyes focused on the path ahead—which was no path at all, just untrammeled fields and the occasional fence and other obstacle—I started west, remembering that town I'd seen when I'd come ashore, and hoping I could make it there and find a way south before too many more hours elapsed.

25.

I came into the nearby town over fields and uneven ground on a downhill approach. The field of stars above had dimmed its majesty the closer I got. It didn't look like a particularly big town, but it was big enough to contain probably five thousand people or so. Maybe more, for all I knew; it was tough to judge from this perspective.

It was quiet, a few lights on in scattered houses visible from where I was. Not a shop or store with them on, though, at least not that I could see. It was the dead of night, and this place was heavy on the "dead" part of that. A dog barked in the distance, the lone sentry awake around here.

I decided that walking through town was my easiest bet, just strolling in like I owned the place. From my perspective on the hill, I couldn't tell much about the town, but I was either looking for a rail depot where I could hitch a ride south or else a car I could steal in order to head that way myself. The second option was somewhat more suspect at this point because I would be driving in the middle of the night on unfamiliar roads.

But if this town wasn't big enough to justify a rail station… well, I couldn't exactly wait around until daybreak for the bus.

Dawn was, fortunately, still hours off in my calculation. That lone dog barking in the distance lent a spooky aura to this little hamlet. My footsteps as I skipped the last fence on a pasture and hit a road heading into town sounded incredibly loud to me, like a rocket re-entering the atmosphere and making a couple sonic booms in the process. It was, obviously, not that loud, but it sure felt like it to someone like me, sensitive to the slightest sound.

I started my casual walk along the road. My sodden Stranglers t-shirt was stiff from the seawater, and my stolen, way-too-long pants were hanging awkwardly on my frame. My boots, which I'd stolen from the cop I'd mugged yesterday morning, fit surprisingly well, for which I was thankful. There'd be nothing worse than looking terrible and having ill-fitting shoes.

I only hoped that the bedraggled look I now wore like a vagabond could be passed off as the UK version of a hipster rather than something more sinister. Because the only person probably awake in this town was a local cop on night duty, and flagging their attention would tend to be somewhat bad for my health. And my plans.

The street I was on was residential, but it fed into a more main street. I passed quaint little houses with a 1950s look to them, a kind of post-war, we're-at-peace, chicken-in-every-pot vibe to them. It was the UK version of what I saw in Minneapolis in the sections bordering the first-ring suburbs, or in Eau Claire, Wisconsin in the parts just radiating out from the downtown. I'd seen houses like them in a hundred cities in the US, and London, now that I thought about it, and even though the style was different, the feel was the same: like someone had come in and tried to create the 1950's feeling of home. They looked cozy. I think they might have hit the mark.

Or maybe it was just because they reminded me of my house before it had burned down.

I hit a main avenue that fed farther into the town, a few commercial buildings popping up down the way. This was going to be a long, uninterrupted walk down this street, and I was starting to feel just a little nervous about it. In the distance, I could see a lone car making its way toward me, gradually.

My breath caught in my throat. If it was a cop…

Hell, if it was a person who had a brain in their head…

They were going to pass right by me, and in the process their lights would illuminate me for a few seconds. When that happened, I'd need to shield my face while playing that I'd been blinded by the light, or that it at least was uncomfortable, without making myself look too suspicious. That was a pretty tight rope to walk, but it was what I had to do.

I was drawing some pretty ragged breaths, maybe even holding them. My heart rate spiked, thumping in my chest. The car's headlights reflected a bright glare off a storefront two blocks away.

It was drawing closer.

I looked down, and my heart jumped in my chest again. "Bedraggled" didn't fully cover my present look; it was obvious these clothes didn't quite fit me. I only hoped that kids in Scotland—what? I'm kind of a kid, still—wore really baggy clothes sometimes. And had long, stringy, completely disastrous hair. Because I was rocking that look, too.

At least…I hoped the kind that would be out walking and causing absolutely no trouble at three in the morning would be dressed in baggy clothes. Because otherwise, I was about to tip someone's suspicions hard.

I tried to steady my breathing, but I couldn't. This was going to be a moment of truth, and I didn't know if I could handle the truth. It wasn't like I could carjack them either, because unless I took this person hostage, it wouldn't be safe to use their car to get to York.

This was what my life had been reduced to: vetoing carjacking someone because it would alert the cops to my movements.

I never thought I'd say this self-pitying thing, but…FML.

Readying a hand to hold it up to block my face and eyes from the bright lights approaching slowly, I kept my steady pace. My boots clicked along the sidewalk as I headed toward the main street—high street, I guess they called them over here. I waited for the trouble that could come soon, imagining the squeal of tires as this car pulled over, and turned out to be cops.

But they signaled a left turn a block ahead, and I was left on the empty street, my heart still thundering in my chest.

Part of me wondered if I was going to die of a heart attack before anything bad actually happened to me. I almost stopped right there, to lean against a storefront and breathe. I'd been pursued for a while now, but what Rose had done in tapping out my powers…

Well, she'd made my flight more of an actual run, one I had to undertake because I couldn't really stand and fight anymore. And she'd cut off my best avenue of retreat in the process, the ability to just fly off when things didn't go my way.

Now I was stuck fleeing on foot anytime things went bad, like some street criminal in the US. I mean, one that could run faster than a car moving at low speed, but still…not optimal.

My nerves were still jangling, the lit street lamps providing an orangey-yellow light for me to walk by, but those tangled thoughts in my head cried out that maybe I couldn't do it this way; that maybe taking the direct approach had been…well, dumb.

I was breathing loud and hard, again, and I didn't think it was going to stop anytime soon. I'd been through battles, through a war with people trying to exterminate my kind. But sneaking through a Scottish town in the wee hours of the morning while a seemingly unstoppable succubus and Police Scotland chased me?

I might have finally found the thing that did my poor little heart in.

There was an alley up ahead, and I looked down it as I passed. It was confined, only ten feet wide or so, and seemed to come to a dead end at a fence. I ducked inside and found a good, thick shadow midway down, and crouched within its depths, sheltered next to an abandoned cardboard box that was filled with recyclables someone had apparently failed to get to the bin.

Sitting there in the darkness, my heart beat like a bass drum. I squatted down, closing my eyes, putting my back against the brick wall. "It's okay," I said to myself, wondering what the hell was wrong with me. I felt so damned weak in that moment, and it pissed me off.

For years now I'd been the most powerful being on the planet. Not invincible, as much as I sometimes wanted to believe I was, but strong. I had powers no one else could claim, or at least in combinations no one else could.

Even without those—without the souls that came with them—I was still an indefinably bad badass. I'd killed a lot of people, almost all of whom had totally deserved it, and all of whom had at least kindasorta had it coming. I clenched a fist and held it tight against my chest, feeling my heartbeat ripple through the muscle in my hand.

Sitting in the darkness of that alley, I discovered a little truth about myself that I hadn't really realized until that moment. I'd gotten pretty damned arrogant about how good I was. I'd even bragged that no one could stop me, something I'd stopped saying after I'd taken a bullet to the head in a bank in Florida a few months ago, but which sentiment still sort of rested somewhere in my heart—this youthful feeling that I was, in fact, untouchable, that no one could beat me because no one could fight harder than me, was stronger than me, was as damned unyielding and indefatigable as I was.

Man. Did I let that arrogance get out of control or what?

It was bad enough that I'd somehow thought I was invincible, but now that those powers, those souls, were gone? The empty hole they left behind, the abilities that I really could have used right now? It was almost like fear was rushing in like a tide into a hole in the beach, filling it and replacing the courage and power that I'd had before.

My hand was shaking, even though it was clenched.

I'd heard somewhere once that fear of loss was a more powerful motivator than the idea of gain. I believed it now, because since I'd lost what I'd had—my power, my souls—I was running harder, trying harder, more willing to cross lines, maybe, than I had been before. If Rose sent a meta against me right now that had some enviable power, I might even have felt compelled to drain them dry and take their abilities, try and turn them against her.

"Shit," I whispered. I didn't even want to contemplate that.

I stood, still in shadow. My breathing had slowed slightly, but not by much. There was a definite tightness in my chest, and I didn't care for it at all. Part of me wanted to curl back up, to just sit there in the darkness and pretend I was trapped on all sides by metal rather than get up and get moving, trying to find my way to York.

It was really, really hard to get moving.

It was almost like there really was an invisible box around me. I breathed as slow and steady as I could, comparatively. "We're going to make it out of this," I said, wondering why I was saying "we" when I was plainly alone for the first time in years. "I'm going to get you all back," I said, answering my own question. "I will find a way."

I pushed off the brick wall behind me, and stepped out of the shadows. I wasn't going to wait here all night. I needed to move under the cover of darkness, because this was who I was now. For the time being, anyway. I started to step toward the mouth of the alley—

And engine noise stopped me. I froze, just a step or two out of the shadows, and a light ran along the side of the building opposite me in the alley. It didn't look like normal headlights, though I could hear the car. It felt more like…

A car cruised past the mouth of the alley, and as the headlamps passed the open aperture, that light didn't stop moving down the alley walls. There was another light source coming from behind the headlamps, and it only took me a second—a second too long—to realize what it was.

A spotlight mounted on the driver's side mirror.

It shone down the alley and lit me up. I put my hand over my face like I'd planned, but I knew how I suspicious I must look, hanging about in small-town Scotland in an alley in the middle of the night.

A car door opened, and I stayed frozen.

Who had spotlights mounted on their car mirrors?

Cops.

I'd been found.

26.

Reed

I landed outside the office, wishing I'd just used my powers to fly back from Texas rather than trying to feign calm on the jet ride with Angel. She'd been a decent traveling companion, staying gracefully quiet the entire way, unlike any of the other options I might have been presented with. She hadn't even protested when I had flown off toward the office without her when we landed. Miranda would have groused that I was breaking the law, since the governor had yanked my free flight status over Minnesota airspace.

I was so beyond giving a shit.

Opening the door, I found Casey sitting behind the receptionist desk. "Hi, Reed," she said, all chipper.

"Morning," I said, more wood chipper, a little below a snarl. I had things on my mind. Also, it was more like evening at this point in the day.

I didn't even make it through the hallway into the bullpen before Miranda seemed to spring out of a nearby wall, making me wonder if she'd been waiting in ambush, a paper in hand. "What the hell is this charge for a charter plane for an international flight?" She wasn't angry, exactly, but she was clearly of a mind to work out the financial detail on this one.

"I have business overseas," I said coolly, making my way up the aisle through the middle of the bullpen rather than skirting the edge. Heads were popping up—Augustus, Scott, Friday, even Veronika, Colin, and Kat. I guess the B team had made it back from their latest sojourn to California.

Also, I wouldn't have called them the B team to their faces, because Colin was scary fast, Veronika was just scary, and Kat could pull tears out—guilty, terrible, pretty tears—at a moment's notice.

"Hey, Reed," J.J. called from his cubicle. He was peeping out of it like a groundhog on February 2nd when winter was about to go away. "You got a second?"

"No," I said, clipped, and turned my attention back to Miranda. "Don't worry about it, okay? It's not credit card fraud; I chartered it myself. I'll be back in a couple days."

She gave me the raised eyebrow. "Where are you going?"

"Tahiti," I lied, only a few steps from my office.

"That doesn't sound like a business expense," she said.

"Find a way to justify it," I said, not turning back to answer her, "and if not, I'll just pay the company back out of my own pocket." I really didn't care, but I didn't have a credit card that could be charged for the hundred grand or better it had taken to get the plane. I doubted they were going to accept a personal check either, and I didn't feel I had the time to explore other payment methods.

"I don't think you realize—" Miranda started to say, but I slammed the door to my office and shut the shades.

That done, I stood there in the pale dark, twilight peeking through the slits in the closed blinds. I took a long, slow breath. I was about to violate a whole heaping ton of laws. Not exactly a first for me, but definitely the first time in a while. I clenched my phone in my hand.

How the hell was I supposed to explain this to Isabella?

There was a knock at the door, a brief and done thing that ended as someone opened said door and slipped in. I turned to find J.J. standing there, closing the door behind him. His hair was puffy, his look serious, and he said, without preamble, "I know where you're going."

"J.J…" I started.

"Dude," he said, brushing my objection aside. "Really?"

"I'm not going to—"

"I know where you're going," J.J. said. "Do you have any idea how big a flag you raised around here by doing this?"

I hadn't considered that. My crew was tight, and if they knew I booked a charter to the UK…well, then they knew almost everything. "Dammit."

"I covered it up," he said. "When the pilot files the flight plan with ATC, I'm going to change it in the system so it looks like you're going somewhere innocuous, like Sacramento. But you need to be careful on these sorts of things." He lowered his voice. "You don't know who's listening, even in here." He wasn't speaking meta low, but I realized he'd never said my destination out loud, even though he surely knew it.

Damn. In the heat of the moment, I'd forgotten that in addition to the Scottish authorities watching the hell out of things on that end, the FBI was probably still surveilling us on this end. We had the office swept for bugs regularly, but that was hardly a thing you wanted to hang your life on. "When was the last sweep?" I asked.

"Checked a few minutes ago myself," he said. "It's easy once you have the gear. But dude—I still wouldn't go speaking it aloud anywhere you can avoid it. Remember Ca—uh, that really smart lady who could use targeted words to hear our conversations about her?"

"Got it," I said, nodding. He meant Cassidy Ellis. "Listen… I need you to tell Isabella for me."

He made a face. "Dude…you think I'm not coming with you?"

"J.J.…" I said, exasperation popping out. "This is serious, man. I have to do this alone."

"Are you nuts?" J.J. asked, waving a hand behind him to encompass the bullpen and all the people waiting within it, probably straining hard to hear our conversation through the door. "You gotta be joking right now. You're gonna take the team and leave me behind?"

I froze. "I'm not taking the team."

He squinched his face up further. "Whut?"

"I'm going alone," I said. "The team is staying here."

J.J. adjusted his glasses, giving me an "oh no you didn't" sort of look. "You're going to ditch everybody? You're going to go—extract our friend—and you think you can just go solo, no one rolling with you?"

"No one is coming with me," I said, hesitating.

"You heading into trouble?" J.J. asked, like I was dumb, and it was obvious.

"Hopefully not."

He cocked his head. Again, I got the feeling I was dumb. "You're going to her. She's wanted. She's—I assume—in some kind of trouble—"

"She got disempowered," I said, not sure why I said that. It just sort of popped out. "She ran into another succubus," I went on, when his eyes blew up wide, "a stronger one. This other girl...she ripped the souls right out of her, left her...weak. Turned the cops against her. She's..." I ran a hand through my long hair. "It's bad."

J.J. just stared at me. "All the shit we've been through, and you think that the crew is going to stay behind on this one?"

"This is off books, J.J.," I said. "This is not the mission, it's not their job. I don't have the authority to ask this of them, even if I wanted to. They shouldn't have me dragging them into this—"

"It's Sienna, man," J.J. said. "We're all in this."

"No, we're not," I said. "She's my family. *I'm* in this. But the rest of you? This is your private lives, man, and what we're talking about here is the opposite of what we do here for work. This is lawbreaking, doing wrong—this team doesn't do that. They aren't a group of bank robbers or mercenaries. And when it comes to this kind of illegality, these kinds of life-changing, ruinous consequences, they don't answer to me—"

"THEY WILL ANSWER TO THE KING OF GONDOR!" J.J. shouted, almost rattling the door. His eyes were on fire, wild as I'd ever seen them. "Dude. The beacons are lit AF, okay? Sienna calls for aid—"

"You guys aren't Rohan," I said, trying to keep an even keel. J.J. was plainly worked up, speaking in geek metaphor that—yeah, I got it, but…I wasn't exactly proud of the fact. "This isn't your fight. This is the reason Sienna has kept us all at arm's length for the last several months. Everyone who goes on this trip is asking for a prison sentence if things go wrong, if we end up getting into a fight. Let me handle this—"

"Hell no!" a voice cracked through the door.

"Nuh uh," came another.

"What the—" I went for the handle and J.J. moved aside. I opened it to find the crew out there, not even making a pretense of working. Augustus, Scott, Kat and Jamal were standing right out there, Veronika, Colin, Abigail and Friday about a half-step behind them. Not one of them looked shame-faced, though Chase was lingering back a ways, as was Miranda.

"Man, Sienna put this team together," Augustus said, and before I could say anything to that: "You ain't got grounds to deny it. We all know she's been behind the scenes on this from day one." He looked at Miranda significantly. She didn't admit anything, of course. She was a lawyer who'd been taking orders from a wanted fugitive; she'd be dumb to open her mouth, even here. Augustus looked back at me, all sincerity. "She's saved my life more times than I can count. If she's in trouble, if she's powerless I don't care whose damned law is standing in the way. I'm going. Because if I got my ass in it up to the neck, you know she'd be there to help, even if the law was still after her."

"Here, here," Jamal said, doing a little abrupt clap. When no one else joined in, he stopped.

"Guys—" I started to say, and then Abby shot me a hard look. "And gals," I amended. "There could be serious consequences for this. Life in the cube, and for some of us…it might be a long life."

"Puh-lease," Veronika said, feigning a yawn. "I'm insulted you didn't ask me to come. I mean, I do illegal things all the time."

Augustus rolled his eyes. "Yeah, okay, we get it. You have a wild sex life."

Veronika froze for a second, then threw her head back and let out a laugh. "Oh, I like you, pretty boy. I was talking about how I used to be an assassin, sweetie, and you go full into the gutter without even a nudge from me." She wore a wide grin. "I'm wearing you down, baby."

Augustus made a face. "Did you just Urkel me?"

"Sienna and I have had our differences," Scott said, "but you know...I'm there for her, no matter what. She's saved the world...so many times. And the world turned its back on her? Well, I won't. I'm coming." He clenched a fist in front of him. "If I have to ride the waves behind you all the way, I am coming."

"Like you could leave me behind on this," Kat said, arms folded in front of her, usual smile evaporated.

"I will hack your plane and send you into the ocean if you try and leave me behind," Abby said, completely inscrutable. She had a good poker face. Scary good. "So unless you want to go for a nice swim in the north Atlantic..."

"You'd be okay," Scott promised.

"And then I'd bring down a rain of satellites on you, just to liven things up," Abby said, still inscrutable.

"Or we could just save ourselves the headache and bring the whole clown car along," Jamal said under his breath.

"I'm fighting for Sienna," Guy Friday said, boldly, declaratively, a little sappily, like he was crying under his mask. "For truth, and freedom, and justice and decency and stuff! Because she's my niece! And because I kinda want to drink some Belgian beer right at the source."

"I'm not going to Belgium," I said crossly.

"Oh, well," Friday said, "then for all those other reasons—I AM COMING!" And he struck a pose, massive arms strapped across his inflated chest.

I looked at Colin, then Chase, because neither of them had said anything. Colin looked around, adjusted his beanie slowly (for him) and said, "Yeah…no prison can really hold me, and the cops can't really catch me, so…" He shrugged. "I'm in."

Looking past him, Chase had a hard look on her face. She had her arms crossed, and there was a mountain of discomfort, her brown hair coming over one of her eyes in a pouty wave. "So…Sienna's how I got this job, huh?" She bowed her head. "I shoulda known. Saved my life in Montana, got me the best-paying gig I've had in years." She let out a long breath. "Yeah, okay. I guess I kinda owe her. Plus, uh, y'know, if she's been saving the world…" She shrugged again. "I suppose I've been living on borrowed time or something, so…"

"You don't have to do this, you know," I said. "This is voluntary."

"Yeah, and I'm kind of volunteering," she said. "You guys have been really decent to me, and she's one of your clan, so…" She nodded. "I'm in."

I nodded, once, feeling a little…not astounded, exactly, but maybe a little amazed. "I have to admit…I've worked with most of you for kind of a while now, and…you did surprise me today."

"That's right, baby," J.J. said. "Winger speech and bring it on home."

I ignored him and went on. "My sister is…a complicated person. We all know that. But most us know that the hell that's come her way lately is stuff she doesn't deserve, that she didn't earn. And now this Scottish succubus, whoever she is…she thinks she's got Sienna rocked back on her heels, on the run. That she's isolated, hunted and alone. Well…

"Sienna has saved the world, and she's saved us all, at one time or another," I said, feeling my chest puff a little with pride. "It's our turn now. Let's go save her."

27.

Sienna

I was spotlit.

Caught.

Frozen like a deer in the headlights, blinded by the bright.

Given everything that had happened, all the hits I'd taken these last few months, it was very tempting to just…give it up right here. Toss in the towel. Say, "So long, and thanks for all the fish!" Whatever that meant. (Reed said it a lot)

I was hemmed in by a cop car on one side and a fence on the other. If I ran for it, they'd call it in, and I'd be hounded once more, a whole country of cops—and probably Rose—descending upon me.

I'd lost my souls, lost my powers, and now…I was trapped in an alley in some coastal town in Scotland I didn't even know the name of, and the police were staring me down.

Really…there wasn't much farther a girl could fall. If this wasn't rock bottom, I could only hope it was awfully close.

Faced with a choice of standing there, submitting, surrendering…I like to think that most people who'd been through the hell I'd been through would have just given up at that point. We like to think the worst of others, like to believe we're special. And we are all special, in some ways. Some people are especially stupid, for instance. I might be one of them.

Because whenever the pressure really tended to get on…in clinch time…that was when I bucked up and went bold, in spite of all the clawing, nagging, nasty doubts that had just threatened to drag me down.

I shielded my eyes against the spotlight, cringing away. I couldn't see much of anything, except some police lights flashing somewhere behind the blinding white in my face. "Ow," I said, not bothering to hide my American accent. "Man, that's bright. I'm glad you guys came along though, because—I gotta tell ya—" and I threw in a chuckle here "—I have never been so lost in my entire life. Silly American, I know, making all us tourists look stupid." I started toward them, taking an easy pace, keeping my hands where they—if there were more than one of them—could see them.

"Just stop right there," a male voice with a Scottish accent commanded.

"What?" I asked, still flinching away from the spotlight and hiding my face. "I'm lost, man. I need some help."

"I'm asking you to stop," he said, and his voice was rising. Probably some worry.

"I don't understand," I said, taking it nice and easy. "No comprendo, you know what I mean? You Scots, I don't understand what you're saying most of the time—"

I heard the motion rather than saw it, the sound of the guy drawing something from a holster.

Damn.

I sprang into action, committing both of us to our paths, because I needed to reach him before he drew, and he needed to shoot me before I could beat his skull in (which I totally would not do). He'd erred in letting me get relatively close to him without drawing his weapon—whatever it was. I had a suspicion.

There's a concept in law enforcement that's popularly referred to as the "twenty-one-foot rule." It's not actually called that, really, it's called the Tueller Drill, but if you say that to most people, they'll go, "Huh?" Hell, if you ask most people about the twenty-one-foot rule, their reaction would probably be just about the same. But it's a simple idea, that a human being can cover the distance of twenty-one feet or less in about one and a half seconds—faster than a law enforcement agent can draw their gun, get a bead, and fire a shot.

I was well inside twenty-one feet of this guy, and I could move faster than a human being. I did so, catching him before he could bring up the stun gun he was lifting to bring to bear on target—

On me.

I swatted it out of his hand and made a split-second decision.

I was so tired of hiding, of being pushed back, chased, beaten.

Thrusting my hand against the officer's cheek, I brushed right past his defenses—

And slapped my palm against his face, anchoring it there.

"Shhh," I said, and my will bowled his over, even though I didn't fully have my soul power to bear. He did indeed hush, and it came as a slight surprise.

The burning came a moment later.

It ran through my palm like someone had brushed it with a tickle, then it became a fuller feeling, a sensation of fire running across my skin. I got hot and flushed, and in five seconds I was in, rushing like I'd dove into the officer's mind.

I took great care, not going anywhere that affected his core memories—who he was, his family, his loves and disappointments. It was a boon of my power that I could be a little picky and choosy about the memories I stole, if I didn't take the whole entirety of a person.

Here, I was after a very specific thing, a little thread that was perhaps entwined with the rest of his life but didn't define it. An easy string to pluck, to remove, a tangential detail to his life that he wouldn't miss unless a certain subject came up—

That Sienna Nealon was a wanted criminal instead of a vaunted hero. Heroine. Whatever.

I took from him the memory of where he'd been when he heard I'd gone rogue, and a few discussions he'd had with the people in his life about me being dangerous. He was of the opinion that, of course, I was, but fortunately the news I was in Scotland and causing havoc was still so new that he wasn't going to lose much in the way of memories. A briefing from his commander, a few chats with his wife, comments made idly about "that damned Sienna Nealon" being at it again.

Oh…and the moment when he'd first heard, just as the late news was coming on right before he and his wife were about to turn off the TV and get to their marital business for the evening, taking a brief respite from the sleeping kids. Of course, he ended up sitting back down and watching, a kid woke up, and the moment passed because his wife went to go deal with the crying tot and fell back asleep, leaving the poor guy to—

Well, he wouldn't miss that memory. *Next time*, I whispered in his mind as I took the memory, *when she's ready, to hell with the news*. It's all bad anyway.

I pulled out of the officer's mind and then yanked my hand away from his face. My total time in his head? Probably less than a third of a second. It felt longer, of course, as it always tended to, that dilation effect of reading through synapse and memory like I was living it in the moment. It'd been a near thing, too, getting distracted in this cop's head, especially given how close I'd come to some pretty salacious material. I didn't want to violate his privacy, and besides, thanks to that time I removed Scott's memories, that age-old question of what men thought, of what it felt like for dudes during—y'know—had already long ago been answered for me. My skill game took a major level up after that, if you know what I mean.

Oh, God.

Anyyyyyway. I took a step back from the officer in question and he blinked a couple times, now shadowed by the headlights once again. "Constable," I said, and he focused on me. "Can you help me?"

"Holy hell," he said in a thick Scottish accent (really, was there any other kind? There were Edinburgh accents, which were no accent at all, and Scottish accents, which were close to incomprehensible. That seemed to be it). "Sienna Nealon?"

This was the moment of truth, and I'd soon discover whether I'd effectively removed the problem areas of his memory. I couldn't really see his face since he was outlined by the blinding light, but I had high hopes that I was as good at playing around with memories as I thought I was. I'd certainly had a decent amount of practice.

"That's me," I said, waiting for the results of my memory-stealing exam. I was just standing in front of him, and stooped down to pick up his taser, handing it to him butt-first. "So…I'm in a little bit of a bind here, Constable. Trouble around every corner. Think you can give me a hand?"

He just stared, the dark shadow, and then turned, giving me a look at his profile. It was a little doughy, but he had the kind of face you wanted to trust—and not punch. Which made it so much easier on me a moment later when he said, "Absolutely, anything you need."

"I've got to get the hell out of Dodge here," I said. "Kinda ran into some trouble and I can't fly out."

"Ouch," he said, nodding along. "Where are you headed?"

I held my index finger over my lips and smiled. "Can't tell you. Classified, you know."

"Oh, sure," he said, nodding along furiously. "If you need a police escort—"

"No, no," I said, "I wouldn't dream of pulling you off duty. But I was wondering…do you have a train station in town?" I shivered a little.

"Absolutely. You need a ride?" He gestured back to the shoe car that he had been driving, the damned spotlight still on us. "Trains aren't running this time of night, but—"

"That'd be great, thanks," I said, and started toward the car even before he did. I took care to make sure I got in what was, to me, the driver door, but to the UK was the passenger door, for reasons probably only known to Wikipedia. He got in after me, and now that the spotlight was no longer blinding me, I could see he was smiling. Almost drooling in excitement, actually.

"To the train station, then?" he asked, and I wondered if I should be worried about him peeing on me in his excitement.

"Well, that depends," I said. "You said there are no trains running at this time of night. Did you mean passenger trains?" He nodded. "So…do cargo trains move through in the middle of the night?" He nodded again. "And do you know where I could catch one?"

He didn't even answer, just shifted the car into gear. "You must be in a hell of a hurry, not wanting to wait for a passenger car. I mean, that's dedication, riding the rails on a cargo train. Dangerous too—"

"I scoff at danger," I said, looking out the window as he steered us out onto the street carefully. It was still looking dingy, but he dodged us down a side street and off the main drag I'd been heading down when I'd ducked down the alleyway at his approach.

"You surely do," he said, guffawing lightly, giving it way more humor than the remark deserved. "Can I just say? I've been a huge admirer of yours for a long time now."

"It's nice to be admired," I said, a little forlornly, without looking over at him. It had been nice. Of course, not that he remembered it, but those days were well over now.

"Ye've just done so many amazing things," he gushed. "That meteor over Chicago?" I turned to look at him, and he was staring at me with a glowing face. "I mean, I guess that was never technically confirmed by anyone, but—I mean, everyone knows it was you under that big bloody rock. They don't just hover in the air in the air by themselves and gently come to rest in a lake, you know."

I could remember the weight of it on my shoulders. "Yeah. I know." I kept looking out the window.

"And that first battle in Minneapolis!" He was on a roll

now. "I mean, watching the cell phone footage of that…it was just incredible. You go turning into a dragon and chomping on that Sovereign bastard! I mean, it's like the stuff of legends. I love it." I looked over at him and he blushed. "You know. I admire it."

It had been a long time since anyone had said anything this nice to me, and it stung considering I'd ripped some memories out of this man's mind to make it happen. "Yeah, well…you and nobody else these days."

"Och, you've got just tons of admirers," he said. "I'm sure a lovely lass such as yourself probably has a never-ending line of male admirers seeking your hand."

"Nope," I said quietly. "Not my hand. Nor anything else, lately." If I had any energy, that might have been a lot more self-pitying, but as it was, I didn't have much thought to spare for the deficiencies of my love life.

The ride was a steady stream of gushing, and the officer's excitement at meeting a "real-life celebrity superhero!" only made my guilt at messing with his mind more present in my own. Here I had someone who had been a genuine fan of mine, and yet the knowledge that I had done terrible things had turned him against me. Somehow that made me feel even guiltier for depriving him of his memories, even though they were all misapprehensions about what I'd done.

The police car slid up to the side of the road and stopped, and the officer nodded his head. I avoided looking at his nameplate; I didn't want to feel any more responsible for him than I already was. "Train tracks are right over there."

"Any idea when the next train will come through?" I asked.

"Usually every few hours, I think?" He didn't sound too sure.

"Thanks," I said, and popped the door open. Standing there, I leaned back in. "Hey…you mind keeping the fact I was here between the two of us for a while? It's supposed to be a secret."

He tapped the bridge of his nose. "Just between you and

me. I'll keep it under my hat for a few days, then?"

"If you could," I said, smiling faintly. "Good luck to you—"

"Officer—" he started, extending his hand toward me.

I recoiled from him, and watched the pleasant expression melt off his face. If I touched him again right now, it'd vault him into immediate pain as my powers started to rip his soul out of his body whole. "I, uh—sorry," I said.

"Oh, not a problem," he said, apparently just as embarrassed as I was horrified. "Just wanted to...shake yer hand."

"Maybe next time," I said, and shut the door, walking away before he could come up with another thing to say that would make things more awkward for us both. I could hear a train whistle in the distance, and it sounded like sweet freedom, with maybe just a little tingle-twist of guilt.

28.

I rode through the night, thankfully unable to sleep under the gentle sway of the train on the rails. It didn't feel like it moved all that fast, rattling as I lay atop one of the carriages, staring up at the steadily lightening sky. I had a bad feeling about where we were going, thinking it probably wasn't York. I kept low, laying flat the whole time I was aboard because I figured, being on an open-topped car, standing or sitting up would reveal my profile to any witnesses watching the train pass. There probably weren't going to be many at this time of night, but all it'd take would be one and my chase would suddenly get a whole lot more exciting.

The slow break of day found the train squealing brakes and slowing down, and as I popped my head up, I could see no more countryside around me. Now it was suburban neighborhoods, or the Scottish version thereof. Looking around, way, way ahead I could see Edinburgh Castle perched atop its massive basalt peak.

"Hellfire and brimstone," I said.

I'd been afraid of this when I'd caught a westbound train, but I was running shy of options that didn't involve stealing or co-opting a car to make for York. While I could have gotten the cop back in town to drive me, and it might only have been a few hours, I had these fears about the dispatcher trying to reach him and failing, and sounding the alarm. The same applied to me stealing a car right now. I might get away with it, but all it would take would be someone noticing it before I reached York and they'd be looking for me. I didn't know how integrated Police Scotland was with the UK police services—it could have been very integrated, or suffer from a total lack of cooperation—and didn't feel like gambling my escape on it.

But the closer I got to York, the less of a gamble it would be. The closer I got, the more it'd be an issue of navigation rather than risk of discovery. But not being able to find where I was going was a very real concern, and it made me wish I'd brought John Clifford's map with me, even though I knew it wouldn't have survived my swim in the Firth.

The train continued to slow, chugging down to what felt like twenty miles an hour. Pretty soon, I had a feeling, it would stop, and that was a vexing thought. If I'd had a complete map of Edinburgh in my head, it would have made things easier. As it was, I needed to figure out how to find a southbound train, preferably without strolling right into the middle of Waverly Station and buying a ticket.

Oh, the woes of being a fugitive.

The sky had adopted a blue-purple haze, clouds strung across it. I'd seen prettier dawns, but I couldn't recall when. It was a strange sort of stray thought that smacked at me, recalling to mind that over the last few years I hadn't exactly taken a ton of time to stop and smell the roses, even before I was a fugitive. I'd been so busy building up my agency, trying to do my job, that I was doing a pretty piss-poor job of living my life.

No time for that now, though. I looked out across the Edinburgh neighborhoods around me, and realized that this was probably going to have to be the time to dismount, much as it sucked. It was probably somewhere between four and five in the morning, and the longer I waited for this train to chug me on into the station—or the train yard—the more likely I was to be seen.

So I hopped off, landing heavily on an embankment made of big pieces of grey rock where they'd built the tracks up off the ground. The dismount might have broken my leg if I hadn't been a meta and thus already pre-conditioned to be a little tougher than a normal human, because YEOUCH! That landing stung. My palms hit the ground too, as my legs bent, helping take the impact for me.

I popped back up and immediately ran to a nearby clump of bushes. I'm sure that didn't look suspicious at all, a dark-haired, squat lady jumping off a train and hiding in the bushes. Well, what were my other options? Stroll through town like nothing was happening? That was probably going to have to be my play when it came to my next move, because darting back and forth between shrubberies in eastern Edinburgh wasn't likely to work all that well.

What I really needed was access to a map, or better still, a phone. With a mobile phone I could look up routes to York via train, figure out the quickest path, even figure out the likely train tracks where such trains would pass. I mean, I was heading on a westerly course now, but who knew where Edinburgh's southern spur line was? It could have been behind me for all I knew.

This was information I needed, and I needed it urgently. There wasn't anything for it; I was going to have to steal a phone, and quickly.

The mere thought of that caused the nervous buzz in my stomach to heat up to a bubbling boil. The last time I'd been in Edinburgh, it was like the city itself had turned against me, delivering Frankie—Rose's catspaw—right to me on several occasions. Looking back, it could entirely have been Rose, using a GPS in her phone to constantly send her location to him.

Buuuuut, enough other weird stuff had happened around here to make me wary of accepting the easy explanation, the one that would essentially make Edinburgh slightly more friendly to me now (not that it would be *friendly* friendly, given that the cops were still looking for me, but…relatively less hostile, I guess).

All I needed right now was a bunch of Edinburghers dialing up 999 or calling Rose directly if she somehow did control them through Siren powers. And that was a fear that was circulating in the back of my mind, moving closer to the front all the time.

I emerged from my clump of bushes and found myself behind a few businesses. There was a McDonald's in front of me, and also an optician's office in a couple low-slung, one-floor commercial buildings. They were situated on a two-lane with some nice shoulder margin on the side road, and I could see cars coming in either direction, but sparingly, maybe one every minute or so.

The McDonald's was open twenty-four hours, which I regarded as an unfavorable sign. If there was good news in all this, it was that I had perhaps a few customers to blend in with, maybe one of whose cell phones I could steal if they were being very unattentive and I was feeling particularly sneaky. I didn't love the element of chance in all this, but what the hell else could I do? I needed access to Google, and now.

I sauntered up to the door of the McD's like I owned the place, and surveyed the inside before opening the door. I was in luck, but I couldn't decide whether it was good or bad.

There wasn't a soul in the place except for the employees, and that gave me an idea.

Walking in, I found myself in a very standard-ish McDonald's. Long counter up front, an electronic ordering kiosk (!—That was new, or at least new to me) back from the counter about ten, fifteen feet. The menu looked a few degrees off what I would have seen in an American location, but that was fine. My stomach was rumbling again, and I was determined to get whatever I could get here, and be quite content with it. I could already smell the fries, and they smelled…mmm…good.

I slid on up to the counter after making sure there truly was no one here out in the main restaurant. I didn't want to pretend I had very long, because a customer could have been beelining toward me right now, heading for their normal morning coffee and inevitable rendezvous with troublesome destiny (i.e., my fist if they were unlucky).

Looking around like my head was on a swivel, I sauntered up to the counter. There was definitely someone back there, but I had a feeling that with the ordering kiosk, they were maybe just making food or taking drive-thru orders. I heard them humming a happy song, and it sounded a little like Taylor Swift's Shake it Off. It was a good choice, unlike deciding to come to work this morning.

I jumped the counter and suddenly I was in the Employees Only area of the McD's. I didn't have time to reflect on my rulebreaking though, because I hurried back behind the equipment—fryers and whatnot—to find an employee working with their back turned and oblivious to my approach.

Drawing a deep breath, I fell on them immediately, seizing hold of them by the neck. I realized a little late that the employee in question was a dude, albeit a shorter one. I didn't let him turn around, clutching him firmly by the back of the neck the way you might grab hold of a particularly disobedient and struggling cat. My hand was squarely on his skin, and I held him tight as he screamed for the next few seconds until my power kicked in.

There was no nice way to do what I was doing, or at least no nice way that didn't involve me being a stereotypical succubus seductress, and that just wasn't going to happen, so I woman'd up. It didn't take more than a few seconds for me to brainhack him, removing his memory of this encounter as I lifted him and positioned him back toward the front of the service area. That done, I gave him a little shove forward and he toppled over, missing the memory of why he'd fallen—it was a pretty traumatic thing, being assaulted from behind, after all—as well as his memory of what had happened to his cell phone and his favorite hoodie, both of which I now knew were in the employee break-room just between the kitchen and building's rear exit.

Sweeping out of the kitchen as I heard the guy I'd assaulted swearing at his unexpected fall, I tried to creep as quietly as I could, snatching a sandwich off the rack as I went. I hit up his locker and "borrowed" his cell phone and hoodie, slipping on the latter and unlocking the former with the passcode I'd stolen from his mind. I felt some mild discomfort at my act of Robin Hooding his stuff, but unfortunately his life wasn't in danger from lacking a cell phone and a disguise, while mine very much was.

I headed out to the road, and started walking along the sidewalk, pretending I was just another modern day zombie, my face stuck in my phone, a McD's bacon, egg and cheese—British bacon, so basically ham—bagel in hand, and my hood up high to block anyone from seeing my now-ratty hair. I stared at the screen as I punched up a map of Edinburgh first. The GPS locked onto me, and boom! Now I knew where I was.

Then I got to work on the secondary problem, my feet tapping along the city sidewalk, the green row of hedges across the street slowly lighting up in the dawn. I pulled up a train schedule for Scotrail, trying to figure out how the service worked from Edinburgh to York as I munched on my sandwich, which was the first thing of reasonable healthful benefit I'd eaten in quite a while. Which was sad to say.

What I found was interesting, and took a little map study to work out. The easiest path from Edinburgh to York actually went quite a bit east out of Edinburgh and then hooked south through Berwick-upon-Tweed (what a funny name), Newcastle upon Tyne, and so on, down to York. Travel time looked to be about two and a half hours, which wasn't terrible if I could hide on top of a carriage during the whole trip.

When I checked the GPS, it said I was 1.4 miles walk from Waverly Station, which was the closest and the one the train from York departed from. I wondered if there was a closer station, but I couldn't see it on my map, and the schedule I'd gotten for this one trip seemed to suggest there were no other local stops. Of course, the website wasn't the most navigable I'd ever seen, especially for a Luddite like me, so that wasn't a definite guarantee or anything. Still, 1.4 miles was nothing, really.

I picked up my pace, continuing to use the phone as cover even though I was no longer looking at the screen. Luckily for me, the fast food employee had charged the thing fairly recently, giving me a nice 95% charge to work with. The last thing I needed right now was for it to go dead on me when I might actually need it. I figured right about the time it died or around noon today, I'd need to chuck it, because my mark would get wise to its disappearance and either report it stolen or cancel the service. One of those was much worse than the other, assuming the police took time to investigate its usage. They probably wouldn't, but when confronted with a city that seemed to be run by Rose and which promised horrible death should I be found…who would want to take the chance of being found out?

Keeping my head down and my eyes sweeping for trouble was an easy enough thing to do. The city air was chill and coming alive, the purple sky turning gradually more orange. My heart was hammering in my chest as I looked around surreptitiously. The traffic on the road steadily increased as time wore on, and I was stuck to a human walking speed to avoid making trouble by revealing myself as a meta by breaking into a car-speed sprint.

According to the map app, it was going to take me about thirty minutes to walk to Waverly, and I was going to get to pass by the Queen's house. Yay, scenery. Hopefully they didn't take their security too seriously, because getting caught out in front of Holyrood House would be embarrassing.

I stalked along Lower London Road, according to the map, which then said it turned into Kirkwood Place. I was passing four-story apartments now on my left, rows of cars parked in every single space. The city was starting to wake, and that was bad news for me, in a way. I might have looked a little more unusual skulking along in the dark, but there were fewer eyes to scrutinize and take notice of me. That would have been a plus, especially given how many people were looking for me right now.

Heading up the hill, I had to hang a slight right at the split of the road, passing a beige apartment building. This area looked to be in good repair overall, but was desperately quiet in a way I didn't care for. The hum of cars in the distance made it seem like an aura of menace hung over the city. Trees rustled in the wind every now and again.

Someone spoke behind me, and a door slammed. My pulse spiked, and I looked back. Just a couple guys coming out of a flat, laughing and talking to one another. They didn't seem like zombies working for Rose, but then, maybe they wouldn't have. They went straight to a car and got it, driving past me without so much as a look a moment later.

My heart rate slowed. If I didn't get out of Scotland with Reed, this was going to be the new normal. Always fearing the next corner, the next person I passed. Always worrying what was waiting for me just over the horizon, in the next five minutes, and the five after that.

That kind of certainty was a taste of fear I hadn't known in a long time.

It had been slowly ratcheting up the last few months before I'd left America. It had hit what I thought was the fever pitch when President Harmon had sent the entire US law enforcement and military infrastructure after me, but then that had died down for a while after I'd beaten Harmon.

When it kicked into high gear again after the LA explosion…I'd left. I'd thought I'd found a way to take the heat off by coming to the UK.

Now I was in Scotland, disempowered, with the entire law enforcement apparatus after me, nary a friend in sight and scarcely in contact (Reed being the exception) and somehow things had, once again, gotten ever so much worse.

A car went by, and I thought I saw a face staring out at me.

I looked, out of habit, and realized after one heart-stopping moment that it was a kid looking out a car's back window. I sighed, the wind rushing through the trees to my right, and kept walking.

I checked my phone. Now I was on Abbeyhill. Road? Street? The app didn't say, and I didn't care. I was following the blue line and trying to ignore the fact that I was having to walk under a shadowy, forbidding underpass that lasted only twenty or so feet. That there was nowhere for a threat to hide beneath it mattered little. Somehow, walking in shadow was now cause for fresh worry.

But in fairness…almost everything was cause for fresh worry right now.

I walked a few minutes more, through some tight spaces, below an even darker underpass that caused my little heart to pitter-patter wildly. Once more, no harm came to me, though the sound of a bus shifting right as it went by would have caused me to explode in flame if I'd still had that power. As it was, it just almost caused me to lose bladder control. Which was kind of the opposite of fire, really.

It took me another few minutes of following Abbeyhill to reach Holyrood House and Scottish parliament. I recognized the latter from overflying it when I'd been in Edinburgh a few days earlier, and it still looked like a deconstructed and reconstructed pile of jangly, messed-up angles. I wasn't sure who the architect was on it, but it felt like they might have taken a lot of inspiration from Pablo Picasso. And maybe some LSD, too.

I watched the guards and police outside the parliament building with a wary eye. The last thing I needed at this point was to get my ass snared in a normal security perimeter for a high security location like this. Talk about your avoidable acts of incompetence.

Taking the fork onto Calton Road, I got a slightly queasy feeling as I checked out the map. I hadn't intended it this way, but my route was taking me past the Calton Heights Burial

Ground, where Rose and I had enjoyed (or rather, she'd enjoyed and I'd gotten my ass kicked) our last climactic showdown before she'd done the metahuman version of spaying me.

The mere knowledge that I was approaching this place was bad enough, but the road I was taking to get there was making it so much worse. The segment of Calton Road I was walking along was surrounded on the right by a high stone wall that looked like it was a remnant from the 1700s or earlier, a product of old Edinburgh at its finest, an archaeological masterpiece from the days of yore.

It was also boxing me in on that side. Rows of flats were providing a similar service on my left, which was disquieting in that if Rose came thundering down on me out of the blue right now, I had nowhere to go but maybe into an apartment building in hopes of fleeing out a window or door out the back. Not the surest of escape routes, and when you're fleeing for your life, any uncertainty save for that of capture is generally bad. Because it can lead to capture.

The surroundings added another tremble to my heart as I walked. This was the kind of worry I didn't really need, the knowledge that not only was I in a hostile city, but my escape options were severely limited. If the cops pulled in front of me and behind right now, I was out of luck. Block the street over through the apartment buildings and I was even more high and dry.

None of this was good news, and it was the sort of thing that my brain liked to dwell on and imagine, doing me surprisingly few favors in the process.

Passing a black iron gate to my right, a little break in the wall, I was treated with a view of the Burial Ground.

My stomach dropped to my feet, lurching, as I couldn't keep myself from stealing a glance inside.

There was a fair amount of damage from my battle with Frankie and my subsequent ass-kicking by Rose. I didn't dwell, just taking a mental snapshot of what I could see and moving on, but…

It was enough. Enough to send my stomach swirling and churning.

I could almost feel the trauma, the event, like it was inside me, welling up, almost close enough to touch. I didn't cry out in alarm, but I did feel some small measure of nausea as I remembered lying there, staring at the black sky, head swimming, as Rose held her hands to me, my skin burning like someone had lit it afire.

The block wall passed to my right, and I tried to stare at the individual blocks of stone as I quickened my pace. I kept it in the realm of human possibility, breaking into a light jog. I saw movement ahead, someone walking past out of a gateway from another round of flats. They caught sight of me and stared for a moment, and I realized I wasn't staring down at my phone anymore.

I'm just a jogger, I thought, trying to match my form to what I'd seen from people who I'd seen running in the past. I clutched my phone, kept my head down, tried not to stare at the person who was now watching me intently.

Shit.

I passed them as they raised their phone to their ear, and I listened intently as they made a call, waiting to see if it was going to be something bad. I was almost prepared, mentally, to assault this person—a guy, I realized dimly, still trying not to look directly at him—if he said something that sounded like he was dropping a dime on my location.

He said something about being late for work but being on his way now, and I didn't relax when I heard it. I had to keep jogging on, past the building, which was replaced with a short wall on my right and the hill leading up to Calton Heights. The smell of fresh dirt reached me here, where Frankie's attacks had churned up the ground inside the cemetery. Taller buildings with a more commercial bent were springing up on my left now as I got deeper and deeper into the city proper.

The buildings started to blend together as my mind raced, worrying about what was happening, what I was seeing. There were more people now, all along Calton Road. According to the map app, I was now only five minutes from Waverly Station, which presented another question: What the hell was I going to do when I got there?

It wasn't like I could just board the train, after all.

On the other hand…I was pretty sure the ticket kiosks for these stations were unmanned. If I could keep my head down, maybe…

No. Too dangerous. If my ticket got checked in the train—which was likely—I'd probably be recognized and caught in a hot second. Then I'd be trapped in a train with plenty of time for the staff to call the cops and whoever else.

Plus, I didn't exactly have a ton of money with which to buy a ticket. That was hardly an insurmountable problem, but still…

I glanced back, and once again, my stomach dropped. There were people behind me, walking extremely quietly. It wasn't just one or two, either; it was a whole heap, a mob, like twenty or thirty.

Leading them was a big man with light blond hair, fair-skinned, with a leather jacket and a pair of jeans that were so ragged I doubted they'd ever seen better days. They might have just started out shit and gotten progressively worse over time until now, where they lacked even the structural integrity of a collapsing building.

When he saw me looking, we made brief eye contact, and a spark of recognition in his eyes gave way to a predatory grin.

Yep, he saw me.

Yep, he knew who I was.

Two minutes run from Waverly Station and I had a mob behind me, led by someone who was actively seeking me.

Edinburgh, you've screwed me again, I thought as I broke into a run, desperately trying to reach the train station, and whatever faint hope of freedom it held, before they caught me, hoping against hope I could lose them in the crowds.

29.

Reed

The plane cruised steadily at about 35,000 feet, the gentle hum you might expect in a commercial flight a little louder on the smaller aircraft. The engines roared outside, taking in air and forcing it out the back in great jets, slipping along at over four hundred miles an hour.

I could the feel disturbance (not in the Force) created by the engines. I hadn't really been able to before Harmon had overclocked my powers, but now I felt it keenly, just another added benefit of the expansion of my abilities. I glanced across the Gulfstream's aisle at Scott, who was pensive, staring straight ahead at the seat in front of him. I wondered how keenly he could feel the moisture in the air—or maybe lack thereof at this altitude.

Everybody was engaged in some kind of avoidance behavior. Distraction was the king of pursuits for those of us waiting for whatever might happen once we reached York. It wasn't that we expected hostilities, but given what Sienna had told me...

Well, I'd warned them all to be prepared, and it looked like most of them were taking the hint.

Except Friday and Kat. They were sleeping. And one of them was snoring. (Kat, surprisingly.)

"The sleep of the innocent, huh?" Chase chucked a thumb

at Friday and sat down next to me in the empty seat that everyone else had left abandoned. It was like they could sense my mood, or maybe read the *'F off'* written all over my face.

"You've known him longer than I have," I said with a little amusement. "How innocent does Friday strike you?"

"I never knew him as Friday until I came here," Chase said. "What's that all about?"

"Hell if I know," I said with a shrug. "I think Sienna came up with it. Guy Friday or something, because he used to follow our old boss around so close that if Phillips stopped too abruptly, Friday would have fallen in."

"That's interesting," Chase said, looking back over her shoulder at where Friday sat alone, but hopefully for different reasons than me. His head was back, his mouth was open, and he looked pretty much dead to the world.

"As interesting as anything related to Friday can be, I guess," I said.

"Can I ask you something?" Chase showed her nervousness by scratching her arm. "Everyone else on this thing—" she just plunged right ahead without waiting for my answer on the previous question "—is all full of hearty conviction that they're running into a worthy cause. Can I just ask…is there something I'm missing about Sienna and this whole Eden Prairie thing? Keeping in mind I'm the new girl, and don't really, uh, know anyone that well yet, so I miss all the good gossip."

"The Eden Prairie thing wasn't Sienna's fault," I said, letting my weariness seep out in the form of a story. It wasn't a story I tended to tell very often, mainly because no one seemed to want to hear it. "The Supreme Court issued a ruling—probably influenced by President Harmon, who hated Sienna—that turned loose all those criminal metas she'd put away over the last few years—"

"Yep," Chase said. "I read about that. But, I mean, the official reports talked about her losing her damned mind and nuking a commercial park filled with reporters and innocent people."

"And killing all those criminals she'd released," I said, "who'd turned up at our office for a spontaneous protest in the middle of the night, masquerading as a lynch mob. One of them turned the reporters into a bunch of feral animals, sent them after her. She broke their control, but she got overwhelmed by all those criminals afterward, and…they had her down, so she…went off like a bomb, I guess."

"Huh," Chase said. "No wonder the LA thing went over like a lead balloon. I was kinda out of the country working when the Eden Prairie deal went down."

"They didn't have the internet where you were?" I asked with a snarky smile.

"Not at that time, no," she said, utterly serious. "So…if Sienna dusted those crooks in self-defense, why is she still public enemy number one?"

"Because President Harmon was a meta running a scheme to take over the world by boosting his metahuman telepathic powers so he could mind-control everyone." She raised an eyebrow, then the other, and I felt compelled to further explain. "That…sounds really stupid when you just blurt it out that way, doesn't it?"

"Little farfetched, yeah," she admitted. "Boosted powers? Telepathic president? Man…you people deal with some weird stuff."

"You can say that again."

Chase got a little gleam of mischief in her eye. "You people deal—"

"We do, we really do," I said, nodding along.

"So why is everyone avoiding you like you're a black hole?" Chase asked. "Like you're a bomb on the plane. Or a snake on a plane."

"Probably because Samuel L. Jackson isn't around to announce me as such," I said, looking around for J.J. He'd supply the Samuel L. Jackson line if he heard Chase reference it, I was sure of that much. "Look, Chase…"

"Oh, man. Is this the part where you shut me out because

this isn't any of my business?"

I took a deep breath, biting down that first instinct, because…it kinda was her business. "No," I said. "You're riding into this storm with us, so…it's totally your business now. The reason they're avoiding me is probably—and I'm just guessing here—because I'm projecting a black hole, and no one wants to ask how I really feel, even though they can hear us talking."

"As usual, you're amazingly self-aware," Veronika announced from a couple rows back. "You keep it up and you'll be self-actualizing in no time."

"That sounds dirty," Friday said. In his sleep, I think.

"We're having to sneak into the UK," I said, looking Chase right in the eyes. "Do you know why?"

"They've got a metahuman ban," she said. "The whole EU does." She laughed grimly. "I've had to dodge it for years for work."

"Do you know how it happened?" I asked, smacking my lips. She shrugged. "Out of the country and away from the internet when it went down?" She didn't react save for a subtle hardening of her attitude to tell me she wasn't amused. "Fine, I'll tell you—it's because I went to Rome and got into a fight just outside the Vatican with a meta who wanted to create a nation state of his own in Italy, starting with killing the Pope and taking over the Holy See to make it his evil fortress."

Chase's eyes widened subtly. "Seriously? That plan? The weirdest shit. Grandiose much?"

"I don't choose my own villains," I said with a sigh. "Anyway, I stopped these guys, with help from, uh, the Goddess Diana and another Poseidon who was a priest. But it was a pretty ugly incident, and so the EU decided they'd had about enough of meta shenanigans, and just slapped a blanket ban on us. It was still pretty early days for our kind being out, and they'd lost most of their meta population in the war, so…anyway. Meta ban. It's on me." I thumped my chest lightly. "So anyway…when we get to York…"

"We're going to have to kinda…lay low, aren't we?" she asked, getting it.

"Like a snake on—not a plane—its belly." I leaned back in my seat. "This rescue mission? Would have been a lot easier if not for my mess in Italy a few years back. So, you want to know why people are avoiding me? It's because I'm a pit of worry for my sister, who I have the luxury of knowing is innocent, and who is as powerless as she's been since the end of the war, is trapped behind enemy lines, basically, in an EU country, and might not even make it to the rendezvous. But if she does," I said, finally drawing close to the grey crux of worry that was hanging around my neck right now, "I don't know that we're going to easily be able to hang out waiting for her, because the minute we pop off this plane, if anyone recognizes us—"

"We're in the soup," Chase said, nodding along. "And not good soup either, like chicken and wild rice. Probably bad soup, like that thin, crappy tomato stuff that tastes like watered down ketchup."

"Close enough," I said, giving her that one. And I just let her think it over, as I looked out the window and saw the coast on the horizon.

We're coming, Sienna, I thought, but didn't dare say aloud for fear someone would hear me and think—I dunno, decently of me, maybe. And for fear that maybe…in spite of all the things she'd done wrong in her life…it would be my screw-up that ultimately killed my sister's chance to escape the UK.

And just maybe…kill her, too.

30.

Sienna

I was screwed over by Edinburgh again, and I didn't really have a lot of options available to me that I liked.

The mob behind me broke into a run as soon as I saw them, so, naturally, I broke into a run too, pounding down the street at meta speed, cries of angry and disgruntled people starting to bellow out from behind me. Waverly Station was right ahead, and there was no point in politely pretending I wasn't a meta when a randomly assembled street gang of people dressed in...

Whoa.

While my lead pursuer might have been dressed in quite the, ah...aesthetically displeasing ensemble, what with the shredded jeans and all, his fellow members of the Kill Sienna Gang were not following his fashion example. I saw men in suits, women dressed for the office, two people looking like they were homeless, someone who might well have been on their way to a punk rock concert...

I was about to be killed by horde of Edinburghers who probably wouldn't have associated with each other under normal circumstances. Yay for bringing people together. I was a unifier.

Waverly's triangular roof stuck up straight ahead, and I tried to decide whether it'd be better to leap the wall and try to hide in the crowd or dodge this lot and circle around to the main entrance. Hopefully they hadn't hacked my stolen phone (a very Jamal thing to do, but hopefully not a very Rose one) because if so, the damned game was up on my current destination and also my final one.

My boots thudded against the sidewalk and I shoved past an old lady wearing a head scarf. She let out a cry of shock as I jetted past, almost knocking her over just by momentum. I looked back to see her astounded face...

And also my tattered jeans pursuer running a hell of a lot faster than a normal human would, leaving the rest of the angry mob behind.

Okay, well, that gave me something to work with. I might be able to outrun most of them if I could just get rid of this guy.

I decided, screw it, and vaulted the wall, finding myself landing in the Waverly Station carpark. That seemed like a fine option for a game of hide and seek, which was what I was planning to play with Mr. Blonde. I knew the next train to York was leaving in twenty or thirty minutes, but that was a long time to try and dodge him.

I cursed when I landed, because not only did it hurt, but this wasn't actually a car park at all. I must have misread the sign, because instead I found myself in a passenger drop-off zone. I could even see a damned train, though it was just behind a fence.

Shiiiiiiit. This did not help at all, really.

Deciding there was not a lot of point in being coy, I broke for the train and sprinted. With a short, controlled leap, I made it over the fence into Waverly proper, and found myself not on a platform. I was on the damned tracks, and there was a train in front of me, pulling slowly into the station, driver gawking at me open-mouthed.

Getting run over slowly might have been a metaphor for my life of late, but it wasn't really going to work for me, so I sucked it up, ignored the pain in my ankle, and leapt again, skittering over the roof of the train, staying below the arched glass that made up the ceiling to the station, and slid off onto the platform on the other side.

I almost landed on a guy who looked at me with visible alarm. "Where'd you come from?" he asked in thick Scottish.

"My mom said heaven, but everyone else says hell," I quipped, and started to walk away like my little leap over a train was nothing. "Actually, my mom probably agreed with everyone else, now that I think about it." I turned and started to run down the platform. This was not the train I was looking for. This one was heading for Inverness.

A grunt behind me caused me to turn from my run. The blonde man had landed, and he'd done so on that poor, unsuspecting Scot who'd asked me where I'd come from. Mr. Blonde was up in a hot second, grimacing in pain from landing his ass on the pedestrian's head or something, I imagined.

For my part, I suspected the getting was about as good as it was going to get, provided I wanted to finish this incident quickly and not start another. I leapt over the next train and Mr. Blonde followed, about ten yards back from me. As I slid over the roof of the carriage, I knew what I was looking for–

An empty aisle or space between trains where I could pull out my old ass-kicking skills and put old Blondey down hard so I could catch a train. Maybe I'd even change up my look by borrowing his shirt. My hoodie was probably well-identified by this point, after all, so it wasn't going to function as an effective disguise for much longer.

I came sliding off the train and down onto the tracks below. I landed with all the grace of a sack of potatoes, but Mr. Blonde didn't do much better. I wondered if there was a third rail here, brimming with electricity and ready to bring this fight to a shocking close. I resolved not to touch any of the rails, though that would be a hard resolution to enforce if I got into a scuffle. I'd been shocked to death before though, and had no wish to reprise that particular exit from the mortal coil.

Blondey landed a little more solidly than I did, letting out another grunt as he pulled himself to standing. He was staring at me with a look of such intensity that I couldn't help but comment on it.

"What's the matter?" I asked, feeling a little tingle in my heart, in my legs, in my guts, but unwilling to show it to one of Rose's flunkies. "They don't make laxatives in Scotland?" I mimed his expression. "I mean, you look like you need to sit down and pop a squat, really take a load off, bro—"

He glared at me, then cast a look over his shoulder at the purple- and blue-painted train car behind him. I followed his gaze, because when you're fighting a meta and you don't know their power, it's not wise to look away from their eyeline, cuz odds were—

Yep. The train wall flexed and bowed, metal squealing in a loud echo through the vast open spaces in Waverly Station. The side of the train started to swell like a pimple, growing larger and more distorted the longer he stared at it. Within a few seconds it looked like it was ready to explode. "Uh oh," I said, and waited until the last second before—

It popped like a zit and shrapnel came shooting at me, little fragments of metal that filled the air like buckshot. I threw myself back up on the platform, but that wasn't exactly cover. I was gonna hoof it to one of the nearby benches, but a quick look back over my shoulder made it obvious that Mr. Blonde had now taken control of these fragments of metal and was steering them like tiny bullets.

At me.

I dodged them as they shot by. Well, most of them. A few little shards caught me on the arm and shredded my hoodie sleeve like it was nothing. I sucked in a pained breath, realizing that no, the good times were indeed not going to roll right now. I was going to roll, though, and I did, going low and sliding under a bench before coming up on the other side, breathing a little heavily.

The bench slid away along the concrete with a screech as Mr. Blonde worked his power on it. It skittered away, revealing me lying flat on my chest. "Oh, man," I muttered, popping back to my feet in an improvised flip that left a trail of blood on the concrete floor.

Blondey grinned and then brought the flotilla of makeshift bullets at me again, hard and fast, and this time I flung myself backward, just fell and caught myself in a bridge, hoping that he'd gotten them moving too fast to steer them into me.

He had, more or less. The "more or less" being two or three fragments that sliced across my exposed midriff and made me fall out of my bridge. I landed on my back, and propelled myself back to my feet with a quick shoulder roll.

"I want your blood," Blondey said, grinning like a shark who smelled—well, blood in the water. He was advancing on me, and I'd been in enough fights to recognize a distraction when I saw one. He still had that angry swarm of shrapnel, after all, like his own personal squadron of bullet bees, and unfortunately they did not buzz.

"A lot of people have wanted that over the years," I said, trying to get control of my breathing. The run, the jumps, this fight…none of it was proceeding as well as I might have hoped. I looked around the platform, hoping for something, anything I could use as a weapon. There were green-painted steel poles holding up the electronic screens to announce the trains, and a few advertisements on those big, back-lit screens. Everything in sight had metal in it, and thus would make a poor weapon against this guy. "You guys should consider just scheduling a blood drive and inviting me. I'd totally donate, since it's for a good cause—"

I heard the shrapnel rather than saw it, since it was coming in hot at my six o'clock, and I threw myself forward. I had high hopes that he'd have to stop it before it completely perforated him—actually, I hoped he'd suck at controlling it and that would solve my problem for me by ripping him to shreds with his own petard—and thus lose track of me for critical seconds wherein I would—

Coming to my feet, I was ready to make my attack. Except

I'd executed a forward roll, and hadn't been able to plot out my approach exactly. I wasn't going to come at him directly, because I didn't want to step into the path of the shrapnel, so I'd gone sideways left, at a forty-five-degree angle, figuring I'd come back at him hard from just outside the shrapnel cloud—

Except he'd stopped the shrapnel cloud and spread it out above me, something I didn't realize until I started to come to my feet and felt a mighty stinging right at the top of my head—

I'd jumped right into the metal shards, hanging perfectly immobile right above me like a minefield.

Blood sluiced down my face and I stopped my upward movement as soon as I felt the sharp pain. It was a little too late though, because I hit another shard with my shoulder, another with the side of my ear, and another sliced right down the back of my head.

I hit the ground hard, blinded by both my blood and the astounding level of pain that comes from a partial skull fracture. I'd heard the bone crack upon impact with the shard I hit most directly, and it had done some serious damage. I landed on my tailbone, adding another element of agony, which ran up my back like someone had pulled the pain fire alarm and it was ringing all up and down my body.

I didn't even realize how badly I'd been hurt until a few seconds later, when Blondey was already on top of me, a dozen other people around him. The mob had caught up to us while I'd apparently been stunned out of my senses.

They surrounded me, swarming me, and Mr. Blonde and his grin were the most frightening part of it all. They closed in, and all I could see were shadows blotting out the sunlight coming in from the windows above as hands started to grab at me, angry, like the shrapnel, intent on tearing me apart.

31.

I was being grabbed by a hundred hands, roughly, angrily, fingers digging in, and somehow I knew that when they delivered me to Rose, it didn't necessarily guarantee I'd be conscious or in good condition. I might have pieces missing, because Rose would have told them I could heal from just about anything they did to me.

Unfortunately, this knowledge of my healing ability was not as much of a consolation to me as you might think.

There was so much blood in my eyes I could scarcely see. It ran down my face, covering my vision like a crimson cloud, finding my nose and pooling on my upper lip, a metallic scent I couldn't gag away from. My body hurt everywhere, but the top of the skull in particular was screaming from what had happened to it.

Someone kicked me, and that set the whole ball of the mob beatdown rolling. I had just started to come back to myself when the punches began to land, and none of them were what I would call gentle. They were hardly the practiced blows of a professional boxer, but there were a lot of them, and what they lacked in quality they damned sure made up for in quantity.

I wasn't the type to lie there and take a beating though, so I swept out an arm, blindly, but with all my strength, and heard the satisfying crack of someone's knee joint bending in a way it shouldn't have. I heaved out in the other direction and was rewarded with another cry as I caught another knee and turned it wrongside-right, probably sending their kneecap to the back of their leg in the process.

That lessened the assault on two sides for a second, because the two people whose knees I'd broken fell back into their mob brethren, probably surprising them or knocking them off balance. I didn't care which, so long as they stopped for a freaking second.

Lashing out with my feet, I did a little breakdance maneuver just as someone kicked me hard in the thigh. It kinda sent a numb tingle down my leg, but I didn't need to feel it in order to dish out harm with it. I swung my legs around in a high-speed, vicious sweep, and was rewarded with grunts as I took the legs from under three or four people. The thud they made as they landed was a satisfaction all its own, and I swirled my legs up above my own head, kicking another couple people and forcing them to step back, giving me enough room to leap, somewhat blindly, to my feet.

I wiped the blood out of my eyes and got probably sixty percent of it, if that. I got enough of it that I could see again, albeit not well. My head was woozy from the skull trauma, I was still surrounded by a mob, and I'd mostly just made them take a step back, not driven them off. Driving them off was going to be harder, especially if they were somehow mind-controlled by Rose.

Even the injured were pulling themselves back up, looking at me with loathing and fury, angry and ready to attack. They were about a quarter of a second from surging at me like a rising tide.

I threw myself into their midst and swung with everything I had. Not one to wait for the attack to come rolling in, I seized the initiative and started dishing out skull fractures of my own. Screams of pain cut the air in Waverly Station, and I was back in the beatdown business, selling but taking no returns. I popped one guy in the jaw so hard he'd be drinking through a straw for a while, caught another one in the stomach so hard he bowled over the three people behind him.

Spinning because I sensed others closing on me from the rear, I caught two eager beavers with a spinning kick, my heel just about sheering their faces off and sending them flying to the side and into a clutch of assholes swarming at me. This wasn't a fair fight—for them—but if they kept at me in a zombie horde, I wasn't going to be able to put off the pain that was closing in on me forever, and they'd notch a win by sheer numbers alone.

I caught a glimpse of Mr. Blonde behind a couple of these jobbers that were coming at me in waves. He was lifting his hands, and I didn't like the look of that, so I kicked the only non-metallic weapon on the platform at him—one of his mob co-conspirators.

Mr. Blonde's eyes got big right before this dude with a bowl cut went sailing into his face. As a succubus, I was still faster and stronger than most other metas, and I could send a bastard at him pretty quick. He didn't quite dodge in time, and ended up catching a shoulder to the nose, which slowed his roll.

"This has been fun, guys," I said, hearing a train squealing a couple rows over. I slapped a big guy right in the face and shoved him, hard, against a little crowd behind him, bowling them all over. "Let's never do this again." I hurled myself forward and back down onto the tracks, wiping blood again as I heard the cries of the mob, a kind of guttural screaming, rise behind me.

I leapt the next train, landing on the roof and sweeping a quick look over the entire station. Apparently, station personnel had been oblivious to the rumble going on in their midst, because everywhere else in the station, business looked like it was proceeding as usual. A train was pulling out, and I was a little too disoriented at first to figure out which way it was even going.

Hell, I didn't care. I needed to be anywhere but here.

Vaulting to the next train and then down onto the platform beneath, I realized I had about fifty yards and two more trains to leap before I could get there. I didn't know what Mr. Blonde's recovery time was, but I had a bad feeling it wasn't going to be forever, which would have been a nice change from the way my luck had been running these last few days.

Screams from the mob got my attention as I dismounted and hustled across the wide platform ahead of me. They got louder when they saw me, like tiny, angry ferrets when they— I dunno, saw ferret food. They came streaming after me, a little too slow, thankfully.

I jumped the last train and started to hop over to the one pulling out when something whistled behind me. I threw myself down and a glittering swarm of metal bees shot over me. That damned shrapnel cloud again. It hovered there, closing slowly down, inching toward me where I lay, flat, against the train roof.

The son of a bitch had just imprisoned me; I couldn't sit up, couldn't get up, and couldn't even roll to the side without ripping myself to shreds on his immobile minefield.

Dammit.

"STOP!" a woman's voice cracked through the station, and it had that aura of command that expected to be obeyed. It also had an accent, and I damned near had a cow right there, because I thought it was Rose.

The metal fragments came tinkling down around me, dropping in my face and on my arms, sprinkling me like a metallic rain. Gently, too, not like bullets at all.

I looked up and found the little minefield gone, the train's rattling loud in my ears as the one next to me continued to chug its way out of the station. There were only a few cars left and then it'd be gone, leaving me behind to face the mob, as well as Rose—

I sat up and looked across the platform. Most of the mob had stopped moving, a flow of people that had congealed in a mass, now looking back toward the origin of the shout, seeking direction. I stared across the platform and saw a woman standing there, just a thin slip of a girl, strawberry blond—

Not a redhead.

Not Rose.

She was standing next to Mr. Blonde, who looked like he was about to drop to one knee and propose. Other guys from the mob were there too, standing before her as though she were Queen Guinevere and they were about to swear their swords to her.

A woman's face, purple with fury, popped up over the edge of the train nearest me, screaming as she clawed her way up to me, and, without thinking, I punched her in the nose. Not too hard, but she plummeted off the side of the train and thumped to the concrete ground below.

I stared at the blond woman in the distance, and she stared back at me. She raised a hand, and that was all I had time for.

I leapt onto the departing train, catching the last car right before it pulled out of the station, clattering down the tracks to a destination I didn't even know.

32.

I didn't ride that train for very long, because it became quickly apparent that I was heading west, the opposite of where I wanted to go. My stolen cell phone had been wrecked during the great Sienna beatdown back in the station, which left me with only the knowledge I'd Googled before I lost it—that the train to York went east, through Berwick-upon-Tweed and Newcastle upon Tyne (seriously, these names).

That meant I was in the wrong place, heading the wrong direction, so as soon as I saw a train passing in the other direction, probably only a mile from the station, I hopped over immediately, as lightly as I could, and lay as flat as a pancake upon the roof of the carriage.

We pulled back into Waverly a few minutes later, and the place was all abuzz. I rolled over as the train doors whooshed open and people began to stream out. In the distance I could see a big, black sign with yellow LED bulbs telling me where each train was going. To get to York, I'd need a different train, probably on the other side of the station given my luck.

When I studied the list, and then my platform number, I realized I had gotten a break—a very small one; the platform I was seeking was only two down, and the next train to York via Berwick and Newcastle was only ten minutes from departing.

I lay on the roof of that train, flat as I could, for nine of the longest minutes of my life.

Little breaks of conversation reached me, stuff about how there'd been a fight on the other platform, probably a gang or something, but they'd cleared out as soon as they heard the boys and girls in blue coming. Boys and girls in yellow vests, I reckoned, given what I'd seen of Police Scotland. It was a fun little bit of gossip, but fortunately I didn't hear the name "Sienna Nealon" mentioned, so that was a plus.

The station announcement started to warn me that the train for York was departing. I leaned over; the platform next to me had more or less cleared, so I rolled off and landed lightly on the concrete, looking around as surreptitiously as one can look when you're trying to figure out if a mob of angry, mind-controlled people is lurking somewhere, waiting to tear you apart.

I made my way slowly toward the train to York, trying to act casual and probably failing because I was all bloody and my sleeve was dangling on my right side where Mr. Blonde had torn it to pieces with his metal powers. Lucky for me he was pretty weak, comparatively, or he might have just hurled a few trains onto me and called it a day.

The York-bound train started to pull out of the station just as I was moseying up. There was no sign of security personnel, and no one was waiting here now, so I started to slowly walk the length of the platform as the train started to chug out. I looked away from the windows, where the passengers were sitting, some of them staring out but most of them looking at books or their phones.

I waited again until the last car, and then, with a look back to make sure no one was watching—they weren't, the platform was clear—I took a running start and leapt onto the top of the train to York, going flat as quickly as possible.

With any luck, that mob had run back to Rose and told her I was headed west while now I was going east. Of course, that girl—the one who waved at me—she was an odd addition to this formula. It had almost been like she'd pulled them off of me, but…if she had, it was probably only to keep them from murdering me into tiny pieces before Rose got her chance.

No, everybody still hated me and either wanted me dead or wished me serious ill, that I was pretty sure of, this blond girl notwithstanding.

The train rattled and rolled over the Scottish countryside, and I watched it go by for a while before I closed my eyes, and let the rough ride and the sound of the rails sing me off to sleep.

33.

The ride to York was long and breezy, the train rolling along under a grey sky. No chance of a sunburn for my pale skin here; I was going to bask in the lack of warmth atop the rattling carriage as I waited for it to get to its destination.

We passed through Berwick-upon-Tweed, I presumed, then Newcastle upon Tyne, the cities rolling by like a slightly older version of what you'd find in the heartland of America, but with an old-country kind of feel to them. The stylistic differences were striking, and it drove the point in like a stake to my heart that I was far from home and my return was still uncertain.

Rose was out there, somewhere. It was surprising I hadn't seen her show up in Edinburgh, sending that metal-shooting guy in her stead. Of course, Mr. Blonde could have been a meta hired gun, along with the blonde lady, maybe financed by the US government since they were after me. I'd tossed the shattered cell phone I'd stolen just in case, sinking it in a river as we'd rolled past.

My geography of the UK was a little hazy, but I was pretty sure that once we'd passed Berwick we were back in England. I would have let out a little sigh of relief—hell, I might have; I was still breathing heavily—but I wouldn't have been able to hear it over the rattle of the tracks.

York station was a long, barracks-like half-tube, with arching apertures for trains to roll in and roll out. I saw it from a ways off, smaller than Waverly and fairly obvious even before I heard the announcements rolling over the speakers inside the train car declaring we'd reached our destination. The train shuddered to a stop and the doors opened to disgorge the passenger cargo.

I waited, the hum of people moving about a pleasant background noise. No chance of falling asleep now, I thought, my pulse quickening. Some passengers were getting off, others were getting on, and I decided that the time had come for me to make my escape.

Rolling off the back of the train, I once again avoided contacting any of the metal on the tracks, even though I was fairly certain that the power was supplied by an apparatus up top. That done, I jumped casually up onto the platform, drawing only one set of eyes, a frown and a shrug from a woman passing by who didn't look too closely at my face, instead turning her roller suitcase and heading off toward the exit.

I tried to keep my right arm—scene of the worst of the shrapnel injuries, though there were a few good bloodstains on my belly too, coupled with some cuts to my shirt and hoodie—huddled away, as though someone might come by and give it a good slap on the wound. The injuries themselves were just about faded away now, but the blood remained because I lacked a facility to clean myself up.

York Station had already grown quiet, the passengers having filed off quietly, and the ones going to this train already mostly onboard. I walked past people that were largely focused on their smartphones, and was thankful for the lack of scrutiny. I needed a break.

I was still thinking that when I made it to the exit and found someone standing there, waiting for me with a stern look upon his face. Grey hair, a silver mustache, and leaning on a cane like an old British lord or something.

Wexford.

"Hello, Sienna," he said quietly, standing like an oak

planted right in my path. He wore a tired smile, and one that I found—for the moment—incredibly reassuring. "I hear you've run into a spot of difficulty."

34.

Reed

The plane touched down on the tarmac in York with a little bump. I tried to smooth things as much as I could, canceling out the crosswinds that had threatened to buffet the plane on the approach, but our pilot apparently lacked the expert-level skill most of the private plane pilots tended to have, and he bounced us good one time, eliciting not a sound from his meta passengers, who were used to their fair share of bumps in the course of our duties.

Sliding across the tarmac, the Gulfstream hit another bump, this one in the pavement. I cringed, and glanced at Augustus, who shrugged. "Didn't know I was supposed to smooth everything out too," he said. He closed his eyes and concentrated. "There," he said when they opened again, "pavement fixed. That ought to make it a little easier on us the rest of the way."

"Where are we going?" Jamal asked. "Up to a jetway?"

"You know that's not how this private service thing works," Veronika said with a smirk, a whiskey she'd poured during the flight still in hand. "They roll you up to a hangar and bring your car right up to you." She threw a glance at me. "Limo, I hope?"

"We're not staying," I said tightly, because now we were in the dicey part of this op. We'd had no contact with Sienna since the last time I'd slept, which was almost twenty-four hours ago. Or something. The change in time zones and all the waiting we'd done between Texas and Minneapolis and here was throwing me off. "Most of us will stay on the plane."

"I like the way you say 'us,'" Scott said, leaning forward in his seat, "like you're going to be one of the ones who stays."

I swallowed heavily, because he'd heard me right, and I hated that I'd even said it. "I am staying on the plane," I said quietly. "I'm known here. If I go outside and get seen, hell is gonna be descending on us from the UK authorities about ten seconds later. We need to send out people who aren't known here, who aren't known associates of Sienna Nealon." I glanced around the cabin. "Veronika, Colin, Chase...you're up."

"Lucky us," Veronika said, draining the last of her whiskey and getting to her feet. "I'll lead this soiree, ladies." She looked at Colin, who had cocked an eyebrow at her. "You're an honorary lady, Colin. Take that as the compliment it is." She waved them forward and ducked the bulkhead as she headed down the aisle toward the door. "Come on."

"And we just sit here?" Augustus asked, raising an eyebrow at me.

"Not all of us are just sitting," Jamal said, head down on his tablet.

"Copy that," Abby said, her laptop on, well, her lap. "Some of us are working."

"I've got the traffic cams around York and I'm scanning facial recognition," Jamal said. "No sign of Sienna yet."

"He's so good at this," J.J. whispered to Abby. "Why do we even bother to show up?"

"So we can keep tech geeking when he switches from a support class to a mage," Abby said.

"Right," J.J. said. "You're smart and beautiful, did you know that?"

"I'm really more of a druid than a mage, which covers both," Jamal mumbled, but they didn't hear him. I did, and am embarrassed to say that I thought he was pretty dead on with that assessment.

"Anything we need to know before we make like a fetus and head out?" Veronika asked, opening a luggage compartment and pulling out a bag. She knew what she was after, and she'd slid a case out of it seconds later, popping an earphone into her ear and then handing one each to Chase and Colin. When she looked at Colin she said, "Might want to hold that in if you go for a run."

"This is not my first time using one of these," Colin said, getting a little irritable at her constant condescension.

Veronika just smiled back and beckoned him forward as she waited for the flight attendant to open the door now that we were at a stop. "You get off first, before anyone sees you, okay? You're recon. Chase and I are going to hit the ladies' room."

"That's good cover," J.J. said. "Very realistic."

Veronika just smirked. "Of course it is, genius. I actually have to go. You?" She looked at Chase and got a nod. "Yeah, I figured."

"You know we have a bathroom on the plane?" I asked.

Veronika just shrugged. "I got a thing about preferring to have my feet on solid ground if I can. It's a thing." The flight attendant lowered the ramp, and Veronika headed off, a second after Colin whooshed out past them all.

"What...what was that?" the co-pilot asked, his hair blowing over his forehead. Apparently he hadn't been paying attention to our entire conversation, which I realized a little belatedly had been held entirely in the open.

"A strong wind," Veronika deadpanned, and headed out. "We'll be back in a little bit, once the plane's refueled." I'd already talked with the pilot about this, and he was clear on how we were working this: we were parked here until I said otherwise.

"Hm. I'm getting something," Jamal said, staring intently at his screen.

"The mage is a power player," J.J. said. "He has a serious INT bonus, and that gives him a minus five to all hacking attempts."

"I think it's more like minus twenty, honestly," Abby said.

Kat snorted, sighed, and rolled over in her sleep a couple rows back. I had kinda forgotten she was even on the plane, honestly, because she was apparently still on California time.

"What have you got?" I asked, taking up the mantle of the leader by asking the question that Jamal had just begged. I stood up and moved to look at his screen, laying hands on the stitched leather seats as I levered my way over.

"I've got Sienna at the train station," Jamal said, and he blew up the screen to show me footage of Sienna with another guy—a little older chap, very British-looking—walking side by side out the front doors. "Who's that?"

"Don't know," I said, staring intently at him. "She had some contacts over here. Maybe he's one of them."

"Who's the threat?" Scott asked, leaning over the seat to peek at Jamal's screen. "We should probably be on the lookout for trouble since I'm guessing we can see farther than her right now."

"All I know is that it's a succubus named Rose," I said, staring at my sister's digitized face on the display. She was severely pixilated, the camera not doing the best job of rendering her. She was still recognizable, but it wasn't exactly HD.

"So it's a she named Rose and that's all we know," Augustus said. "Scottish, right?"

"Yeah," I said.

"We're looking for a white girl with fair skin in a country largely of white people with fair skin," Augustus deadpanned. "That'll be easy to find."

"From what little Sienna told me, I get the feeling she'll find us before we find her," I said quietly. "She's drained countless metas. We have no idea what her power profile is, but I think we can safely assume it's obscenely strong." I heard the murmur of discontent. "Hopefully we won't run across her at all; we can just extract and bail before she even knows we're in country, since no one likes to go into a fight overmatched."

"I love it when I'm facing enemies that can totally annihilate me without much thought," Augustus said. "I mean, I look back on how we fought Sienna in South Dakota last year, and I think—why don't I go courting more ass-whoopings like that? Because now we've got a succubus with all those powers she used to lay the beatdown on us, plus more still. Good times." His face was pure snarky amusement.

"I get the feeling we're going to be using those beefed-up abilities of ours if we cross this Rose's path," Scott said, a little ominously for him. He was usually sunnier than that these days.

"Seems likely," I said, stepping up and grabbing the box of earphones that Veronika had left behind. I snugged one in my ear and held it out, offering them to the rest. Augustus took one immediately, and so did Jamal and Scott. J.J. and Abby followed, while Kat let out a gentle snore and turned over in her seat. She was wearing a black sleep mask and I wondered if she even knew where she was right now. I doubted it. "This is Reed," I announced, "online."

"Geez, champ, you coulda waited to say anything until I was done emptying my bladder," Veronika said. "I think you just settled the issue for me, thanks. That was some splashing."

"Uhm, how do I mute this thing?" Chase asked, her voice echoey.

"Let's focus on something other than the ladies in the bathroom," Augustus said, voice a little thick with embarrassment. "Yo, Colin, how's the view from York?"

"I'm a little out of town," Colin said, and I could hear the wind rushing past him. "Nice scenery. You know, I always figured I should try running across the ocean, but I can never quite get manage to get across Puget Sound without eventually falling in, so…probably not a great idea, huh?"

"You can still swim fast though, right?" Augustus asked.

"Pretty well, yeah," Colin said. "Water offers a lot of resistance. Hey, I'm in York proper now."

"Where were you before?" I asked, sliding open a window

shade. This wasn't a proper airport. Not that it mattered. Sienna would figure out what was going on and find her way to us.

I hoped.

"It's kind of a run," Colin said. "We're a ways outside of town. Where did you say Sienna was?"

"She was at the train station," Jamal said, and I could hear his frown without even looking at him. "She's not there anymore, and I'm hard pressed to figure out why."

"Hey guys," Colin said, and he sounded a little breathless. "Did we ever figure out what this enemy of Sienna's looks like?"

"We don't have a description, no," I said, a frown of my own puckering my brow. "Why? You see something?"

"I'm not slowing down enough to see much," Colin said. "I'm running around this wall that circles the old city. Kinda cool."

"Are you...doing touristy stuff?" Scott asked. "While the rest of us are stuck on the plane?"

"Why, do you need me to get you a York hat? Coffee mug? Tea mug?" Colin cracked. "Commemorative panties that say, 'Mind the Gap'?"

"Ooh, I want some of those," Veronika chimed in.

"Done," Colin said. "Knew you would."

"Colin, she's somewhere near the train station," Jamal said, still intent on his screen. "She ducked into a blind spot of the cameras or something, I don't know—this is weird."

"On my way—I think," Colin said.

I settled my hand on the back of Jamal's seat and gave it a squeeze. "How would Sienna have known where the blind spots are in the camera system?"

"She shouldn't have," Jamal said, still focused on his screen. "I mean, some cameras are obvious, but others are really well hidden, and sometimes you can get a look from blocks away. I don't see how she did it, because the coverage here is pretty good, but...she damned sure found the blind spot. Almost like she—or that guy she's with, more likely—knew exactly they were doing."

"Lends credence to the idea it's one of her UK sources," I said, coming up again and nearly braining myself on the low-hanging bulkhead. "Colin, if you find her, can you extract her here?"

"In less than two minutes," Colin said cheerily. "You find her, I'll...uh...unwind her?"

"Unbind her," Abby said. "It almost fits."

"Lined her," J.J. said, thinking out loud, "kind her, mind her, pined her—"

"Rind her," Scott said with a smirk. "Like a watermelon."

"Tined her?" Jamal asked. "Tinder. No! Wait, definitely not Tinder."

"If you find her, get her the hell out so we can pop smoke, okay?" I offered, trying to steer past the rhyming police.

"Rogerwilco," Colin said.

"Veronika?" I asked. "I know there's not much going on here since Sienna's in town, but do you see any activity?"

I waited a moment, got distracted staring at Jamal's screen. He was still playing with the cameras around the train station, zooming out and trying to catch Sienna. His face was all screwed up in concentration, but he had a whole lot of nothing going on, that I could see, in the results department.

I paused, listening. "Veronika?"

"Yeah, boss," Veronika said, the tension ratcheted up in her voice. It was obvious as the nose on my face when I actually concentrated on it.

"How are you doing out there?" I asked, experimentally.

"Oh, we're doing just fine," she said stiffly, and I almost swore. Instead, I motioned to Jamal, trying to get his attention. I caught it, and he looked at me quizzically as I pointed to his tablet, then brought my finger around to encompass the world around us, forcefully.

He got it, and touched the base of the tablet. The screen flickered, and then switched to something else.

A view of a plane on a tarmac.

Surrounded by men with guns, creeping closer and closer to the Gulfstream with the open door sitting in the middle of the runway.

Our plane.

We were surrounded.

35.

Sienna

"This is a safe house," Wexford said as he bolted the door behind us. He'd led me into a nearby hotel just a couple hundred feet from the train station, a pretty swank-looking place that had looked like it might be one of those rare European hotels that had so much lux going for it I'd want to stay there rather than the cookie-cutter American chains I preferred while abroad.

"Oh, good," I said. He'd led me up through the servants' entrance and stairwells to this room, on the third floor, and we'd seen not a soul along the way. "Because I've been staying in unsafe ones these last few days and it hasn't been working out so well for me."

Wexford smiled thinly, leaning against the door. "I sense you've had a rough go of it."

"Can you read my mind again?" I asked, making my way over to the bed. My clothes were still shredded, I was soaked in blood—including, still, my face despite my best attempts to use spit to rub it off. I couldn't clean what I couldn't see, after all.

"Indeed," he said, a little wearily.

"Then you know what's happened," I said. There was a certain comfort that came from arriving here. Even seeing Wexford standing there at the train station had been a relief of sorts. With the exception of the cop I'd brainwashed to forget I was a criminal, I hadn't exactly been sunning in a sea of friendly faces these last few days, and they'd been a little stressful.

He seemed to think for a minute, then nodded. "Yes, now I see. Rose, her name is?"

"Rose, her name is, but by any other name she'd be thorny as hell," I agreed, stepping through into the bathroom before I could see his reaction to my witticism. I turned on the cold tap and looked in the mirror. My face was bloody, all right. I got to work on it. "I went into this thinking the perp was an incubus. I guess that shows me not to assume. And as you've no doubt ascertained from poking around in my skull, she's royally pissed at me and I have only suspicions as to why. All I know for sure is that she's gone to some rather extreme ends in the name of vengeance for…whatever the hell got her panties in a twist."

"Perhaps I might shed some light on that," Wexford said, and I caught sight of him standing behind me in the mirror. He moved, and on the bed behind him was a manila file. "For your suspicions do seem to be correct."

I turned off the tap and almost lunged for it. When I opened it up, I found surveillance photos of Rose, all from a distance, all from cameras she didn't know were there. Digging a little deeper, I found candids of the sort families took of their kids—her with other people, smiling. A mother, a really old dad or maybe grandfather. I looked up at Wexford. "You know her?"

"She's known to us, yes," Wexford said with a nod. "Rose Steward. She lived in the metahuman cloister in Scotland…at least until—"

"The war," I said, my legs delivering me onto the bed with a gentle thump. "That cloister—"

"Was wiped out by your old friend Weissman—"

"That shitbird was no friend of mine."

"—and your Great Uncle Raymond," he said, looking over my shoulder at the file.

I processed that. "Look…that sucks for her and all, but…why is she so pissed at me? I didn't kill her family, and I didn't really like the people who did."

"It would be difficult for me to speak to her motivations without seeing inside her mind," Wexford said, pacing back and forth in front of the bed crisply, with lordly precision. "All we can say for sure is that she is indeed, for some reason, quite obsessed with you, and has…done a number, I think you call it, on your abilities and your…person." He seemed to wince at the sight of me. Having now seen myself in the mirror, I couldn't blame him.

"Nice way of saying she's ripped me eight new ones," I said, falling back on the bed. Here with Wexford, I felt oddly safe again. Maybe it was his mind control working, but I didn't think so. There was something about human conversation that was a pleasant lubricant to the spirit after a hard series of mental hurdles. I'd been on the run for months, but Rose had upped the game on me, and damn if it wasn't taking a toll. I wanted to sleep again, but I fought off that instinct easily, sitting back up. "And you had no idea what she was doing up in Edinburgh before I went up there?"

"Indeed not," Wexford said, turning to look at me. "If it's as you see it in your mind—that she has 'taken the city,' nearly—then this comes as quite the surprise to Her Majesty's government. I am the only telepath that I know of in the government, and while we always have a decent traffic of officials coming back and forth from Edinburgh, they would hardly notice…whatever it is you've noticed."

"I've noticed mobs chasing my ass through the streets," I said. "Fearless, angry, seemingly controlled by other sources. Meta sources, presumably. Rose, if she's behind all the stuff I've seen…" I shook my head. "Your country lost a pretty decent amount of citizens to her."

Wexford's face fell, and I could tell he was feeling it. "Indeed…" he said softly. "It seems we've missed one of the tragedies of our time as it happened upon our very soil."

"You really did," I said, let my head sag as I stared at the patterned carpet, which had an older look to it. "How did you find me, by the by?"

Wexford almost smiled. "For one with direct access to most levels of government, it isn't terribly hard. This whole island brims with security cameras, after all."

"Mm," I said, then frowned. "Hey, how high a level would you have to be to see—"

The door to the room blew open, shattering as it flew out of the frame. I ducked my head instinctively, rolling off the bed as a spray of wooden shrapnel blew overhead and the door shot into the room, launched like it had been blown out of a cannon. I didn't see Wexford, since I was trying as hard as I could to mush my face to the carpeting, but as soon as I was down I immediately sprang up again, pushing to my feet in time to see—

Wexford had taken the door head-on as it had flown into the room. It had split him almost in two, and his eyes stared dully at the ceiling, the wreckage of his body leaving me in no doubt…

He was dead.

"Ye did miss one of the greatest tragedies of our time," Rose spat as she hovered her way into the room, hair floating and her face blazing red, "you great ruddy idiot. You and the whole government missed it, with your heads up your arses in London. You missed the slaughter of a whole people, nearly, your own people—you didn't give a fig, hiding in your country estates—" She practically spat at Wexford's corpse, which lay still and silent on the ground beneath her as she hovered in.

I was frozen in place, Rose looking darkly at him, and then she swiveled to look at me. "And you," she said, bleeding that malevolent loathing out in my direction now, "you…you were as responsible as they were for it, you and your high and mighty self…"

Without a thought, I turned and sprinted for the window, hurling myself through the glass at high speed, thinking only one thing—

Run.

36.

Reed

"Oh, hell," I muttered as I mentally assessed the situation.

Veronika and Chase were captured.

Colin was out in York.

A plethora of gunmen were creeping up to our airplane.

And Sienna, who we'd come here to rescue, was nowhere in sight.

"Uhh, Reed?" Scott asked, nudging me out of my short mental break from reality. I wasn't quite screaming in my own head, but close. This was a real damnation of a situation.

"Augustus," I said, "blow up the tarmac at their feet. Non-lethally. They look like cops to me."

"I can do that," Augustus said, stirring out of his own open-mouthed surprise at our situation, "but then we're not going to be able to roll to the runway."

"One massive problem at a time, okay?" I turned my attention to Jamal. "I need eyes on Veronika and Chase."

"Got 'em," Jamal said, and his screen flipped to an interior view of an office. There was a firing squad vibe to what we were seeing, Veronika and Chase standing there with their hands over their heads, guys with lots of guns pointing at the two of them. The only other things in frame were a desk next to the window and a potted plant.

Veronika was staring right at the camera, probably because

she could hear me and knew we were watching. "Anytime, boss." She didn't even say "boss" sarcastically.

"Let me—" I started to say.

"I got this," a soft voice said from behind me, and I glanced back to see Kat, her sleep mask up on her forehead.

"You—how?" Augustus asked.

Kat just pointed at the plant.

"That's like a baby ficus," Augustus said.

"You worry about your concrete and let me deal with this, okay?" Kat said, patting him on the shoulder. Then she closed her eyes.

There was no sound on the camera, but I could hear a loud CRACK! in my earpiece, corresponding to what was going on in the room where Veronika and Chase were being held. On the screen, we had a grainy view of the potted plant just shattering as every gunman in the room turned to look.

"Did you just—" Augustus said.

"Tarmac," Kat said, concentrating. "Also—I ammmm GROOOOOT!"

The damned plant leapt out of the wreckage of the pot and attacked the nearest black-garbed tactical guy. It caught him full in the face and he ripped off a few rounds in the air out of sheer surprise. The plant seemed to stretch, limbs reaching out and grabbing the next nearest team member, dragging the two of them closer and smashing their heads together with a THUNK! so loud I heard it over the headset.

Veronika and Chase sprang into action on the screen, and I buried my instinct to say, "NON-LETHAL!" because what the hell was the point? Chase shot her lightsaber power out of her sleeve and cut the guns out of three of the twelve SWAT guys' hands while Veronika fired plasma bursts at three more, rendering their weapons inoperable.

That still left four more, counting the two that Kat had, uh…treed? Bushed? I wasn't sure what to call it.

Two of the remaining team members were all over the shrub-related incident that was afflicting their team members.

The damned plant grabbed the guns out of their hands with vine extensions, and then whipped at them with the gun butts. Here they were, SWAT-looking guys in full black tactical gear, and a potted plant was strangling two of their number, had disarmed two more and was now smacking them in the helmets with their own weapons.

I could hear the chaos in the office. It was a hell of a thing.

"Augustus, you standing by?" I asked, trying to make sure the next thing I needed done was going to get done in time.

"Whenever you're ready," Augustus said, eyes closed. I guessed he was gripping at the tiny pieces of stone and rock in the tarmac, which—I was just guessing based on how my control of the winds went—was not the easiest of things.

"Colin," I said, "I need you to find Sienna and get her the hell back here." I waited a second. "Colin." Scott looked right at me, concern rolling down his face like a falling curtain. "Fannon, report in."

"That's worrying," Scott said.

"J.J.—" I started.

"Way ahead of you," J.J. said, clipped. "I'm tapping into Jamal's feed and putting it on my screen. I have nothing on Fannon, though." He looked up at me. "He's gone dark on comms. Signal lost."

I swore under my breath, then looked back at Jamal's screen. "Find him." The gunmen were edging closer to the plane. Another few seconds and they'd be close enough that any attempt to blow up the tarmac under their feet might cause damage to the plane. "Augustus, take these guys now."

"Yep," Augustus said, and there was a moment of quiet.

Then it sounded a little like an earthquake outside. The plane shook lightly—and only lightly, thankfully—and then a whole lot of screams started flooding in through the hatchway.

"Tangos down," Jamal said. He wasn't exaggerating. The camera view of the tarmac had shown what looked like a swarm of mosquitoes launching out of the ground for a second, then every single guy with a gun hit the dirt. The tarmac seemed to be alive, ripping their weapons out of their hands and swallowing them. I even saw the asphalt reach into their holsters and take their sidearms, the weapons disappearing into the black tar and gravel like they'd been eaten whole.

He flipped the screen back to Chase and Veronika, who were just wrapping up with the last couple of guys. Veronika had guns in hand and was slinging a couple more over her shoulders. "You bringing us presents?" Augustus asked.

"I didn't have time to stop off at Harrods," she quipped, "and I'm guessing after this trip, I won't be welcome there anymore. Thanks for that, by the way," she said acidly. "This is all the tourist memorabilia you get from this trip."

"We visited York, UK, and all I got was this lousy submachine gun," Scott said.

Veronika popped out of the office, Chase hot on her tail, and a few seconds later they appeared in frame on the airstrip. "I appreciate the chaos you've created here," Chase said, tightly, as they emerged, heading back for us, "but I gotta believe this is going to attract the wrong kind of attention."

"They were here waiting for us," I said. "We've already attracted the wrong kind of attention."

"You think this was a setup?" Veronika asked, huffing as she ran. She and Chase were picking their way over the fallen, writhing SWAT guys.

"How else did they know we were coming?" I asked.

"If this is a trap, you'd think they'd have laid it better," Augustus said.

"Yeah, like with coverage from snip—" Kat started to say.

A booming crack echoed outside so loudly that it seemed enter the plane like a man kicking a door down. Veronika staggered in her run, and Chase caught her right before she stumbled. A hazy energy field appeared on Chase's right-hand side, like a shield between her and Veronika and the harm that was coming their way from the sniper. She picked up Veronika with her left arm and flat-out ran for the plane. Another crack echoed, and Chase faltered. She tossed Veronika unceremoniously up the ramp, and then backed up it double-time herself, another boom lashing our ears as she came inside and hit the button to raise the stairs and door.

"You okay?" I asked, rushing to pull down the shades on the plane. J.J. and Abby were doing the same on the opposite side, and Kat and Scott joined in, trying to hide our bodies from clear view while doing so. It went quickly thanks to meta speed, but I didn't draw a breath until it was over.

"Fine-ish," Chase said, breathing heavily when she saw I was done. A bloody streak was cut down the side of her head, a slice that looked like someone had knifed her. She saw me looking and said, "One of the sniper rounds. My refraction shield isn't strong enough to stop something like that. It just pushed it a little off course."

"If it hadn't, your brains would be all over the pavement right now," I said, and then turned my attention to Veronika, who was clutching her side and bleeding all over the carpet.

"Yeah, no, it's cool," she said, wincing, as we stood there. "You worry about Chase and her little cut to the head. I'm fine." She pulled her hand back from clutching at the wound, which was squarely in the middle of her chest. "Looks like they missed the heart by maybe a quarter inch, based on the bleed pattern." She grimaced. "A little to the left and this would be a lot worse."

"Kat," I said, but she was already there, hands on Veronika and working to heal her. A muffled shot rang out from outside, and there was a crack in the cockpit.

"The pilot," Veronika said, pain turning to panic. "Reed, our escape—"

I was on it. I vaulted forward, lurching toward the front of the plane. I opened the door and—

The pilot was dead, his brains sprayed all over the place, a spiderweb of cracks in the center of the windshield. The co-pilot was just sitting there, mouth agape, like he might die of shock—

His head exploded a second later, spraying me with red and opening another massive hole in the cockpit window.

I slammed the cockpit door and hit the deck, barely breathing.

"What's the word from the front of the plane?" Abby called. She had a strain to her voice.

I swallowed heavily. "The pilot and co-pilot are dead," I said, the realization I'd just led two innocent men into their deaths not quite hitting me fully yet. Colin was missing. Veronika and Chase had been shot.

And we were trapped on a runway, still surrounded by enemies…with no sign of Sienna.

37.

Sienna

I burst out of the safe house window pissed off, heart beating a mile a minute, reflecting on a few hard realities. First, it really wasn't a safe house at all, was it, in either sense of the word? Like, it was a hotel, not a house, and it ended up being not safe at all, dammit.

Second...Rose was on my ass like white on Conan O'Brien, and that was, to understate things massively, not good.

I hit the ground and rolled, running toward a city wall that was just standing there in front of me. A few tourists were speckled along its length, and I didn't even bother finding a staircase. I spider-manned my way up it with a good leap and by using the footholds provided by the uneven nature of the stones used to build the thing. My hands scraped and dug against the rough stone but I made it, vaulting above the crenellations at the top and onto a walkway.

An astonished tourist gaped at me. "You're—"

"In a big damned hurry," I said, pushing past him without doing him injury. Sounded Italian.

I ran down the wall at a furious clip, trying my best not to look back too much.

I failed.

Rose was easily keeping pace with me, just floating off about twenty feet, looking at me pityingly as I bolted along.

There wasn't so much as a fortification in sight, but there was a bridge ahead a little ways, and maybe I could—

"You can't be serious with this," Rose called to me, just drifting along, watching me. "Where d'ye think you're going to go?"

"Well, I've made it to York," I said, wondering if she was going to close in on me or just deliver color commentary until I died of boredom or exhaustion. It was feeling like it could go either way.

"I let you make it to York, darlin'," she said, almost piteously.

"Yeah, okay," I shouted. I was still heading for the river bridge. If I could make it…

Well, I didn't know what I'd do next if I made it. But if I could submerge, slow Rose's momentum down, take her fire out of play…

That'd just leave her with off-the-chart energy projection skills and the strength to squeeze me to death without much effort. Totally even odds.

Sigh.

The wall was curving to an end, heading to the right up ahead where it returned to ground level to meet up with the bridge to allow pedestrians to cross the river. Rose was easing closer, but I decided to liven things up and add some destruction of public property to the charges against me, so I launched a kick against the tooth of the wall fortification, the crenellation archers would duck behind while shooting arrows in the days of yore.

I hit the crenellation with gusto, and it shattered the old stone, sending a chunk flying right at Rose.

She moved right out of the way, dipping slightly as she did so. "You remember when you used to be the most powerful meta in the world? Sad to think those days are gone." She made a tsking sound, then laughed, loud and high and kind of like a mean girl from the high school I never went to but always imagined.

"I mean, what are you supposed to do, now that you've peaked and are on the downhill slope?" Rose asked, putting the fear in me that she was, indeed, going to color commentate me to death. If I wanted to go out that way, I'd watch ESPN. "I'd imagine a prideful girl like you…you've got to be just stinging right now. Feeling the burn of your ego being hit hard. Speaking of—"

She launched in at me and clocked me in the jaw so fast I didn't even see it coming. One minute I was ready to round the corner and get on the downslope to the bridge, the next I flew into a crenellation, and hit it a lot harder than the one I'd just kicked at her. It impacted along my back, stars flashed in front of my eyes, and I swallowed a tooth.

I staggered up, hearing the gasps from visiting tourists, or maybe from me trying to get my wind back after she'd knocked it out of me. Rose was at a distance again, and I couldn't see her very clearly, because she was blurry from the hit I'd taken, but I knew she was smiling. "Oops," she said with much glee.

Dragging myself forward, I didn't bother to launch a counterattack, because now that I didn't have my other souls or a gun, my only long-distance offensive weapon was basically to throw shit at her, and I was all out of shit to throw. A gorilla in a zoo with a handful of its own feces had more effective means of holding off Rose at this point than I did, which was a sad thing to admit.

"Did you really think your little friends were going to come swooping in at the last second and save the day for you?" she asked, and it turned my blood cold to hear her reference Reed and—others, I presumed, people he might have brought with him. Augustus. Scott. Jamal. Maybe Kat.

I slowed, not that I was moving very fast anyway. An old lady with a cane down the way was escaping more quickly than I was, and it took me a second to realize that my left ankle was broken and screaming at me anytime I put weight on it. That was bad: I was hobbled, and healing instantly was a thing of the past. I was also pretty sure I had a few broken ribs.

Rose moved a little closer, but not so close I could have even spit on her. Her leer was apparent now. "Oh, yes, I know about your little friends. They're the reason I've let you go so far, that I let you run away like this. They're out there at the airfield right now, getting surrounded, getting shot, probably—I told the lads I sent to be careful, but you know how hard it is to find good help."

I didn't say anything to that, but she must have read the fear in my face. "Oh, come now," she said, leaning on the Scottish. "You didn't think you were actually beating me by just running away, did you? I've been one step ahead of you all this time, darlin'."

I kicked out at the wall again in rage and sent another chunk of stone at her. It hurt like hell, and I keeled over after it was done because I had to put all my weight on my broken ankle for a few seconds to pull it off, but I sent a piece of block right at her smug face—

And she gravity'd it off, sending it shattering to the ground below like it had been snagged by the event horizon of a black hole.

I threw myself to my feet again and started forward at a hobbling run, which was still faster than anything a non-meta could have pulled off. There was a massive building behind her with a white facade and a bunch of small windows. Maybe if I could get inside, hide, evade her—

She swept in front of me and crashed into me again, this time striking a glancing blow against my belly that felt like someone had popped my stomach.

I staggered back again, and Rose had inched a little closer this time, now only about ten feet away from me, but still hovering off the ground. Her red hair caught the wind coming off the river, and the malicious joy in her eyes now that she was revealed was completely unlike her persona when she'd pretended to be my sidekick.

"I think it's about time to finish this up," Rose said as I wobbled, my legs weak beneath me, my head swimming from the beating I'd taken. "Give her the goodnight kiss, will you, darlin'? So I can go deal with her little…family?"

I wondered what she meant by that, and then I saw a blur that slowed down right in front of me. I caught sight of a beanie and bright eyes that locked onto me like a missile.

Colin Fannon.

He was coming right for me.

I wanted to let out a breath of relief, but didn't want to tip her off. She was about to see, anyway, when he caught up to me and I disappeared. Then she'd know that we'd—

Colin blurred at me, not slowing down. I braced myself, figuring he'd grab me and off we'd go—

But instead, as he came to halt, I caught motion at his side as he lifted his arm—

And leveled me with a punch to the face that put my lights out.

The fact that he was here had seemed such a relief; a friendly face come to aid in my salvation.

The fact that he'd just turned on me at Rose's command?

That was…so not good.

I lost consciousness, slamming into the wall behind me but only dimly aware of it.

The last thing I managed to think was that Reed was here…in York…that he'd brought Fannon here to save me.

And if he didn't know Fannon had turned…

Then he was in even more danger than I was.

I passed out into the dark of unconsciousness, thinking only of my brother.

38.

Reed

My decision was a split one, born of the fact that Veronika was bleeding in front of me, a ton of advancing gunmen had just gone down outside because of Augustus's assault, and Colin Fannon was MIA somewhere in York.

Stay to save Sienna, whose whereabouts we didn't even know?

Or—

"SHIT!" Jamal shouted, thundering through the cabin. "Sienna's clashing with this other succubus in York, and it's— shit!"

I stole a look over his shoulder as my brain raced with what to do. "What?"

"She's getting torn apart," Augustus breathed, hanging over the seat. Scott, next to him, looked grey in the face.

"NO!" Jamal shouted again, matched a second later by a similar imprecation from Augustus. Scott remained utterly silent.

Jamal looked up at me, eyes a little teary. "Fannon just turned on Sienna." He swallowed visibly, and looked to the floor. "She's down."

"What the actual…?" Veronika said, struggling to her feet. "Bullshit. Fannon wouldn't do that."

"He just did," J.J. said, and turned his own laptop around to show Veronika.

261

"Reed," Scott said, and he looked more pained than I could recall ever seeing him.

"We have to get down there," Augustus said, pushing off the back of Jamal's seat and ripping the leather in the process.

The sound of a bullet spanging off the body of the aircraft seemed to pressurize the cabin.

"We fight our way out—" Augustus said.

"Come out swinging, lightning in hand—" Jamal said.

"I'm gonna pulp some heads," Friday said, already swelling. He'd been silent for a while, and I'd thought him asleep, but his eyes were cross and furious.

"I'll rip up every blade of grass between here and town," Kat said, and looked at J.J. "What's that thing you say when I start using trees to fight?"

"The Ents are going to war," J.J. said solemnly.

"I'm gonna plasma-burn some mofos," Veronika said. "To ash."

"You guys," Scott said, and he was so quiet. "We can't."

A moment silence fell in the cabin, marked by another booming shot outside that made a ringing noise when the bullet impacted the body of the aircraft.

"What do you mean we can't?" Augustus asked, bearing down on Scott with a brow curved in anger. "I know you've got your issues with Sienna—"

"This isn't about issues," Scott said, almost whispering. "We go out there now, we all die. Bravado aside—this is a suicide scenario."

"Then let's make it the charge of the damned light brigade," Veronika said.

"If it would do an ounce of good," Scott said, voice rising, "yes. I would make a glorious end of it." He turned to me. "But it won't. We will all die, and Sienna will still be the prisoner of that—that kilted bitch."

"She's not wearing a kilt," J.J. whispered to Abby. "Do women wear kilts?"

"They're called skirts, dear," Abby said.

"If you've got one shot," Scott said, and he was still speaking to me, "you don't pull the trigger when you're fifty miles from your target. Sienna would tell you that. She'd understand." He looked right at Augustus. "And she wouldn't want us to die, stupidly, right here, running out into gunfire so they can pick us off from a mile away."

"Who's going to rescue her if we don't?" Augustus looked like he was about to lose his mind.

"Who's going to rescue all of us if we're trapped together?" Scott asked. "This succubus, Rose…I think she's got it in mind to hurt Sienna real bad." He looked at each of us, in turn, coolly. "Can you think of a better way than peeling the souls out of the only people left on the planet who still care about her?"

That cold notion washed down me in a sickening torrent.

Sienna was trapped.

And we were bait.

No…not bait.

We were the human sacrifices that this Rose intended to use to bring Sienna to hurt, to pain, to…

To agony, basically.

To her knees.

"Not today," I whispered, and gathered my wits about me even though my skin was cold and my hands threatened to shake. I tried to get the wind, and it took me a couple tries to summon it up properly.

The plane rattled as I started the winds beneath it. It lurched as it took to the air, my plan all along being not to worry about the tarmac below, because I could just lift us up and start the engines—or simply pump out a few hundred mph of air in their place if need be.

"No!" Augustus looked at me, eyes flaring in disbelief. "Reed, *she's your sister!*"

"And you're my team," I said, straining as another bullet hit the fuselage. "I won't sacrifice your lives in vain, Augustus. Not when we've walked right into a trap."

I thought he was going to lunge for me for a moment, but he didn't. He looked like he wanted to.

Jamal just sat there, staring at his screen, but I don't think he saw anything of it. Friday shrunk, his muscles reducing down to their regular size. He collapsed in his chair like his knees went out from beneath him.

I righted the plane and jetted high-powered air out the back of the engines, creating an artificial draft. The plane shot forward, one last parting bullet hitting us in the underbelly as we rocketed away from the airfield at several hundred miles per hour.

"We...we just lost her, didn't we?" J.J. asked. It sounded like defeat. Abby just touched his hand.

"Get on ground radar, J.J.," Scott said, issuing a command I might have thought of if I hadn't been propelling a plane toward the stratosphere with nothing but my will and my powers. "Look for missiles. We don't know what kind of control this Rose has over the UK military."

"Yeah, that's not the sort of thing I can just do—" J.J. started to say.

"I've got it," Jamal said. "I'm tapped into their comms, too—throwing that over to you, J.J."

Kat was still holding her hand over Veronika, who was standing in the middle of the aisle, staring past me, eyes unfocused. Chase stood just behind her, quiet relief slipping out on her face.

"Rose definitely has at least local control over the military," J.J. said. "They're coordinating a response."

I turned the jets up harder, and motioned to the cockpit. "Someone needs to start the plane so I can go from flying to just giving us a good tailwind."

"I'm a pilot," Chase said.

"I'll ride shotgun with you," Veronika said. Her voice sounded like it was ground out, full of menace and anger at the fight not going as she planned. She and Chase vanished toward the cockpit.

"You left her behind, Reed," Augustus said into the silence that followed.

"What else was I supposed to do, Augustus?" I asked. "Sacrifice all of us to this Rose? Because I don't think she had intentions to do anything with us but maybe torture us to death in front of Sienna for her own kicks."

Augustus slumped back in his seat, staring out the window. "We could have saved her, man." But he didn't sound sure.

"We've got missiles in the air," J.J. announced.

"I'm taking us low," I said, trying to orient the plane. I thought I'd been sending us west, but I couldn't really be sure. "When they get close, I'll feel them. Veronika," I called warningly to the cockpit.

"She's working on it," Veronika called back. "I don't think these things are meant to be cold started while in flight." She threw one of the pilot bodies unceremoniously back into the aisle, then the other.

"This sucker is gonna hit us in like thirty seconds," J.J. said. "Wait, maybe less."

I floored the wind currents behind us, maintaining the ones beneath us. The plane shuddered, hitting a speed its engines were not rated for. I felt a little like I was donating blood, my very life running out of me as I pushed the plane forward.

"Relax, Reed," Scott said, easing up next to me. "I've got this one."

I could feel the missile as it started to close, cutting through the air faster than we were. I couldn't tell what kind it was, just that it was there. "How are you going to do this, Scott?" I asked, my voice straining as I tried to concentrate on keeping us aloft and moving forward while still mentally tracking the missile that was coming to kill us.

"Easy," Scott said. "It's raining."

I could actually feel it now that he said it, the water coming down outside the cabin. It was a light one, but enough that I felt it when a ball of liquid condensed and pulled together, streaming toward the missile. I could feel the wind running over its surface, and then, suddenly, for a second I didn't.

Scott had flooded the missile with water, the additional weight messing with its ballistic characteristics, and then it dragged down, losing us as it fell to the earth below, engine puttering out.

"Uh, bad news, guys…like ten more incoming," J.J. said.

"One at a time, partner," Scott said as I drove us for the coast even faster. The smart move would have been to dive us for the deck, but I wasn't sure I could keep us low against the total resistance that being at that altitude would provide. I would have liked to have pushed us higher, to the open skies and far from the higher air pressure below, but that wasn't realistic given what I was combating.

Which was fatigue from lack of sleep, and flying a plane without any engines across the north of England.

"Bringing the engines online now," Chase called from the cockpit. "Not sure how well this will work…"

I rolled my eyes and killed the airflow into the engines to essentially recreate their grounded, at rest state. It was a lot easier than continuing to thrust us forward, which I was having to do, or keeping us aloft, which was mostly being done by our forward momentum and the wings now, thankfully.

"Engine start!" Chase announced. "Whatever you're doing, keep doing it for a few seconds while I get 'em warmed up."

"Sure, no problem," I said, straining a little. I'd dispelled hurricanes, and lifting a plane wasn't too difficult, but the missiles flying toward us from behind were a little concerning.

"Bogey only a hundred yards out," J.J. announced. "Two more close behind it, and, uh…like twelve—no, fifteen—more after that."

"Like walking in the park," Scott said, and his forehead was showing a little sweat now. "Splash one."

"Literally," J.J. said. "One down. No, two—three."

"Damn, waterboy," Augustus breathed.

"If you wanted to throw some rocks up at the ones

following, he probably wouldn't object," I said, sweating a little myself.

"If I could see them, I would," Augustus said. "Or feel them."

"I think I have this," Scott said, straining.

"Four and five down," J.J. said. "Six and seven closing…"

Something blew up a little ways off, and I felt it.

"Sorry," Scott breathed.

I felt something else, too—sudden, supersonic, cutting through the air toward us from behind.

"Uh oh," I said.

"Something else on radar," J.J. said. "Unidentified… small…faster than the missiles…"

"It's Rose," I breathed, as the engines outside thrummed to life.

"She's closing on us, man," J.J. said, looking up at me, wild-eyed. "What are we going to d—"

"Scott…" I said, "lay off on the missiles."

"Done," Scott said, collapsing on the seat behind him. Kat came over to him, putting a hand on his head, but his pallor didn't really improve. "That…was not the easiest thing ever. The welds on those things—"

I concentrated on those drifts behind me, on that supersonic object cutting through the air toward me.

There was a break of fury in my mind, like blood ran in front of my eyes.

I reached out with my mind, with my powers, and seized every single one of the remaining missiles in a furious wind—

And sent them right into a perfect convergence on the Scottish woman following us.

The Gulfstream issued a rough shudder as the explosion's shockwave ran through the plane.

"Got her!" J.J. shouted. "She's losing altitude…"

"I know," I said. "I can *feel* her."

Rose ceased her supersonic flight, dropping back, falling to earth. I pushed her along, slamming her into the ground as we rushed forward, away from her, away from the ground as Chase turned the flaps and added power to the engines and we left the ground behind.

I fell into the nearest chair and put my head back against the soft seat. I was pretty sure I hadn't killed Rose, not if she was the premiere badass she seemed to be.

But maybe, just maybe, I'd given Sienna a break.

I consoled myself with that thought as I pushed the plane with a hard tailwind back across the Atlantic...and wondered if I'd ever see my sister again.

39.

Rose

Alistair McKinney was Rose's date for the evening. They walked along the summery streets of Edinburgh, trees green even in the evening dark, her giving him coy looks, him giving her hungrier ones. His hair was silvery, but he was eager and bordering on lecherous. The air had that brisk scent to it, and the lights were shining out from the flats in the buildings all around them as they went, his arm hooked in hers, his suit jacket's rough cloth rubbing at her elbow like this whole evening had chafed at her mind.

She'd felt a bit strange about this at first, but that had been easily soothed. Because honestly, it felt so damned good when she touched a person, it practically made her ravenous for more.

This is fine, Granddad said. *He's just a man, and not a very good one at that.*

Aye, Tamhas said, *he's a right bastard. I've known him for a long time, and this one—this one's going to set you up for life if you can just get hold of his bank accounts. It'll make things easier.*

Just keep an even look, Hamilton said. He'd been advising her on being natural in moments like this, when she was deceiving. He'd had her practicing faces in the mirror. Doing exercises. Finding the emotions on command.

"Ahh, you're such a pretty thing," Alistair said, stroking his

269

fingers through her hair as they walked.

Give him a little bit of hope, Hamilton whispered.

Rose did, flashing him a ghost of a smile. He went for her hand to hold and she brushed him, escaping while still keeping him on the line.

They were walking through the New Town, a lovely place that Rose had already developed a little affinity for here in Edinburgh. It was grand, she thought, filled with history and mystery, and a sort of magic that she might have felt more acutely with other company.

Like Graham, who had spent these last months…silent.

That's it, Hamilton said, breaking into her thoughts. *Now get him inside.*

"My flat's just up here," Alistair said. They passed the rows of lovely older buildings, beautifully maintained and surely of finest quality within.

And in spite of their surroundings, part of Rose, deep inside, below the hammering heart, wanted to throw up.

Alistair hopped ahead, legs lively as he went up the steps to unlock the door to the flat. He took them two at a time, that short riser from the sidewalk up to the older apartment building. It had grand arches and recessed windows, a lovely and elegant old building. He held the door for her, and in spite of the summer warmth…

Rose felt…cold.

Go on, Granddad said, and Rose tottered up the steps in her heels, feeling very much out of place. All her life she'd have dreamed of looking as lovely as this, to be dressed to the nines this way, to be here in Edinburgh, and yet now here she was, her last pounds put into the dress, the heels, the hair…

And she was about to use it all to ensnare and kill a man to live.

It had a cold comfort, trying to figure out how to make it outside the village these last months. The voices in her head were loud, all the time. Maddening, even when she was trying to sleep. She'd wake out of a sound dream—always a nightmare, always the same one, people howling at her, clawing at her, ripping at her clothes—in the tiny flat she'd rented, gasping in the night, afraid everyone could hear her the world over.

Afraid that somebody would be coming. That Weissman, or Raymond, maybe. Maybe both.

"Let me show you inside," Alistair said with a wink as he held the beautiful, glassy front door open for her. She stared; he was waiting.

She wanted to walk away. To stride off down the street with nary a word, and leave Mr. McKinney to his posh flat, to his fancy life. She didn't want to touch him, and she didn't to take his thoughts or his bank account information or anything else, really.

This wasn't what she wanted at all.

Get in there, you stupid, worthless cow, her mam said.

Mechanically, Rose walked up the steps, and into the flat.

They'd had this conversation before when the money started to run out. She'd tried a job, but sometimes the voices would act up and she'd shout out in the middle of work. It came on like a fit in the middle of the store. Headaches so bad they'd drop to her knees, arguments between them so harsh that she'd cringe away from a customer.

She'd been sacked a few times before she'd realized that no one wanted to work with a crazy person.

And she had become a crazy person. Voices in her head completed the circle.

"You want a cuppa?" Alistair asked once she was inside. The apartment was indeed posh, grand staircase leading upstairs, the entire building his. She was living in a one-room flat, and he had a whole building. She looked around, feeling that intense desire to run again, like she didn't belong here among these riches, these hardwoods, these leather-lined books and fancy people. She stared at Alistair and felt nothing but sick at his leer, one-sided as it was.

Answer him, you stupid cow. Her mam's voice rang out in her head again, sharp and harsh. Had it ever been any other way? Rose had a hard time imagining it now.

"No, I'm...fine," Rose said.

Alistair eased up to her, and she felt strangely like a shark was circling her. "Would ye like to go...upstairs?" So full of meaning.

Her own mind, faint and buried somewhere, said no, but the other voices said yes, and that was what came out of her mouth. She followed him up that grand staircase into the darkness waiting above.

He guided her up, a hand on her arm, light and gentle. And yet still it felt horrifying, like she was walking, wide awake, into a nightmare. *Just a little farther*, Tamhas soothed.

This is nothing, Granddad said. *You've read enough books to know—girls your age have been doing unpleasant things to secure their prospects for all of time. This is one of those, but so much easier. You don't have to marry the old bastard, or even spend that much time with him. You can take him any time now.*

Just touch him a little, Hamilton urged. *The charade is over. Put your hands on him, pretend to be really interested, to keep him from screaming, and then...just take what we need, and break his neck.*

Rose gulped. Alistair led her into a darkened doorway and clicked on the light. She blinked back from the intensity of it, then her eyes adjusted it. It was a bedroom, furnished in grand style. A four-poster was the centerpiece of the room, turned down like a maid had just left.

That's a good lass, Granddad said. *You can just follow his lead. He'll take care of it himself soon enough, if you give him enough time. All you'll need to do is hold on.*

Rose wandered into the bedroom after Alistair, who was unbuttoning his shirt. When it came off, she saw that paunch that extended slightly over his belt, the gnarly trail of hairs that pathed down his belly. His chest was flat, sloping down to his gut. He shed the shirt, letting it fall to the floor, and a vague hint of revulsion ran through Rose even though he was ten feet away.

"Now you take yours off," he said, quiet, voice dripping with suggestion.

Just go over to him, and give him a kiss, Hamilton said. *Touch him. Something. Keep him on the hook, lass.*

Rose wobbled over to him, following the command. When she got close, he did it for her, brushing his lips against hers. His breath was fowl, garlicky, and strong, and she nearly gagged but managed to hold it in at the last.

Keep it together, her mam's voice said. *Don't raise an alarm now, not when you're so close.*

He pawed at her, and she took it for a moment before pulling away. He grinned, looking her over. "You're nervous, aren't you? It's all right."

She nodded without saying anything, feeling ashen.

"Is this your first time?" he asked, coyly.

She brushed her fingers against her lips, wishing she could wipe away the feeling of what she'd just done. She just nodded, that sick feeling rising in her belly, along with the bile.

"It's all right," he said, "it's not my first time. I can show you the way. We'll take it nice and easy. Hm?" He awaited her approval, and as he did so, touched her arm.

It was all she could do not to recoil in terror. He had already turned away, busying himself.

Touch him now, and it'll all be over soon, Granddad said. *If you let this drag on…ye just might regret it.*

Aye, you're going to have to go along with what he wants in order to avoid alarm if you don't seize this moment, Tamhas said. *Get on with it.*

Alistair turned on the TV, then dropped the remote to the bedside table with a clatter. "A little background noise," he said with that same smile, and unbuttoned his pants. They slid to the floor and he shrugged out of them, then came back at her again.

I could tell you what to do here, you worthless shite, Miriam Shell said, her own disgust boiling over, *but you'd just cock it up.*

Finish him, Graham said quietly. *There's no need for all this*

*show, Rose. Just…be done with it if you mean to do it. You don't need
to let him keep backing you into a corner. You'll have to play along if you
don't, and I know you don't want that—*

Rose turned away from Alistair, freezing in place.
Something about what Graham had said, about Miriam's
goads…they got to her. She kicked the straps off her heels,
then slipped the dress straps from her shoulders, her head
rushing as she did so. That sick feeling in her stomach was
replaced by a breathless hunger, a twisted anger let loose,
driving her on. That she could feel it when Graham's own
heart dropped—not that he had one anymore, but the feeling
was still present—was all the sweeter.

She turned back to Alistair, down to her bra and knickers.
He looked her up and down, his eye wandering. "Shall we get
into bed, then?" she asked, trying to live up her voice. It still
sounded dull to her.

He bought it nonetheless, and lifted the covers, as if
opening a door for her. She slid in and moved over to halfway
across the bed, pulse racing. The TV was going quietly in the
background, a rerun of some show playing like muzak in a
shop.

Alistair slipped out of his own briefs and slid into the bed,
letting out a hearty sigh as he let the covers drop after him.
She'd seen, because he'd shown off, briefly, before sliding in,
as though the mere sight was something that would fascinate
her. It had the opposite effect; she was vaguely repulsed,
though she kept a lid on it.

"Now then," he said, staring at the space of inches between
them. She was on her side, facing him, and he was opposite,
facing her. "What shall we do?"

Rose swallowed hard.

Go on, Granddad said.

Get it over with, Tamhas said.

Ye've got him now, Hamilton said.

Finish this, worthless girl, her mam said.

And somewhere, in the back of her head, a quiet whisper

from Graham: *You don't have to do this.*

Rose leaned forward and kissed him, closing her eyes and pressing her lips to his. He ran his hands over her, fumbling at her bra, drawing her close, pulling her like he was a big strong bear and she was a weak little thing. He touched her, put his hands on her, and she did the same.

He released her bra and she shrugged out of it, heart beating, but somehow it didn't matter. She was beyond fear now, into spite, into fury, and she didn't even care about the man who had his hands on her body in ways no one ever had. He was an empty vessel to her, a dagger to stab at the ones she very nearly hated.

She kissed him again, and again, and started to feel the burn on her lips, on her fingers, in the places where he touched her. He gasped, clearly feeling it too, and she pushed up and straddled him, putting her bare palms on his hairy, flat chest.

She could feel the burning now, and Alistair McKinney's mouth was wide. It was a smile, of sorts, though crossed with pain, too, as it started to take over. "Hush now," she said, and he did, as his eyes rolled up and the feeling started to take over.

Something broke in on Rose as she started to let it loose, to let that—that demon feeling take her over. She was atop him, rubbing against him through her panties, and her skin was afire. She didn't care that she didn't like him; in fact felt it all the richer. She was alive with pleasure, and that it was this man—this disgusting, old, sloughing-skin man—it was all the better. She hated him, though she barely knew him, hated what he represented, the desire to use her like others had used her. He would have come to hate her after he'd come anyway, probably thrown a few pounds at her to get her to leave once his animal needs had been sated.

It was like all these arseholes in her head. They hated her for what she was until they needed her, and now—now they just hated her again, and all the more because they were trapped inside.

Rose, what are you— her granddad said.

The news broke through her fog of pleasure, and she turned her head.

"The American president announced the existence of a race of humans with superpowers—"

What?

She refocused her attention on the television and away from Alistair McKinney, who was gasping.

"…an employee named Sienna Nealon managed the agency response to the crisis…"

That name.

She knew that name.

Weissman had said it that night—that, that horrible night when—

"…Harmon has declared her a hero, responsible for saving the world from a dire threat…"

She barely felt her fingers on Alistair McKinney's chest, but he was choking now, being ripped out of himself. The little numbers she needed, vis a vis his banking information, came tearing out along with the rest of him, and she knew it was there. He was twitching under her, but she didn't care; she pushed down on him, the last bits of his mind ripping free of his body now. She couldn't have pulled a hand off now if she wanted to; her entire self was on fire with pure, uncontained joy—none of that fear that had torn at her when she'd been in the throes of it at the village that night.

This was the beauty of what she had, and she wanted to use it, wanted to do this every time she could.

Rose stood almost as soon as she knew it was over, leaving the corpse of Alistair McKinney behind. The news was still talking, but she didn't care.

Sienna Nealon.

That name.

Sienna Nealon was the reason she didn't have a bloody home anymore.

Sienna Nealon was the reason she didn't have a life anymore.

Sienna Nealon was the reason she couldn't even think her own thoughts, alone, anymore.

Rose stared at the dark-haired girl, the camera following her as she walked to a car. Then they cut to the US President, Harmon, talking about metahumans, outing them there on international television.

I can't bloody believe it, Granddad said. *A secret that's lasted countless human generations and he just…throws it out there.*

Rose was standing near naked, and for some reason…she no longer felt self-conscious at her skinny body, thin thighs, almost no chest and knock knees. What did that bloody matter, anyway? Any man who touched her was going to get a dose of what Alistair McKinney got, and it'd be all to her joy and none to his.

The world is about to change, Tamhas said. *And this girl, this…Sienna Nealon…she's going to be right at the forefront of it.*

"To hell with her," Rose whispered.

You could be right at the forefront too, Hamilton said. *Look at what they're doing to her: making her out like one of those comic book heroes people are so damned fond of. You could—*

"To hell with that," Rose said, slipping her bra back on. She stooped to get it at the side of the bed where Alistair had dropped it, ignoring his hand hanging limply next to her.

Don't be stupid, Graham said. *She's a succubus, like you. And she's got other powers at her disposal—*

We should learn how to do that, Granddad said.

"Oh, we're going to, all right," Rose said, strangely cold again. She slipped back into the dress which she'd left puddled near the entry and picked up her heels. For some reason, now, when she put it on, she felt…

Different.

You be a good lass, her mam said, sounding a little more tentative than she had with her previous pronouncements. *You can have power now. Walk openly now. Do great things—*

"To hell with your great things," Rose said, spewing it out as she walked out the bedroom door and headed for the staircase. "To hell with you all—you clingers, you shites, you. I was worthless to you until your own lives were about to end and then suddenly, suddenly Rose has use again. You're the plague that is humanity, aren't you?" She breathed heavily, spite oozing out with every breath, as she walked, with a purpose, to the door.

"Well, now I've got money," she said, "and I've got powers—I'll figure out how to use the powers like this Sienna Nealon." And she let a mighty fury rage over the souls in her head, and felt them scream in a way they never had before. Usually it was her screaming, but seeing that girl—that Sienna Nealon—she knew, somehow she knew—that determined look in her eyes as she'd been led out of her house—that she needed to be hard. Relentless. That it was all necessary...

In order to destroy Sienna Nealon.

"Everybody who ruined my life is dead except for one," Rose said, opening the door and casting one last look inside Alistair McKinney's grand house. Maybe she'd come back, make this place her own. She needed to know things first though—how to use those other powers. How to manipulate others who weren't as malleable or stupid as Alistair McKinney, for one.

A babble of voices broke out in her head.

You can't think this is the way— Granddad said.

You can do better, be better— Tamhas said.

You can have the whole world— Hamilton said.

You're gonna nozz it all up anyway, you wee scunner, Miriam said.

Please don't do this, Graham said softly.

You're such a disappointment, Mam said.

"Fuck all of you," Rose said, hard eyes determined. She'd run this city, run this country, and someday—she wasn't particular about the when, just that she'd do it—someday she'd bring this Sienna Nealon down on her knees and leave her naked and scared shitless for her own mortality, the way she'd left Rose out at the village. Terror would be the point. She'd need to feel it, really feel it the way Rose had, and then, eventually—

"I'm going to kill her, too," Rose said, and she walked out the door into the warm Edinburgh night, feeling alive again, and unworried, mind free, for the first time in months.

*

"Oh, God," Zack said. They were all standing around the scene of Rose's innocence, lost like a piece of crumpled carbon paper tossed on a fire. He'd watched her make her choices with a steady, growing horror. "This is…"

"It feels like when Sienna killed us, doesn't it?" Eve asked with an even tenor.

"I watched it happen," Zack said. "With this…kind of cold horror. She plotted it all out, and came after you one by one. It was like watching someone drive a truck toward a pedestrian, not veering off."

"And she got us," Bastian said, looking around the foyer and up the stairs toward where the body remained. "Just like this girl got him."

"Sienna was more calculating," Gavrikov said.

"We were pushing her into it, too," Bjorn said. "Just like these souls moved this Rose."

"So they've got a common thread," Zack said, looking at their newest addition. Graham hadn't said much; he looked like a paler shadow of the healthy young man they'd seen in the earlier visions. "More than one, actually."

"Have you ever been so angry at the world, or at something," Graham said softly, "that the next thing you ran across that tripped your trigger ended up getting all your ire?" He nodded at the door Rose had shut on her way out. "That's your girl to Rose. She heard the name, believed the worst, and made her decision. She's a stubborn one too, not willing to back off it for a moment, even if she had heard something better, something that might change a lesser mind. She's kept a good mad on for…years now." Graham shook his head. "Now she's all in. And your girl…she's about to be on the way out."

"This still doesn't help us," Harmon said, pacing the foyer. The usually calm politician was starting to show signs of wear. "I expected her to make a slip by now. To let us see…something other than this dull purgatory of her past idiocies." He let out a hard breath. "I don't care about her poor, tortured soul. Lots of people have traumas, trust me. I know. This is hardly the worst I've seen, but this reaction…'to hell with the world, to hell with Sienna'—this is a bratty girl being twisted and self-indulgent because she's discovered she has godlike powers to back up her angst."

"Makes you grateful Sienna didn't take a worse turn, huh?" Zack said, a little lighter than he felt. "Especially given the, uh…influences she had on her compared to Rose."

"What's that supposed to mean?" Bjorn asked, eyes narrowed.

"It means she's had a serial killer and you in the forefront of her mind all this time," Gavrikov said. "And me. Can you imagine a dimmer view of humanity than the one I hold? I don't care for any of you, save one."

"Yes, your precious Klementina," Eve said dryly. "We've heard."

"Unaccountable power is the bane of human existence," Gavrikov said. "I watched my father isolate me and my sister, and then torture us at his every whim. If he felt in a cruel mood, he was free to be as cruel as he wanted. He trampled all over us. This girl—" he pointed at the door "—she is like that. Unsocial. Powerful beyond the ability of men to control. Working quietly in the background, nothing bold or flashy, that would bring condemnation from the world of men. She is the very definition of unaccountable power. Like any petty tyrant in a fiefdom in which they have full control and no detractors with any, she has a left a trail of victims to correspond with that power."

"She has detractors," Graham said, and there was a faint howl in the distance, outside the house, almost like the wind. "But they are…I suppose 'powerless' would be the word.

Compared to her. In this place..." He bowed his head and shook it. "She's a goddess, and we're the worshippers."

"And I'm agnostic," Gavrikov said.

"Then I suspect you will end up believing in her before long," Eve said, "because she doesn't strike me as the type who's going to go light on the wrath. That will be enough to convince you sooner or later, since you're just waiting for a display to give you faith."

"I don't think she's going to show us anything," Harmon said. "We're mushrooms down here, unable to even see out the nearest window."

"Yeah, we're a long way from the Lido deck on this ship," Bastian said. "It's like one of those troop transports where you don't even get a porthole to see out."

Harmon showed a flash of irritation at the military metaphor. "Yes, like that, only not stupid. She's surely used her powers by now—"

"She has," Graham said. "She's using them constantly, all the time."

Harmon honed in on him. "You can see? See out through her eyes?"

"Aye," Graham said. "You might too, given enough time to learn your way around her head. But I'll warn you—it's not going to be pretty when you do. It's sort of like...drowning beneath the waves." He got a far-off look in his brown eyes. "And just as you think you'll never taste air again, you break the surface...and find yourself in the middle of flaming wreckage, like a ship exploded around you or something."

"I've had that happen," Gavrikov said.

"How do we do that?" Harmon asked. "I need to see, to feel in order to be able to...push my way out." He seemed desperate, his pacing continuing unabated. If he could have worn holes in the floor of Alistair McKinney's foyer, he would have, Zack was sure. "In order to get us out," he said quickly, but Zack caught the implication.

"I get the feeling," Zack said softly, "that when it comes

time to jump ship…none of the rest of us are going to get a life preserver, or a boat of our own."

Harmon's eyes flashed, cagily. "You know how to keep crabs in a bucket? It's easier than you think. You just put them in there. Every time one is close to climbing out, the others will pull him back down. It's a strange animal instinct, one I always thought was more appropriate for humans; it's like the very embodiment of envy. 'Oh, you can get out of this prison—let me stop you right there.'" He turned away, seething, his control slipping. "If I can get out with all of us, I will. If I can get out by myself, in an instant—" He turned back around, and anger and determination split his face. "Can any of you blame me for seizing that kind of opportunity?"

"I always expect a rat to escape a sinking ship if given a chance," Gavrikov said with a faint smile.

"You're such a worthless turd, Harmon," Zack said, his own anger rising in him, blinding him. "I'm still sorry I voted for you."

"Well, the campaign is over, my friend," Harmon said. "No takebacks. Which is a rule that extends to life, and ours has ended. Now we're here, trapped together, and—be assured, I hate you all as much as you hate me right now."

"You'd sell her out in an instant, wouldn't you?" Zack just shook his head.

"Rose?" Harmon frowned. "Of course I would. I have no loyalty to her and neither do y— Oh. You didn't mean Rose."

"I meant you'd sell Sienna out to Rose in an instant, if you thought there was an advantage in it," Zack said quietly. "You'd use those telepathic powers of yours to her benefit without thinking twice."

Harmon blinked. "We're stuck in her head, genius. She can compel me to help her through pain, and unlike you, perhaps, you brave soul, I'm not used to being tortured. I would almost certainly fold given about five seconds. I know myself; I know this to be true. So why would I put myself through prolonged agony when I could just give up and spare myself the trouble?"

The image of Sienna flashed through Zack's mind, and a cold truth fell over him as he stared at each of those trapped with him in turn. "You wouldn't, I guess," he said, hollowly. "You have no reason to."

"Just like Wolfe in that regard," Harmon said, turning away again. "And speaking of…where is he?" He turned back again, to Graham this time. "With her? Is he her new favorite?"

"Aye," Graham said. "He'll be with her all the time now. Top of mind, because of what he can do. She's got others like that." He stared at Harmon. "Given what you can do…she'll probably come for you, next. She's got plans right now, though. Hasn't slept in a couple days, but…when she gets a breather…she'll be on you, I expect."

"Oh, goodie," Harmon said, but it rang hollow, sarcasm like an ineffectual shield for the small dose of dread that leaked out.

"She's got thousands of us in here," Zack said, looking right at Graham. "Why are you the only one that's talking to us?"

"I'm the only one that cares, I guess," Graham said. "Most of the new ones…you wouldn't believe the state they arrive in. They come in ones and twos, no connection to each other, hardly. Those that do know each other before she absorbs them—families and whatnot—they're huddled together like you lot, unless she splits them off. Which she does sometimes. Isolates them." He folded his arms uncomfortably. "I guess what I'm saying is…not many know their way around like I do, being here since the beginning. It's a big place now, not like it was when we started. Every soul she absorbed…it's like they added a little space to the world. Now it's so big, a new person would get lost without a guide."

"Are you our guide?" Zack asked.

Graham looked right at him. "Maybe. I'm a bit caught between worlds, you see. She doesn't want me with the others from the village—for obvious reasons, I suppose." He looked away, and the regret was almost a tangible thing, the roads not taken plain to Zack—for he had a few of those of his own. "So I wander. Most people are shuddering fools when they get here. Hardly a will of their own, being newly minted metas when they're absorbed. She cows them quick, breaks them down if she needs them. They become servile little slaves to her mind. And that's that." He stared at each of them in turn. "You're the first ones she's brought in in a long while that had minds of your own still. Which is funny—" he smiled "—because you haven't had bodies of your own in a long while, too. You should be just about dissolved to your succubus's will, I would have thought."

There was an uncomfortable silence, with Eve and Harmon looking away, Bjorn and Gavrikov staring down. Bastian answered for them: "Sienna...wasn't like that."

"That's nice," Graham said. "But ultimately pointless now." He extended his hands out. "Welcome to your new world. Bid adieu to the old. Because this is your new normal," he said, and he was rueful as anyone Zack had ever heard. "You're here now, with us now..." He shook his head, looking once more at the door that Rose had closed on her way out. "She's got your girl, by the way...and that end is coming up soon." Zack felt his heart catch in his throat, but Graham did not stop. "So you might as well give up hope of rescue...because this—" and he looked around again "—this is where you are from now on." He looked pointedly at Harmon. "And escape? Is a fanciful dream." The president's eyes dropped. "You may not like it, but this is simply the way things are." Graham's voice was low, bitter, and streaked through with sadness.

"This is how it's going to be," he said, a little sadly, "forever and ever. And no one...not your girl Sienna, and not any of you...will beat Rose. You're here forever...and that's just a fact."

40.

Reed

"Reed?" Her voice like a hollow thing, brittle and easily broken, on the edge of cracking.

"Sienna?" I asked the question of the darkness, because I couldn't see her. It was all darkness, all around us, deep in the dreamwalk. It always a little dark, but this was an inky, all-consuming sort of black that threatened to drown me in its depths.

The last thing I remembered was sitting on the airplane, the thrum of the engines the background noise as my brain worked through the impossible fact that we'd been ambushed, that we'd lost Colin somehow, and that we'd nearly lost Chase and Veronika, maybe would have lost the entire crew if we'd disembarked fearlessly.

"I'm here," she said in a hushed voice. I still couldn't see her.

"I came for you," I said, and it was a plaintive sort of excuse. "I was in York, and—"

"Did she get you?" Sienna's voice was quiet. Terrified.

"We got away," I said. "I managed to get the plane in the air. We lost our pilots, but…everyone made it out okay except—"

"Colin," she whispered.

"I sent him after you," I said, still probing the dark. Why was there no light?

Why couldn't I see her?

"He betrayed me, Reed," Sienna said. Now she was cool, almost resigned. "He took me out when Rose had me on the ropes."

"I might have gotten her, Sienna," I said, hoping I was right. "She was coming after us, and they'd sent missiles. I steered them into her. Maybe...maybe I got lucky—"

"You didn't." The air of finality was punishing.

"How do you know?" I asked.

"Because it wouldn't have finished me."

"You're not invincible," I said, then strained, feeling like that was a poor point to make at this juncture. "And she's not, now. You killed Wolfe. You've killed...or beaten...everyone you've come across."

"She got me, Reed," Sienna said, and I still couldn't see her, no matter how I tried. "I'm...she got me."

"I'm gonna come back for you," I said, listening to that thin, reedy desperation. I couldn't remember a time when the hope had so gone out of Sienna's voice. "I will—I'm going to find a way and—"

"No."

"You can't stop me," I said with a smile of pure, false bravado. "The others—we're not done, Sienna."

"If you come back," she said, "Rose will capture you. And she'll kill you in front of me."

I gritted my teeth, bearing down against the darkness. "Sienna, listen to me—just because I can't reach you right now—just because it looks like there's no hope—"

"There's no hope." So quiet.

So final.

"You need to hold on," I said. "You have to—"

"It's over, Reed," she said, and it was like the darkness got more complete. "I'm sorry."

"You don't have to apologize to me!" I shouted, and it echoed in the space we were in. "Sienna—I know who you are, even if you're forgetting. No one beats you! You don't let them! And this Rose—she's not going to w—"

"I think…" And she emerged out of the dark, a haggard figure, bloody and bruised. "…we should say goodbye now, Reed." Her eyes were red, but clear, and the slump of her shoulders just…killed me. "Because I don't know that we're going to get another chance."

"Sienna…" I tried to grab at her, but she was just out of reach. Tried again, and she slipped farther away. "This isn't over. It doesn't have to be. You can still fight! You can still—"

But the quiet was all-consuming, and my sister slipped back into the dark, her voice a mere whisper.

Now she was broken.

"It's over, Reed. I love you."

And then she was gone.

Without even saying goodbye.

41.

Sienna

I was jarred out of the darkness of my dreamwalk with Reed, leaving it on perhaps not the greatest note, but the one that fit for the moment.

It was dark in the dreamwalk because I was in the darkness, the world around me shrouded by black cloth that was wrapped around my head.

I was bagged, like a hostage, except...

No one was going to pay the ransom for me, because Rose...didn't give a damn about money.

The world moved around me. A thump, and I realized I was in the back of a vehicle. Probing with my feet, I found the boundaries of my world, and they were large. I seemed to be in the back of a van or truck, my feet sliding around and making contact with metal walls. I was as gentle and quiet as I could be, trying not to let whoever was driving know that I was awake.

No need to raise the alarm, after all.

Just as I was starting to get an idea about the limits of my little world, the vehicle bounced to a stop, and I thudded my head against the rubber floor. My arm made contact with it, skidding slightly as the rubber resisted against my skin where my sleeve had been torn by Mr. Blonde hours before.

The sound of someone killing the ignition, then opening a

door up front of me, came through the metal walls, muffled, but clear enough. The squeak of doors opening below my feet came next, and strong hands reaching in and dragging me out. I fought a little, but not too much. Token resistance, really, because blind and bound in metacuffs, there was no easy way to fight back.

And I was going to fight back, in spite of what I'd told Reed.

I had to.

But I also had to try and convince him not to come back. Rose had known he was coming this time—any one of a thousand things could have tipped her off, but the sudden betrayal of Colin Fannon was a worrying one—and I needed to at least try and keep Reed and the others clear of this giant mess I had gotten myself into.

Because otherwise…he'd come back, and Rose would be waiting.

And the next time…I wasn't so sanguine about his chances of escaping her.

Case in point. Here I was, trussed up and hooded, being led across snowy ground by rough hands—

Wait.

Snow?

In summer?

The crunch of snow beneath my shoes was unmistakable, the gentle chill of winter tickling my flesh and raising goosebumps that were, for once of late, not related to the hair-raising predicaments I seemed to keep getting sucked into.

"Take that off of her," Rose's voice sounded from somewhere in front of me, and suddenly the world brightened as the black hood came ripping off. The light was blinding for a few seconds, but I got my bearings again pretty quickly.

Rose was hovering ahead like an angel—fallen one, maybe—smiling benignly upon me. Colin Fannon was at my shoulder, the black hood in his hand. At my other shoulder was Mr. Blonde, that jag who'd cut me open at the train station in Edinburgh before that mystery girl called him off.

She didn't seem like she was around to save my ass from harm this time though, which was just as well for her health, cuz Rose didn't seem like the type to tolerate lesser bitches in the pack.

"D'ye like it?" Rose asked, raising her arms to indicate the massive snowfield we were standing in the middle of. There were curving-topped mountains in the distance, but this little stretch of plain had been blanketed beautifully and perfectly. "I wanted you to feel a little at home, y'see. I know your native land is a bit like Scotland in this regard—the big snowfalls."

"Gee," I said, clinking my cuffs behind my back, "thanks. I appreciate the effort." Pure snottiness. I wouldn't let her think for a second she'd actually beaten me, even if she skinned me alive an inch at a time.

She shrugged lightly. "For someone with the power of a frost giant at their disposal, it's an easy thing." She floated a little closer. If I could get the meta cuffs around her neck and pull hard enough, I could take her head off. That'd put an end to her pretty swiftly.

"Uncuff her and leave us be, will ye?" Rose gestured to Fannon and Mr. Blonde. "It's time for some real talk." Her green eyes glittered, and she shot me a malicious and dazzling smile. "Some girl talk."

They had me unlocked in a hot second, falling over themselves to execute her command. They were gone a second later, taking my best weapon with them. "Thanks for nothing, Fannon," I called after him. He didn't even acknowledge me, and when I looked at his eyes, they looked...

Blank.

I'd known Fannon a little bit. Probably the least well of nearly any of the associates at the agency. He was a lot of things—kind of a hippy, into being vegan and environmentally conscious...

Blank-eyed and empty? Not so much.

"You've got a lot of sick puppets," I said, watching their

retreating figures head back to the van. They got in, started it up, and began to pull away, leaving tire tracks in the snow as they crunched their way across the field.

"Excuse me?" Rose asked.

I turned back to her. "Uhh…sorry…I think I made a mistake. Sock…sock puppets, that's it. You've got a lot of sock puppets." I waved at the van driving off. "You've got your hand up a lot of asses, Rose."

"I do have a certain way with people," she said, absolutely straight-faced. "You could say…I know the secrets of their souls." She drifted a little closer to me. "Like you, for instance."

"You don't know shit about me, Rose," I said, looking sideways, pretending to be bored. I was actually hanging on her every word, hoping she'd give me a seed with which to destroy her, or get close enough that I could take a reasonable chance to choke her to death.

"You really hate me now, don't you?" She drifted closer and closer, only a few feet away now, grinning madly. "Good. I've hated you all this time. Had to fake my way through it while I was hanging about with you."

"You're a wonderful actor," I said. "I bought it. You're a master at feigning sincerity."

"That's not me," she said, still smirking. "That's Hamilton. He's classically trained. I just draw on him anytime I need his skills. He's been in the theater since the days that Medea was performed live."

"Blah blah blah," I said, pissing on her little reminiscence. "What now?"

She cocked her head at me. "Now…you're going to try and kill me, of course."

That felt awfully on the nose. "Oh?" I asked. Of course I wanted to, but the fact that she'd just casually suggest it…

"See…" Rose said, drifting even a little closer, "what we have here, is a couple of succubi with a dispute over who's the best. I don't really care that I'm stronger than you—because I am. I don't really care that I'm better than you—because I am.

What I care about…is you knowing, in your heart, in the depths of your empty, soon-to-be-ripped out soul—" this she said with a rising ferocity "—that I own your arse—" and she darted in faster than my eye could track her and slapped me right on it, making me jump "—wholly and completely. You belong to me now, Sienna Nealon. You're going to attack me so that I can show you—eliminate that little doubt, that hope that's feeding your soul, the one that says, 'Yeah, you can still beat her.' we're going to knock that right out of you, starting now." And she smiled. "So…strap it on, lass, and let's have a go. Give me everything you've got. I'll even give you the first hit for free."

I debated whether to do it or not to rise to her goad, but I'm me, and there was no way I was going to pass up a free hit against someone who'd caused me this much agony, especially when I judged that if I sat there passively, she'd eventually starting pounding on my ass anyway, and if I was going to take a beating, I at least wanted to deserve it.

So I slugged her in the face with a couple fingers sticking out in a point, not pulling the punch as I drove it right into her eye socket like an old pro. Her eyeball disappeared under my assault and Rose took the hit with a shock.

I didn't stop there, either. I hooked my fingers into the cartilage behind her nose and I ripped it out as I yanked my hand back, following up by dragging her toward me and elbowing her in the other eye as hard as I could. A hit like that from a normal human would cause trauma; my strike caused so much overpressure that her other eyeball exploded and she was blinded, half her face hanging off.

Not wasting any time, I seized her by the hair, taking care not to spend much time touching her skin, and lifted her off the ground. I was going to drive the back of her head down into the point of my knee, shattering her skull and spilling her brains all over this pretty white snowfield she'd created. I had a grip on her by the small crater I'd created in her face and was yanking her down when, very suddenly, she slipped my grasp.

"Oh my," she said, floating eerily back up into the air, blood racing down her pale chin and cheeks from the gaping places where I'd torn muscle, tissue and bone. Her eyeballs reappeared first as her skin knitted itself back together, and she rasped, "That's not nice, Little Doll." And her green eyes sparkled as she was left looking almost as flawless as before, save for a few streaks of blood.

Something about the way she said it almost knocked the knees from beneath me. It was pure Wolfe, speaking through her. She'd just used his powers to perfectly heal from my assault in a matter of seconds, which meant...

He was with her now. Really, truly with her, doing her bidding and repairing her face from my near-lethal assault.

I swung at her again, coming at her with a series of punches and attacks designed to showcase my martial arts expertise. She fought back, flawlessly, her form perfect, her speed and dexterity miles beyond my own—

And she finished me with a perfect counter that swept aside my punch, turning me around, and landing a shattering blow against the small of my back.

My legs went out, numb and as good as dead. My face hit snow, cold and bitter, and my chest followed. The landing drove the breath out of me; she'd broken my spine, I could tell from the way I couldn't move anything below the waist. I tried to push up—

"Now, now." She landed heavily on my back, putting a knee right between my shoulder blades and then dragging me over. She was still smiling. "If you get too out of control, I'll break your spine just below the neck, really give you something to heal over, aye? I want to talk now—"

"I've got nothing else to say," I almost spat.

"Good, because I'm the one who's talking," she said, putting a hand over my mouth for a second and mashing my lips so that one of them split open. She did it so casually that I almost believed she was simply too strong to fully appreciate how easily she could hurt me. "So zip it."

She settled, staring right down at me. "You know why I hate you? Did the Englishman tell you?"

"You lived in the cloister here in Scotland," I said, roughly, not wanting to dignify her question with an answer but not feeling like this was not the conversational hill where I wanted to make my last defiant stand.

"Aye, I did," she said. "It was a village, y'see. I was raised there my whole life. Never left until…after." She looked out into the distance. "When…your great uncle came, along with your friend Weissman—"

"Weissman was no friend of mine," I spat. "I tried to kill his ass."

"You should have tried harder," she said, then thumped me on the chest, breaking eight of my ribs. "I looked into things, after I first heard about you. Interviewed some old Omega folks—I shouldn't say 'interviewed'; I actually stole some of their memories, you know, before your pal Philip Delsim cut them to pieces—and so I know what happened." She leaned in closer. "You decided to stay in London and make your stand there, with your little friends…" Her expression darkened. "…Instead of helping me and mine.

"You could have saved my family," she said, voice getting harder and colder by the moment. "My village. You could have fought your uncle with us, there, instead of in London. That's just typical though, innit? Your family and friends lived—" and here she became even frostier "—and mine died. And now…" She smiled, but it was thin, and pained. "It's time to pay the piper for that choice, my darlin'."

She forced her hand down on me, pressing it against the skin of my cheek. I tried to wrestle away from her, but she thumped me again with her knee, and my head went blurry. My skin started to burn where she touched it, then everywhere else. It spread down my face, down my neck, like someone had doused me in gasoline and lit the fire. Trapped between the cold of the snow and the heat of her touch, I burned.

Rose was there, invading my mind, my thoughts, swelling

inside me like she might come bursting out of my chest. It lasted for forever, or for a moment, and then she pulled her hand away, eyes rolled up in her head like she'd just had a grand old time.

She let out a long breath, and then wiped her brow of non-existent sweat. "Whew. Have ye asked yourself what would happen if you didn't take the whole soul from someone? If, instead—" she looked down at me, and licked her lips "—you just…disciplined yourself…and took a little nibble every day, or every few days?"

Rose leaned her face in close to mine, til we were practically cheek to cheek. "You get a little piece of them at a time, like I just took from you." She stroked my cheek and it burned immediately, her power going to work overpowering mine, carving off another little slice of me.

"What…did you take?" I asked, my breathing taxed and heavier than hers. The cold here burned my lungs, and my breath steamed the air.

"Nothing you'll miss," she said, eyes glittering. "Just a little memory from your past, something from your teenage years, some embarrassing, unimportant lesson or two. I steered away from the good stuff—your friends, your loves, the things you really value, because…" She leaned in again, almost brushing me but whispering in my ear instead. "I want to take those things from you in front of you…I want you to watch your friends die, knowing how much you still love them, how much you secretly care…something most people wouldn't have known about you, but…I see you now, darlin'." She put her teeth on my ear and bit it just hard enough that I flinched. "I've got a little piece of you now, and I'm going to come back on the regular to take another—and another—" She bit me again, and this time it hurt, because she ripped through the cartilage and took a corner of my ear, then spat it on the white snow, which was already turning crimson. "Soon enough, there'll be more of you in me than in here." She touched me on the sternum and rested her hand on my shirt.

"I'm going to take a piece of your soul at a time," she said, standing back up over me. "I'm going to take every friend you have left in your little family." She looked around. "I'm going to make you suffer. Make it so you never see your home again." She smiled and leaned down again. "Welcome to Scotland. You're free to wander about the land here, knowing that—just like the last few days, I'm never more than a heartbeat away." Then she stood up and started to walk away.

I lay there in the snow she'd made, breath steaming the air, hurting like I'd never been hurt, the memory of everything I'd done to her...she just shrugged off.

I'd thought I was invincible, had told my souls that...but I was wrong.

Rose had taken everything from me, almost.

And now she was going to take the rest.

A piece at a time.

"Enjoy your stay," Rose called back, over her shoulder, as she walked away. "You know, as much as you can given that I'm always watching. It's pretty country, even though it's not your home." She looked back, and her eyes glittered. "I doubt you'll ever come to love it here like I do, but...that's all right. It doesn't really matter, after all, whether you like it or not...

"You'll die here just the same."

Sienna Nealon Will Return
and the Scotland Trilogy will conclude
in

NEMESIS

Out of the Box
Book 17

Coming December 1, 2017!

Author's Note

If you want to know when future books become available, take sixty seconds and sign up for my NEW RELEASE EMAIL ALERTS by visiting my website at www.robertjcrane.com. Don't let the caps lock scare you; I don't sell your information and I only send out emails when I have a new book out. The reason you should sign up for this is because I don't like to set release dates (it's this whole thing, you can find an answer on my website in the FAQ section), and even if you're following me on Facebook (robertJcrane (Author)) or Twitter (@robertJcrane), it's easy to miss my book announcements because…well, because social media is an imprecise thing.

Come join the discussion on my website:
http://www.robertjcrane.com !

Cheers,
Robert J. Crane

ACKNOWLEDGMENTS

Editorial/Literary Janitorial duties performed by Nick Bowman and Jeff Bryan. Final proofing (and some Britishing) was once more handled by the illustrious Jo Evans. Scottish proofing was done by John Clifford, who you might notice also gets a cameo in this one. Any errors or weird Americanizations you see in the text, however, are the result of me rejecting changes to try and make things decipherable to an international audience.

The cover was once designed by Karri Klawiter of artbykarri.com.

Once more, thanks to my parents, my in-laws, my kids and my wife, for helping me keep things together.

Other Works by Robert J. Crane

World of Sanctuary
Epic Fantasy

Defender: The Sanctuary Series, Volume One
Avenger: The Sanctuary Series, Volume Two
Champion: The Sanctuary Series, Volume Three
Crusader: The Sanctuary Series, Volume Four
Sanctuary Tales, Volume One - A Short Story Collection
Thy Father's Shadow: The Sanctuary Series, Volume 4.5
Master: The Sanctuary Series, Volume Five
Fated in Darkness: The Sanctuary Series, Volume 5.5
Warlord: The Sanctuary Series, Volume Six
Heretic: The Sanctuary Series, Volume Seven
Legend: The Sanctuary Series, Volume Eight
Ghosts of Sanctuary: The Sanctuary Series, Volume Nine
        (Coming 2018, at earliest.)

A Haven in Ash: Ashes of Luukessia, Volume One
        (with Michael Winstone - Coming Fall 2017!)

The Girl in the Box
and
Out of the Box
Contemporary Urban Fantasy

Alone: The Girl in the Box, Book 1
Untouched: The Girl in the Box, Book 2
Soulless: The Girl in the Box, Book 3
Family: The Girl in the Box, Book 4
Omega: The Girl in the Box, Book 5
Broken: The Girl in the Box, Book 6

Enemies: The Girl in the Box, Book 7
Legacy: The Girl in the Box, Book 8
Destiny: The Girl in the Box, Book 9
Power: The Girl in the Box, Book 10

Limitless: Out of the Box, Book 1
In the Wind: Out of the Box, Book 2
Ruthless: Out of the Box, Book 3
Grounded: Out of the Box, Book 4
Tormented: Out of the Box, Book 5
Vengeful: Out of the Box, Book 6
Sea Change: Out of the Box, Book 7
Painkiller: Out of the Box, Book 8
Masks: Out of the Box, Book 9
Prisoners: Out of the Box, Book 10
Unyielding: Out of the Box, Book 11
Hollow: Out of the Box, Book 12
Toxicity: Out of the Box, Book 13
Small Things: Out of the Box, Book 14
Hunters: Out of the Box, Book 15
Badder: Out of the Box, Book 16
Nemesis: Out of the Box, Book 17* (Coming December 1, 2017!)
Apex: Out of the Box, Book 18* (Coming Early 2018!)
Time: Out of the Box, Book 19* (Coming Spring 2018!)
Driven: Out of the Box, Book 20* (Coming Summer 2018!)

Southern Watch
Contemporary Urban Fantasy

Called: Southern Watch, Book 1
Depths: Southern Watch, Book 2
Corrupted: Southern Watch, Book 3
Unearthed: Southern Watch, Book 4
Legion: Southern Watch, Book 5
Starling: Southern Watch, Book 6* (Coming Fall 2017!)

The Shattered Dome Series
(with Nicholas J. Ambrose)
Sci-Fi

Voiceless: The Shattered Dome, Book 1

The Mira Brand Adventures
Contemporary Urban Fantasy

The World Beneath: The Mira Brand Adventures, Book 1
The Tide of Ages: The Mira Brand Adventures, Book 2
The City of Lies: The Mira Brand Adventures, Book 3
The King of the Skies: The Mira Brand Adventures, Book 4*
    (Coming Late 2017!)

Liars and Vampires
(with Lauren Harper)
Contemporary Urban Fantasy

No One Will Believe You: Liars and Vampires, Book 1*
    (Coming Fall 2017!)

Forthcoming, Subject to Change

CPSIA information can be obtained
at www.ICGtesting.com
Printed in the USA
LVOW10s1626130218
566429LV00011B/626/P

9 781976 141744